"A sharply drawn psychological thriller of uncommon emotional depth, *Under a Dark Sky* is a rare treat—and no less than I've come to expect from Lori Rader-Day. Both an irresistible locked-room puzzler and a finely wrought examination of friendship, love, and loss, this is the kind of book you can't help but read too fast. You can't wait to find out what happened, no matter that you never want it to end."

—Elizabeth Little, author of *Dear Daughter*

"Seven individuals gather *Under a Dark Sky*. How many ways are they connected? How many patterns are waiting to be found? With a delicate yet steady hand, Lori Rader-Day traces the lines that join these old friends together and the barriers that divide them, to reveal a constellation as inevitable as it's astonishing. Splendid stuff from a master of the genre."

—Catriona McPherson, author of *Go to My Grave*

"I don't know a writer who captures better the insecurities and damaged and damaging relationships of ordinary women."

—Ann Cleeves, *New York Times* bestselling author

# Praise for *Under a Dark Sky*

"A brilliant concept, brilliantly told! *Under a Dark Sky* is a novel that you simply can't put down. Populated by living, breathing characters and filled with fresh prose and sharp dialogue, we thrill to spend a harrowing, yet redemptive, getaway with our wonderful protagonist, Eden Wallace. I guarantee this book will resonate with you. Because, let's face it, aren't we all afraid of the dark?"

—Jeffery Deaver, *New York Times* bestselling author

"Lori Rader-Day is a modern-day Agatha Christie: her mysteries are taut, her characters are real and larger than life, and her plots are relentlessly surprising. *Under a Dark Sky* is a stellar addition to her award-winning catalog. The closed-door mystery echoes the claustrophobic atmosphere of Christie's *And Then There Were None,* and there are enough breakneck twists to captivate modern readers. A dynamite late summer read!"

—Kate Moretti, *New York Times* bestselling author
of *The Vanishing Year*

"*Under a Dark Sky* by Lori Rader-Day is an atmospheric and absorbing mystery with an intriguing cast of characters. You'll want to read this gripping novel with the lights on."

—Heather Gudenkauf, *New York Times*
bestselling author of *The Weight of Silence*

# Under a Dark Sky

Also by Lori Rader-Day

*The Day I Died*
*Little Pretty Things*
*The Black Hour*

# Under a Dark Sky

*A Novel*

## Lori Rader-Day

*wm*

WILLIAM MORROW

*An Imprint of* HarperCollins*Publishers*

P.S.™ is a trademark of HarperCollins Publishers.

HarperCollins books may be purchased for educational, business, or sales promotional use. For information, please email the Special Markets Department at SPsales@harpercollins.com.

FIRST EDITION

*Designed by Diahann Sturge*

Library of Congress Cataloging-in-Publication Data

Names: Rader-Day, Lori, 1973– author.
Title: Under a dark sky : a novel / Lori Rader-Day.
Description: First edition. | New York : William Morrow Paperbacks, [2018]
Identifiers: LCCN 2017049911| ISBN 9780062560308 (softcover) | ISBN 9780062846143 (hardcover) | ISBN 9780062845832 (large print) | ISBN 9780062360315 (epub)
Subjects: LCSH: Widows—Fiction. | Murder—Fiction. | Psychological fiction. | BISAC: FICTION / Mystery & Detective / General. | FICTION / Psychological. | GSAFD: Suspense fiction. | Mystery fiction.
Classification: LCC PS3618.A3475 U53 2018 | DDC 813/.6—dc23
LC record available at https://lccn.loc.gov/2017049911

ISBN 978-0-06-256030-8
ISBN 978-0-06-284614-3 (hardcover library edition)

18 19 20 21 22  LSC  10 9 8 7 6 5 4 3 2 1

*To Greg, forever*

# A *few years ago*

In the dim of the truck's dashboard lights, Bix's hand reached toward the steering wheel. "Hold on a second," he said.

"At ease, soldier." I swatted him away and kept my eyes on the road. We'd already had this argument back in the parking lot of the bar where we'd met the guy from his old unit and his wife. Out of earshot, of course, closing ranks. He usually drove—he couldn't stand to be a passenger—but he'd had one too many at dinner. Three too many. Even so, I'd had to go low to get the keys from him. *You get a DUI*, I'd said. *I'll have to drive you everywhere for a year.* I didn't know if that's how it went or not, but neither did he, and also he was drunk.

"Take a nap or something," I said.

"Eden, pull over."

"You getting sick?" I let off on the gas, pulled to the edge of the road, and unlocked the doors. Bix stayed buckled. "What?"

"Just . . ." He squinted out the windshield. "I don't know. Is that weird?"

Our headlights picked up a pair of bright eyes in the brush. Beyond that, an empty field. We were stopped in the home-bound lanes of the divided highway, still more than an hour away from our front door. A black sky wrapped around us. A car approached, but it was distant.

"What? Is what weird?" I said.

When he didn't answer, I looked over at him again. He was shadow. "You going to puke or what?"

"Just . . . hang back," he said.

I put the truck in park with a sigh. Drunks. I wanted my bed, the fresh sheets I'd put on. We should have left the bar hours ago, as far as we'd had to travel. Of course there were a lot of stories to get through, a lot of inside jokes until the guys were all red-faced and drawing attention. The wife I'd known from base housing in Fayette Nam, as we called it. Me in North Carolina back when Bix was on the ground in Fallujah. She had as much patience as anyone could expect for dinner and nostalgia, but even she had started yawning into the back of her hand. Rounds got poured. Things got late. And now—well, Bix could take the guest room, if he was going to be sick all night.

He blinked, squinted past me. I was admiring him, my handsome husband, when I realized how bright the night had become.

Out the windshield, the headlights of the approaching car had grown intense—far too bright and too quickly. In the moment I realized what was happening—

"What the—"

—the car rushed past us at speed, on our side of the highway instead of its own, almost in our lane.

We shook, and dust and debris lashed against the truck.

Bix whipped around, pulling against his seat belt to watch the car's red taillights disappear.

"—hell," I said.

"Dude's having a wild night, that's what the hell."

It was Army to both respect the rules and scorn them. But I was not Army, and neither was Bix, anymore. "He's going to kill someone," I said. I put the truck in gear and pulled onto the road. Bix tucked his arms across his chest and let his neck cradle into the sling of the seat belt. He mumbled something.

"What?"

"If he was going to kill someone . . ." He swallowed the rest of it, his head lolling back.

"What?" I said again.

He had begun to snore. I turned on talk radio to keep me company, but it was still a long way home. I kept myself alert trying to figure it out. *If he was going to kill someone . . . what?*

When we got home, I shook him awake, gently, to go inside. His eyes opened, red and bleary, and I wondered what kind of night we would have. Scale of one to ten. But then he unbuckled the seat belt and opened the door on his own, walked a straight line to the door, and patted his pockets for the keys before he remembered he didn't have them. He waited for me, sheepish. An OK night, then, at least.

"What did you say about that car?" I said, yawning. "About if he was going to kill someone . . ."

"What are you talking about?"

"The car," I said. "On the highway. You know."

"Weren't there a lot of cars on the highway?"

He didn't remember. He didn't remember the car, the near miss, or what he'd said that I couldn't hear. I let it go. I needed an OK night. I just wanted the sleep.

# Chapter One

*June*

The first sign that things would not go as planned was the tableau that awaited me at the bottom of the open staircase: a pair of boxer briefs hanging from the newel post, as out of place as if they'd been dropped from the sky. Still life with underwear. After a moment, the boxers resolved into a pair of swimming trunks, which was a relief but not a full pardon. A mistake, easily. The last week's renters must have forgotten them. But I wasn't satisfied, because I had already noticed the other car parked outside, an expensive model with Ohio plates. I stood at the bottom of the stairs with my suitcase and camera bag at my feet, waiting for the swimming trunks to make sense. It was one thing for the owner to forget them here. It was another thing altogether to think the cleaning service hadn't bothered with them, or with the pool of water forming on the hardwood floor below.

The pool of water couldn't be a mistake, could it? How could the system that turned the guest house over from one week to the next—every week of the year—break down so completely?

The rest of the place seemed tidy and reassuring: a big airy front room with wide windows filled with sunlight and a kitchen stocked with silver appliances reflecting the shine. In all this aggressive daylight, I felt safe and entirely at odds with why I had come.

I'm not sure how long I stared at the mess, unable to decide what to do about it.

A footstep sounded above and then a man, young, bare-chested, stood at the top of the stairs, speaking back over his shoulder. "I said we'd figure it out later," he said. "I thought I heard Malloy—"

He'd seen me now and was eyeing my suitcase in the same way I'd calculated the puddle on the floor.

"Hello," he said. He was gorgeously brown, South Asian, maybe, with smooth, hairless arms and eyes so dark I couldn't quite look into them. His black hair was wet and swept back from his forehead in a sheet. The owner of the swim trunks, no doubt. He came down the stairs almost regally on bare feet.

"Are you late getting started on your way?" I said.

"Are you from the cleaning service?" he said at the same time.

"No, I'm . . ." For some reason I didn't want to say that I was here to stay the week. I had a bad feeling that who I thought I was and who he thought he was would clash, unrecoverable. I had enjoyed a certain kind of avoidance of conflict since my husband had died. Dodging disagreement was a symptom, though, not the disease. The truth was that I was a decorated solider in the fight against decision-making, and since Bix had died, I had given up all patience for the clockworks of life and the world around me. The casualty had been friendships, then family. Strangers, of course, had been the first to go. I didn't like talking to them, or having them talk to me. In most situations—and I hadn't known this until I'd had the chance to practice it—I could end any conversation I didn't want to have and walk away. Midsentence, if necessary.

Of course I had lived a bit of a rarified life, no children, not having to work, not having to settle any disputes or answer to any demands. Not after the funeral and the first rush of mourners had stopped fussing at me. Not after that. All the systems of my life had been set up well beforehand, and they continued to *tick-tick* toward infinity. Or, actually, not infinity at all, as it turned out.

"I'm the renter this week," I said finally, no way around it.

"Paris," the man called loudly.

"What?" The voice came first, then the woman, lithe, showing off long brown legs in tiny shorts and a substantial décolletage in a strappy bikini top. Her black hair bobbed in thin, tight braids, some of them decorated with beads, gold to match the delicate gold ring in her left nostril. She provided another royal descent down the stairs, an African queen. The frown on her face projected that she wasn't going to accept whatever there was to find out. She had made up her mind. She looked me up and down. "What's going on? Where's Malloy?"

"This is our week, right?" he said. "In the house. You're absolutely sure."

"Of course it's our week. We already checked in, remember?" She turned to me, shapely arms folded across her chest. "We've had it booked for weeks."

"My reservation was made almost a year ago," I said.

They exchanged a glance, in which it was confirmed that anyone who would make plans so far in advance was clearly disturbed and probably the one at fault. The one most likely to get the date wrong, anyway.

For a moment, I let myself wonder if I *had* mixed up the date. I hadn't been sleeping well. Plans, thoughts, promises, memories—at times it all went a little fuzzy at the edges. My mind would wander from the moment and deep into another place I couldn't pinpoint or explain, and then I would come back to reality with a click. A click, almost audible, like the click of a camera shutter. Not my camera, the one I had been carrying around since I'd started the lessons Bix had signed me up for. On my camera, the shutter noise was a setting I could turn off, and so I had. But that was the sound I heard when I came back from wherever I had gone, and maybe the person I'd been talking to would have shifted or even moved away. *Click.* Sometimes the problem in front of me took care of itself.

But I knew I hadn't messed up this date.

"My husband," I said. "He booked it for our wedding anniversary—"

The man's eyes flicked behind me to the door, empty. I hadn't gotten used to that little glance over my shoulder. It still hurt. He should have been there, backing me up. Though backing me up had not been his best quality.

"Before he died," I said. It was hard to explain, the loss. Nearly nine months later, I was still trying to figure out which words people needed to hear first. Or at all. People wanted the story. They often felt the details were part of something owed to them. For these two strangers standing in my way, simplicity was best. "He made the plans, but he didn't live to keep them."

"We're so sorry," the man mumbled, but the woman wasn't having it.

"It's an anniversary for us, too," she said.

"Pare," he scolded. "Don't."

"Well, it is," she said, though she looked slightly abashed. "And besides—it's *also* the anniversary of when we graduated," she said. A toddler pout crept onto her face. She was used to getting her own way. "Almost. It's been forever."

*Forever.* People liked to throw around words like that, the meaning stripped away. The younger they were, the more easily they pitched the phrase. What did *forever* mean to someone for whom the word *anniversary* was tied to leaving a school?

"High school?" I said.

"College," he said. It came out apologetic. "Five years."

"Oh." I had only a handful of years on them, six or seven. An age difference that didn't matter from my side but might from theirs. They seemed even younger, actually. But that was probably the grief talking. Grief had its way with you, time-wise.

I was already tired of having to talk with them. They shouldn't be here. I had fought my despair and inertia and doubts to drive up here and face up to a few things, and these people had no role in it. For a moment, I felt the tug of home. This was the permission I needed. I could get back in the car and, if I drove quickly and made no stops, be home before dark. I could see our tenth anniversary through as I had all the days since he'd gone, locked up tight inside a house with all the lights blazing out into the darkness.

Except it couldn't continue this way. A set of house keys had been placed in the hands of a keen real estate agent who had encouraged me to vacate so that he could inventory all the ways in which our history could be stripped out of the place. At the end of the week, I would decide. Did I give him the go-ahead to stage the place as a showroom, or did I return and figure out how to live there on my own? He had tried to call me three times during my drive north to the park, but I hadn't answered. There were no emergencies left in my life. Except—

I imagined sunset stretching shadows into my path on the long ride home. Except that one.

"Let's find the park director," I said, throwing my camera bag strap across my chest. "We need to settle this before it starts to get dark."

"Why?" the woman said, trading in her pout for a sneer. "I thought we came here to be in the dark."

"But when it gets dark here, it's going to be *really* dark," the guy said, turning to me. He was trying to be nice, but I felt his hope radiating toward me that when we worked this out, I would be the one to get back in my car. He wanted things to go well but he wanted things to go better for this woman and himself. "She wouldn't want to start for home in that kind of dark," he said, and he had no idea how right he was.

"Welcome to the Straits Point International Dark Sky Park—oh." The young woman at the main office recognized me right away. When I'd checked in less than a half hour prior, we'd had a little trouble with the process. Something in the paperwork, and the reservation being under Bix's name—

anyway, we had worked it out at last. Wallace, party of one, not two. Now the woman waited to see what more trouble I could cause, her smile as pinned on as her name tag.

The couple came in behind me, arguing in close tones and letting the screen door bang. I had learned on the way over that the man's name was Dev. "It means divine," the woman, Paris, had said, as though it anointed them both.

Neither of them stepped forward, so I did. "We're hoping you can clear something up for us," I said, leaning in close to read the woman's name tag, "Erica Ruth Neubauer."

"I can try," she said. She was young, too. Maybe the whole world would seem that way to me now.

"The guest house seems to be a little, uh, crowded," I said. "This nice couple believes they have it for the week, and I'm pretty sure I do."

Erica Ruth looked among us. "That's right."

I suddenly saw the third option, the one I hadn't wanted to consider. On the wall over Erica Ruth's shoulder, there was a head-and-torso photo of a man with a thoughtful expression. He was handsome, with the sharp collar of his shirt framing a clean-cut, masculine jaw. He had something of the accountant about him. All business. A metal plate on the bottom of the frame read *Warren Hoyt, Director.*

"Is the director around?" I asked. "We need to get to the bottom of things pretty quickly here."

Erica Ruth turned her back on us to put a page through on a walkie-talkie, then we all waited in awkward silence. I felt the rays of sun diminishing as we stood there shuffling our feet. I was always keenly aware of what time it was these days.

"How many bedrooms are in the guest house?" I said, fidgeting with my camera bag. It was heavy on my neck.

"Three upstairs plus the suite," she said.

"Which suite?" Paris demanded. "What does that come with?"

Erica ran through a few details without enthusiasm. "They all come with access to the lake," she said, shooting for cheerfulness.

At the sound of tires crunching outside, we gave up on talking and waited. The man from the wall's portrait, his face just as thoughtful in real life, appeared in the doorway and entered with a sigh. "Let me guess," he said. "Both parties thought they had the entire house for the week."

He was a tall guy, muscular in his adult version of Boy Scout khaki gear, a green polo shirt buttoned to the collar. Warren. There was no easy nickname for Warren that I knew of, and people without a path to a nickname put me on notice. The faux-military aspect of his uniform also got my back up. Bix had been career Army, master sergeant, decorated, twenty years and retirement by age thirty-nine, with stints guarding the DMZ in Korea and active deployments in both Iraq and Afghanistan. As someone who had dated, then married into the strain and fall-out of the actual military, I didn't expect much from this proto-scout. Either sell me some cookies or get off my porch.

Plus, I had heard the guy's transference of the problem back on us. A management move. "So we're meant to share it," I said. "Is that what I'm hearing?"

"Share it," Paris moaned. "Dev, do something."

"If this misunderstanding occurs often," I continued to Warren, "perhaps the language you use to talk about the arrangements isn't clear."

"The contract is clear," he said. All business, indeed. "Do you make it a habit to sign documents you don't read in full?"

"She didn't make the arrangements," Dev said, kindly.

"Did you make your own?" the director said, giving him the full weight of his attention now. "You also seem to have misunderstood."

"We have six people coming," Dev said. "I thought—"

"Six? *Six?*" For a moment my mind couldn't move past the concept. I could feel my mouth opening and closing. "*Six?*" I had meant to spend the week alone, not in a frat house. Not in a barracks, for God's sake.

"Our good friends from school, Malloy, Sam, and Martha," Paris said. "Malloy's girlfriend. And us. Six. Which is why we wanted the whole house."

"You wanted three bedrooms," Hoyt said, sliding behind the desk. He pulled out a clipboard and flicked through a couple of pages. "I can check your request in the system, but save me the time. Three bedrooms?" Dev nodded. Hoyt put down the clipboard. "Three bedrooms were available, and I'm sure someone would have told you the suite was *un*available."

"Oh," Dev said. "I didn't—I didn't realize that's what that meant. I guess I thought the suite was another building." Paris sucked at her teeth.

"But surely my husband would have asked for the whole house," I said. I didn't get to use that phrase—*my husband*—much anymore, and it felt like a soft blanket around my shoulders. I had always liked saying it. All the Army wives used it, every time, because you never knew when your last chance would come. Plus, my husband outranked a lot of theirs. "My husband would have asked for the whole house," I said. "It was our—"

It would have been a romantic getaway, a tenth wedding anniversary. Dev, reading my mind, blushed and looked down at the sandals he'd put on for the walk over from the house.

"Well, he didn't pay for the entire property," the director said. "You have the suite at the back of the house. A bit secluded from the rest of the living quarters, with its own bathroom and entrance."

"But shared kitchen and living room?" I said.

He didn't want to admit it but nodded. "It's communal living," he said, brightening his voice into brochure copy, into a halfhearted sales pitch. "We're a family-friendly place. We get a lot of grandparents with the whole brood, vacationing families. Intimate—" He cleared his throat. "More private retreats are probably best suited for the hotels in town. Only a few miles away."

I glanced at the other two. They probably didn't mind communal living. That's what they'd come for. And they probably wouldn't let a little communal living ruin any private moments they had planned, either.

Why had Bix chosen this place? In the last few months of his life, he had picked up a small interest in the night sky, flipping through a magazine or two, but with no patience, as usual, for reading. Out on the town, he might complain about the orange glow of light pollution. His interest in a wide sky coincided with a few other changes, including a few that I had welcomed. He'd been in the process of chilling out, and if a little astronomy was all it took, so be it. Among the many knotty mysteries of paperwork he'd left behind, this reservation hadn't been the toughest to solve. The dates were just ahead of our tenth wedding anniversary, and he'd put away a little stash of cash, too. The money had come in handy while I'd figured out widowhood and how to take control of our finances. I had considered letting the reservation pass by, of course. I had been letting a lot of things pass by. But by the time the dates rolled around, I was ready for the change in scenery, for the chance to get out of that house. For the chance to get out of the rut I had created for myself.

This was too much, however. Six people.

I looked around. Everyone was looking at me, impatient. Maybe I had let the silence go on too long. "I'll be on my way. Home," I said. "Not to some backwater Motel 8, thanks. I can be back in Chicago before it gets—if I leave right now, I can get back tonight. I'll need a receipt for my refund."

Paris's chin rose triumphantly. Dev looked relieved. But Erica Ruth and her boss grimaced in exactly the same way. I had a feeling this conversation took place more than once in a while. "We have a no-refund policy," Erica Ruth said.

"Also in the contract," Hoyt said. "The one your husband didn't read."

I was angry and, worse than that, I was going to have to spend at least one night here on principle alone, refund be damned, and worse even than that, I was scared. I hadn't known if I could go through with any of this on my own, and now I would have to find out what I was made of in front of an audience.

"He might have read the contract," I said, forcing my voice through the smallest window possible, the fit so narrow that it creaked. "He might have understood it completely, but he's dead now, so I can't ask him."

Faces around the room fell. If misery was good for anything, it was for reminding other people that their problems were petty and ridiculous. It was good for getting people to shut up.

"I'm so sorry," Warren Hoyt said, and he might have even meant it.

"But not sorry enough to help me," I said, and pushed past Paris for the door.

## Chapter Two

I stomped past the park's green Jeep, kicking as much gravel as I could displace as I crossed the lot back toward the guest house. Bix had done this to me. He had somehow managed to trick me into this predicament and also into being mad at him again, all from the grave. Duped me into being mad at him for something other than dying. Duped me into feeling something other than fear and betrayal.

The thing was, I was afraid of the dark.

I hadn't always been this way. I used to be a grown-up. Or, I thought I was. It's hard to remember. In the time since Bix had died, I had lost track of the woman I might have once been. She seemed like a person I'd met or read about, instead of some earlier incarnation of myself. She might have been an adult, or she might have been someone who tagged along after her husband from state to state, from one desolate life milestone to another. I'd been too busy to piece her back together. Too busy mourning, I guess, and not just the man but the life I thought I'd been living.

I was shaking from the interaction in the office, from having brought up Bix in broad daylight. I hardly talked about him anymore.

I had, at first. I talked about him all the time. I used up all the sympathy of friends, of family, of my entire world, talking about him. No one I knew had lost everything. They ran out of glib cheerfulness, and then the check-in visits stopped, the calls. The invitations. Talking about Bix drained people dry. I had to believe it was more than boredom. Maybe they didn't want to admit that this thing that had happened to me—this annihilation—was possible. Maybe they didn't want to admit it could happen to them.

Bix's mother was the only person who never tired of me. We sat around cups of tea getting cold and took turns saying his name. Between the two of us, we forgave him almost everything.

At the funeral, some of his buddies had wanted to tell stories, funny ones, stories that would have lifted everyone's mood. But I hadn't wanted my mood lifted, not then. I had just learned a great deal about Bix that I hadn't known. And by the end of the day, I would feel even less like having a laugh.

So for a long time, when it happened by accident that a smile might find itself on my lips, I let it fall away. No. I wrenched it off before anyone could see it. I was a widow. Widows weren't allowed to smile.

Eventually, though, I got tired of my own grief, or of the person I was when I was mired in it. I got impatient with myself, with the role. With the story of Bix's death, with the people I had to meet and talk with, the papers I had to read and sign, read and initial here, here, and here, with all the things he'd left behind for me to sort through, discover.

By six or seven months, I had started to see an opening. I wanted to talk about something else. I didn't want to stay in it the way I was, trying to spite the guy who hadn't even survived to see how angry I was at him. I wanted to forgive him, really forgive him, and so I began to try. At some cost, because other people couldn't. That, apparently, was why some people had stayed away in the first place.

I wanted to laugh. I had once liked to laugh, or I wouldn't have been with Bix. And now, nine months later, I wanted— something. A way back. A way forward.

I was stuck. So I didn't talk about him much anymore, a relief to the few who were willing to be around me. And I tried not to think about him as much, either.

Except—at home, in the night, no matter what I allowed myself to think about or talk about, every light source in our house glared out into the dark. It was the only way I could face the long hours of the night alone. The lights were keeping more than the dark at bay.

Now, in this far-north refuge, the sky was still bright and would be for hours. But when the sun fell, these woods would close in around the guest house without the benefit of artificial light. Here in this dark sky park, one of only a handful in the world, all efforts had been made to keep lights minimal and those that were necessary turned toward the earth to avoid light pollution. All this so that we mere humans of the twenty-first century could gaze upon the pristine night sky as our ancestors had done.

The ultimate prank.

Bix had booked this getaway without knowing, of course, what it would mean to send me into the dark. He would have been with me, watching for the stars to sprinkle the black sky to the horizon, for shooting stars to dart over our heads. The visible Milky Way. When I'd discovered the reservation paperwork, I'd pictured the two of us sitting at the edge of the lake, our fingers entwined in the dark. Imagined days spent taking photographs of the ripples in the water, of leaves waving in the trees. A few nights in a strange bed to invigorate the marriage, who knows?

The trip had seemed like Bix's apology to me, a promise he was making to himself and, without my knowing, to me. It had all seemed terribly romantic.

And it might have been, if he had lived. If he had lived and I hadn't developed a real fear of the dark. And if six total strangers wouldn't be ruining my chance of breaking through that fear with their presence. With their rowdy, happy lives.

I was almost upon the guest house before I realized there were more people moving into it. Two more cars had pulled up behind what I assumed was Dev and Paris's fancy Jaguar. All the vehicles had Midwestern plates—Ohio, and now Michigan and Indiana—and empty racks on top from which all manner of athletic gear had already been dislodged. Two bright yellow kayaks leaned up against the picnic table to the side of the house, warming in the sun. I reached for my camera.

Maybe they'd be out all day on the lake. Maybe it would be fine.

Through the viewfinder, I framed the shot, the kayaks like giant pieces of fruit resting against the rim of a bowl. But I didn't take the photo. Instead, I lowered the camera and tucked it back into the bag.

Six people. Six boisterous athletic types in their sexual

primes, at the beginnings of their lives and relationships, before anything had to be faced or managed or gotten through. I couldn't imagine spending another minute among them. Not for money. Not even on principle. So what if they were on the lake all day? It wasn't the daytime I was worried about.

My phone rang in my pocket. I hadn't had more than two bars of service since Grand Rapids. I pulled the phone out, peered at the service. Spotty. The real estate agent, again.

I braced myself. "Hello?"

"Eden, hell-oh. Where've you *been*?"

"On the road, Griffin, what's up?"

"Just checking in to see if all that driving has given you any *clarity* about what you want to do here," he said breezily. "I know the plan—*Tuesday*—but just in case *epiphanies* came to you."

Griffin had a way of talking that made me think less of myself for listening to him, but he had a good track record of sales and a sense of style that I lacked. He had a sense of ambition that I was missing, too. The reception was bad. His voice seemed to be coming from inside a barrel, and the words cut out.

"No rays of light or thunderbolts," I said, examining a bruise on my forearm. I didn't remember hitting my arm on anything. Was I a danger to myself, as my sister had suggested? "Is there some urgency?"

"Well, I took a look around the house again—" He cut out.

"And?"

"—to get my hands on the place—just move some teeny tiny things—"

"You're breaking up terribly. What are you moving?"

Nothing.

"Griffin? You're not coming through well."

"The sofas. All of them," he said. "They're out of here. You say the word."

"And this is going to help sell it?"

"I'll bring in a few—just—it up a bit—"

"I'm not following you," I said. I'd tried my phone at the front of the park on arrival. No bars. Texts were coming through. I could see I'd missed one from my sister, but I didn't want to answer that right now. She would have too many questions for a text conversation, and the phone option was clearly not working well. "I can't really tell what you're wanting to do to the place. But what if I decide to stay? Remember the part where we are just thinking things through? Until Tuesday?"

"We could—" He cut out again.

"Griffin, can you please just leave the teeny tiny things where they are for now? Can you hear me? Just until Tuesday, OK?" I looked at the phone to see if we had disconnected. "Hello?"

"A *love* seat—set off the—"

"Tuesday, OK?" I said. "I'll talk to you then." I hung up the phone. He would probably use the bad connection to justify doing precisely what he wanted. The phone buzzed in my hand. A text from Griffin: Just one love seat? A shame that texts were getting through at all, really.

I put the phone away.

My suitcase sat somewhere inside. The car with Indiana plates had blocked mine in. Home was at least five hours away. And, even there, at home, teeny tiny things were already changing.

I was suddenly magnificently tired. I put the heels of my hands to my eyes and pressed, letting time march toward sundown and darkness and my own reliable terror. If I could just relax for a minute. If I could just get some sleep. I had not gotten enough sleep since—

And then the woman from the funeral appeared whole cloth in my mind. Navy dress, crumpled tissues in her hand, hair a bit mussed, slept in. The dress was too tight, stretching over her hips. That's what I had to fall back on, the memory of that ill-fitting dress, after she said who she was. *You think you're the only one who lost someone—*

"I'm sure it's not all that bad," a man's voice said. "Not the end of the world, at least."

I dropped my hands, not sure how long I'd been standing there. He was coming around the end of the house and past the kayaks toward me. Presumably he was one of the four additional expected guests and likely the same age as the pair I'd already met, but he seemed somehow older. He had startling good looks, the kind that hardly ever occurred in normal life—chiseled jaw; straight, bright teeth; and chestnut hair that had grown a little long, curling around his ears. He moved like someone comfortable in the world and, even though he wore far more clothes at this introduction than Dev had at his, I found myself imagining the skin underneath. I was staring. I pulled my arms around myself and looked toward the woods. A cloud passed over the sun overhead, its shadow dragging over us.

I shivered. "It might be."

"It might be," the man agreed, cheerful. He passed me and reached inside the open window of the car with Indiana license plates, the one keeping my car from leaving. He brought out a thick metal watchband and strapped it around his tanned wrist. The watch was a statement piece, the kind of thing that came with a yacht, maybe, not a kayak. Not a beat-up Volkswagen. He pushed the watch up his arm, shook it down to his wrist, then pushed it back up again. "It might be the end of the world," he said. "But it's probably not. Almost nothing is."

Something about him reminded me of Bix, though they looked nothing at all alike. There was no sense in it, really, but I felt a shift in this man's favor for the similarity, whatever it was. "Did you lose the love of your life?" I said.

The guy stopped and considered the question. "Well, strange you should ask," he said, letting that sentiment drift between us without anchor. "To be honest, I just found her."

For a moment I thought he was flirting.

It wasn't out of the question. A few guys had tried since Bix's death. I was young for a widow, for one thing, not yet thirty-five, and Bix's benefits, insurance policies, and stashed cash had left me set up for a life of leisure that attracted a certain kind of attention. I had bumped up against single men—and married men who tried anyway, for sport—in all of the photography courses I'd taken. Lighting 101, portraiture, still life and tabletop photography. I'd had to skip darkroom techniques, obviously. In each of the classes, there were always men readily at hand who treated the course like a singles' mixer, who thought I looked pretty good or at least pretty available. I could recognize the attempts, but didn't allow them. I'd had to stop the classes, anyway. They were a waste of money at this point, given I couldn't seem to take a single frame since Bix had died.

I didn't want men around me, anyway. Those swimming

trunks on the newel post of the stairs inside had been doubly startling because they were so—male. I hadn't kept any male company, hadn't wanted any male attention. Yet, I wasn't immune to a good smile.

Here was a good smile. I caught my distended reflection in the windshield of the nearest car and ran my fingers through my messy hair, windblown from the drive and maybe a little more carefree than I actually was. I'd had no chance to admire a reflection in a long time but now I did. There she is. How odd that that woman was still there.

"There she is," the guy said. I looked up, startled. He was watching over my shoulder. I turned to find another beautiful creature approaching from the lakeshore, this one with a sheet of sleek honey hair and milky pale skin. The hair was probably dyed, but who could argue that she shouldn't bother? My own pale reflection couldn't compete with that. Not now, not ten years ago. "Hon?" the man called, waving her in. "Come meet someone."

"Hey," the woman said, smiling wide. She had a crooked eyetooth, but the flaw only made her prettier. I liked that she had decided to let that crooked tooth have its place. She leaned in to shake my hand. "I'm Hillary. You must be, uh . . ." She looked uncertainly toward her boyfriend.

"No, I'm—"

"A new friend," the guy said.

"Are you staying in the park, too?" Hillary asked.

"That's, uh . . ."

"We're so excited about tonight," she said. "I want to sleep all day until it gets dark so I can stay up all night."

This was pretty much the same schedule I'd been keeping, minus the part about sleeping at all.

"Hills has been studying the constellations to get ready," the man said. The way he looked at her made me think of long-ago feelings. The trouble with marriage was that time accumulated over top the things that had brought you together and hid the gleam of those first shiny impressions. Here was brand-new love, pink and fresh as a newborn.

"Malloy," I said, pulling the name from memory.

His attention wrenched from the girl. He seemed to see me for the first time. "Yeah," he said. "I—wait, are you with—? Have we met? I can't place you, I'm sorry."

Dev and Paris were coming along the back of the cars. She pouted, and he petted at her. She wore a hefty diamond on her left hand but no band. Theirs was a relationship with at least a few miles on the odometer. I looked back at Malloy and Hillary, who clung to one another. The first couple would ruin the second. It would be tiring to watch, like a nature program marathon, predators tearing cute little rodents to pieces all day.

"You don't know me," I said. "I was just leaving."

Paris squealed and ran up to Malloy. She tucked herself against him for a hug. He had to untangle himself from Hillary to make it work. Over Malloy's shoulder, Paris eyed the other woman.

"At last," Malloy said, turning himself out of Paris's embrace. "Pare, Dev. I want you to meet Hillary. Hills, you've heard me talk about—"

"But now he only talks of you," Dev said.

"I'm so excited to meet you," Hillary said, shaking Dev's hand.

"I don't want to interrupt your reunion," I said. "But could I get you to move your car?"

"You're not staying at the park?" Malloy said.

"Only," Paris said, crossing her arms, "to stay at the park would mean she was staying with *us*. Some mix-up."

A fierce feeling of ownership of the suite rose inside me. Just because there were more of them, didn't mean I had less title to the room and the shared spaces. Paris had left out the part where they'd made the same mistake Bix had.

"Oh, yeah?" Malloy said. He pulled Dev in, pounding him on the back a few times the way men did to keep their embraces active and sportsmanlike. "That's great. The more the merrier. The sky is pretty big, after all, so there're plenty of stars to go around."

I WENT TO fetch my suitcase. Malloy was the openhearted one in the group, that much was clear. But after I let the wave of indignation pass over me, I saw Paris's side. Friends trying to recapture their youth and sense of belonging— they had no need of an extra. I could leave now and be done with all this. I'd have to find another way to get back on track. Some other way that hadn't already occurred to me. I opened the door.

"—thought we were supposed to be honoring memories here or whatever the hell we're doing. You can't hide in the bathroom the whole week."

Upstairs, another young man sat sidesaddle on the bannister, his black sneakers dangling in the air. He was bearded, stout. Behind him, a door was open. Inside, another woman stood at a vanity and fixed her face in the mirror, her curly red bobbed hair turned to him.

"I can't believe he—"

"Martha." He'd had his hands raised, gesturing, but, seeing me in the doorway, dropped them and hopped off the bannister. He hurried down the stairs. "It's great to meet you," he said, drawing out the words as he reached for and pumped my hand. "We missed you guys getting in. We've really been looking forward to this, haven't we, Martha?"

Martha emerged from the bathroom and laid her hands on the rail overlooking the downstairs, another queen surveying all she commanded. She had a wild smile forced onto her pale, freckled face. Her eyes locked with mine, and the fake smile, painted a vibrant red, turned into something else. Her eyes lit up, feasting on me as she took her time down the stairs, one finger trailing along the railing. "You're not Hillary."

Hillary and Malloy were just behind me, so entwined as to have difficulty getting through the door. They laughed their way in.

"Oh, right," the bearded man said. "I'm sorry— Who are you?"

"This is our new neighbor," Malloy said. "Roommate, actually. She's in the suite in the back."

"The suite?" Martha said. She and Paris exchanged looks.

I was starting to understand the alliances and divisions: The group of friends, tight in college, all the stars in their constellation swirling around Malloy and his easygoing grin. And then Hillary, the new girl. It would be just like old times, except not at all. Not with new people.

Malloy's wuzzy gaze on Hillary hadn't wavered. He didn't care that another stranger was in the guest house because he couldn't see anything but her. Another stranger, in fact, helped cut the tension.

"So you're . . ." the bearded man said again.

"Eden," I said. "Eden Wallace. There was a mix-up with the reservations."

"There was?" Martha said, looking toward Dev. He shook his head.

"Oh, that's fun. I think it's one of those things," Hillary said, her eyes on Malloy. "Like in the movies?"

No one knew what she was talking about. Martha and Paris fought down smiles.

"The meet-cute," Hillary said. "I think that's what they call it."

"*You're* cute," Malloy said. "This is Eden, everyone. Eden, this is everyone. And this is my darling Hillary. Isn't she wonderful?"

THE REST OF everyone turned out to be Sam, with the beard and the belly, and Martha, she of the pin-up lipstick and red curls. They were not a couple, as it turned out, just friends from college who hadn't brought anyone with them and had agreed to share a room to make things tidy.

Of course, without me in the suite downstairs, lodgings might have been just as easily divided up.

There were hugs between the friends and more careful introductions between Hillary and the others as I stood with my suitcase at my feet. I had meant to be gone by now, but the car from Indiana still sat behind my car's bumper. I glanced toward the kitchen, where a yellow-faced clock over the stove ticked away the minutes. A window allowed a beam of sunlight to wash over the kitchen, but the angle of light was getting tricky. If I left now, I might get stuck in traffic. I would definitely get stuck in traffic. I lived in Chicago, where getting stuck in traffic was the price of admission. What I hadn't been caught in, in even the shortest days of winter since Bix had died, was darkness. What would I do, if the sun went down while I was still driving?

Pull over, turn on an ineffective overhead dome light? Wait all night as the battery on the car died and the darkness enveloped me? I pictured, instead, reaching for the door handle and flinging myself into oncoming headlights. And then the swirling lights of emergency, the news cameras catching it all for the sake of those at home. News at ten and eleven.

I didn't know where the end of my sanity was, but I thought it might be just there, in the near shadow of nightfall. But hadn't I come here to face that possibility? That I might not ever make it back from here? And if I did, could I even be returned to the woman I was before I was this small, cowering rabbit of a person? I had to get back to who I had been—or who I would have been without Bix's influence. I had no other choice.

I pulled up the handle on my suitcase, clicking it locked. The group went quiet, then rallied. Paris pulled Martha away and toward the kitchen, and Sam followed.

"Come on," Malloy said to me. "You have to stay one night. Get what you came for."

He had no idea what I'd come for and how likely it was I'd fail to achieve it. Or how many night terrors might arrive in the meantime. "I came here for different reasons than you and your friends," I said at last.

"We just came to . . . get to know each other, have fun," Hillary said. Malloy pulled her in tighter and put a kiss on top of her head. She looked uncertainly to where the other women were whispering heatedly in the hallway on the other side of the kitchen. She seemed to buoy herself. "And to see the stars, of course."

"I didn't actually come to see the stars," I said. Without Bix to guide my sight upward, I probably would have failed the test anyway. I might have attempted to take a few photos during the day, but I couldn't really imagine how I would have broken through the fear that kept me locked up tight under bright lights each evening. And even this new plan of somehow talking myself through a single night of darkness, unaided, was a tall order. I took a shaking breath. "It's hard to explain."

"Her husband died," Dev said from the couch.

Hillary made a sound, her hand shooting to her mouth. I had lost track of Dev since we'd gotten through introductions—or more to the point I'd forgotten he existed. I shot him a look. I hadn't wanted to bring up Bix again. Not in front of young love. Young, delicate, exposed, pink-belly love.

Malloy's face was a mask when his smile was tucked away. "I'm sorry to hear that."

It had been long enough now that I often tried to brush away condolences. What to say? "Thank you—"

"This is their anniversary," Dev said.

Hillary made another sound.

"Well, uh, Tuesday, actually," I said. "But this—yeah. This was his surprise for me. Surprise."

"Oh, no," Hillary breathed. She moved toward me, letting Malloy's arm drop from her shoulders. "Oh, no, now I get it."

Dev shrugged and let his head sag to the back of the couch.

"You do?" I said.

"You wanted to be alone," she said.

I was surprised that she, out of all of them, seemed to understand it. Not that it made any sense at all, since alone was all I ever was. The scenery. I had banked on the change of scenery taking me somewhere I had literally never been. I had the SLR Bix had bought me slung around my neck, a gift to get me started learning, and I had. But now the memory card on the camera was empty, brand new. I hadn't taken a single shot since his death. He had given me this life, these ambitions, and now this place. He had made this all possible. Surely, if nothing else, I could find the gratitude not to waste it.

"Alone with the sky," she said. "With heaven, maybe?"

I couldn't help it. I laughed. Over on the couch, Dev snorted, coughed, and joined me. Once I had started I couldn't seem to stop. "I'm not—" I tried. "I'm not a—what's the word? I don't even know."

"Pilgrim," Malloy said. He wasn't laughing but he had taken Hillary back under his arm to make her comfortable with the hysterics. "We're all pilgrims."

Dev shook his head and lay back again, the hint of a smile still on his face. Sam wandered in to see what was so funny. The women, I assumed, had gone to see the suite, to make Paris at home there before anyone else thought to stake a claim.

I had been thinking *zealot*. "Did you go to some—what school did you all go to?" I said.

"State," Malloy said. His grin rebuilt itself. "Not some weirdo religious enclave, if that's what you wondered. I meant on this earth. We're all pilgrims here upon the earth, sometimes not for long."

If anyone else had said it, I would have torn through him with cynicism. But Malloy seemed to mean it, to understand our fleeting situation here in this house and in this world better than anyone else could. I couldn't quite laugh at him. For some reason, what he said comforted me, more than most of the platitudes I'd already accepted as condolences. *Pilgrim* made sense to me. I felt like a lowly traveler, anyway—temporary and small against the coming nightfall. My life had shrunken to the tiniest pinprick, like a solitary and distant star in the night sky. I had come here for—something. Bix had wanted us to be here. I wanted to understand why, and when I did, by Tuesday at the latest, I wanted to call Griffin back and tell him what to do about the house. Very tall order.

But to figure it out—well, I couldn't go back home just yet. That's where it all waited. All of it: his things, the bills I soon would not be able to pay. The failures of our life lived there as well as my absolute loss at how to move on.

How many lights could I leave on in the suite without the rest of them noticing? Without some well-meaning ranger coming to tamp down the glow, which would surely go against the park's rules, if the light leaked outside. It was too late to get home before dark now. I'd been lulled by Malloy's smile, by Hillary's innocence, by their brand-new, bright-eyed relationship.

The house was silent, somehow strangely respectful. Malloy squeezed Hillary to him. They couldn't bear to be out of touch with one another's skin, even as they waited for me to agree to gate-crash their first night.

Love. It made no sense.

Wait until they knew. About Bix. About everything. Wait until I had to explain the anniversary was a milestone I wasn't sure we would have reached if Bix had lived to see it.

# Chapter Three

Malloy rolled my suitcase through the kitchen and into the back hallway. Paris and Martha slid out of the suite ahead of my entrance, snickering and avoiding eye contact with me.

"Did you see the weird self-guided tour markers on the way in? The silhouettes?" Malloy said. "We drove down to the viewing area and they're all along the way, these strange flat people standing along the road, pointing out facts and stuff. Historical figures, I guess, but—damn, they are creepy. I kept thinking someone was running out into the road. Braked hard every single time."

Inside the suite, homey and fussily decorated in beach house whites and blues, I inhaled deeply. The room had one tall window with sheer curtains. It would have to be covered. The breath came out as a sigh.

"Look, don't stay if you don't want to," Malloy said, taking the case across the sitting area to the foot of the bed. He looked around. "Nice. But so what? It's a nice room and we're fun people, but if you'd rather go home, don't let me bully you into staying."

I hadn't decided what I'd rather do, but I found myself going along with this plan. One night. I could do one night, couldn't I?

It cheered me up to think I might. This man. His confidence was catching.

"I hardly think you're a bully," I said. "Malloy. Is that your first or last name?"

"The only name I answer to," he said. "You know what I mean, though. We can roll this suitcase right back out, if you want. I can stop trying to convince you that you should stay. I've, uh, been known to talk people into things sometimes. There are people like that, you know? Some of them not as good intentioned as I like to think I am." He raised an eyebrow at me and I nodded. I knew about that. "Anyway. You should make up your own mind."

I had no problem imagining this guy convincing a woman to take a chance on him or talking one of his friends into whatever scheme he had in mind. "Was this group trip your idea, then?"

"Not even close," he said, turning to the window. He seemed to think better of his tone and softened it. "I brought the kayaks. I'm nothing if not game for a week on a lake. But apparently we have some things to work through before we can enjoy ourselves. There's an *agenda*, God help us."

"It sounds like you're here for group therapy," I said. "Paris said it's the anniversary of your graduation."

He turned a wary smile my way, as though waiting for a punchline. "Yes, it's that," he said. "Five years. In June."

It was June now. I waited.

"*Next* June, five years a year from now," he said.

"So it's the anniversary of something else."

He made a sound in his throat. "When your husband died," he said, "did you ever find yourself having to console other people? Like, instead of getting on with the greatest loss of your own life, you became responsible for everyone else's grief?"

"Oh, yeah." I sat on the edge of the bed. "They want you to give them permission to be fine with it. Meanwhile you're not fine."

"Or you are, because life goes on. Eventually. Even when you thought you didn't want it to. But some of us," he said, nodding his head to the other room, "have not had our fill of mourning." He sucked his teeth for a second. "That sounded so cruel. I'm such an asshole."

"So who was it?"

"The love of my life, as a matter of fact," he said. I remembered what I'd asked him outside at his car, his answer, my misunderstanding. I felt myself blush. He *had* been flirting a little, though. Handsome men liked to keep their hand in, their skills sharp. Maybe I was cute enough to flirt with. Or maybe I was safe, a few years older, a widow, his girlfriend nearby. Someone to humor and jolly into a better mood.

"Really?" I said, nodding toward the door, through which his gorgeous girlfriend could be found.

"I thought so, for a minute or two. Youthful obsession, more like. But apparently second chances do exist. Hey, maybe you'll stay long enough that you'll learn the sordid details." He flicked at the ID tag on my suitcase. "Chicago, huh? Good place to be from."

I wasn't from there. Bix was, and so when he'd retired, we settled there. When we'd first arrived, I couldn't believe I lived under such a skyline—I couldn't believe that the skyline actually existed outside films and television, outside dreams of what a city should look like. I had come from a much more suburban area: sprawling, without center, ugly. Chicago was lovely. The high-rises were jet-black blocks against the night sky, everything lit fiercely and defiantly. Lights left on, welcoming, beckoning, except to the east, where the city came to an abrupt halt at the crescent shoreline of Lake Michigan. To the east of the city, the lake lay dark, the sky to the horizon.

I walked to the window and drew aside the curtain. There it was. The far side of the same lake, though we were up against the very northeastern tip of it. It seemed like the end of the world just now.

This is why I'd come. To expand the world that had turned so small. To come to the end of something and step over into what was next. To see the damn stars as Bix had wanted, and then kiss them all, and him, good-bye. To get over him, at least enough to get on with things, whatever those things turned out to be. To get on with life and what was left of it.

There was too much of it left to live it out hiding from the night sky. And, more damning, there was far too much of it remaining to ride out the money Bix had left me. All those systems set in place, and the clock was winding down, even so.

"Chicago's nice," Malloy said, fidgeting with his watch again. Up his arm, down his arm, rattle around his wrist. He didn't seem to like the feel of it on his skin. "But you can't see any stars there."

"A few," I said. "But I guess not enough."

MALLOY LEFT ME to go reattach himself to Hillary. I sat down on the bed and pulled the camera bag strap over my head. The bed was comfortable, laid with a fluffy comforter I was sure would be no comfort to me. Not at night, anyway. I could hear low voices in the kitchen and wondered how much of the conversation was about whether or not I would stay.

I wouldn't have wanted me here, in their place. I didn't want me here now.

One night. I could make it through one night.

I would have to cover the windows. There were extra blankets folded on the chair in the seating area. They would do. I went to the door and tried the switch for the overhead lights. Weak. Far too weak.

A radio sat on the nightstand. I turned it on, fidgeting with the dial until something local and boring came on, then turned it off.

"Hello?" Hillary stood at the door, raising her knuckles to knock and then dropping her hand when she saw me. "Oh, wow, this is so cute. Look at this little living room you've got. It's so homey."

"I probably won't stay more than a day," I said. "Maybe you and Malloy can grab this when I go."

She tilted her head, smiling. "I don't think that will be the way it goes."

"I don't know," I said. "Seems like you're the first lady of this place."

She laughed. "If you mean because Malloy is so—well, he's just so much himself, isn't he? I've never met anyone like him."

Hillary had done it again. She had such an innocent way of slashing through to the truth and now she'd struck gold again. So much himself—yes, maybe that was the thing about Malloy that had reminded me of Bix. Even though he'd been through so much, even at the end, when things weren't quite what they seemed, he had always been so much himself. And that's what had bothered me most. Lying should leave a trace.

Hillary went to the window, murmuring over the view of the lake and woods. I watched her hair slide over her narrow shoulders. I had never been a woman like this, the porcelain kind, slim at the wrist. I hadn't met too many of them, either. On base, they might show up, young, married, deer in head-lights. They were rare creatures, tottering around on slim legs and heels too high to be practical. Most of us were practical. You had to be. And if you couldn't protect yourself, you didn't last long, not out in the field and not among the wives on base, either.

"Are you nervous to be inserted into the family this way?" I said.

I hadn't meant to be unkind, not consciously, but it must have sounded that way. She turned from the window, a furrow between her eyebrows. For a second, she looked older, harder. And then the moment passed. "Is it that obvious?" She shrugged. "I mean, they just love him so much, you know? You can tell how protective they are of him."

"Possessive," I said. But then I was again thinking of Bix.

"That, too," she said, without the smile this time. Some-where in the other half of the house, one of the women laughed. "But there's no question how close they are. They want to be around him so much. One of them is always calling, and this trip, well, I think it's been in his calendar almost as long as I've known him." A strange, blank expression passed over her face, but then she rallied. "Hey, we're going to do a bonfire down by the lake tonight, maybe. We— Malloy and me—we want you to join us."

That was clearly out of the question. "I might make it an early night tonight," I said. "It was a long drive here and it will be a long drive back tomorrow."

"Tomorrow? You're really not staying?" She seemed honestly disappointed, and then I remembered the other two women pulling each other around the house to get away from her. In other circumstances, I'd feel bad for her. "Don't you want to see the stars before you do, at least?" she said.

Paris suddenly stood in the door. She gazed over the suite, the open curtain to the lake, my suitcase on the bed. "Did either of you bring a corkscrew?"

"They don't have one in the kitchen?" I said.

"I guess it's such a *family* place," Paris said. She turned and we followed. I had a feeling Paris was accustomed to being followed at every turn she made.

In the kitchen, the group had begun an attack. Sam and Malloy pulled at drawers and opened cabinets methodically from one side of the room to the other while the rest of us gathered around Dev. He stood with the neck of a wine bottle between his knees, prying at the cork with a screwdriver.

"You found a screwdriver but not a wine opener?" I said.

"Martha had it with her," Paris said. "She's handy like that."

"It's from her trunk," Sam said, stretching for a high cabinet.

"Hey, keep your mind off my trunk," Martha said. Behind her, the back of Sam's neck turned bright pink. "A single girl's gotta be ready to take care of things herself." She looked at me. "You know how it is."

Dev had chipped away some of the cork.

"Oh, poke it through," Paris groaned. "A little cork never killed anyone."

Several fabric carry-alls with slots for six bottles of wine apiece sat on the counter. I tallied the bottles visible in the room. "The *cork* may not kill you," I said. "But your ambition might."

Sam looked to see what I meant. "You don't like wine?"

"Sam is a distributor," Martha said, bumping him out of the way to open a drawer that had already been checked. She pulled out a silver cake knife with an intricate, tarnished handle. "Look at this beauty. Now we need some cake," she said, and then slid it back. "Sam's been working on us for years. He's got us all talking tannins and vintners. I can't believe I just said 'vintner.'"

"I don't mind wine," I said. "Occasionally." Martha looked at me with pity that I probably deserved. "I just didn't plan on replacing all my body's fluids with it this week. You won't be driving anywhere, right?"

"And we have lift off," Malloy called, pulling a silver corkscrew out of the back of a drawer and raising it over his head to cheers from the others. He ignored the bottle Dev had been battling, took up another bottle, and pulled the cork with a practiced skill. Dev set the bottle with the screwdriver stuck in the cork on the counter more heavily than I thought was warranted.

"Now," Malloy said, "who remembers which cabinet had the glasses?"

"Sam is our wine hookup," Paris said to me. "He gets the good stuff."

"I guess now's as good a time as any," Sam said, turning to the cabinet door over the sink and taking down glasses. There were six matching ones.

"What do you mean?" Malloy stretched beyond Sam's

reach to the uppermost shelf, where one oddball wineglass sat, neglected. He rinsed it out and poured the first dram of red. Sam watched as his friend took a sniff, sloshed the wine around the bowl of the glass, and finally sipped. The sort of thing I would have made fun of to amuse Bix, but I could tell from Sam's hungry eyes that he cared. When Malloy gave them all a satisfied grin, Sam launched back in. "I . . . left my job. I might do something entirely different."

"You're serious?" Martha said, her perfectly painted lips opening and closing a couple of times as she decided what to say. "But . . . but you love that job."

"It's just a job," Sam mumbled.

"You'll still get your discount, though, right?" Paris said.

"You mean, do *we* still get his discount," Martha said without looking at Paris. "But why, dude? I thought you were going for that promotion—" She glanced all around, her eyes landing on me as Malloy handed me the first serving. He had kept the mismatched glass for himself. If none of them noticed, I did. "I'm sorry," Martha said. "Maybe you don't want to talk about it."

"Well, I don't really, but I thought you should know. No, I do not get the discount anymore," he said. "I'm a *civilian*."

Malloy had served the women. Martha took a sip and exclaimed over it. Now Malloy opened another bottle of the same label and poured for the men, Sam first.

"None for me," Dev said.

"Oh, shit, I forgot," Sam said. "I meant to bring you a greez and I forgot."

"A what?" I said.

"Pinot grigio. I'm allergic to red grapes," Dev said.

"So he drinks wine like a very fine lady," Martha said, winking at him.

"Every time I'm with these guys, I'm two seconds away from an EpiPen," Dev said.

"He can't even kiss me when I've had red," Paris said. It hadn't stopped her from sipping at her glass.

"We'll swing into town for some reinforcements tomorrow," Dev said.

The staggering amount of wine on the counter was not enough.

"So, Sam. What happened with work? We talked about you going for the gold at that place," Malloy said. "Did it not work out?"

Sam looked my way. I got the hint and set down my glass. I hadn't wanted it, anyway. I'd lost the taste for alcohol but hadn't wanted to explain. "I'm going to grab a few things from my car before it gets—" I stopped and tried again. "I'll be right back."

Outside, the air had turned cooler. Shadows drew across the clearing and over the cars. I went to mine and pulled open the back door. I'd brought a few snacks from home to subsist on until I could run over to the town for the week's staples. Now I wouldn't have to go shopping, and I wouldn't have to make things last. I grabbed the bag and shut the door. After a moment of hesitation, I locked the car with a beep of the key fob, convincing myself that I would have done it anyway. Even in my secured garage in Chicago, I locked my car. So why did I feel as though I was warding off something? Or someone?

I stood next to the car, surveying the scene. The guest

house's design was flat and uninviting from this side. The woods—pines, cedars, a peeling birch or two—crawled up to the property and dangled branches near the roof. On the far side of the house, the land dropped away. The lake, then. If I only had a few hours here, I might as well take advantage of them.

Out of the corner of my eye, I sensed something moving. But when I turned my head, there was nothing there but a stirring among the branches from a breeze. I hit the lock on the button again and headed toward the kayaks and around the house. There was a ridge and then the low grass of the guest house's yard gave way to long wisps of sea grass before thinning to sand. A wave slid among the pebbles that rimmed the shore, which stretched off into a public beach to the north. A handful of people punctuated the curl of the beach as it turned in on itself, a wide-open cove. Just to the south of the guest house, a skinny strip of natural peninsula struck out into the water, a headland protecting the shore from rougher waters. This must be the so-named Straits Point.

Above, the sky was a bright blue with only a few thin clouds. It was a shame, really, that this place was so dedicated to darkness. The park's daylight was highly underrated. Everywhere I looked, a postcard-worthy photo framed itself. I hadn't brought my camera outside with me, but who was I kidding? I wouldn't have pushed the shutter button, anyway.

I walked along the curve of the land to the south and out onto the slim promontory. It curled around on itself, a finger beckoning, a half grin of land jutting into the water. The curve protected the beach and, at its tip, brought me face-to-façade once again with the guest house. For a house that faced into a scenic waterfront, west, probably into a perfect sundown every day of the week, it had few window openings in this direction. I shaded my eyes. Someone moved quickly out of view in one of the windows.

I kicked a rock into the shallow water. There was something about the peninsula that made me think of walking a pirate ship's plank. Turning to the lake again, I could almost believe I was alone.

Why had I so wanted to be alone here? Maybe only because that's what I'd expected. Would I want to spend a week in a house with strangers, even if I could?

Even from this distance, I could hear them chattering inside the house, moving things around in the kitchen and laughing. A lonely sound, the laugh of a stranger.

I knelt at the water's edge at the point of the peninsula. The water here was clear, the sand below fading quickly out into the depths. I looked around at the image I would not capture with my camera: clouds, a sailboat out in the wind, tipped so that the sail was a bright knife of white into the water. I ducked my head and found the right angle on the gray-green lake to show its flatness to the horizon, unadorned by bird or boat. Empty. After a few minutes, I rose and walked back to the mainland.

To the side of the house, a group of Adirondack loungers encircled a fire pit. I sat in one and fed myself cheese crackers out of my stash. From this viewpoint the guest house's style was architecturally interesting and angular, though overly modern for my tastes. But it was a handsome place set upon the very land's end. The fingernail's edge of the mitten state's middle finger. Bitterly cold in the winter and sold to the world as a winter wonderland in radio and television ads and on buses careening down Chicago's snow-packed streets—who needed more exposure to snow and brisk wind? We had plenty of that in Chicago, thanks, enough for a lifetime every single winter until we started to question our sanity for living there. But then came the spring and it was just as scenic and seductive as this park was now. Someone must have been quite enchanted by all this land to have offered to enclose it as a state land package, and many more must be drawn here for the trees, the waves, and now, with the special park designation to regulate the lights, the dark sky above.

Bix had been taken in, somehow. Without him here to serve as docent to all the wonders before me, I couldn't say I was. We had this lake back home.

Hillary was mincing down the yard toward me. "Can I join you?" she called, not waiting for the answer.

So much for having a moment to myself. "Sure," I said. "Cheese cracker?"

"Thanks." She took a few and nibbled at one like a rodent. "Sorry if you thought they wanted you to leave."

"They did," I said. "It's fine. I don't really care if Sam gets a new career. Do you?"

"I do, a bit. Malloy talked him through some decisions he was making about it a few weeks ago. A pep talk for his promotion. He spent a lot of time . . . But I guess it didn't work. And now we'll have to talk about it some more. I guess we have to talk about *something*. So what do you do?"

Do? I fell asleep as the sun rose, spending most of my efforts trying to catch even a few hours of rest, rushed around in the last hours of daylight to try to live a life, and then I incarcerated myself behind an arsenal of lamps and light fixtures until the first rays of sunrise the next day. I hid behind my dead husband's forethought and planning. I struggled to see what was next.

"I'm not working at the moment," I said. It was a sore subject every time my sister brought it up. Michele hated that I didn't work. No kids, no job, and now no husband.

I'd had a job, once. It had been hard to build any kind of career, trailing behind Bix base to base. But in Chicago, I'd gotten the kind of job that I might have done for the rest of my working life, without ambition. But Bix hadn't wanted me to work in the insurance office. Low-level administration as a concept made his head spin. Since he left the Army, he'd run his own company—sales, service, and chief bottle washer, as he liked to say. He worked with his hands, met new people every day, never had to sit more than a half hour behind some desk. He worked hard, or at least he seemed to. My lack of ambition had made him inexplicably angry, even though I'd had to keep any ambition I might have come by tucked inside because of *his* job. To teach me some kind of lesson, he'd bought insurance policies through me—life, accident and dismemberment, disability—hoping it might light a fire inside me for sales. It didn't.

Even worse: if I dared to voice a desire or interest, he was quick to suggest I pursue it. Caught watching a baking show? I should go to French pastry school. Reading an article on some type of crafting? Why don't you set up an online shop? If we listened to a radio story on therapy dogs, he would soon be researching what it took to train them. For me. He was happy in his own choices, but had boundless energy for any idea that might wedge me loose from where I was—he thought—stuck. When I said I might want to take up photography, that was it. The camera was researched and gifted. I quit the job with his blessing. With his insistence, really. My sister had a lot to say about that, too.

The photography was not a career. Not mine, anyway. When I sold the house—*if* I sold the house, but of course I probably had to sell the house—I would have to start over in some job, but I had no idea what that would look like. In addition to having suffered his death and the rest of what he put me through, what I had learned, thanks to his insistence, was that I was not the kind of person Bix thought I could be. *Should* be.

*Click.* I came back from where I'd gone to find Hillary reaching for another cracker, giving me a curious look.

"Life insurance comes in handy for giving you some time to think," I said, finally, and this was the truth. We had all those policies he'd bought, after all. Bix was not normally the guy who planned for eventualities. His military training had made him reactive, all fall in, never leave a man behind. He was good in a snowstorm, in a flat-tire situation. But he was not naturally an organized, thinking-ahead guy. He was live-for-today, might-die-tomorrow Army, through and through. All those policies had resulted from his one-man feud with my lack of drive. This, I now understood, was his guilt talking. All the pushing and prodding into decisions, into progress and change. He'd been trying to find a way to make things up to me, though I hadn't yet discovered the things for which he would pay and pay dearly. "I'm a photographer," I said, finally.

"Oh," she said. "Portraits or . . . ?"

"Weddings," I said. It was a lie, but the lie had occurred to me before the truth.

Hillary blinked away toward the lake. "That seems like it would be difficult . . . I mean since your husband died. I can't imagine. I mean, if anything happened to Malloy, I don't know what I would do."

"You would live," I said.

Her expression went hard. "Not very romantic for a wedding photographer. And that's a cruel thing to say. Jeesh, how did your husband die?"

"I only mean that I did. I lived. You would, too, if you had to. You've not been together all that long," I said. "It would hurt. It would be a while before you wanted to go on. But then you would."

She narrowed her eyes at me. "How do you know how long we've been together?"

"I don't. I'm just guessing."

She folded her arms and glanced back at the guest house. "They weren't talking about us before we got here?"

"I didn't say that. What? A month? Two months?"

"Three," she said, narrowly. "Not that it's any of your business."

"Nope, it sure isn't." I popped a handful of cheese crackers into my mouth and turned back to the lake. My sad life was none of hers, but that hadn't stopped her asking about it.

I should have said news photographer, documentary film. No, something boring—corporate handshake photos for the e-newsletter of Such-and-Such, LLC, delivered to in-boxes and filed into e-trash cans twice a month. Or I could have gone the other way and said I was a crime scene photographer, something that would drain away all this useless chatter. Who cares who I am? I'd be gone as soon as I could.

"There you are," a male voice called. And here came Malloy down the lawn toward us, of course. At three precious months, they couldn't be out of one another's sight for long. "Everything OK?"

"Just getting to know each other," Hillary said, tucking herself under his arm and flashing me a look I couldn't interpret. She'd learned enough.

"You're staying, then," Malloy said to me. "That's great."

"Just tonight," I said.

Over Malloy's shoulder, Sam and Martha approached, arguing in low tones. And behind them, of course, Paris and Dev, also having a few close and hissing words. One night was all I could handle. The sun was already getting low over the lake, but it would take a while to reach sunset, this far north, this late in June. I settled back and passed the box of crackers down the line. The gang was all here. Again.

# Chapter Four

S o . . . you all went to State?" I said, to keep the silence
from getting too enjoyable. Maybe if I pried for their
stories, they'd leave mine alone.

"Except Hillary," Paris said.

"Hills went to the University of Chicago," Malloy said,
squeezing her up against himself. "She's kind of a brain."

Sam peered around Malloy with the box of crackers in his
hand and crumbs in his beard. "Oh, maybe that's it," he said.

Hillary looked his way. "What?"

"I keep thinking you look familiar," he said. "I'm from
Chicago originally. My sister went to U of C and I used to
visit campus a lot. Maybe you knew her. What year did you
graduate?"

Hillary tucked herself deeper into Malloy. "Small world,"
she said. "What was your sister's major?"

"Biology," he said. "What about you?"

"Business."

"She's tops at her office, aren't you, babe?" Malloy said.
Hillary reached for the crackers and put a handful into her
mouth.

Sam mugged an impressed expression, then glanced around the circle of his friends. Martha, studying Malloy and Hillary, set her wineglass on the arm of her chair and turned her attention to Paris and Dev, who had pulled away a few feet, still in nearly silent combat. "Come on, you two," Martha said. "Let's not have a couple's spat this early in the week. It can't be that hard to be happy on this gorgeous day in this beautiful place."

"Like you would know anything about being in a couple," Paris muttered.

"Ouch," Sam said. "She would if anyone was good enough."

Martha glared his way and folded her arms. "Thanks, *friends*. So, Pare, what's up with that lifelong commitment you're supposed to be making?"

"We actually do have plenty of time to fight this week," Malloy said. "No need to do it all today."

"We're thinking next summer for the wedding," Dev said. Paris turned her chin toward the water. "Probably in Ohio, can't get around that. First thing, we need to narrow down the guest list from ridiculous to slightly less ridiculous."

"Indian weddings are, like, a week long," Paris said.

"It takes longer than hopping over a broom, I'll grant you," Dev said. At Paris's stormy look, he amended. "Which I'm totally willing to do. My parents are going to be so confused about that broom."

"If I have to paint henna doily designs on my skin that no one will be able to even *see*," Paris huffed, holding out her dark forearms, "then your parents can learn a little African-American history. I will send them a book."

"You know you're the only woman I would wear a bridesmaid dress for, Pare," Martha said. "If you need me."

"Oh," Paris said, blinking. "Oh, that's so sweet of you. But my cousins, you know I have eight girl first cousins—"

"And that's part of the problem," Dev said. "We're not even starting from common sense. If you have *eight* girl first cousins, let them take up a pew or two and sit the hell—"

"And the colors would be brutal for you," Paris said, tumbling in again. "I was thinking yellow because of the cousins, you know—"

"Apparently colors are important in these decisions," Dev said to Malloy.

"—and I have to include them—my God, my grandmother would die all over again if I didn't. But I don't know if you'd—"

"I would look terrible for *you*," Martha said.

"Let's set a date first, and then maybe things will fall into place," Paris said. "You'll all be the first to know." The promise drifted off. It seemed like a remnant of a long-ago conversation.

"How long have you been engaged?" I said.

"A few years," Dev said, a little tight in the jaw. He didn't specify or look to Paris to winnow it down further. No further math would be tolerated, no more talk of colors and henna patterns or brooms. I wasn't on the guest list. "We're getting set in our careers, and it seemed—we didn't want to rush into anything."

Martha laughed. Malloy fidgeted with his watch.

"Hey, you two," Sam said. "Cheesers." He held his phone aloft toward Hillary and Malloy. They pulled together, raising their glasses toward him. "I'll send it to you," he said, thumbing at the screen. "If I can get a single bit of service. Ever."

"So, Eden, tell us about yourself," Malloy said.

"Ah," I said. More of this? "There's not much to tell. I've lived all over the place, just got settled in Chicago about five years ago."

"She's a photographer," Hillary said.

"A hobbyist," I said. I might have been blushing.

"You have to follow your passion," Malloy said.

"And hopefully it pays the bills," Dev said.

"What do you do?" I said to Malloy.

"I'm a farmer," he said.

"Well—" Paris started.

"Really," I said, taken aback. "Weed?"

"Dairy," he said, laughing.

"I thought you were going to try something else on your own," Paris said.

"My dad is turning the family farm over to me," he said. Purposefully, it seemed to me, not looking in Paris's direction. Hillary beamed up at him. "I'm committing myself, and maybe that makes me the lunatic in the asylum, but it's a done deal. So I'm a dairy farmer. Paris is in tech. Martha's in law, as soon as she gets past that big bad bar exam." She gave him a wink and a click on a finger-gun. "Dev's a doctor. Soon, anyway, right? And Sam's in wine."

"Every chance I get," Sam said, raising his glass and taking a deep drink. And then he seemed to remember he was leaving the business and sighed at the glass in his hand.

Everyone held a wineglass except me and the guy with the allergy. That seemed like a good excuse to leave them. "I left my glass inside," I said and started to stand.

"Let me," Paris said. "I'll grab the bottle." She handed her glass to Dev and was off to the house before I could think of a good reason to refuse the favor. Dev watched after her as she hurried to the house and disappeared.

"Oh, thank God for you," Sam called after Paris. He sipped at his glass and smacked his lips at Martha. "Do you like this cabernet?"

Just then her elbow knocked into her glass of wine. It landed in the grass, splashing toward her skirt. "I liked it better when it wasn't on my dress," Martha said.

Sam retrieved the goblet, miraculously not shattered. "Get you more, dollface?"

"I don't deserve more," Martha said, pouting. Then she smiled, dimples deep in each cheek. "Later. I'm going to run in and soak this before it stains." She hurried off, too, leaving her shoes behind.

"How's the doctoring going?" Malloy said.

"Huh? Oh, fine." Dev seemed distracted.

"How soon before you get a leather couch?"

"It's just a residency rotation," Dev said. "I might end up in family practice."

He sounded thrilled.

"How *are* your parents?" Malloy asked.

"They are team plastic surgery, as always," Dev said, shoving his hand into the cracker box and coming out with a fistful. "They don't think I can save any lives. They wouldn't want me to try, anyway." Malloy and Sam exchanged glances while Dev's head was turned toward the house.

"So when do we see these stars I hear so much about?" Sam said.

"I think they just show up," Malloy said. "In the *sky*." He reached into his pocket and pulled out his phone, glanced at it, then at Hillary and around to the others, me, and up to the house. A strange expression passed over his face. He put the phone back in his pocket, glancing Dev's way. We fell into silence. I, for one, enjoyed the sound of the waves. I had always liked to listen to the sound of water, of wind rising through trees. Maybe that's why Bix had wanted to bring me here.

After about ten minutes, the back door's banging rescued us from what had become an awkward silence.

Malloy whistled. Martha, dressed in a long, low-cut sundress that showed off her impressive cleavage, was coming across the yard. I couldn't help thinking that the back door was supposed to be my private entrance and exit, but said nothing. She twirled once before taking back her seat. "What did I miss?" she said, batting her eyes.

"The stars," Dev said.

"Those old things," Martha said.

"There's a viewing area up the shore," Hillary said. "Malloy and I took a peek on the way in from the road. It's just a clearing where the trees don't get in the way, but I can't wait."

"Hillary's been studying up on this place," Malloy said. "The constellations and everything. She's got a real knack for it. Maybe she'll go pro."

Hillary smiled hopefully but no one said anything for a long moment. Dev cleared his throat. Martha glared at Malloy. "Pro . . . what now?"

"Just joking, Marty," Malloy said.

Martha twinkled at him, the dimples deepening, and leaned back. "It's good to be all together. Photoship is no substitute."

"Photoship is an excellent substitute," Sam said. "And for confirming that everyone's life is better than yours."

In the photo class I'd taken, all the other students used

Photoship to share their photos online and take in feedback from each other and their friends. I'd signed up for a profile since it was free, but I'd only put a few images up before my enthusiasm dwindled into self-consciousness. Anyone could see scenes from your life? For what purpose? A few of my classmates had gotten photography jobs from their posts—weddings and headshot portraits, mostly—but I had no hopes. My photography wasn't the kind of work that got wedding gigs. Posting there was pissing into the ocean, anyway. It had only made me feel alone and unconnected, and I had that pretty well figured out on my own.

"I loved the photos Paris posted from your visit to Indiana," Martha said.

Hillary looked at Dev. "Oh, you should have come by and seen us."

Dev turned heavily lidded eyes on her. "We visited Malloy," he said. "Not sure you were even in the picture then. We should have thought to have you over the same weekend, Martha."

Martha waved off the comment. "Well, I had just been there. My grand tour. I saw Malloy in Indiana and then I came to see you right after. Just didn't post any pictures of it, I guess." Dev turned back to the house. "You know what they say about that, right? When you're taking photos, you're not truly in the moment. You're wasting your life."

The rest of them looked at me.

"So how far up the shore is this clearing?" I said.

"Less than a mile," Hillary said. She shaded her eyes and pointed. "Where that stretch of land curves out?" No one else seemed at all interested in challenging her position as expert. She had a role among them at last. Tour guide.

Malloy, who had been staring into his glass, raised his head. "We should go check it out," he said.

"Now?" Martha said.

"Let's wait for Paris," Dev said. He glanced toward the house, then started for it. "I'll go get her."

Malloy smiled at the ground. "Yes, let's wait for Paris," he said, almost to himself. "Martha, what's new since I saw you?"

"Oh, you know. Just kicking ass and taking names."

"Wouldn't have believed any other story," he said. "Now, Sam—"

"What's everyone think of this cabernet sauvignon I brought?" Sam said, raising his glass to the light. "Are you getting the cherry note?"

The wine, to hear them talk, was a six-course meal. I found myself wanting that glass I'd left behind.

"Here they are," Malloy said, as Paris and Dev appeared around the corner of the house, marching side-by-side. Paris held the promised wine bottle, but not my glass. "What's the word? Are we off to the viewing area?"

"I thought it was nighttime when we're supposed to care about the view," Paris said, passing off the bottle for refills. She drank from her glass, looking at me over the rim.

What was the point of rushing off in a lather to do me the favor and then not following through?

I stood up and without discussion started toward the viewing area. I wasn't great at decisions, but this one didn't need six extra votes. Anyway, I wouldn't be seeing any of it in darkness. This was my only chance to see what this place was about. And these people. This might be my only chance to get away.

# Chapter Five

The beach was thin, the greenery growing up almost to the water. I walked carefully along the shore, watching for the kind of rock that might twist an ankle.

I glanced over my shoulder. Sure enough, Malloy and Hillary, holding hands, followed me. Beyond them, Paris with her heels hooked in her fingers, Dev, and the rest.

I didn't wait for them. With the sun positioned as it was, I had to start thinking about the dark. This walk had to be brisk, the visit to the clearing fast. A clearing? Who cared? Why not turn and go to my room and let them have the clearing to themselves? Wildflowers and a grassy patch for lawn chairs and stargazing—it would be nothing much to see in full sun. But I had been in the car for hours and would be again tomorrow. My legs needed the stretch of a walk, and so I pressed on, pausing only to take off my own sandals and squeeze the wet sand between my toes.

A gentle wave rolled in, the lake lapping at my ankles.

All right, Michigan tourism commercial. I see you.

The sound of the water sent my thoughts back to Chicago's shoreline, where long stretches of beach attracted tourists and natives alike. I never liked the water as much as Bix. We both sunburned easily and were miserable and grumpy with it, hot and uncomfortable in our own skin. But he was always ready to pack up the car again next time. Memory loss, almost, how easily he forgot consequences. That was one of the things I loved about him, though, his inability to cling or rail. He didn't hold grudges, not against the sun and not against whatever I might say in the heat of an argument. He was ready to forgive me any little fault. I was the one who remembered it all. The sting of sunburn that would make the next two weeks unbearable, the mistakes of marriage and friendship, the fight itself, every harsh word he'd ever said, the terrible nights, each and every one. I had always served as scorekeeper.

I guess that was another reason I had come to the park, even if the darkness scared me, even if I knew being here would bring up memories of Bix. While I was busy being bad cop, he'd been trying to nudge me toward happiness. Probably because he felt terrible about his own misdeeds, to be sure. There were plenty of those and more I hadn't even known about until too late. He was a good apologizer. He had to be, right devil that he was. But in certain moments, he was also ridiculously sweet, like the time he found a scarf in that particular shade of blue I loved and brought it home for me, no reason.

He was full of surprises—had been. Finding the reservation paperwork among his things was a good example. Why had he planned something for us so far out on the calendar? So out of character, but I'd finally backtracked what must have inspired him.

Once, I'd told him about camping under the stars as a

kid, the one thing I remembered doing with my parents that helped me see them as regular people, just trying to do their best. One of the few fond memories I had of my dad, actually, was the two of us sitting on a picnic table—the tabletop, not the bench—throwing old Halloween candy corn to raccoons.

There's another story I'd told Bix that he must have forgotten, or he wouldn't have thought to bring me here. After our dad died, Michele and I were shuttled around the aunts and cousins for a couple of weeks. "She's not well" is what the women would say to each other over the tops of our heads, meaning our mother. After a week with our mother's cousin Dab—Dab Holt, I'll never forget—who had a cigarette in her hand every second of her waking life, we finally were allowed to go home. We arrived in Dab's land-cruising boat of a Buick, smoke roiling out when the doors opened. We hadn't had a chance to grieve, not with Dab on the case. Life had been too different those last few weeks to notice that life would never be the same. That first night back home when I wandered, crying from a nightmare, into my mother's room, she took me right back to my own bed. "We're not going to start any bad habits," she said, but she left the light on for me. I hadn't been afraid of the dark, but afterward I made up any story to keep the lights on. I didn't have to try hard. Leaving the lights on was easy, and so my mother let it go. It was a very bad habit, actually, and it took until I went to college to talk myself out of it, to love the night sky, finding freedom in walking home from a party with friends. Drunk, we'd point out the constellations we remembered. "Which constellations did you remember?" Bix had asked when I told him this story. By then we lived in Chicago, where you couldn't see many stars at all. *Just the guy with the belt*, I had said.

My parents were both gone by the time I met Bix. He wanted to hear the stories of them, even the terrible stories, when they hadn't been doing their best, not by a long shot. Michele would barely discuss our childhood. Hers was different enough, anyway, being five years older. We never talked about the other guy with the belt, or the welts across our legs for slight offenses. Michele liked everything and everyone tagged and filed away.

But Bix had wanted to know. It was only fair, given the number of tales from the front I had absorbed: impossible stories, impossible nights, each one of them. How many nights had I cradled him while he cried and choked over what he'd been put through over there, over all the terrible things he'd seen? He suffered, those nights, and I suffered with him. Sometimes, in the middle of one of his night terrors, I was the enemy. All the lights on, small comfort.

So one night, lying in bed, I told him how the raccoons lined up at a safe distance and begged on their haunches, their little fists greedy for the candy. It had started out a charming story, fun. And then I found the heartbreak in it. That's how it felt, I told him, to lose a parent so young, even a bad parent. You sat back and watched from a safe distance as the world passed, your hand outstretched for sweetness. Why were those raccoons the only thing I got to keep? And then he'd held me while I sobbed about all that was lost, all I might have remembered if I'd only been paying attention. *Nobody pays close enough attention*, he'd said, stroking my hair. The lights, on.

But he had. The blue scarf. The photography lessons. This trip.

All the times I'd left the lights on for him, he must have decided we could both use a date with the nighttime sky. Finding the reservations and the socked-away cash, I had had the most overwhelming feeling of gratitude for Bix and for who he was. Who he really had been, despite everything.

Make no mistake: the score would never be even. Since the funeral, I'd had a hard time not looking back over our entire relationship, turning over every episode with suspicion. Turning over moments that I'd thought I had forgiven. This trip reminded me of the moments when we got things right, when we had been paying the right amount of attention to each other.

*Click.* When I came back, blinking, to this world, I stood at the water's edge. The sand shifted in the retreat of a wave.

Hillary's voice, impatient. "Eden, *hello?*" I turned around. I'd passed the opening to the clearing. She was waving me back to where the others were already climbing inland from the beach.

The clearing was as I'd imagined it, a wide patch of closely clipped grass surrounded by a crescent of woods. A rocky ledge separated the clearing and the beach, lined with brush and dotted here and there with the flowers of prettier weeds.

"Well," Paris said. "This was worth the trip indeed."

"Now we know where it is and where the opening is," Malloy said. "So we can come back in the dark." He had his arm, predictably, around Hillary as he spoke, bolstering her physically and against anything his friends wanted to say. They pulled away from the group, sat on the grass, hip to hip, and turned inward, their faces tipped toward one another.

On the other side of the clearing, Dev lay on the grass and coaxed Paris down next to him. Martha and Sam wandered down to the rocky barrier. He still carried his wineglass and offered it to her. She shook her head, curls swinging.

I was left in the center of the clearing, alone. Across the water, a blue-gray whale of another shore drew my attention. More Michigan? I had lost track of my geography. Above, the sky had gone a bit gray, too. Without a turnaround in the weather, there would not be much to see of the stars tonight for anyone.

I had not had much practice with sky gazing. Normally, the sky was a painted plane of blue and, from what I remembered of night, black, dotted with the sparkle of tiny white specks. A theater backdrop on which lives played out. But now, maybe because the dark sky park had forced me to consider it, I had a feeling of the sky's vastness. It was not a landscape, a surface, but—everything else. When you thought about it, when you let in the concept of deep space, of stars, of our galaxy and those beyond it, of a universe without end, of *forever*—what *forever* really meant—it was too much to take in. My tiny understanding of it rested upon my skin until, without warning, the wide abyss sank in and then stretched out from me in all directions. The creeping loneliness I had been keeping at bay rose up in my throat, a choking panic.

I held the back of my wrist to my mouth to keep from making a noise. The others didn't need to know I was losing my mind.

I let go of the sky and focused instead on the in and out of my own breath, on the steady ground, the prickly grass against my bare feet.

The water, all the way to the horizon. The wide-open sky.

Breathe in. It would pass. Breathe out.

These episodes of panic, though more rare, were worse than the minutes I'd been losing to my drifting focus. In these moments, I was present, all too much, every second experienced fully and horribly. I could feel the strangulation of my airways, each capillary end shriveling, every dying cell fraying out. The forward march of life and its eventual end, keenly felt as it happened.

Breathe in. Breathe out.

When at last I recovered myself, I took a deep, shuddering breath and glanced around. Only Dev seemed to remember I was there. He raised his eyebrows at me. I had dropped my sandals in the grass.

"That's enough nature for me," I said when I knew I could speak clearly. I grabbed my shoes and headed for the opening again.

At the beach, I looked back. Malloy and Hillary were following, Paris and Dev dusting themselves off to come along, Sam and Martha turning to join them. Ducklings, and I was mother.

I didn't get it. They were supposed to be the best of friends, old friends desperate to be together again. I'd seen how Bix's Army buddies were when they got near one another. Wars would be refought and won, right there at the dinner table, and maybe if we stuck around long enough, someone would say something real and people who rarely cried in mixed company—Army and non-Army—might shed a few tears. They were tight. They would have died for one another. Some of them had. And once you felt that way about someone, you pretty much did forever.

And yet these people didn't even seem to know how to enjoy one another's company. They didn't even know how to be at a lake house. Only Dev and his wet swim trunks on the newel post had dipped a toe in the water. But he'd done that before the rest of them had arrived. Now that they were all here, they couldn't be separated for more than a few minutes before roll was called, before the one who got away was rounded up and nosed back into the group. They seemed to be waiting for something to happen, or not letting it happen by keeping vigil.

Tomorrow. Tomorrow I could leave and never think of them again.

Inside, the wineglasses were topped off. Malloy chose a long couch and stretched out, leaving room for Hillary to nuzzle up next to him. Paris and Dev took the love seat but didn't cuddle; Sam slid an ottoman from the corner over into the group. Martha stood by until Sam offered her a corner of his seat, then made herself comfortable on the floor with her back up against the couch underneath Malloy. He reached forward and ruffled her hair.

My box of crackers had been left open on the counter, empty. The scavengers. The bottle of wine that Dev had attempted to open still sat on the counter with the screwdriver sticking out of the cork. The corkscrew had been tossed to the side, kept handy. Their plan was to subsist entirely on squashed grapes?

I tossed the box into the recycling bin. In the living room, they were finally starting to talk. I edged out of the room as they peppered Malloy about work, his family. My experience told me Malloy was a man used to people wanting to know all about him. And maybe he'd been trained to expect such attention from this collection of friends. They folded in around him, disciples.

Bix had had that way with people. He hadn't been moviestar handsome the way Malloy was, but he had a different kind of magnetism. People wanted to talk with him. They wanted to tell him their stories. If I sent him to the convenience store for a gallon of milk, he'd come back a half hour later than expected with a tale from someone he'd met in the checkout, or from someone whose car he had jumpstarted in the parking lot. He was always helping someone, always handing over ten bucks to a sob story. It was kindness. It was fine. We had ten bucks to give, certainly. But it wasn't the money or the missing half hours here and there I'd come to resent. To other people, Bix was a hero. But he gave himself away. He was picked to pieces by all the people who relied on him, asked things of him, saw a sucker coming from a mile away. What was left, at the end, wasn't much.

That little bit leftover, I'd had to share. Of course, I hadn't known it at the time or I might have put up a fight. At least, that's what I told myself.

I listened to the friends' low voices for a few minutes, poured out my glass in the sink, and turned toward the suite.

"Not staying up to see the Dippers and stuff?" Malloy called after me.

"I'll catch them next trip," I said. He smiled at me as though he thought I was joking. I was joking—I would never come back to this place—but I was also going to my room. "Nice meeting you. Good night." The rest of them didn't bother to try to talk me back.

In my room, I found my phone facedown on the floor near the bed. Must have dropped it. I checked the time and then the service. Nonexistent. I might have been able to text my sister to tell her what a cock-up Bix's plan had turned out to be. But I didn't have enough bars to take the call she would have made in response. My sister leapt at chances to talk about Bix's mistakes.

I turned on the radio and listened to the calming voice of the local announcer. Live? Probably recorded. I lay down on the bed and went back to my phone, trying to get Photoship's app to load. No good. The signal was that weak.

On the radio, the voice was talking about the dark sky park. I sat up. ". . . In the greater scheme of this galaxy of planets and stars, we are specks of stuff bumping along and into one another," the voice said. "All the things we have and have built, more dust. If you think a galaxy is a big playing field, consider the universe we know beyond ours, and galaxies we know that spin out there, all the way out into the great unknown. You may think of it as nothingness, but then you may have also looked up into our own clear blue sky today, high of seventy-six degrees the guys down at the weather station tell us, and thought it empty." I snapped off the radio before I could hear anymore. I didn't need any dust-to-dust nonsense right now.

My phone churned. Not enough connectivity to see Photoship. All I'd left on there were the odds and ends of the early photography efforts, anyway. Bits and pieces, literally. My specialty. The corner of something, the edge, a close-up view so zoomed in as to make the object foreign. I liked surfaces and textures, the bright shine of the sun on a tabletop or a reflection in a window, glint and glare filling the viewfinder, everything obscured, everything lost to the light.

I had taken all the photos of Bix down.

And the accidental self-portrait, from when I first received the camera. That had come down first, of course.

I'd taken it by sheer ineptitude, like someone who checks to see if the gun is loaded and shoots themselves between the eyes. In the photo, my eyes are open and curious, my lips parted. The effect is of a moment, an honest moment in a life. It wasn't attractive or artful. And yet I posted it to Photoship and for a while, before I had learned things I hadn't known about my life and taken it down, I had enjoyed that photo and my wide-open countenance. Now when I thought of that photo, I knew it showed a woman about to be shot between the eyes.

A WHILE LATER I woke from a doze, fully dressed on top of the still-made bed. The room was bright. It could have been any hour of the day—noon? No, early morning, still dark. My eyes darted around the room, checking the lamps. All on, all good.

I'd been dreaming that I was standing among the friends in the kitchen. I had the sense of an unfinished conversation, of wanting to go back and finish what we'd had to say to each other, of being pulled away.

I heard a noise in the other room. I sat up, blinking. Someone bumping into one of the chairs at the counter in the kitchen. Then a voice, a whisper, and another noise, this time a low groan that I hoped wasn't sexual. Hadn't I called it with this bunch?

The extra blanket I'd hung over the window facing the lake had fallen to the floor in a pool. I slid off the bed to fix it up again, fighting off a wave of nausea at the sight of the dark window behind the thin drapes. Hands shaking, I tucked the edge of the blanket back over the curtain rod and pulled it down to cover the night.

Another noise, this time closer, in the hallway outside my room. I looked toward the bedside clock. Two in the morning was not a late hour for a group that had come to see the stars. Not for a group of people planning on a bonfire by the beach.

But then the suite and its separate entrance was mine, if only for the night. I hadn't been firm enough on that.

I went to the door and reached for the handle, ready to scold. But the image of the dark hallway beyond rushed at me and I froze. Footsteps sounded on the other side of the door, quick, and then a door, the back door, wrenched open and flung against the wall.

I raced to the window, hesitating only a moment before pulling the blanket and the curtain back to reveal the tiniest sliver of blackness. My eyes caught the rush of someone moving off north toward the public beach, but it was far too dark out to see who it was. And then I couldn't hold the night back anymore. I let the curtain back and pressed the blanket to the edge of the window frame. When I stepped back from the window, my breath was ragged.

I crawled back into bed, still fully clothed but this time under the comforter. I lay in the bright room staring at the ceiling.

Who had a late-night fight? Paris and Dev seemed the likely pair, since they seemed to run hot that way. Paris did, anyway. Dev ran whichever way Paris wanted him to. Funny that they'd ended up together at all. Not that I cared—a couple where one person had all the power didn't interest me. Marriage was supposed to be a pairing, not an ongoing strongman competition. But then a lot of what I knew about marriage I'd learned after I'd already signed up for it. A lot of what I knew I would never wish on anyone. You learned as you went when it came to love, and some of the lessons came by way of the roughest road.

I could feel myself drifting off into that delicious place between sleep and wakefulness. Maybe it was the long drive in the day before or maybe the guest house had lulled me into a sense of security I hadn't known in a while. I hadn't taken any of the pills I carried around to make myself available for sleep and yet I was drowsy, comfortable.

Dreams crept back in. Bix lay in the bed next to me, and I threw my arm around him, tucking up against his warm back. My dream self cuddled in for the night, but in my sleep I began to feel uneasy and angry. We were in our bed, but also at the park, just as he'd planned. What was he doing here at the lake, after all he'd done to me? All of it, but also the dying, the being dead. These were unforgivable actions. In the dream, I noticed the moon glowing through the open window, and then I woke, choking.

The window in the real room was covered. If the moon had risen since I'd last dared look outside, it was hidden. The clock said that the long night I had suffered since I last woke was only a half hour.

The shadows, just out of my sight, crept toward me, on the move. When I looked directly into the corners, everything was what it should be, but when I turned my head—

And then came the scream.

## Chapter Six

I ran to the door. But then I stood there, hand reaching toward the doorknob.

The scream had come from the front of the house, maybe as close as the kitchen, but the hallway just outside my room would be pitch-dark.

Elsewhere in the house, other voices rang out in alarm. Someone shouted, but I couldn't tell what he'd said. One of the women shrieked and shrieked. No one comforted her, or if they tried, no comfort could be found.

A band of light appeared under my door. A pathway. I wrenched the door open to find Dev, backlit, leaning into the hallway from the kitchen. His voice, when it came, was strangled, breathless. "Eden, are you OK?"

"It wasn't me," I said.

He reared back, almost hidden behind the door. "*What* wasn't you?"

"The screaming," I said. "What's happened? Who's yelling?"

"Just about everyone," Dev said, opening the door wider so that I could see him better. He wore only boxers. Ashen-faced. "You'd better come out. You're alone, right?"

I was still out of sorts from the nap and the dream. I glanced back at my bed. Some of the things that hadn't been real had felt very much so, and now this moment of reality had the aftertaste of nightmare. "Of course I'm alone," I said. "What's going on?"

The screaming had stopped, but I heard someone crying, the kind of desperate sobbing that produced a catch in my own throat.

"It's Malloy," Dev said, and gestured me through the door to the kitchen. I wrapped my arms around myself and moved toward him.

"Is he—" But before I could get the words out, I could see for myself. A hand, the fingertips bloody, lay open on the kitchen floor. I saw the hand first and concentrated there, even as the rest of my attention took in Malloy's body stretched alongside the island, the swipe of blood along the wall to the floor, and then the screwdriver from the abandoned bottle of wine from earlier now stuck into his neck. "Oh, God." A pool of blood darkened the floor there. "Oh, my God. No, oh no—"

I pulled my gaze off Malloy. Paris clung to the newel post at the bottom of the staircase, gazing in dumb horror into the kitchen. Sam stood nearby, wearing a robe and a mask of terror on his pale face. Martha, in a short pink nightie, stood nearby, clutching herself by the elbows. Dev stood to one side of the doorway to let me through, pulling at his hair.

Finally I saw Hillary. She crouched on the floor on her knees in a T-shirt that might have been Malloy's, her face low to the ground and her hands in claws, wracked with sobs that had gone silent. Then she caught her breath and came up from the floor with her mouth wide and wailing. The noise was wordless for a long while, and then formed itself into a long, beseeching question. "Why?" she cried. Over and over, while we stood by and did nothing. "Why?"

Martha took a shuddering breath and sank to her knees next to Malloy.

"Martha," Dev said. "No—"

I jumped in. "I don't think you should—"

Too late. She crumpled forward into Malloy's chest, crying.

Malloy. It didn't seem possible. But his skin was waxen, pale. His eyes, open and staring. They said death was peaceful but then when you witnessed it, you knew it couldn't be. Not this kind of death—early, violent. With men like Malloy and Bix, the lack of life was too startling, too hurtful and unnatural.

The air was thick with the smell of wine. The bottle that Dev had tried to jimmy open lay spilled on top of the kitchen island. The wine opener lay in a shallow pool of cabernet that ran over the edge of the counter. I could just hear the last of the stream of wine dripping onto the floorboards.

"Why?" Hillary implored, her face pressed into the floor again.

"The better question is who," Martha said, rising from Malloy's chest, her voice congested and accusatory. The front of her nightgown was heavy with blood.

Paris gasped. It was hard to argue anything had happened here except murder, given the screwdriver, but they all seemed too dazed to take it in.

In contrast, I felt sharp. I had slept in the night for the first time in months. After spending so long not sleeping well or at all, after months of treading through days, of making mistakes, of words coming out of my mouth that I myself didn't follow, I felt as though I could see through walls. I felt as though I were up above the room, looking down on everyone's movements.

"You," Hillary said, sitting up. The wail was gone, and her voice was guttural, animal. We all turned to her. "You did this." She had pinpointed Martha as the target for this assault.

Martha sat back on her heels, looking from Hillary to me to Sam, the others. "Wh-what are you talking about? I just—"

Hillary got to her feet, wiping her face with her hands. "You. Or you," she said, turning on Sam, then Dev. "You or you. Does it matter which one? All of you are at fault."

"That's not fair," Dev said. "None of us would have done this, Hillary." But he sounded nervous.

"You're the one we don't know," Paris sniffed.

"And *her*," Martha said.

The room went silent. I had been staring at the screwdriver, plunged up to the handle in the soft flesh of Malloy's neck—I couldn't help it—when I realized she was talking about me. In their silence I heard their agreement. I was the one they didn't know. Hillary at least came vetted by Malloy, which was the only endorsement anyone needed. "I had no reason to kill your friend," I said. "I didn't know him, or any of you."

"Maybe you're just that special kind of psychopath," Paris hissed.

"Paris, come on," Dev said. Every word he uttered in Paris's direction shaped the world to his desires—either to get her the thing she wanted or to keep her in bounds of what was polite or right. He was like one of those dogs herding sheep back into a paddock. I would have said she didn't deserve a guy like that, but then I didn't think a guy like that was much of a prize.

A guy like—

"I saw someone," I said. "Someone ran out the back door and woke me up. I thought it was one of you, but maybe it wasn't. Maybe it was—"

"Who?" Martha said, standing.

"Any one of you," Hillary growled.

"Come on, Hillary," Sam said. "You can't possibly think that we came all this way to see everyone, planned this trip for—I don't know—weeks, just to kill Malloy." He looked down again at his friend's body. "Oh, my—Malloy is really dead. He's—he's—"

Sam stumbled backward, hit the couch, and slid to the floor.

"We need to call the police," I said.

They all looked at me, uncomprehending. They were all as affected as Sam by the reality of the situation, stunned, and I was mother duck again. I looked around the kitchen. No landline. "Does anyone have their phone on them?" I said. No one moved, so I started back to my room.

"Wait—" Paris said.

I waited. We all did, all of us probably hoping for sense and order.

"I think we need some kind of—system."

For a moment, we all stared at her. Then I knew what she meant. A buddy arrangement, of sorts. Truthfully I wasn't sure I wanted to be on my own, either. My eyes drifted down to Malloy's body, the bloody fingertips. I was the only one who hadn't brought a date to this murder.

"Nobody can leave these two rooms without someone with them," Paris said thickly.

"Like a bodyguard?" Dev said.

"Like a witness," Martha said. She looked down at the horror of herself. Dev handed her a towel from the counter. "I agree."

They all looked back to me. "Well," I said. "Who's coming to witness me getting my phone?" I turned on my heel and made for my door, not waiting to see how the straws were pulled.

It was Dev who appeared in the door, blinking into the blazing light of my room. He shielded his eyes. "You doing surgery in here?"

I was digging through things on the night table for my phone and didn't offer him an explanation. I'd had the phone in bed, I remembered, though I hadn't called anyone. Little reception, and no reason to call, except—I hadn't told anyone where I was going. I hadn't told anyone I was keeping Bix's plans. I should have texted someone, at least. His mother. My sister. I had a few friends left who might care if I lived or died. I should text someone now. That worked, right? Even if I couldn't call someone, maybe I could text? Somehow, the fleeting second of connectivity a text needed to travel might be found? I finally located the phone in its bright pink case hidden in the bedcovers. It registered the symbol for a couple of missed calls and one bar of service. No. Zero bars. I held it out and turned in a circle.

"Maybe outdoors?" Dev said. The bright pink case seemed to catch his attention and then his disapproval. He looked up. "What's wrong?"

I had stopped spinning. Outside? Outside would be dark as nature intended, the lake as black as a bag over my head—

Dev grabbed my wrist. "Are you OK?"

"I can't—"

I couldn't go outside. I couldn't say that I couldn't go outside, either. I held out the phone to him. He took it, held it high, low, out from his body. His eyes flickered to the window, to the blanket hanging over the curtains, to the floor lamps I'd pulled to my bedside, lit to full capacity. The package of 150-watt lightbulbs I'd brought with me to replace all the lesser values lay on top of my open suitcase. He registered the detail, was confused by it, blinking. At last his face cleared, illuminated. "So, you're . . ."

"I don't want to talk about it."

"How do you get any sleep at all if you can't—"

"I'm not, OK? Hardly any at all."

"But that's—"

Crazy. He wanted to say *crazy*. That's what my sister called it.

He looked at me a long, uncomfortable moment.

"Look, I'm a doctor," he said. "It's not healthy to miss that much sleep, to never let yourself be in the dark. It's bad for—oh, whatever. I won't lecture you on circadian rhythms when we have a— I'll take this outside to see if I can get better reception." At the door, he glanced back and then was gone. I heard the back door slap the wall, just as it had earlier in the night. That figure racing from the house— was that the person who had killed Malloy? And why? But what if—

Here I stopped and thought over the last day, the complicated friendships I'd seen in action. What if Hillary was right? What if it had been one of the people in the house, running from what they'd done and then sneaking back inside in time to feign surprise and horror?

I closed my door behind me and returned to the kitchen doorway. "Dev is calling the police," I said. Nobody wondered why Dev was allowed to slip away from the buddy system.

I stopped at the threshold of the kitchen and avoided looking at the floor. I wrapped my arms around my elbows to keep myself in place.

The rest of the friends had shifted positions. Sam had been pulled up and moved to the couch, reclining in pajamas like a nineteenth-century lady with the vapors. Martha tended to him. She was now wrapped in Sam's robe over her bloody nightgown, the dusty soles of her bare feet poking out below the hem. Paris sat nearby with wet cheeks, her knees skinny in shorts. Only Hillary stood where I'd left her, staring at the body.

"Did anyone—did anyone check his pulse?" she said.

"Hillary," I said. The blood near Malloy's body was dark, his face progressed to a shade of pearl. There would be ways to tell how long the poor man had been lying alone, dead, in the kitchen, but that's what he was. "I think we're far too late for that. Martha already—"

"Please," she whispered.

I understood. Of all the people in the house, I knew best what it was like to hold out past the point of hope.

I stepped closer to Malloy's body and crouched in front of him. Bracing myself for the horror of touching him, I reached for a spot on his neck opposite the screwdriver. For a moment I thought I might feel the flutter of a low pulse. I peered at him more closely. His lips did seem to have some unexpected color. But then I realized the pulse was mine, the blood rushing through my own fingers against the dead man's cold skin. His lips, sauvignon-stained.

The room was drenched in wine and smelled of it, but at this close proximity, I could smell the nickel scent of blood and beneath that, the tender smell of another human being, salty and soapy. I held my fingers at Malloy's throat, putting in the time so that Hillary couldn't say I hadn't given him a chance. I realized after some time that I had stopped thinking of the body as Malloy's and had traveled back to the funeral parlor in Chicago and the body of my husband. The last touch, the last chance before the casket was sealed. A bad moment at the end of many bad moments.

Then the moment clicked back into place. Hillary had stretched her neck to see me. God, how long had I kept her in suspense? I pulled my hand back and rested on my heels. I shook my head. She reached behind her for the wall and sagged against it.

"I thought I had all the time in the world," she said.

Martha and Paris turned to listen.

"Everybody thinks that," I said. "Everybody's wrong."

"Some are more wrong than others," she said. And I couldn't argue with that.

## Chapter Seven

Dev entered the kitchen from the back hall and pressed my phone into my hand. I noted again the missed call and text notifications but didn't check them. Now was not the time. Dev and I waited on the other side of the kitchen, listening to Hillary crying, the others occasionally sniffling. Within minutes, the sound of a car outside attracted Martha to the door. No sirens.

"It's the park director, I think," she said.

I looked at Dev. He shrugged. "I remembered the number."

"But you called 911, right?"

"Yeah, of course. I just thought we'd need to alert him, too." He ran his fingers through his hair so that it stuck up in the back. "It made sense at the time."

Warren Hoyt stood in the doorway in street clothes, though his version of everyday wear was just as nipped and tucked as the uniform he'd been buttoned up in earlier. At the sight of Malloy's body, the expression on his face traveled between horror and disappointment in us all.

He gazed forlornly around the guest house, as though making sure there were no additional corpses, and found Sam looking wan and Paris, drippy. He took a long look at Hillary, crying up against the wall, and then me. "I hear sirens," he said, standing uncomfortably among us with a pleading look in his eyes. "So we'll just . . ."

This was either a man who had had no experience with death or far too much. Maybe this wasn't the first body in the guest house. Maybe this was something that happened all the time. I didn't like to think so. The water lapping quietly against the shore, the scent of the lake in the air, the crickets chirruping in the trees—or maybe those were frogs, I didn't know. All of it was beautifully tranquil. Tranquil enough that I'd forgotten, just for a few hours, that I didn't sleep. I ached to get back to that soft bed and try it again. For someone who hadn't yet seen a single star and now stood watch over a dead body, I was a highly satisfied customer of the park's facilities.

Hoyt wiped his face with his hand. "No one, uh, moved the, uh, gentleman, did they?"

"I think the police will handle the investigation, Mr. Hoyt," I said. The sirens were quite loud now, anyway.

A pained expression crossed his face. "Yes, I suppose."

"What is it?"

"Nothing, only . . ." His eyes roamed over the rooms again.

"Worried about your family-friendly marketing plan?"

"No, of course not," he mumbled, reaching for the top button of his shirt and finding it already fastened.

"Maybe I imagined that you were worried about the police being called here?"

Again, the pained look.

"No, it's—nothing. The local constabulary, you see, doesn't get much opportunity to solve, uh, this sort of thing," he said, turning as the sirens cut out and several car doors slammed within the yard. "They're much more accustomed to . . . accidents."

The word covered an awful lot of ground. "What kind of—"

"And it was going to be such a nice week, so many guests. The Perseid shower," he said mournfully.

"*What*—"

But then the door opened and the uniformed men and women who gathered there drew all attention.

"What in God's creation," the first man started. He was red-faced and soft-jawed. Prone to bluster and disbelief, I decided, watching him take in the balance of us in the room and the mess of Malloy's body. He stood back and held the front door, bowing like a valet. "If you don't mind," he said, "this is a damn crime scene. Get out. Except you two."

Everyone, reacting quickly to authority, had stood and rushed to action and had to stop to see which two needed to stay put. Martha's robe swished against her legs. The officer was pointing across the kitchen to Dev and me. "You two find another way out and try not to touch anything in the meantime."

"The back door," Hoyt said unhelpfully and shuffled along with the others out the front.

Dev pulled at the shoulder of my T-shirt to propel me away from the kitchen and down the back hall. I put on the brakes. The back door was hanging wide open, leaving the screen door as the only barrier between me and the darkness.

"I can't."

Dev sighed. "Look, I don't know what your . . . *deal* is, but you'd better figure it out fast."

My deal. If it were my deal, I would have redistributed the cards to give myself a better hand to play. I would have cheated—believe it. "That's what I was trying to do."

"That's why you came here? To get over your fear of . . . the dark? Or whatever?" Dev looked out the door toward the black lake. "That's rough immersion therapy, right there. No wonder you wanted the place to yourself. Did your husband help you through this kind of thing? Is that what you were coming here for? Both of you? I don't get it."

"No, it's—" The dark square of the door pulsed at me. I couldn't think. Words failed.

"Oh," he said. His voice had dropped its edge so that now I heard a hint of kindness I hadn't before. "He caused it. By dying."

The warm turn in Dev's voice calmed me. It created a small bubble of hope in which I found that I could speak. "It doesn't make any sense to me, either."

"So you can't go outside?"

"I'm not sure I can."

"What if I help you?" he said.

"How?"

"You tell me."

I had never tried to defy the fear, to walk out into it. I hadn't had any plans for how plunging myself in the park's natural darkness would fix the problem. But I hadn't had time to devise a plan since I'd been here, either. I didn't want the darkness to touch my skin. It made no sense. The darkness had no weight, no texture, no heat. And yet it burned me almost physically only to think of stepping out into its embrace.

I opened the door of my room. The bright glow of my army of lamps was such a relief I wanted to run to the bed and leap in. As welcoming as the lamps were, I might cover my head and hide.

*Cover my head.*

I went to the bed and pulled the comforter off the top and then went to my suitcase and dug around the edges until I found the large, heavy flashlight I'd brought along and the long sleeve of batteries for it. I tested the current batteries with the button, flashing the light, on, off, on.

"Is that going to work?" Dev said.

I looked up. The circle of light from my flashlight landed upon his chest like a target. "Maybe."

"Let's go, then," he said. "Do I need to tell you how suspicious it's going to look for us to be hanging out back here after they told us to get out?"

I grabbed my car keys, just in case, and wrapped the blanket around me, pulling the edge down over my forehead. I turned the flashlight on myself, lighting my chin upward. The effect was immediate. I couldn't see much of anything with the glow of the light beaming over my cheeks skyward. I was light-blind, probably the only way I would get out of this house tonight.

Dev made a noise in his throat at the sight of me. "I guess we'll work with it." He turned for the hallway and I followed, trying not to trip over the blanket or anything else on the way out.

At the open door, I hesitated again. I felt the weight of the blanket shift, a tug. Was Dev pulling the comforter? Had he stepped on the hem? "What are you doing?"

"Picking up your train, milady," he said, dropping it. "Never mind, just go."

I stepped forward, thrilling a bit at the idea that I had done it. I was outside. I didn't need to stay a week. Under the comforter, I could feel the chill in the air. A fish or animal splashed at the lakeshore. Outside. I was outside, at night.

But then I heard voices coming around the back of the house. Dev turned toward them, and I lost the thin cord that connected us and allowed me to believe this might work. I teetered there at the threshold, unsure. What would the police do if I lunged for the door and barricaded myself in the suite? Maybe I could keep them at bay until dawn.

And then they'd take me to jail.

"Sir," the man's voice said, "we need you and the lady to come around— What's this about?"

"The lady is having a little bit of a . . ." Dev said. "Uh, panic attack?"

Perfect. That was a role I could fill. I had an escort then, was hustled around the side of the guest house and to a waiting ambulance. The response, the concern, the hurry—I didn't have much time to actually panic or to see what the rest of the group thought. The bay doors of the ambulance hung open like shutters and inside all the panels and instruments gleamed in a bright, otherworldly, medical light. I reached toward the interior of the rig, moth to flame, and let myself be packed inside.

Outside the ambulance, as the doors closed the night away from me, Paris said, "And why does she get to escape this nightmare while we stand here in the dark?"

FROM AMBULANCE TO emergency room to triage room, curtained off from view, I let them shuffle me from bright space to bright space. I tried to justify the attention. To say nothing was wrong with me—that was a lie. But was it something I needed a doctor for? Was it something that could be fixed?

And yet all I had to do was think about being set out of the hospital into the night, and my blood pressure skyrocketed.

"Are you experiencing any stress?" said a concerned nurse. She watched the latest spike on the monitor over the top of a pair of reading glasses and made a note on a clipboard.

"A man was just murdered in the house I'm staying in," I said.

Her eyebrows rose into her hairline and her glasses slid down her nose, but she kept writing. "Seems like that would do it," she said. "Friend of yours?"

I didn't know how to answer that. "He wouldn't have to be my friend for his murder to upset me," I said. We both listened to the tone of my voice, the words hanging in the air. "Sort of," I said.

Malloy had called me a new friend upon introduction—before he had known my name or a single thing about me. It had nothing to do with me. I could have been anyone, but that was not how Malloy saw the world. And would his real friends—the ones with whom he was having one last good time before adult responsibilities and marriages and new careers pulled them apart—would they have been so fond of him if he'd been any other way? I had discovered the Malloy-ness of the man, the thing that made him so much himself, just like Bix. It was openness. It was the willingness to be only what you really were, pilgrim or otherwise. That open quality was one I missed, though it was the same quality that might have been at the heart of my life's current state.

"Yes," I said, finding myself tearing up. The nurse looked at me strangely. "He was my friend." Or he would have been by the end of the week, if either of us had lasted in the house that long. I had a moment of regret that I would never know Malloy better. He had seemed smart, kind. Maybe if I'd stayed the week, he could have helped me find the path through the decisions I needed to make. I was nothing if not a pilgrim to men like that.

The nurse made another note on the chart. I was picking up diagnoses as I went.

When she left, the hospital noises closed in on me. I had nothing to read, had turned over my phone and my keys before the ambulance bay doors closed, and had left everything else I owned behind. I couldn't sleep, even with the brightness of the room.

A strange despair came in a wave over me—gut tender, throat clenched. I had been here before, but for reasons that made more sense. I turned away from the nurse and wiped at my eyes. Malloy? He was someone's son, someone's lover. His death was a tragedy, but for someone else. Bix again?

I peeled back another layer on what was bothering me, though, and found an unexpected nerve. The park. Even though I'd made it outside into the absolute darkness of the park, I still hadn't gotten to see a single star. And that was Bix again—his expectations, his dream, his plans kept secret from me, and now I would fail to see them through. His stupid idea to come here. I didn't even like surprises, not anymore.

An hour or more went by while people in varying shades of surgical scrubs came to ask me the same three or four questions. Observation, this was called. Which was fine, as I had nowhere else to be. I lay back for the pressure cuff once more and glimpsed through the curtain a dark sleeve just outside the room. A police officer? I wasn't just under observation. I was also under lock and key.

I'd left my car behind, for crying out loud. I had turned over my keys, my phone. Where did they think I'd run off to, if I had something to hide besides my own crippling neurosis?

But then the sleeve slipped out of view and a pair of eyes darted a look through the part in the curtain.

"You can come in," I called.

Warren Hoyt appeared at the gap, clearing his throat but not saying anything.

Even fully clothed, I felt suddenly exposed and fragile in that hospital cot. I pulled the thin blanket up to my shoulders. "I thought they had a cop stationed outside my door for a minute," I said. "You're not deputized, are you?"

"You mean the conservation officer," he said, not a hint of humor visible. "The district officer will probably want an accounting of all this later, but of course it's the Emmet County Sheriff's Office investigating."

"The ones who are more accustomed to accidents," I said, "than murders."

"The lake," he said. The strict veneer dropped a bit to show what was underneath: hopelessness. "Horseplay, someone loses their balance and falls out of the boat. The whole group drinking—" His face darkened. "Wherever people are off their guard and the beer bottles stack up, you can be sure there's potential for an accident."

A wave of memory washed over me. I closed my eyes, but the image of twisted metal rushed in. I took a deep breath and willed it away. "This was no accident," I said, my voice shaky. "That screwdriver—"

"Please," he said, easing himself down on the edge of the bed, pale. I scooted up on the mattress to make room for him. "I'm trying to get the screwdriver out of my head."

That provided a different image. Hoyt winced at his own words, so I could tell he'd heard it, too.

He was a prim specimen. A forty-something-year-old guy who probably talked to two people a day in the course of his work duties. No wedding ring. No guts for blood. No evidence of an interior life—or maybe his life was all interior. What was his story?

"Have you had any other accidents like this one?" I said. "The not-an-accident type of accident?"

He stared at the floor for a moment. "Never anything quite like this. Not in living memory, anyway."

"Not like that hotspot of criminal activity Mackinac Island," I said.

"They do see their share."

It had been a joke. "Seriously? And how do the villains get away? On bicycle? By horse cart?"

"By ferry," he said, frowning.

The man had never met a joke before, that much was clear. My desire to see his surface cracked, just once, was distracting me from Malloy, the guest house, all those people back there, the dark sky.

The machine behind my head gave a dramatic beep. Hoyt looked over at it, concerned. "Is there something wrong?"

"Blood pressure," I said. High blood pressure could probably be blamed for the headache I had acquired. I rubbed my forehead. "I had a . . . panic attack, I guess."

"Lucky you didn't have it in the water," he said. Now I had the image for what an accident on the lake might look like. So much in life could go wrong—that was the thing you could go several decades of your life not understanding. Things could go wrong. And then they all did.

The problem was that when you were young you could assume that someone else would take care of everything when things slid sideways. But the older I got, the more aware I was that no one would be riding in on a white horse if things went sour. There was no safety net. If the local cops were better at fishing drowned bodies out of the drink than investigating an actual murder, then Hillary wouldn't get satisfaction. She'd have to suffer it out, and maybe there was nothing anyone could do about that anyway.

Bix was dead, and nobody had been able to take a dent out of that. But I was the one left standing.

I was standing.

Figuratively, at least. I lay back in my hospital bed and let my eyes close. The events of the night rushed over me until I was dizzy. I had no notion that I would be able to sleep, not after all that had happened and would continue to play out, not with a stranger sitting on the edge of my bed. The Emmet County sheriff would want a word, if this machine ever stopped beeping at me, and I would probably have to see the rest of the group again before I could make my way back home. I would have to figure out how to reclaim my life in well-lit Chicago, but perhaps for the first time since Bix died I thought I might be able to do it. The house? I would figure it out.

Just before I dropped into sleep, I had two simultaneous visions that banged together like cymbals but were too late to keep me awake. Warren Hoyt, sitting on the edge of my hospital bed, and Hillary, wailing on her knees.

What was Warren Hoyt doing at my bedside? Why had he attached himself to me? And then: How could poor little Hillary make it through this, if I hadn't been able to?

I'll help.

I'll.

## Chapter Eight

I jumped awake to the curtain around my cot being whisked open. Standing in the wide gap was a police officer. A real one this time. I sat up, bleary. My eyes were drawn to the woman's belt and the gun at her hip. "They said come get you," she said, speaking around what I hoped was chewing gum. She hadn't taken off her hat. Her hair stuck out from underneath, a frizzy halo of blond curls.

"What time is it?"

"Six or better."

The sun was up. Thank you, Michigan summers. Thank you, bright morning sun, the only star I would get to see on this trip. I was getting back to the park, fetching my things, and racing back to Chicago at speeds that might be unseemly and highly illegal. The sun wouldn't set until after 10:00 p.m. here on the tip of the mitten state, but I would be long gone. All thoughts of Hillary and Malloy and of conquering my own fears had flown from my mind. Being able to go out at night was overrated. If I could only go home, I would forget these people and their murderous problems. I would get on with things as well as I could in the daytime.

A small life, boxed in by the hours of sunlight. It was fine. I could live with it.

Warden Warren had left at some point. I stretched, yawning but clearheaded. I'd slept a couple of hours again, and in a hospital bed, of all places. Over the course of this one night, I'd probably gotten more sleep than I had in any single night since Bix had died. It was like a miracle cure. I hated to let it go.

"Come on," the officer said. "They got some papers for you to sign."

Many papers and a startling invoice later, I was released to the officer's custody. Her badge read *Bridget Cooley*. She was straight-waisted, not just because of the belt and holster, with round, childish cheeks made rounder on one side by the bubble gum.

The lobby doors swished open for us. Outside the air was cool and soft. I took a deep breath. The sunlight, the sleep. I was renewed.

She led me over to a county cruiser. "I don't suppose you'll confess to killing the fella."

I stared at her. "No," I said. "I won't be doing that."

"Then you can sit up front with me." She opened the door. "The back's for killers. And dogs."

The cruiser smelled mostly of the latter. When she slid into the driver's seat, I said so.

"I said it was for dogs," she said. "My partner, Gruff, had to be put down last month." Her voice got thick but she recovered. "The county might not swing for me to get a new pup. The training, you know. It costs."

I rolled down the window. "Will you have to get a human partner?"

"Cheese and rice," she exclaimed, her mouth falling open and the pink wad of gum inside revealing itself. "I never once thought of that. What if they make me drive around with one of the guys? Rather be guarding the fudge shops at Mackinaw Crossings than share a car with some of those . . . farging ice-holes."

It wasn't an act, this innocence. I was used to a different sort, Bix and his buddies, who didn't hold back on colorful turns of phrase. I wondered how the Irish lass had gotten through the police academy without taking anyone's name in vain at the very least, but decided it was rude to ask. "How long have you been a cop?"

"Three years almost. I thought about being a CO but I don't like to fish, like, at all."

"CO? What is— Oh, is that a conservation officer?" What had Warden Warren said about them? That there was one, somewhere, keeping the peace in some way. What did that make Hoyt? A paper-pushing administrator, my guess. An accountant in shiny new hiking boots without a speck of dirt on them. What was so special about Hoyt that he was in charge of the vast night sky of the Straits Point Park, seemingly without naturalist or ranger pedigree or a shiny badge?

"Yeah, watching for poachers out of season and nabbing swells out fishing without a license. Bo-ring." She had a lot to say about poachers for a while, enough that the subject seemed less than boring, actually, to her. I closed my eyes, pretending to sleep so as to avoid learning more about the daily duties of conservation officers, but despite the pretending and the sleep I'd gotten, I did doze a bit, because for a moment or two I believed I was in the car with Bix.

He was driving fast, as he did, and we were late. We must have been meeting someone, and Bix was worried that this person would have to wait on us. *Who is more important than me?* my dream self couldn't bring herself to say. *Why are you endangering my life because someone else might wait five minutes?* And then we were driving to his mother's for the holidays, having the fight we'd been having since I'd started the photography classes. He'd pushed me to make a change, to take the time, but then suddenly he'd decided I'd had enough training and should have been looking to turn the photography into a job.

"What job is that?" I'd said, when we'd had the actual fight the first time. It stung. No strings had been attached but now I was derelict of duty.

"You could do portraits," he said. "Families, pets. Maybe you could get into taking those stock photos you always see."

I was picking up a sense of urgency that was counter to every promise he'd made. All those times I'd moved with him from base to base, starting over. Now that we were settled in Chicago, couldn't I have a minute to myself?

"I just got started," I said. "Are we in some kind of money trouble? Is there something you need to tell me?"

We'd saved smart all those years. What was it? Gambling? I didn't follow the stock market. Maybe I had missed some big news.

"No, I—" His hands patted the wheel as he tried to find words. I waited. He was sick? Dying?

"What is it?" I said. He was freaking me out.

"Nothing, Edie," he said, and he was back to himself. He reached and took my hand. "Nothing's wrong. What if something happened to me? I want you to be able to, you know, stand on your own two feet. And don't you want to be able to make a go of this with your pictures?"

"Someday, maybe," I said. "I mean, I'd love to, of course, but it's probably going to take some time. And— Bix, I don't know if I'm any *good*—"

Reassurances came, but I was not fully reassured and he'd spent the evening out distracted and moody. Everyone had noticed. It wasn't a terrible night, but it wasn't a fun one, either.

In the dream, Bix was driving and I was the passenger. I was nervous for some reason, telling him to turn around. This is the way, he said. When I turned forward, headlights bore down on us, brightness filling the windshield—

I jerked awake, reached for the door handle to steady myself.

"OK, then?" Officer Cooley said.

My mouth was dry, my head fuzzy. We passed a couple of roadside hotels. These must be the spots Hoyt had promised for "intimate" getaways. I had come back to myself enough to feel embarrassed for him having said it.

And then, as we drew away from the town: green. Trees, fields, more trees. I sat up and rolled my neck, stiff from the short nap.

"What do people here do for fun?" I said.

"The lake," she said. "Skiing and all, and then in winter, snowmachines all over. They're crazy, swishing all over the place until someone drives in front of a semitrailer. And drinking, of course. Well, drinking all the time, and then the semi."

I swallowed hard and lay my head back on the seat. The accidents Hoyt mentioned were suddenly less abstract. Twisted metal. Rolling lights. A television announcer's bobbed hair-cut swinging as the casualties were listed.

Inside the park, Officer Cooley slowed her car to a crawl. The patient curve of the drive lulled me into inattention—until a figure leapt to the side of the car. I jumped and grabbed at Officer Cooley's sleeve before realizing it was just one of the silhouette markers, a little girl, holding a stack of books.

"Just one of them stand-ups they got all over," Cooley said. "That one is the kid that named Pluto. There's like ten of them, but she's the one that gets me. I always think it's some dang kid jumping in front of the car. Some of them are creepier than her. Bigger. They'll really make you jump."

We pulled in at the park's office alongside a green park Jeep, another county cruiser, and an old maroon civilian sedan with a bumper held on by wire and duct tape. The rust bucket had a Darwin evolving-fish sticker in the back window.

Inside stood the matched set of drivers: Hoyt, the blustery police officer who had shooed us out of the guest house the night before, and Erica Ruth, chewing her nails behind the front desk.

"Well, look who's back," said the red-faced cop. "That was quite an exit you orchestrated last night."

Warren Hoyt raised his chin, smiling. We were friends now, apparently. Over his shoulder, his stoic portrait looked out from the wall.

Erica Ruth's eyes darted around the room. She seemed afraid to let them alight on me.

"I had a panic attack," I said.

"Convenient," the officer said.

"It isn't," I said. "I'd rather not have . . . the problem." We were still in the realm of truth. I had been panicked at the thought of going outside and Dev had produced a good cover story. I owed that guy. "I assume you have questions for me."

"That I do. Hoyt?"

Warren nodded toward his office, and the policeman pointed his tubby belly in that direction. "Cooley," he bellowed over his shoulder. I followed him, with the younger officer trailing behind.

In the office, the guy in charge chose the chair behind the desk. I pulled a straight-backed chair from the corner to sit in front of him, noting a couple of photos framed on Hoyt's desk but not having the right view to see who he kept nearby. Officer Cooley closed the door behind us and stood at the wall.

"Name?" he said, gesturing to Cooley. She pulled out a notebook.

"Eden Wallace," I said.

"Maiden?"

"What?"

He glowered at me. "Your maiden name, ma'am."

"Cannon. I didn't catch your name."

He looked as though he'd rather not bother with answering. "*Sheriff* Jeffrey Barrows. Address?"

I gave him the address in Chicago, the house teetering on the chopping block. He raised his eyebrows. "That's a nice neighborhood," he said.

"You know Chicago?" This tiny outpost on the tippy top of Michigan's mitten seemed another world.

"Can you tell me what time you retired to your room last night?"

"Early," I said. "Before ten. Maybe nine thirty?"

"You came all this way to see the stars and sacked out before ten? It's not even dark by ten right now."

"I was tired after the long drive. And with the mix-up—all the people in the house, you know—I had decided to go home today. Another long drive." I glanced over his shoulder at the reassuringly bright window.

"You're leaving?"

"As soon as I can put this mess behind me."

Sheriff Barrows's pink face grew pinker. "A man's life is not some mess to be swept away."

But a man's life could be a mess, especially after he died. I swallowed hard. "Of course not," I said.

"Tell us about your evening. Start with what the whole group was doing before you turned in for the night."

I drew the scene for him, the friends convening in the kitchen over wine, the walk up the beach to the clearing, the gathering in the living room where I'd left them. Any conversations I remembered. Who was where, at what time? Who was arguing? Who sat near whom? No matter how I sliced it, I was the odd man out. "And then I turned in. They were all still in the living room when I left them. They might have gone out to the fire pit, after, or the beach. There was a plan, but it was cloudy. I fell asleep," I said. He had no idea how unusual that was. "Then someone started screaming."

"Who was screaming first? Could you tell?"

"One of the women," I said. "I just met them, but for some reason I want to say Paris. But—I think she came down last, because she was still on the stairs when I came out. Martha or Hillary, then. And then there was more shouting and screaming, and Dev came to my door and told me to come out."

The sheriff waited for Officer Cooley's hand to go still over her notebook. "Why do you think he did that?"

"What do you mean?"

"Why did he have to?"

Now I saw the problem. People had been screaming bloody murder in the room next to my bed and I stayed behind a closed door until someone came to check on me. "I was scared, I guess," I hemmed. That was the truth, if a lesser one. I wondered how soon Dev would tell the police about my weirdness. It was a character flaw, but perhaps a motive if you dug deep enough. Mental illness. He was probably telling the rest of them now. You'll never guess, he'd say. She can't even come out of her room, not even for a murderer—

"Oh," I said. "I forgot—there was someone in the hallway before the screaming started. I heard a noise in the kitchen—oh, God, do you think I heard—" I stopped and swallowed the bile in my throat. That whisper, that moan, that stumble against the chair. I might have heard Malloy being killed. What, after all, had woken me up? "—and then footsteps, and then the door hit the wall, and I looked outside and saw someone—"

"Who?" His jowls shook. "Man? Woman?"

"I couldn't see. Someone fast, and it was dark," I said, shivering a bit. "I didn't get a good look, just—shadows. And of course I had no idea how important it would be . . . and then Martha started screaming. I think Martha, but it could have been . . . So I was on edge, I suppose. That back hallway belongs to the suite. I was surprised out of sleep by one of them being back there—"

"You thought it was one of the group back by your room?"

"Well, it only made sense at the time," I said. "I had no reason to believe anyone but Malloy and his friends were in the house with me. Now? I don't know. It could have been a thief or—Malloy might have surprised someone in the act, I don't know. Do you get a lot of break-ins up here?"

He ignored me but I saw a look pass over Officer Cooley's face as she wrote. They got a lot of break-ins up here.

"Take me through it again," he said.

I went through the timeline again, adding details as I thought of them. "Two in the morning," I said. "That's when I was woken by someone in the hall. I looked at the clock and it didn't seem that late, given what people come to the park to see. And then I fell back asleep. It was about a half hour later the screams started."

He sat back and sucked on his teeth for a second. "Forgive me, but you don't sound like a stargazer."

"Not really," I said. "Not even close, actually."

"And your new roomies? Are they?"

"I didn't get the sense they were there as scientists," I said. I went back over what I knew about each of them. "The girl-friend, Hillary. He—Malloy—said she studied up on the constellations in advance of the trip, but they didn't seem all that serious about the sky as a group. I left them in the living room, inside, before full dark, remember. They weren't set-ting up telescopes."

"Maybe they all had long drives, too," he said.

"They seemed far more interested in drinking wine," I said. "A lot of wine. A troubling amount of wine." Officer Cooley scratched at her notebook.

"So why here, then? If none of you are much into stars?"

"I don't know why they chose it," I said. "They went to

college together in Michigan. I guess I assumed it was nostalgia, an old favorite place, or maybe an equidistant drive from where they live."

"And you?"

"My husband chose the location."

Barrows looked at Cooley. "Where's the husband? Why have I not heard from this guy? Get him in here."

"He's dead," I said. It sounded particularly harsh, under the circumstances. "Deceased," I tried.

"Oh, yes?" Barrows said. He looked at me sternly over the fat of his own cheeks. A long moment passed. I began to think there was a real question that I hadn't heard, wasn't answering. At last he folded his hands together over his belly and sat back with a creak in Hoyt's chair. "A dead husband, you say. By any chance, did he happen to fall into a screwdriver?"

## Chapter Nine

I was sent out to the lobby while the police conferred—over my guilt, I supposed. As I walked into the room, Erica Ruth looked up, then nervously away. Hoyt was gone, and that was fine.

They kept me waiting, on and on. I wandered to a bulletin board and glanced over a list of events in the park: night hikes, viewing of upcoming star-gazing activities, all hosted by the director of the park. His stoic face stared out from the poster. The activities read like movie listings, as though the sky had planned a show for ticket holders. I had seen the viewing area. Nothing special. Why come out to the park to see the stars when any old patch of land offered the same view? The lack of light, I supposed. The park had been set aside and planted with those educational silhouette markers—but those were visible only during the day. The lakeshore? Is that why people came here? But we were standing on the mitten-shaped Lower Peninsula of Michigan, surrounded by lakeshore. The whole damn state was a viewing area for some kind of nature or another. I didn't get it.

"Do you get a lot of couples here?" I asked Erica Ruth.

At first she said nothing.

"Romantic getaways?" I said. "Anniversaries?"

"Some," she said at last. "A lot of people seem to get engaged here."

"Ah," I said, just to keep the conversation going. "And they stay in the guest house? With other people?"

"Sometimes," she said curtly. "Sometimes they stay in town."

"Sure," I said. Speaking to her was a balm on my nerves. She treated me perfunctorily. I was someone she couldn't be outwardly rude to, but she could treat me like a recurring checkbox she had to mark off. But even this bit of human interaction made me feel as though things would be fine. Things would be, someday, normal. "I bet the rooms are difficult to get here, anyway. That's why you have to reserve them so far in advance."

She shrugged. "Sometimes people just like to plan ahead."

She didn't know how out of character it would be for Bix to alight on a plan and follow through. Military training or not, follow-through wasn't his strong suit. A leader of men, sure, but he usually had his troops to do the work. On his own, he didn't always see the end of things. Unless he was really serious about the goal and had to make his case. He'd once planned and saved for a motorcycle I didn't let him buy. I thought it was too dangerous, that he would wreck and kill himself.

"What?" Erica Ruth said.

"Nothing, sorry." I turned back to the bulletin board. Night hikes. Perseid showers. Whatever that meant.

OFFICER COOLEY DROVE me back to the guest house to grab a change of clothes. The others had been allowed to take a few things out the night before while I was in the hospital.

At the house, all was quiet except an officer stationed at the back door. He lifted the yellow police tape for us with a warning to stay away from the kitchen. Not a problem. The warm penny smell of the blood seeped through the closed door. Cooley watched while I collected the fewest items possible. "My camera?" I asked.

"Leave it. They're still sifting through evidence." She noted on her pad what I'd taken with me.

And then she drove me toward town. We had been relocated. At the outskirts of Mackinaw City, she nosed the cruiser into the parking lot of a two-story motel with a dilapidated sign announcing our arrival at the Hide-a-Way.

"Is this really necessary?" I said.

"Sheriff wants you all to stay put one more night at least," she said. "And there's the matter of your other bed being next door to a crime scene."

"And tomorrow?" I said. "Will I be allowed to go home tomorrow, by a reasonable time? It's a long drive to Chicago, you know."

"Never been," she said.

"There's a wide world out there, Officer Cooley," I said. "You should get out there and learn some decent swear words."

"No need for that," she said, turning her bubble-gum cheek toward the motel. "They have a room for you, but anything extra you gotta pay yourself."

The motel's façade was dingy, the neon sign flickering. The parking lot around us, desolate. "Extras like what, exactly?"

"One of us will come get you tomorrow, so stay close by."

With my phone and car keys still in police custody and my only mode of transportation stuck out at the guest house, blocked in by a dead guy's car, I didn't have much choice. There was nothing left to do but accept the Hide-a-Way as my home for the next evening.

I got out of the car, carrying my armload of clothes and a plastic bag of toiletries. The nearest neighbor was a gas station with two of the four pumps out of order. Somewhere not far from here lay one of the Great Lakes region's greatest tourist treasures—Mackinac Island, and a sleek wire suspension bridge to the Upper Peninsula you could see for miles coming into town—and yet nothing at these coordinates could convince me that anyone would come here willingly.

In the motel's office, a surly man checked me in with another warning about the luxurious extras I needed to avoid. Using the phone, it turned out, was extra. I had an upstairs room, along an outside walkway. After I had stowed my belongings in the spot in my room I deemed least likely to be infested with bed bugs, on top of a luggage rack, I hurried back outside, out of the stale air. I felt as though I had been holding my breath all day, and I hadn't eaten in a long time, nothing since the cheese crackers the evening before. I wasn't sure what I could count on in the next few hours. Except nightfall. I could count on the sky turning black and my ability to function failing me.

In the parking lot, I stared long and hard at the sun's position in the sky and then at the distance between where I stood and what I thought might be some quaint, small-town commerce. And then the sun again. It wasn't late yet, just midafternoon, but I was tired. I couldn't imagine sitting at a table, ordering from a menu.

In the end, I went across to the gas station and shopped the hot dogs rolling inside the countertop machine and the dusty bags of chips and cookies hanging side-by-side with packs of batteries, toothpicks, air fresheners. The lights overhead tinted everything an eerie green. My own skin was a pall, otherworldly. Behind the counter, a guy of indeterminate age wearing a trucker hat over his greasy hair watched the silent TV in the corner.

I considered the ice cream cooler, and took out a pint container from a local creamery for a closer look. *Halloway's Heavenly*, the carton said over a scene of idyllic farmland. Such hope I had not encountered in some time.

The door of the station beeped and clattered open to voices, streams of voices all trying to rise over one another. I didn't have to look, but I did.

Dev and Paris came first, going at one another again, then Sam and Martha, bickering in the harshest tones I'd heard yet. One by one they saw me and stopped. My face flushed hot. They would know by now. Dev would have told them what a nutcase I was.

"What did you do with Hillary?" I said, choosing the offensive. "Or was she the dessert?"

"Sure, we're supposed to feel sorry for her after she accused one of us of killing our best friend," Sam said.

The counter guy shifted on his feet and pretended to find something about the lottery ticket dispensers to fuss with.

"Which one did she accuse?" I said. "Maybe Malloy told her some things before he died."

An odd silence swept across the group until Paris gained control. She stalked toward me, brushing past on her way to the wall of coolers. "Who's the one with a dead husband back home, huh?" she said, grabbing at bottles of water. "I bet the police will be looking into *that*."

"And they should," I said. "They'll be looking into all of us. I imagine they'll find a lot more interesting things among the people who actually had a relationship with the victim. The skeleton in my closet is a car accident." I had to pause to catch my breath, to push out the image of the car, the police. "How about yours?"

I didn't feel as brave as I sounded. I had a vision of that night in Chicago, at home with all the lights on, waiting for someone who wouldn't come, waiting for the news they'd brought to be wrong.

I avoided looking Dev's way. If he hadn't told them yet, he would, and what did it matter? I would go back to being a stranger, inconsequential, and isn't that what I wanted? Maybe someday I'd be called to testify at the trial of one of them. That is, if Emmet County's finest could eventually pin the murder on the right suspect, or on any donkey at all.

"Look," Dev said, rubbing at his face and eliciting a sandpaper scratch from his five o'clock shadow. "It's been a rough day for us all, and it started pretty early. Why don't we call a truce for now so we can try to get some sleep?" Here, he looked pointedly in my direction. "They'll come get us tomorrow, probably interview us again, probably another rough day ahead. Several rough days for us, with Malloy's family arriving—"

Here, Paris made a small noise of distress and held her wrist against her puckered face. Dev went to her and pulled away the bottles of water. He looked down at the ice cream in my hand, blinked at it. "And," he continued, leading her toward the register. "And I'm not even sure what happens then. A funeral, at some point. Answers, I hope. But for now, I'm not going to fight anymore. Let's go, Pare."

Fight with me? I was hardly his staunchest opponent but once again I was providing the third man in the ring, the one they could all fling punches at. Hillary must have gotten tired of it.

They paid for their waters, Paris's hungry eyes lingering on the ice cream carton in my hand. They marched from the store and turned toward the town, Dev's arm around Paris's shoulder. In their absence, Sam and Martha hurried to get bottles of water and juices for themselves. When they had finally gone, I put the ice cream back. Heaven-sent was too hopeful for me.

In the end, I settled on a package of crackers and some water, too. Dinner. The guy at the register rang me up, clearing his throat several times before giving my total. "You in that mess up at the park?" he said, taking my money.

"Not at the moment."

"Guy killed," he said.

"Yep," I said.

He held my change in his hand, weighing it but not giving it over.

"Did you have a question?"

"My money would be on that bombshell," he said.

Paris. Martha was buxom but no one's bombshell. Paris was the one you couldn't look away from. She was also black, but I hoped we weren't in racist territory here. "I don't have any information," I said. "But she's as good a killer as any-one, I guess."

"It's usually a blonde, though," he said.

"Is it?" I found I was interested in spite of myself. "Usually where?"

"In the movies," he said. He held out my change and dropped it into my hand. Not chancing the possibility of touching me, I noticed. I had blood on my hands, maybe literally.

"The dead guy's girlfriend is a blonde," I said, remembering Hillary's little speech about our all being together in the house, our meet-cute.

He pointed at me. "Bingo."

"She's pretty tiny," I mused. "I'm not sure she could get a screwdriver into him."

"He took a screwdriver?" the cashier moaned. "Where? In the—?" I pantomimed the neck stab it would have taken on myself, an upward thrust. So a tiny person might have been able to pull it off. A strong person, though.

"Nasty," he said. "That's definitely a chick kill, not even remotely gentlemanly."

"Yes, because men are always gentlemanly when they kill," I said, turning for the door. What was gentlemanly or civilized in any of this? What had that group of misfits come to do in the wild woods, anyway?

One of them, it seemed, had come to take a friend's life.

For the first time, I felt scared for my own. The brazen retorts that had come so easily to the group now fell away. My knees buckled. I caught myself with the help of the door.

Across the street stood the lone figure of the blonde in question, scraping her feet as she walked toward the motel. She stopped and stared up at the sputtering neon, and then up at the sad outlook of the place. Down at the end of the building, a door opened and a group of people emerged, laughing and singing. Drunk. Hillary let the crowd pass, then turned in the direction of the bar and picked up her pace.

I wasn't sure why Malloy and his friends had come to the lake, but I knew that Hillary had just made the decision to avoid her room and go get blotto on her own. And why not? The man she couldn't live without was dead.

I was halfway across the gas station parking lot before I realized I was going to join her. And why not?

So many reasons, and yet they were not what I thought of as I chased Hillary's rabbitish movements across the lot and inside. Maybe I wasn't thinking at all.

## Chapter Ten

Inside the bar, it was dark.

I had pulled open the door and then stood on the edge of the gloom, stalled and unable to force myself to take another step. The dim lights over the bar illuminated only a few questioning or leering faces turned my way.

"In or out, lady," said a gruff woman's voice.

"I'm over here." Hillary's reluctant voice was timid against the other woman's. It would not have been heard in any other bar, but this bar relied on just one TV on the back wall and its patrons concentrating on their own drinks and regrets. My eyes adjusted slowly, by which time the customers had lost interest in me. The woman who had first spoken up turned out to be the bartender. She folded her arms over her ample middle, the extra flesh a fierce white except where her neck and chest had started to go pink with impatience. For a moment I could imagine the woman rising to the challenge of kicking me out. She would have to. I was frozen in place.

"Eden," Hillary said, waving so that I could find her. "I'm

buying you a drink. You look like you need one almost as bad as I do."

Now I could pick her out, her head turned over the high back of a booth. With the eye contact, I found that I could step inside the bar and let the day's light close off behind me. I managed the last few shaky steps to the booth and fell in across from her. Seated, I had a view of a reassuring amount of blue sky through a window high in the front wall. I concentrated on that until I could face Hillary.

Her face was puffy, eyes swollen to slits and nose rubbed raw. I remembered my own first hours after the doorbell rang with news of Bix. Nothing would have made it better. No one could have said the right thing. "I'm so sorry," I said. "It's no help that I've been where you are."

She dug into her purse and pulled out a crumpled tissue. "They think I did it."

"The police?"

"Those jerks from the house."

"One of them doesn't," I said. "Just not sure which one." I was flooded with an anger I didn't fully understand. What made people think they could kill and get away with it? Bix had made a mistake and had paid dearly for it—but I couldn't think about what he'd done right now or I would lose the little bit of distance I could impose on this situation. I just needed to get away from this place and these people. This story could go on without me.

"Malloy knew something bad would happen," she said, her hands in fists. "He didn't want to come here. But I—" Her face folded in on itself.

"You wanted to meet his friends."

"Malloy talked about them all the time," she wailed. "He

talked to them all the time, too, phone calls, texts. I just thought . . . people that important to him should be important to me."

"Or maybe you should be important to them," I said.

She sniffed and held the tissue to her nose, talking around it. "So what if I did think that? They didn't own him, though you would have thought they did from how much they asked of him."

I couldn't help my curiosity. I wanted to know. "Why do you think he didn't want to come? Did he single anyone out?"

"I think he talked to every one of them in the week leading up to the trip," she said. "Except Paris. He avoided her calls."

Interesting. "Why?"

"Hey, Sex in the City," the bartender called. "You ladies going to order some fruity cocktails or what?" She was leaning heavily against the bar but when we turned to look, she took in Hillary's swollen face and backed up. "I'll send something over. Good for heartbreak."

"I hope it's bourbon poured over Xanax," Hillary muttered. "How did you get through this?"

"I gave up drinking and bored everybody's sympathy away," I said. "And ate. I gained and lost twenty pounds. Well, I lost *twelve*." I looked at her, calculating how much the truth might cost me. "It also helped that I found out he cheated on me for at least a year before he died."

Hillary's hand dropped from her face.

The bartender came over and set down two shot glasses and a bottle with a thud, reminding me of Dev thumping down the bottle with the screwdriver still in the cork in its neck. Its neck, and then, later, Malloy's. I must have paled. The bartender waved me off. "Drink what you need," she said, quietly. She shrugged at the bar. "On me, but don't tell those losers at the bar I have a plush side."

After she was gone, I poured the two glasses without bothering to see what we'd be drinking. My hand shook a bit. Telling the truth was still difficult. Shaming. I wanted the drink.

"I thought you didn't drink," she said.

"I don't drink as much as some people."

"When did you know?" Hillary said. "About . . . her?"

"Not soon enough to discuss it with him," I said. "I was never not going to be blindsided, I guess. And then his funeral—well, he had more than his fair share of chief mourners." I didn't like to think about that day. That woman, bringing her grief to my husband's funeral. "It got a little crowded near the casket."

"I'll kill them if they come near him," she said.

She'd said it loudly. One of the men at the bar swiveled on his stool and took a long look at us before turning back around.

"Careful what you say right now," I said.

She narrowed her eyes at me. "You don't think I did it. Everyone else does, but you don't. Why?"

"I don't know. You could have done it back where you live, I guess? Why bring him all the way here to stab him?"

"Deeper pool of potential suspects?" She downed the shot and made a face.

Good point. I held my glass for a long moment, trying to decide if this was how I wanted to handle the situation. There was no such thing as one shot.

Hillary watched my hand on the glass. A little social lubricant might help this conversation. I drank my shot and suffered through the flames that rose back up through my throat and nostrils. When I could talk again, I said, "Well, if you did do it, what's your motive? He wouldn't commit?"

"You're thinking of Paris," she said.

"Why didn't Malloy take her calls?"

She waved a hand at me. "He did," she said. "But only about half the time, or after she had tried three or four times in a row. Oh, yeah, she did that. He called it 'war dialing.' Like a spoiled brat. But he always gave in to her."

"Always?"

"Well, not *always*." Hillary reached for the bottle and poured us another round. "She wanted him, and he didn't give in to that. They all wanted him, in their own way, but her demands were pretty straightforward."

"She wanted to sleep with him," I said.

"She wanted to *marry* him. Forever and ever, amen, and nobody else had better ever come knocking." She shot back the drink and I joined her. My gut was warm, and the feeling was starting to emanate out into my legs. I had forgotten that hard alcohol numbed so quickly, and I didn't mind the reintroduction. "She hated that I even existed," Hillary said. "And that poor kid she's stringing along."

Kid. She sounded a thousand years old.

"But Paris wouldn't have killed Malloy," I said. I studied the blue square of the window for a moment. "She would have killed you."

Hillary shrugged. "Or Martha, then. She wanted him, too."

I could believe her story about Paris, the beautiful woman with the accommodating fiancé she couldn't seem to wed.

She had looked upon Malloy with the hungry eyes of a feral cat. But Martha? I couldn't see it. Martha and Malloy were playful with each other—a flirtation, maybe, or a sibling-like closeness.

"What do the guys want?" I said. A third shot waited for my hand. I didn't remember it being poured but reached for it anyway. Magic.

"Sam was calling a lot for a while, about his job," she said. Some of her words sounded fuzzier to me than they should, but was that her speech going soft or my hearing? My hands tingled. When I squeezed them, they seemed to open and close in slow motion. "And Dev. I don't know. He sometimes calls right after Paris does, just to talk. Malloy always picks up the phone for him." She went quiet, looking off into the dark room. "Picked up."

"Favorites," I said. "He played favorites among them." For some reason, I knew that this would have been the biggest insult among their group, to be the person Malloy didn't love as much as the others. To know it, too—to see the light dim as his eyes passed over the one who had somehow failed to inspire the same level of adoration as the rest. "That's what he did."

"What?" she said. Her face was flushed. She held the back of her wrist to her mouth and closed her eyes.

"He didn't love them all the same," I said. "And they all wanted to be the one he loved best. You. You wanted it, too."

"I'm going to be sick," Hillary said. She pushed herself from the booth and raced away from the table. I heard her fumble at a door and the creak as it opened.

I held my head in my hand and let the warmth of the liquor

pulse under my skin. When I opened my eyes, the bartender stood at our table, pulling the bottle back. "Your friend going to be OK?" she said, stacking the empty shot glasses.

"Never again," I said. "He died perfect. He's never going to disappoint her, except by leaving her alone."

## Chapter Eleven

I had to drag Hillary up the stairs to her room, only a couple of doors down from mine, and tuck her into the questionably clean Hide-a-Way covers. Her face was pale against the sheets, her hair hanging across her eyes. I was tempted to check for a pulse—second time in twenty-four hours—but listened instead until I caught the sound of her breath.

I took her room's phone off the hook, at least. The poor woman needed what sleep she could get, even the alcohol-induced kind. It might be her last chance to rest until after the funeral. Or longer. I thought for a moment about the casseroles dropped off, the notes in the mailbox like little individual grief bombs, the dread scent of stargazer lilies in bouquets that kept getting placed in my hands. Longer.

In the bathroom, I soaked a washcloth in cool water for Hillary's forehead and was startled by the woman in the mirror there. I pawed at my lank hair and wiped the powder of old mascara from under my eyes. I had been thinking of Hillary as a sister in grief but it was clear from what I saw of myself now that I would be mistaken for her mother, if anything. Who was I to give her advice? Bix and I had had our run of things—and we'd run them right into the ground. Hillary and Malloy had been on their way up. Maybe they wouldn't have made it, in the end. But that wasn't the point. Her misery could be nothing like mine. Her grief would be her own.

A toiletry bag sat on the back of the sink. I had it open before I even knew I would be taking a peek. Inside, the usual creams and concoctions young women used to field off what was already well under way in my reflection. A new tube of lipstick in a red too harsh for the poor girl's skin tone. *Ridiculous Red*, the label on the bottom said. One pack of birth control pills, taken up to last night. Well, that was one piece of good news. No tiny Malloy on the way as Papa was put into the ground.

Back in the bedroom, Hillary was still passed out. On the chair near the bed sat a cute fabric reusable grocery bag, flowered and adorable. She'd been allowed a bag? When I'd been patrolled like a criminal, distracted enough I'd left my toothbrush behind?

I hesitated, thinking about all the people who had buzzed around me after the accident. They meant well. Some of them had, anyway. I had felt exposed, as though I had just walked into the middle of a wide, empty theater stage, a spotlight trained upon me. What Hillary needed right now wasn't someone snooping around or even hanging around. I should go.

I started for the door, but stopped. What I should do and what I was drawn to do were not the same thing. The desire to know shot through me. The desire to understand what might never be explained. What had happened to Malloy?

I went back to the bag and, watching Hillary, slowly

opened it. Inside, a set of clothes sat folded. Underneath, a thin wallet. I went through it quickly but only found the expected identifications and credit cards. More credit cards than necessary, in my opinion. Tucked into the currency area with a few bucks there was one photo of the two of them, Malloy grinning like a king. He really had been a remarkably handsome guy, though a little too wholesome, if I was being honest. Pilgrim and farmer. Not my type.

Besides the photo, a couple of receipts for gas, fast food. One for a department store I recognized and the item listed seemed to be some kind of lingerie. Malloy would have gotten so lucky this weekend.

Or maybe he had, before he got very unlucky indeed.

*Luck*. The word signified a certain amount of happenstance, but I wondered. Malloy had said the trip hadn't been his idea, but Hillary had planned to make the most of things—meeting his friends, prancing around in something tiny that would remind Malloy not to spend all night out looking at the stars. Whose idea had this trip been? In the end, maybe luck had had nothing to do with it.

Other than the wallet, the bag held little of interest, just some pens, a few forgotten throat lozenges, a ring of keys attached to an ID card with Hillary's photo. I studied the image—her hair darker, her chin thrust out almost defiantly—and looked for any hint as to what the keys might open. Probably doors and cabinets at that job she was so good at, according to Malloy. The keys to the car they'd driven in from Indiana-Ohio-Wherever were presumably under police protection. I put the keys back quietly, glancing Hillary's way.

*I'll help*. That was what I'd promised myself. Yeah, I didn't think she'd see this as helping anyone but myself.

I put the clothes back, making sure they appeared as neatly folded as they had been found. But then I felt something moving inside the bag and yanked my hand out. A square of blue lit up through the weave of a folded sweater. A cell phone, ringing. I was sure we'd all had our phones taken, but maybe Hillary had used her wiles to keep hers. I pulled out the phone and looked at the screen. Angel, the screen said, over a photo of Hillary and a teen girl, their arms thrown around each other's neck, their other hands up in peace-sign *V*'s.

I touched the screen, accepting the call, and put the phone to my ear.

"Mom?" a young woman's voice said. "Mom, what's going on up there? I saw something online—Mom?"

"Your mom is sick right now," I said, after giving the situation a moment.

"Who is this? Where's my mom?"

"She's sleeping," I said. "Wait. Your mom *is* Hillary, right?" The girl went silent.

"Her boyfriend was murdered," I said.

"No," she said. "No, that's crazy—Malloy?" The girl started to cry. "This isn't some joke, right? He can't be."

"Were you close to him?"

She went quiet, sniffed. The true situation was beginning to reveal itself to me. A second phone? "You aren't supposed to exist, are you?"

"Well, I do," she said. "Put my mom on the phone."

"She's sleeping," I said, "and before that, she was—she really needs to sleep. I don't think we should wake her right now." I glanced over at Hillary. Her hair still hung over her face. "Why didn't she tell him about you yet?"

"She was going to tell him this weekend," she said, her voice thick. "After . . . after I don't know."

"When he was in a good mood, hanging with all his friends," I said. Or after he got tired of all their problems and wrote them off? After that negligee was revealed?

"I guess," she said. "She didn't want to wait until—"

Until. Until? A nearly adult daughter seemed like a first-date topic, to me. "Until . . . until he proposed?"

"Maybe."

"Did she think he was doing that soon?"

"She hoped," Angel said. She snuffled and then blew her nose. "We both did."

"But you hadn't met him," I said.

"Well, no, but he made her so happy," the girl said. "Things just seemed to be going her way finally."

Yeah, that part of her life was over. "How old are you, Angel?"

"What business is it of yours?" she said. "Who *are* you?"

Fifteen or so. "So, your mother had you in . . . high school?"

"Look, save your judgments for the church bulletin—"

"Just working out the math," I said. "Your mom must have been dedicated to her education to finish school and raise you at the same time."

The pseudo-praise seemed to settle her down. "She worked *hard* to finish her GED," she said.

"And then when did she go to—"

The phone was wrenched from my hand. Hillary stood, haggard, glaring at me.

"Your phone started ringing," I said.

"You and I are not actually the same person," she said, her voice raw. "You know that, right?"

We both listened to Angel's disembodied voice asking for her. "Mom? Mom?"

"Answer your kid," I said. "She's scared."

"I'm a little scared, myself."

"You don't have anything to fear from me," I said.

"Don't I?" She put the phone to her ear, her face immediately crumpling at the sound of Angel's voice. "Sweetheart, hold on—"

"I'm leaving," I said.

"Wait! Can you not—"

"Not mention your secret phone? Or your secret kid? A motive, by the way. I won't mention it to anyone," I said. "Unless you don't. You have to tell the cops tomorrow, or I will."

"Fine," she said, but it was not fine. The look she gave me was deadly. "Get out."

OUTSIDE, IT WASN'T quite dark, but the distance to my room loomed, just a few feet too far. I hurried, feeling shadows at my back. At the door, I fumbled with the key, dropped it. When I reached to pick it up, the movement at the edges of my vision made me dizzy. The air felt thick around me, closing in. I opened the door and, from the outside, reached for the light switch. When the light was on, I entered and shoved the door closed, locked the dead bolt, and lay against the door with all my weight, breathing in, breathing out.

When the rising feeling of panic finally fell away, I raced around the room, adding the bedside lamps' glow. Low-wattage, all of it, and my pack of lightbulbs hostage back at the guest house.

Still a little fuzzy in the head, I went to the bathroom and splashed my face with cold water, staring at my reflection in the bad light there. Looking at yourself in multiple mirrors and hoping for different results—was that a psychosis? I heard the sound of Paris's voice in my head. Maybe I *was* a special kind of psychopath.

No, I was not the one wielding screwdrivers here. The question: Who was?

Hillary's secret kid—what did it mean for Malloy's death, especially given that he hadn't seemed to know about her?

He wouldn't have needed to, if someone else did. To his friends, Angel would have been just another person wanting a slice of Malloy's time. I thought again of my revelation in the bar. They all loved him so much, he had to die. Wasn't that what we were dealing with? An irrational person. An irrational person whose love was so bright that it blinded him or her to reality.

There was a logic to the illogical situation, which was not as comforting as it should have been.

Or maybe it had just been a break-in, after all. That mystery figure in the back hallway, running away from the scene. Couldn't we leave the mantle of responsibility hanging from that person's neck?

But—neck.

To stab someone in the neck seemed so personal. A stranger could have stabbed Malloy in the chest and gotten away. Even if he had lived, a stranger might never have been tied to the crime. The screwdriver in the jugular was too intimate. Too brutal.

Pried from the neck of the bottle Dev had tried to open, and thrust into the neck of the only person in the house everyone loved without reason. It made no sense.

I tried to picture the scene. The screwdriver was the problem. Surely there had been better weapons in the kitchen, one drawer pull away. Hadn't the wine opener, far sharper, been just as close? The screwdriver was the weapon of a crime of passion and reaction, not a plan. So it must have been already pulled from the bottle, to be the thing to grab.

I sat down on the edge of the tub and closed my eyes. I tried to remember. The wine bottle tipped over, dripping. The wine opener sitting in the puddle. His lips, wine stained. The only reason to pull the screwdriver from the bottle would be to serve the wine.

A late-night drink between friends, a private moment ruined by a rush of anger and betrayal.

Of possession.

No stranger, then. A friend.

I couldn't get the idea out of my head once it was there. I knew what it felt like to want to be the one, the only—and to have those hopes dashed in a particularly public way. I knew. It was the kind of feeling that made you want to kill someone.

# Chapter Twelve

In the early hours of morning, the doorknob to my room began to rattle.

I sat up and pulled my T-shirt and jeans from the floor. My heart thudded in my chest. I reached for the phone, hesitated. Those damn extras.

The night before, I had pulled the desk chair across the room and lodged it under the knob, a precaution that had felt silly even to myself. But I had stayed in a house overnight—almost overnight—with a group of people who had sacrificed one of their own. One of the five of them was dangerous, and the locks on these old hotel doors were low-tech and ancient. A screwdriver, I'd mused to myself as I dragged the chair across the room. Yes, a screwdriver would do the trick. On the lock and then on me.

I tiptoed to the door and watched it shake in its frame. A rasping whisper came from the other side. "Martha," the voice said. "Open the damn door."

It was Sam.

I had been awake practically every second of the night and felt dizzy and exhausted. The few hours of sleep I'd gotten the night before were long gone. I rubbed at my face. "What do you want?" I whispered.

"My room has a mouse," he said. "Let me stay with you. Come on. I brought wine . . . or a reasonable facsimile, anyway. Let me in."

I yanked open the door. "Wrong room."

Sam stammered, blinking into the light. He seemed a little drunk already, but then what else would any of them have done with their time? I'd been a little drunk myself not a few hours ago. Now my mouth was dry and thick.

"I thought— Oh, crap," Sam said. "I don't know which room she's in and now I don't know which room I came from." He patted his pockets. "And I don't have my key."

Behind him, it was that gray hour of dawn. Not dark enough that I couldn't deal with it, but still, I wasn't comfortable. I hadn't slept in a room with a man in nine months. Not that I hadn't had offers. I simply chose not to be alone with a man, not to subject myself to the mess and noise of other people, to intimacy. The intimacy of boxer shorts hanging from the newel post. Sam looked at me hopefully. I gestured into the room.

"Thanks so much," Sam said. "Yours is as dumpy as mine—but no mice, right?" He peered into the corners, nervously pulling at his beard.

"Not that I've noticed," I said. "But I've been awake all night, so I'm pretty sure no, no mice."

"Maybe all these lights are keeping them away." He looked at me sheepishly.

"Dev told you," I said.

"Well, he said—something. I'm not sure I understood it, but—can I be honest? I get it now. I couldn't sleep tonight, and then that mouse chewing, chewing." His eyes were bloodshot, haunted. "I should have left the lights on, except I was afraid I'd see cockroaches."

Something new to consider. I went to the bed and sat on the edge to put my shoes on, before something ran across my toes. "You should have had more wine, I guess."

"That's the plan," he said, walking into the bathroom and coming out with two plastic cups, still in the wrappers. He tore them open roughly, a kid at Christmas. The bottle had already been opened and, I thought, tipped back a few times. He poured the cups full and set one on the bedside table for me. "I should probably give it up."

"That seems unlikely, given your line of work."

He pulled the chair away from the door and sat. "Well," he said. His first drink was not the sip of a connoisseur but the gulp of a parched drunk. "I've worked with wine my entire career, that's true." His entire career, which was only about five years long, but who was I to judge? Me, with no career to speak of. "But I'm ready for a change, so why not explore other interests?"

The line sounded rehearsed to me. "What are your other interests?"

He laughed. "OK, you got me. I live for wine. I have no idea what I'm going to do."

I gave up on the laces of my shoes. They were harder to tie than I remembered. I was so tired. I didn't need wine. My head was already spinning from exhaustion and whatever evil had been in that bottle downstairs.

"So why did I leave the job?" he said, prompting me. "I should work on what I'll say when people ask."

"Let's pretend people just did."

He searched the corners again, for time, it seemed, instead of mice. "I went up for a promotion and it didn't work out."

Malloy had helped him prepare for a move up the ladder. Hadn't Hillary said Malloy had spent the time to give Sam a pep talk, maybe even when he hadn't wanted to? Why hadn't he wanted to? What kind of friends where these? They may have been close once, but I'd seen little evidence they still were. "You didn't get the promotion so you quit?"

"Stubborn pride."

"Very stubborn."

He took a drink, wouldn't look my way. "Unbelievably stubborn, would you say?"

"What really happened?"

Some of the overconfidence I'd seen in Sam and his friends returned. His face became a mask. "I don't know you," he said. "Why would I tell you anything?"

"Do you think you'd like to wait for the office to open, alone in the parking lot? I bet they have rats the size of—"

"Fine," Sam said. He sat forward with his elbows on his knees and talked to his shoes. "I went after a promotion. Malloy gave me some pointers. We went over everything . . . my worth, what I'd brought to the company, all of it. He helped me script it out. I had a really good shot." The confidence was gone, and in its place, Sam was just some slob slumped over bad wine. He picked at a loose bit of the fake leather on the edge of the chair's seat. "At least I thought so, and so did Malloy. To hear him tell it. Malloy has—had a way . . . Have you ever known someone who could pump you up so full of life's possibilities that you think you can do anything? That you think you might be someone else entirely?"

What had Malloy said? That he had a way of bullying people into things?

And, yes, I had known someone like that, in fact, though Bix's good-natured manipulations had been engaged most often to get me to forgive him for being an hour late when he'd said he'd be gone five minutes. He'd had energy left over to try to remake me, to shape me into someone else. I wish I could say I'd been impervious to these efforts. "Did you want the promotion?

"Of course," he said, coming back to himself. "Yes. More money, better title, more travel, managing a few people. It was a step up, a step toward owning my own business. It was everything." He looked at the cup of wine with disgust and set it at his feet.

"But?"

"But I got passed over, of course." He let his head fall into the palms of his hands, pulling his hair back against his skull, exposing how deeply his hairline had already receded. "By a guy with two years' less experience. I trained him. He was younger than me, all talk, knew everything until, you know, you needed him to do something. That shit-for-brains was going to be my boss, so I . . . I quit."

Interesting that the guy with nothing going for him had beaten him out, but I didn't ask. I still didn't understand why he couldn't work in wine distribution somewhere else, but I had the feeling I was missing things that were perfectly clear. I blinked and felt the world pull back and slide into place in slow motion. *Click-kuh.* It was going to be a long drive back to Chicago, if I ever got the chance to do it. "What time is it?" I said.

"Late. Or early, I guess," Sam said, spinning his watch

around his wrist a few times. He had a large nautical device on his wrist, like Malloy's. He studied the face of the watch for a long moment without revealing what time it read. "I'm not sure I'll bother with sleep. We have to be back at the station in a couple of hours." He shook his head in apparent wonder.

"What's it like to think that one of your friends might have killed the other?"

He let the silence go on so long I thought he intended not to answer. And then: "It feels like the end of the world. Like the absolute end of the world."

This was the correct answer. I shook my own head to try to clear my thoughts. "When you said Hillary had accused one of you of killing your best friend—"

"I said *our* best friend," he said. He stood and went to the window. The sun's rays were finding inroads around the thick, stained curtains. "All of us. We're best friends."

"But that's not how *best* works," I said. "Which of you was Malloy's closest friend? Dev? You? Not Paris."

He turned to me, frowning. "Why not Paris?"

"Just—never mind."

"Well," he said. "I guess the obvious answer was that none of us were, not really. Or he could have counted on making it out of this reunion alive."

WE WAITED OUT the long hour in the room until the sun raged through the curtains. I couldn't sleep in the room with Sam there anymore than I'd been able to before he showed up. "Do you mind if I turn on the radio?" I said, and found a soft, droning voice on the local station again. I dozed a little to the gentleness of it, waking to hear about the stars again.

". . . Orion, Cassiopeia, the Dippers, the bears, my personal favorite Cygnus, the swan, which looks like a simple pair of wings, but contains thousands of planets and star clusters," the voice said. "There they are, right above our heads, marching across the sky—nah, of course you know better than that. You've been hanging out on the dial with me long enough to know that's us gliding around on our axis. We're the ballerina up on our toes, spinning. Those stars are as fixed as anything in our expanding universe. But there they are, on schedule, season to season, night to night. Except that some-one at some point charted them out and drew those invisible lines, turning a clutch of stars, distant and unknowable, into characters from the stories they liked. That's something, isn't it? That's like me looking up and finding Sherlock Holmes and his deerstalker cap in the stars. Why not? Orion's belt is up there. Why not a hunting cap or . . ."

I must have slipped off again for a while, because Sam's snoring woke me next. The radio was still talking. "Finding shapes in the scatter of stars is an act of organization in the face of chaos," the voice said. "An act of faith, if you think about it—faith that the little things you do can matter, can mean one da—dang, one darn thing.

"All the visible stars are accounted for, taken up with dogs and crabs and centaurs and stuff. Beyond that, there are stars without name, without number. You and I don't have access to deep space discoveries to put a name to the shapes they make. NASA knows the names of some of them. But the ones we can see? Got named up a long time ago. I guess I wish they'd left a few open patches for us, you know? To point to the sky and say, 'Here's what I see. Here's who I am. These are the stories I like to tell.'"

I sat up and blinked at the radio. The soothing voice was gone and had been replaced by someone reading off commercials for a feed and seed store. I fumbled for the switch and finally got it to shut up.

I was so tired, as though I'd been traveling, awake all night while the world slept. Sam wasn't snoring now. Was he awake? Waiting to see what I would do, just as I waited to see what he would? I couldn't imagine he was the killer. He had successfully lulled me into trust.

The next time I woke, it was to the sound of water running in the bathroom. Through the partially open door, Sam threw back an inch of the dark wine remaining in one of the cups, then filled it with water and threw that back, too. He saw me watching. "Hair of the dog. Can I use some of your toothpaste?"

The full cup of wine by my bed was gone. I nodded and sat up. My toothbrush hadn't made it to the hotel, and his was locked in his room, so we took turns chewing an inch of paste off our index fingers. I avoided myself in the mirror.

Sam used the bathroom again, this time with the door closed, while I pretended I couldn't hear him taking a piss. I decided to change clothes while he was in there and was just lowering my T-shirt over my bra when he stuck his head through the door.

"Oh, sorry." He closed the door again.

"I'm done," I said.

He came through the room, his eyes lowered. I was touched by his gentle breeding until I realized his respectful distance made me feel like someone's old maiden aunt. What was wrong with me? Maybe I'd been without male attention a little too long. Or maybe the quality of that attention, when I'd had it, hadn't been quite what it should have been.

When Sam reached for the door, he looked back. "It's Sunday. Martha had breakfast reservations set up for today," he said. He thought it over for a second. "I'm sure they're still showing up. You should come."

"I don't think anyone wants that."

"I wouldn't mind you being there," he said. "Like that buddy system Paris tried to start up. If we're all together, well, then at least we know where everyone is. Fewer surprises that way."

He opened the door and waited. I didn't like surprises, either. And I was curious. And maybe a small part of me would rather be among them, listening in, making my own judgments. That's how you avoided a surprise—by paying attention, by watching the still surfaces for currents underneath. I stepped out into the cool morning air, fresh after the closeness of the room. I inhaled as deeply as I could and then let it out, feeling better already. Sam smiled at me in a knowing way. We had survived it, this night.

The door opened two rooms down. Hillary emerged, eyeing us. The smile fled from Sam's face. He stepped away from me.

"Interesting," Hillary said. "So now I guess I know how some people get over the grief of widowhood."

## Chapter Thirteen

Hillary, when pressed to join us, said she would rather eat out of the Hide-a-Way's garbage bin. We left her to it.

Martha's breakfast spot was a place deeper into town, in a mostly residential neighborhood with shaded sidewalks and lawn sprinklers already at work. The houses were small, tidy, with flowering plants weaving through trellises at the front doors. The sun was shining, too, the full day ahead and the sky blue. Outside the café, a hand-painted sign welcomed visitors, and a long bench provided room for an extended family waiting for their table. Two little girls, their pigtails jouncing, ran along the bench and into their parents, who patiently provided another round of tickles that sent the girls back along the bench. Sam watched after the girls with a little smile, holding the door for me. Under his breath, he said, "Here we go."

The place was crowded except for the table in the center of the room with Paris presiding over four empty chairs. Her eyes found me immediately and sharpened. Upon arrival at the table, Sam pulled out a chair for me. "I only asked for a table of five," she complained.

"Yes," Sam said. "Harsh reality, Paris. There are only four of us, now. And Hillary—" He glanced at me. "Hillary had other plans."

Paris's eyelids fluttered as she looked away. Dev arrived from wherever he'd been and sat at her left. He reached over and held her hand, but she pulled it away. "Sure," she said. "I guess we'll just fill Malloy's seat with anyone who happens by. I passed a homeless man in a dirty snow jacket on the way over. Why not him, too?"

"If only I didn't join you for breakfast, you could continue your reunion as though nothing had gone wrong." I picked up a menu, though I wasn't hungry. Martha was making her way from the restrooms, her eyes on me.

"Really?" she said to Paris.

"That's what I was saying," Paris said.

Martha sat on the other side of Sam, who reached out to give her a pat on the back. She threw him off. "I suppose this is your doing," she said to him.

"I thought we could risk having some toast together," he said. "What's the harm?"

"The harm is," Dev said, "that Malloy was murdered."

His voice carried a little further than the others' had, and the tables near us grew quiet for a moment. We all stared at our menus and waited for the crowd noise to rise again. Normally my cheeks would burn with shame and attention, but now I found that I didn't care. I was going home today. I was getting away from these toxic people and their problems. How long could this breakfast of the damned drag on?

"Surely you understand our concern," Dev murmured.

"Malloy's death is no fault of mine," I said.

"And you invited the other one, too, I suppose?" Paris said.

"She was just too busy or we'd have the whole sordid gang back together again."

Sam shrugged and held up his hand toward someone behind the counter. "Could we get all the coffee over here? Seriously, all of it?"

Paris glared at his arm in the air but then her face cleared and she turned her attention to the mug in front of her, a strange contemplative look directed toward its every detail. Dev and I locked eyes. Something had just shifted in the air, but I had no idea what it was.

A young waiter who looked as haggard as the rest of us came out with a steaming carafe and worked his way around the table.

"I wouldn't be at the same table as that other one," Martha said, holding her hand over her cup. "Could I get some herbal tea?" she said to the waiter, dimples in place.

"Tea?" Sam said.

"Herbal tea," Dev said. "You know that's not tea, right? It's, like, *flowers*."

"We should be having mimosas," Paris said, watching Sam over the top of her mug.

"Ugh," Martha said. "Not me but you go ahead."

Paris turned her calculating look on Martha.

"So," Dev said. He cleared his throat. "Did anyone get any sleep?"

Sam snorted, and no one else had anything to say. I couldn't decide if their silence came from the awkwardness of my presence at the table or if they would have been just this weird as a table of four. One of them had just been killed, after all. And one of them, perhaps, was a killer.

Without Hillary there, I could feel them all placing their

hatred upon her absence. If they could talk themselves into her having done it, their tiny world was still safe, if lonely and depleted of Malloy's charm. Even I found myself thinking that the danger lay away from this table. When I looked around at them and considered the odds, an itchy feeling began under my skin. I shouldn't have come. But then if I hadn't, maybe they would have spent their breakfast chatter on my guilt instead of hers.

The waiter came back and took orders, but decisions were hard to come by. Finally Martha and I ordered some toast. When it came, the jams were shared between us. Martha nibbled sadly at her plain buttered toast and wouldn't ask me for the pot of jam. The others picked over plates of eggs and bacon. Martha made a face at Sam's heaping plate. "What?" he said. "It's going to be a long day."

"Terry and Clare might arrive today," Dev said. "We'll need our strength."

"Terry and Clare?" I said.

None of them wanted to talk to me.

"His parents," Paris finally said, her voice soft.

Martha threw down her toast and spit the bite in her mouth into a paper napkin. "I can't—I literally don't know how to face them," she said, flapping her hands at her eyes to save her makeup. "I mean . . . what do we say? What if— Oh, God, what if they think we had something to do with this?"

I pictured that screwdriver in the bottle. They'd be fools to believe any other theory. But remembering Bix's mother and all the long days we had spent with one another coming to grips with the way the world had gone on without us, I felt a wave of sorrow for these unseen parents. They might have thought the dangers were all behind them. Malloy hadn't choked on something too big for his infant throat, hadn't waddled into a neighbor's backyard as a toddler and drowned in a pool. He hadn't lost a game of chicken on a dark road as a teenager, hadn't fallen in with the wrong crowd.

Or at least, that's what they must have thought.

And now he was dead. What a waste.

"Stop it," Martha shouted.

The restaurant went quiet in the wake of her voice. She was looking at me. "What?" I said. "What am I—"

"You're mourning him, and you have no right," she said.

I glanced around. Most of the other diners were trying to recover themselves, but some were taking no pains to hide they were watching. "I— It's hard to explain," I said. I tried to pull my voice down to the level of our table. Dev, at least, leaned in to hear me. "Once you've experienced it, you have a lot more empathy. I was only thinking of his poor parents—"

"You're not the only one who's ever experienced loss," she said. The sharpness of her voice cut through any attempt of the other diners to get back to the business of breakfast. For a moment, I was standing back at Bix's funeral, watching the woman in the navy blue dress approach, knowing something terrible would come out of her mouth. *You're not the only one.* "So save the lectures," Martha said. "They are special people with a special son—" She started blinking and flapping again. "I just saw them a couple of months ago, and they—they were so . . . They are amazing people. They don't need you thinking about them or talking about them."

"They do," I said. I dug into my purse for some money and threw it down on the table. "Try to imagine how much loss you feel and compound it by—no. There's no number. They lost their son. Maybe their only child, I don't know. Think about that before you try to own all the grief over Malloy."

I stood up. The restaurant watched, as one.

"Let's just all go," Dev said, looking uneasily around the room.

Martha picked up her toast and sat back. A red curl over her forehead bounced. "I'm not done yet."

"I'll stay with her and pay up," Paris said. "You can walk ahead."

Dev frowned at them in turn. "Sam?"

"There's still bacon on my plate," Sam said. He was looking at Martha in a way I recognized. Who had been not good enough for Martha, in particular? "I'll be there in ten."

Outside, the long benches in front of the restaurant were empty except for one woman still wearing a coat she must have decided on earlier that morning, when it was cooler. Her head turned to watch as we passed. The coat was bright blue, the color a child would pull from a pencil box to color the sky.

The sky overhead tried to cooperate, the day warming up. We stood on a peninsula of land, water in every direction. Hundreds of people had made plans to be here, soaking in the sun, taking the ferry over to the island, sunning themselves, generally wringing every daylight moment out of their lives. We started walking toward the police station. Not for the first time, I wondered how I had come to be this person I was, stunted and helpless to the ticking of a clock, while the world spun around me. I had never been the person squeezing more out of life.

"I'm sorry about that," Dev said after a few minutes of walking. I was churning hard, making him stretch his stride to keep up with me, but he was doing it, and taking the exercise better than I was. At a street crossing, I stopped and wiped at my hairline.

"You people have an interesting idea about the bounds of friendship," I said. "I don't think I've ever had a friend so devoted a zookeeper as Martha."

"Martha's OK. She's just . . . lonely, I guess."

I gave him a look. I knew lonely.

"No, you know how when you were young—"

"*Thank* you."

"—I don't mean just you. When you're young, everything is so vital and vibrant and wild and out of your control, and all those relationships are volatile," he said. "You feel everything so intensely, right? Stay with me. But then with time, with real life, with love and work and all the things that life brings, you start to wonder if you're doing something wrong. You still love your old friends, all those old relationships that were so fiery and passionate and maybe, OK, maybe a little bit fueled by drama and alcohol and crushes—" He shook his head and started across the street again. I followed, hurrying to keep up with him now. "Nothing in adult life blazes quite like your memory of the way it was."

"Except that memory is faulty."

"I remember the bad, too—the intensity, good or bad, that's what I remember." He seemed to want the confirmation, so I gave in.

"If it's intensity you're looking for, I hear parenthood is a pretty good distraction from the humdrum of adulthood," I said.

"Wrong," he said. "That brings on a new kind of mundane. And if your kid turns out to be other than you hoped—" He seemed to go somewhere else for a moment and then he shook his head and continued. "If anything, having kids must cut down on spontaneity, time, focus. Where's the passion you used to feel for where you might go in life? Where's the awe of learning something new? What happened to the way your gut used to drop when you thought about kissing someone for the first time? What happened to meeting new people and staying up all night talking through your philosophies?"

"I don't drink that much anymore," I said. "Philosophies at midnight are for people who pack multiple cases of wine and no food for a week at the lake." I hadn't had quite the same youth Dev had, and now, of course, I didn't think of things like first kisses.

He scoffed and walked faster while I thought about the vehemence of the rant. "Are you having second thoughts about marrying Paris?"

He stopped abruptly, nearly tripping me up. "That is not what this is about."

"OK, great. You're madly in love."

"I am."

But was she? We stared at one another. I would never ask, though he was daring me.

"OK," I said, at last. "So Martha . . ." I was reminded of Hillary's theory that each of the women wanted Malloy for her own.

"Martha wants things to be the same as they always have been. She is to be pitied," Dev said. Then a wry smile. "Except—except didn't I just say the same thing? That it was better then, in a way, than it is now? It was certainly better two days ago."

We turned and kept walking, this time in full silence. I was remembering all the times I'd had to pack our lives and move across the country. By the time Bix retired from the Army, all I wanted was to go somewhere and stay. I wanted things to be predictable for a while, stable. The same. I just wanted to stop time for a minute. It all went so fast. It wasn't exactly the same thing that Martha wanted, but I could see her point. The good old days, though, were never as good as you remembered. Maybe that was Dev's position. Of all of them, he seemed like the one ready to move on, get married, live a life. He was only stopped by the fact that Paris was the least ready.

At the front of the police station, he straightened his shoulders and held the door for me. Another gentleman. Breakfast, forgotten.

# Chapter Fourteen

The police station was like a dentist's office in a bad neighborhood. Dingy, but clinical. The front desk was protected by bulletproof glass, all conversations forced through a slot low over the counter.

We each had forms to fill out, typed statements to annotate and sign, but first they wanted us to wait. That seemed to be the plan, anyway. Dev and I sat in the waiting room alongside a slumped man in a zip sweatshirt with—best guess—dried vomit at the shoulder. I wondered who he might be picking up, who would be in worse straits than this guy, until I saw that he had been handcuffed to his chair. I forced Dev to slide down a seat.

Twenty minutes went by before the door to the street opened and Paris, Martha, and Sam appeared. Sam sat next to the sleeping man, noted the handcuffs, and then stood, offering the seat to the ladies.

Paris gave Sam the kind of look given to a child who had soiled himself and seated herself on the other side of Dev. "Have they told you anything?"

"Just to wait," Dev said.

"Has anyone seen Terry and Clare?"

"Nothing yet, hon. Just waiting," he said. She popped back up again and went to the window, where a young male officer kept court. He was chubby and pale, probably not more than a few years out of acne. Paris approached like a jungle cat. She was the kind of woman who got a better table with a smile or a flirtatious touch on the sleeve. The others watched. They had probably enjoyed those better tables alongside her. But I trained my eyes on Dev, on his bouncing knee.

When Paris came back, she patted the knee still. "Only a few more minutes," she said.

"So . . . just waiting, then," Sam muttered.

Paris heard him. Her eyes flashed over the group, landing on me. I don't think I was smiling, but I was watching. That was enough.

She turned to Sam. "Maybe I'm just anxious to tell them what I know about certain items missing from Malloy's body," Paris stage-whispered. The word *body* cost her greatly, but she soldiered through.

Sam folded his arms across his chest.

"Pare, what's going on?" Dev said.

"He's wearing Malloy's watch," she said. "That's what's going on."

We all turned to Sam. After a long moment, he unfolded his arms. On his wrist was the overlarge watch like the one I'd seen Malloy pull from his car and attach to himself. I hadn't realized it was the same watch, though it was hard to miss, something more likely to be used to circumnavigate the globe than as a mere timepiece.

Sam's eyes darted around the room. "I didn't take it from the— Who do you think I am?"

"We're not sure anymore," Paris said.

"Pare, come on," Dev cautioned. "Sam, explain it."

The pudgy cop behind the desk had called in a few buddies. They all leaned into the slot in the window to hear the story. Sam stammered excuses about wanting to remember Malloy and keep the watch safe until a door at the side opened and Officer Cooley stood in the opening. "Come on back and tell it to the sheriff," she said.

"I found it in the bathroom, OK?" Sam said. "When they let us in to get a few things. It was on the shelf by the sink and he was dead—I mean he was *already* dead . . . but I would never—"

"You stole a souvenir from a dead man," Paris said. Dev reached for her but she slipped out of his grasp. I had seen this same move—reach, denial—a number of times since meeting them. Dev caught me witnessing it and bowed his head over his sandals.

"Souvenir . . ." Sam gagged. Sweat beaded on his upper lip. "You don't—you don't really—"

Officer Cooley crossed the room and took Sam by the arm. Martha went after him, yelling that she was his lawyer. The door closed behind them, cutting the room to silence.

I was shaking. I got up and went to the bulletin board near the window. Wanted posters for a few local baddies had been stapled there, alongside a poster announcing a community carnival in town and a copy of the flyer listing the latest happenings at the dark sky park. Warden Warren's uncomfortable mugshot looked out from that one.

Behind me, Dev said quietly, "I can't believe you did that to Sam. I didn't even notice he was wearing Malloy's watch. How did you even—"

But everyone in the room save the passed-out drunk knew the answer. Paris spotted the watch because she noticed everything when it came to Malloy.

I darted a quick glance over at them. Dev sat with his hands dangling between his knees, defeated.

"It's a really nice watch," Paris said.

A deep, embarrassing silence enveloped the room.

"He didn't like it," I said.

She turned on me, suddenly taking up more room. The beads on her braids clacked together. "How would *you* know?"

"A guess. He wasn't wearing it until he arrived at the guest house. He put it on but then—I don't know—he fussed with it a lot, bothered at it. Seemed to me like he wasn't used to wearing it. And it didn't look like something he would wear."

"You don't know a thing about him," she said.

"Oh, my God," Dev said. We both turned to him. His face sagged, anguished. "You bought that watch for him, didn't you?"

Behind the window, the gathered officers—more of them than ever—had gone still. The only sound was the squeak of the front desk guy's chair as he leaned closer to the opening.

The door to the side opened. Again, Officer Cooley. She seemed as tired as I felt.

Paris, for the first time since I'd met her, seemed unsure of herself. "I . . . it was a while back. For his birthday," she said to Cooley, then turned back to Dev. "He's a good friend of ours."

Dev pinched the bridge of his nose. "Except I never heard about it. Not from you. And certainly not from him."

"You can't be serious," Paris said, trying to laugh it off. "You can't really think there was something going on between me and Malloy."

"Ma'am?" Officer Cooley said. "I think the sheriff might like to ask you about it."

Paris stopped, waiting for Dev to join her. He stayed in his seat, didn't look up.

"You're just going to let them take me away?" she said. "God, even Sam had Martha running to his rescue."

"Maybe Martha will rescue you, then."

"Maybe," she said, leaning down into his ear, "they'll want to hear about how you wandered away from bed that night."

I looked to see if Cooley had gotten that. She had. Her eyes rose to the ceiling as she seemed to calculate something in her head. She ticked off a count on her fingers. "Yeah, we got enough rooms," she said. "Why don't you all come back?"

"What did I do?" I said. "I just need my keys and phone. And a ride to the park."

Dev stood and took the long way around the chairs to get past Paris. "Like you don't know," he growled.

The door to the street opened and Warren Hoyt entered the room. "Hey," he said to me, looking strangely pleased. "Came to check on you. You should be getting a hall pass here soon, right?"

He was so inexplicably out of place, I'm not sure I would have recognized him but for the fact that I'd just seen his face on the bulletin board. And the tight choke on the neck of his polo shirt. He seemed to be waiting for me—me, in particular—to answer his invitation.

I turned back to Dev. "What are you talking about—I should know what?"

"I saw you," he said.

"You saw me . . . what?"

"Out walking around," he said. "That night."

"No," I said, my voice twisted into a croak just from imagining what he was saying. Me. Walking in the dark. It wasn't possible but he was going to force me to say why in front of all these people. "You know—you know I can't—"

"You were sleepwalking or something," Dev said. "Not all there. But you were up walking that night. I walked you back to your room, but who's to say you didn't come back out?"

"Yep," Officer Cooley said, waving us toward the open door. "Bring it in, team. Nobody's getting a hall pass anytime soon, Warren, sorry."

I looked from face to face. This was a joke. It had to be. Hoyt's face was more serious than even his portrait back at the park office. No joke, then. No joke at all.

## Chapter Fifteen

The interview room was cold and smelled of day-old fast food and body odor. No clocks, anywhere. I began, after a while of waiting, shivering, and going over what Dev had said, to wish for that watch off Sam's wrist.

Sleepwalking. *Or something.* In the dark. It wasn't possible. *Not all there.*

Was it?

My head hurt. I cradled my head in my hands and then remembered that I was probably being watched or filmed. I couldn't look guilty.

I wasn't guilty.

Was I?

There was a lot of wiggle room between accepting the premise that I had been sleepwalking and the idea that I had spent that time stabbing someone. I hadn't had any blood on me, no scratches from a struggle. But then, none of them had had blood or scratches, had they? Still. Even if I had been sleepwalking—

But I hadn't been sleepwalking, surely. I had no history of that, had never woken up with dirty feet or stubbed toes.

Sure, I'd never been so tired in my life. I'd hardly been sleeping at all in the last nine months, and before that—well, my sleep had always been as spotty as the cell phone service at the park. Most of the sleep I'd had since Bix died would have been after sunrise. Had I been stumbling around in the daytime at home? In my neighborhood? In public?

There was that bruise I didn't remember getting . . .

No. Not possible. I didn't kill Malloy in my sleep. It wasn't possible. As for sleepwalking at all—no. Someone would have said something. Except—

Except I hadn't been keeping much company. Who was left to tell me that I was losing my mind?

This was what Paris, Dev, and the others had over me. They clung to their friendships; they fought for them. They had made the time to meet up here at the park, at least. I couldn't remember the last time I'd made time for a friend, my sister, Bix's mom. I had closed myself off in a high white tower of misery.

I forced myself to bring my aching head back to the moment. These friends, the ones still alive, were all lined up in individual rooms in a police station, and now I was among them. Who were these people? What did I know?

Sam. Sam nabbed the watch that belonged to Malloy—after he was dead. Paris had given the watch to Malloy as a gift, a secret from her betrothed. And Dev—Dev knew I couldn't stand the darkness and yet accused me of being out of my room, in it. Martha was a lawyer, which would be helpful for the culprit, when caught. Except if someone decided the culprit was me.

The door opened.

Sheriff Barrows's barrel gut entered the room first. "Well,

now," he said. "Turns out you've been seeing more of the local bounty than you thought, huh?"

"That's what I hear, too. I don't believe it."

Officer Cooley followed and closed the door. She stationed herself at the corner of the table with a notebook and placed a paper bag on the table. Inside the rustle of the bag, I heard keys hit the table. My keys. I felt the air in the room clear up a bit. I was going home.

"It would be much more convenient for you not to believe it," Barrows said, his mouth pulled wider around the words that I thought necessary. "I'll advise you the room's being recorded."

"OK," I said. And then I thought—I don't know my rights. I was so tired. Was this a good idea? Did I have any choice? I wished I could borrow Martha from Sam. "Should I have my attorney present?"

The sheriff's considerable eyebrows rose. "Got one already lined up, huh?"

My attorney handled wills, probate, real estate contracts. "I could get one."

"Shouldn't be any need for that if you keep telling us the truth. All of it."

"I can only tell you the parts I know. I don't think I've ever sleepwalked. Sleptwalked? Sleepwalked? Which—"

Cooley discouraged me with a tiny shake of her head. I sat up straighter. "I honestly don't buy what Dev is saying," I said. "I have—a particular reason to think that I would not be able to leave my room."

"Because of your . . . darkness thing?"

It was getting around, faster than even I'd predicted. "Dev told you?"

"Not that one," he said. "The white fella, beard."

"Sam," Cooley said, checking her notes.

"That's why I didn't come out of the room when the screaming started," I said. "I was scared of more than the noises I was hearing."

"You should have said," the sheriff said.

"And what would you have thought?"

"I still don't know what I think about it. Sounds like an alibi I can't prove."

"Dev opened the door for me. You can ask him about—oh, no."

"Right," Barrows said, bowing his head at how quickly I was catching up. "He's said a few things now and I can't select which of them I believe, can I? Is he lying or is he telling the truth?"

"He's telling the truth about coming to my door," I said. "He turned on the light so I could come out. But the other . . . I don't know."

"You don't know if you sleepwalk?" Cooley said.

"My husband never said so," I said. A small itch of some piece of information wanting to be noticed started up in my mind. I was distracted by the idea that Dev could be telling the truth. Those moments when I slipped away from the track of time and then clicked back in—could I have done that, and deeply enough to be able to walk out into the darkness? Deeply enough to have killed someone? For a moment I let myself imagine that I had done it. No. "But then . . . to be honest, I've slept badly since he died. So I suppose it could be a new problem. But even so, even if I've picked up a secret sleepwalking habit, I had just met Malloy. I had no reason to stab him. I'm not sure I could have gotten the screwdriver out of the bottle, anyway. Even Dev couldn't . . . wait. What was Dev doing out of bed in the first place?"

Barrows waved at Cooley, who flipped through her pages. "He said he went to get a drink—"

"Wine?" I said hopefully.

"Water," she said.

"In the kitchen."

"In the bathroom."

"Downstairs."

"*Up*stairs," Cooley said, firm.

"He says he saw me sleepwalking *upstairs*? How did I not kill myself on the stairs? That railing at the top is too low for my tastes, and that turn at the bottom of the staircase would be a rude awakening."

"He says he was upstairs and saw you *down*stairs," Barrows said. "He was near that railing, he says. He came down, and then Paris came down after him, maybe some of the others as well, sounded like they were all there. He walked you to your room and shut you inside. He says."

"Maybe he saw someone else— Wait! Remember that I heard someone banging out the back door. Someone could have broken in, and that's who he saw."

Cooley's mouth took on a grim set.

Barrows said, "He says he's a hundred percent. It was you."

"A hundred percent," I repeated, but my mind had galloped away, back to the suite, waking up from strange dreams, then opening the door, seeing the dead body. But hadn't I also had that feeling that I'd been among them in the kitchen, that I'd been pulled away from a conversation there? How to explain the bruise on my arm I didn't remember getting? At least I'd noticed the bruise before Malloy was killed. "I can't explain it," I said. "But I had no reason to kill Malloy. Or anyone."

Barrows tilted his head, as though he'd heard a familiar tune. "Speaking of anyone . . . you should be aware we're getting the records sent up from Benedict Wallace's demise. *Bix*, was it?" My blood rushed in my veins and in my ears so that I could hardly hear the rest of what he said. "Just a matter of having complete information, you understand, but I wonder if you'd do us the honor of spending another night as the guest of Emmet County."

I swallowed hard. It made sense they would need to see Bix's records, didn't it? They had to be sure. I could go along with the reasoning. But didn't that mean I was seriously under consideration as the murderer here? And now I was walking around at night, alone, in the dark. So it was said. "Am I under arrest?"

"Not unless you have something else you want to tell me," Barrows said. "But I'm afraid it's not really a request. Let's keep it polite and voluntary. You'll be at the Hide-a-Way again."

"What about another hotel? Surely there are plenty of them."

"Fudgie season," Cooley said. "Tourists, I'm mean. Or did you not notice the million other people all over town?"

"Where are the others staying? Wait—they all have to stay, too, right?"

"Oh, yes," Barrows drawled. "I'm not sure we've reached the bottom of what you all have to offer the files. And some of your friends are hoping to wait out the arrival of the deceased's family."

"They're not my friends," I said.

"They'll all be at the motel, too," Cooley said. "Though we might need an extra room," she said to Barrows, rolling her eyes toward the hallway.

Paris hissing accusations into Dev's ear. The group was starting to splinter.

"Now," Barrows said. "What I really want to know about are these messages on your phone."

He reached across the table for the bag in front of Officer Cooley and slid it toward him. Cooley focused carefully on folding over to a fresh page of her notebook.

"Which messages?"

"Couple of texts sent the night of the death," he said. "Maybe you were sleepdialing instead?"

"No, I— Who? Who did I text, supposedly?"

He rattled off a couple of names: friends, or they had been. But not the friends I might have called on in the middle of the night, on purpose, for any reason. Then: Bix's mother. "Oh, no," I said, instinctively reaching to take the phone. He held it away from me. "What do they say?"

"Lots of interesting things—'need to talk,' mostly. Gibberish, a bit. You sound like a lady in trouble. Some didn't go through. The cell service out there is spotty, but you know that, it seems. Some of them messaged you right back, good friends that they are. Or tried to call."

The missed calls I'd seen and ignored, the messages stacked up. I thought of all the people I would have to explain the situation to—but then I didn't know yet how to explain any of it. Sleepdialing? Was that a thing?

"And then this number," Barrows said, "which received about four texts from you earlier that day." He read the digits, but I hardly recognized anyone's number from memory these days.

I shrugged. "I don't know it."

"Funny thing," Barrows said. "That's an Indiana area code."

"OK . . ."

"And it belongs to our dead friend," Barrows said. "The one who was not your friend. And these four texts to his phone, now, one of them I'll give you as a, what do you call it, butt dial, of one of those—what do they call those little things, Cooley?"

"Emoji," she said. "I think. Is it an emoji if it doesn't have a face?"

"Right. Dumb little picture of an apple, whatever. But the other three, they say . . ." He held the phone close to his nose. "They say, 'Meet me downstairs . . . when she's asleep. Need to talk.'"

"What? No, that's not—*my* phone?"

"Your phone." Barrows looked at me, hard. "Now what did you need to meet that no-friend-of-yours about? And what went wrong when you did?"

## Chapter Sixteen

I had no answers.

We went over the questions again, anyway.

I hadn't known Malloy before meeting him at the park. I hadn't had his number. I didn't sleepwalk—that I knew of. I didn't sleep*dial*. I didn't *sleep*.

It was hard to find time to do many activities in my sleep when I never actually drifted off.

But I had been sleeping at the guest house, I admitted. Pretty well, actually, if only for a couple of hours. I had captured a few winks besides, too, in Cooley's car on the ride back to the park, in the early hours of dawn in the Hide-a-Way.

I didn't think that meant I'd been parading around the lakeshore, calling all my long-lost friends and relatives. In the dark. Texting a man I'd just been met to sneak away after his girlfriend was asleep. I hadn't needed to talk to Malloy. I hadn't known his number. I hadn't known *him*.

I did not *use* emojis.

My eyes stung from weariness. The thought of another missed night of sleep made me want to weep. My body ached, each movement as though I were swimming through time. If I could get just one hour of sleep, I would understand what was going on. I'd be able to crack the code of what was happening. I hoped.

As it was, however, I couldn't tell them why I had Malloy's number on my phone, why it seemed like I had made plans to meet him. Barrows had tucked the phone into the bag and sent it back across the table to Cooley.

Instead of reclaiming the phone and my keys and then my car, another plan was proposed. Numb, I accepted it. I would walk to the motel myself. Officer Cooley would pick me up at a specified time to take me out to the guest house for the rest of my belongings. I was moving into the Hide-a-Way.

My toothbrush. I needed my toothbrush from the guest house. I would agree to anything, if I could only have it.

Which is how I came to be standing in the Hide-a-Way parking lot with the sun burning the top of my head a few hours later. How I suddenly came to the thing that made the most sense: Someone had been playing with my phone.

Who? Whose attention had I caught? And why?

One of the first-floor room doors behind me opened. Paris stepped out. She had changed into her extra clothes. I had, too, but I hadn't had a chance at the shower, what with Sam in my room.

When Paris saw me, she stopped. Her eyes were swollen.

"You're going out to the park?" I said finally.

"Maybe."

It hadn't occurred to me that I would have to face one of them again so soon. They'd hand-fed each other to the dogs so quickly back at the police station. Were they even really friends? I had no patience for being among them. "Maybe you haven't decided? Or you have, now that you know I'm going there?"

"The regular kind of maybe." She sniffed. "I haven't talked to Dev yet."

"I'm sure he'll go wherever you're going to be."

"I don't know," she murmured, pulling a tissue out of her shoulder bag. The big diamond on her finger flashed in the sun. "I might have messed it all up."

Now here was love with a little mileage on it, and a woman who had more sense than I had suspected. "He seems smitten," I said. "When they love you as much as Dev seems to love you, I'm sure it takes a lot to chase them away."

"Like turning in his friend for theft and then suggesting that maybe he himself might have gotten out of bed to kill someone? Yeah. I'm not sure what would cancel the wedding, if this doesn't."

Sam was "his" friend, but Malloy was "our" friend? According to Sam, the arrangement between them was "best," all equal shares.

"He seems very keen to marry you," I said. "And he's been hanging in there for a while . . ."

"Five years," she said. "Almost."

"Oh," I said, too late to avoid sounding surprised.

"Yeah, but it's not that long, is it? If we started dating when we were in college?" Her pretty face puckered in concentration. She pulled one of her braids to her lips and talked around it. "We got together after—well, I was on the rebound from . . . a real mess. So we took it slow. Everyone thinks I've been stringing him along, but we're still too young. At least, that's how I feel."

Not that young. Bix and I were married when we were baby-faced, in our midtwenties. We didn't have a long courtship or engagement. In the military, you had to be married or you got left behind. Of course, any age but my current one seemed young to me now and, anyway, nobody ever got married knowing what marriage would ask of them. "I don't think it was the age that bothered him," I said. "Or even the years of devotion he put in."

She groaned. "The watch. I know."

I didn't have *any* patience for cheating. That watch was damning. "It was just a gift?"

"It was— Oh, who am I kidding? It was whatever Malloy wanted it to be." She sat on the curb, her long brown legs visible as her skirt fell open at a slit. "He could have had me for a song. A song, a nickel, a smile. I was cheap for that man."

My feelings for Paris wavered. I liked her less and, simultaneously, more, for the honesty. Why I was the recipient of it, I didn't know. Surely one of the others was a better audience. But maybe all she needed was an audience, any audience at all. "Really? You hid it *so* well."

"I've been ridiculous. I've been—a fool, an actual fool." She shook her head, the beads in her braids clicking together musically. Her eyes drifted away. "Scheming against my own self-interests, but it didn't matter. And now I've been absent from my life for almost five years, waiting for something to happen that— Did you see that girl?"

"Hillary? She's stunning. But so are you."

"She's the whitest chick I've ever seen," Paris said. She held out her hands to show me the dark skin of her own arms. "If that's the kind of girl he's going to end up with—oh, God."

She folded her arms around herself and bent over them. "He's not going to *end up*—he's dead. He's dead and I keep forgetting. That's not right, to forget."

It was exactly right, in my experience. To think, *Wait until I tell Bix what I heard.* To reach for the phone to text him. I had tried on occasion to call my mother in the years after she died. Like when I met Bix and wanted to tell her about him. With Bix, it happened all the time, still. Sometimes I thought, I want to tell Bix how pissed off I am at him. And lifted the phone.

"No, that's how it goes," I said. "Grief isn't always sad. Sometimes it's weird and wrong—or funny, when you shouldn't be laughing."

"I don't think I'm going to be laughing anytime soon," she said. "This is—it's too much to take in. Malloy is dead. I can't wrap my mind around it. And I can't begin to think—"

"That one of your friends did it."

She squinted up at me. "When Tash died, it was hard to understand, but this—this can't be real."

I hadn't yet heard the story of Tash, but I felt the skin on my arms prickle. This group had already lost one of its own. Tash would have been Malloy's first love, the one lost too soon, the one we had to keep mourning. "How did Tash die?" I said, aiming for casual curiosity, like I hadn't just learned her name.

"Drugs," Paris murmured. "An overdose, they said. Some of them wanted to believe she had overdosed on purpose, but . . . Tash had everything, you know? She was top of our class at school. She would have been valedictorian, with Dev. She was funny and gorgeous and happy. She was dating Malloy and then—well, that didn't work out. I always wondered . . ." She stared off at the gas station long enough I thought there might be someone there.

"What? You always wondered what?"

"Huh?" She blinked heavily at me.

"You always wondered if losing a boyfriend was all it took?"

She shrugged.

"You were all friends at the time?"

She came back to me. "Yeah, Dev and Malloy, Sam, me. Then Martha. Casual friends at first, but then Tash—it changed things. We got tight. Got through it together. I guess that's why it's so hard to be drifting apart now."

"A weeklong vacation together doesn't sound like drifting."

"We haven't all been together since graduation," she said. "And now I guess we'll never be all together again." She put her head in her hands, her face tucked away from me. I found a pack of tissues in my bag and offered them to her, but when she looked up, her eyes were dry. She waved me off, turning a furrowed brow toward the parking lot.

"How did you do it?" she said.

"Do . . . what?" I readied myself for more accusations.

"Live with the impossible. When your husband died."

"Oh." I sat on the curb. "I'm still trying to figure that out."

"But you've made it this far," she said. It *was* an accusation—what was my magic? What secret had I kept to myself? "What if I can't live with the days that come after this? What if I can't live with—what comes next."

What came next was a life without someone she had pinned her hopes on, getting on with that career she'd prioritized, settling in for a wedding—ah. I saw what she meant. One of her friends would be accused, proven guilty, jailed for killing the man she would have thrown her life over for. One of her friends, maybe even the man she was supposed to marry.

"You're worried it was Dev?"

"No!" she said, sharply. "Of course he wouldn't—but what if . . . one of them?"

One of them, but which one? And when it was certain which one, a new devastation, a new friend-shaped hole in the group. Why tease around it? The group was gone. It was one thing to rally around the loss of a college friend dead to an overdose, on purpose or by accident, but this would break them into pieces. Individual pieces. I looked over at the bride. She'd lost them both, the imagined and the real. There would be no wedding. And she knew it.

"I don't have the answer for you," I said. "What's sad is— maybe Malloy might have. He was the one who lost the love of his life and made it through."

She pouted over my phrasing. "Who called her that?"

"He did, actually."

She stood up. "Malloy made it through everything."

"They call it resilience," I said. "It's harder than it looks."

"They call it imperviousness," she said. "Nothing touched him. Maybe even when it should have."

"What you should try to remember was that he was happy," I said. When Hillary's secret came out, I wondered if his friends would allow his happiness to remain a fact. Would they rewrite history to make him a dupe, happy only in his ignorance? "No matter what else comes to light—your friend found happiness again."

"My friend," she said. "I always call him 'our friend,' you know? I guess that was part of the delusion. But he was. He was my friend. But, Eden, come on, don't tell me you didn't notice that body."

"I'm not the dead one." I didn't mention that I had also noticed Dev's.

"OK, then." Paris gazed out over the empty parking lot. "Do you think they forgot that car for us? We need to get out there, get sorted, and get back before it's dark—oops."

I couldn't help it. I laughed. My dirty laundry had passed from hand to hand so quickly. Given everything else going on, who had the time to gossip 'round the watercooler? "Who told you?"

"That block of cheddar cheese they have as deputy," she said, shading her eyes and looking up and down the street. "The woman. It wasn't gossip. I heard her talking to the sheriff."

So news of my lunacy had traveled from Dev to Sam to the sheriff to Cooley to Paris. The circle was almost complete. Shouldn't be too long before my secret got around to Hillary and Martha and then one of them came to inform me, too.

The strange thing was that I didn't mind anymore. I didn't have to hide it or make excuses. Except, when you added it to the sleepwalking theory and now the phone calls and texts, I looked good for actual psychosis. The laugh died in my throat. Those texts were a real problem for me.

But then it occurred to me: Dev. Dev had used my phone to call the police. He'd had the chance to message other numbers, if he'd wanted to. It would explain the random nature of the texts sent out. He wouldn't have known which of my friends I would text in the middle of the night, scared or alone, which ones I would never bother. He'd probably texted the last six or seven people I had texts from, clicking through the queue, one after another. And he was the one who'd witnessed the alleged sleepwalking.

I watched Paris's profile for a moment. "Is there any reason you can think of that Dev would—lie? About seeing me out of my room that night?"

She stood up and slung her bag over her shoulder. "Dev is a good man. You and I are all deep in the shit right now and being girlfriendly, but let's not think you can slur my fiancé. Also, *I* saw you out of your room, too."

She was going to go down fighting, then. And here I was talking to one of the other best suspects. Paris had admitted her feelings for Malloy. What if she had put her desires out on the table and had them rebuffed? Was embarrassment enough of a motive? What if what she couldn't live with was the presence of Hillary in Malloy's life? Of Malloy's life going on without her? Of Malloy's life going on at all.

Officer Cooley pulled up in her cruiser with a *whoop-whoop* of the siren. She had to get out and open the back doors for us, prisoner-style, but let us close ourselves in. In the backseat, Paris sniffed and made a face. "It smells like . . . a circus in here."

"Just the dog act, I think," I said.

"What the—"

I hushed her before Cooley slid into the driver's seat.

"Who's excited to go get all her clothes back?" Cooley said, as she turned the car toward the park.

"We cannot *wait* to go back," Paris said. "There is nothing I like better in a vacation spot than the dried blood of my friends on the wallpaper." She paused, swallowing hard, and then seemed to recover. She dug around in her bag for a few

minutes and then stopped and huffed. "When are we getting our phones back?"

"Can you even get any service up here?" I said. "Mine couldn't pick up a signal—hey. How do I have all those outgoing texts from my phone if I can't seem to get any signal?"

"Which texts?" Paris said.

"Maybe when you were—out walking," Cooley said. "The reception in the trees is bad, but it's good out by the lake. On the shore is the only place my phone works anywhere near that park."

"But I—" We were going to pursue this, even with everyone knowing I couldn't possibly go out in the dark? I put my head in my hands. So tired. All I wanted was to crawl into the loving embrace of the suite's bedcovers. After locking the door and shoving something heavy in front of it, of course.

"So," Paris said, "what happened with the watch?"

I looked up. It was a strangely selfish question but I was curious, too.

"The watch?" Cooley said. "Or the friend caught wearing it?"

"Both," Paris said, giving me a glance. "Of course that's what I meant. What happened with that situation?"

"The watch is being tested for evidence and will be returned to the victim's estate."

Paris chewed at her bottom lip.

"And Sam?" I prompted.

"He's chosen to stay in town for a bit longer," Cooley said. "And the other one, too. The blondey."

"When is Dev coming out to pick up his things?" Paris asked, leaning forward. She looked hopeful.

"Eventually," the officer said.

"And Martha?" I said.

"Right," Paris said. "Where's Martha?"

"I already took her over and left her with the officer on duty there," Cooley said. "Cooley's Taxi Service."

Paris looked out the window. "She didn't want to be in the car with us."

"Didn't say that," Cooley said.

But no other reason was offered.

"You can have the same deal, a half hour to pack up your things," Cooley said. "I got to run back one more time for the rest of them. We only ask while you're in the house that no one messes with the room where, uh . . ."

"Malloy," I said.

"Yes. His room. And the kitchen. It would be helpful if you stayed out of there until we've had a little more time to process the scene. Basically, try to touch as little as possible. Get in, get out."

Paris was smiling. When she caught me looking at her, she turned away. I went back over the conversation until I saw the conclusion she had reached. Cooley was running another trip between the motel and the guest house. Dev would arrive in the next run, and in close quarters once again, she'd have the chance to turn him around.

We passed the entrance to the park and maneuvered along the drive, the canopy of trees hiding the sky.

"Oh!" Paris cried, sitting back from the window. Cooley braked, hard. And then Paris laughed nervously. "Sorry. Those damn . . . people."

We all looked out the window at the silhouette of the little girl standing at an info display, too near the road.

"How do you stand them?" Paris said. "I feel like they're watching me."

They did seem out of place among the roadside brush like that. I didn't like thinking of them out here, somehow, having the run of the place in the dark.

"I guess you get used to them," Cooley said. "But not everyone. One time a visitor out for a walk ran into one of the figures in the night and went *crazy* on it. Hurt himself and had to pay to replace the figure. And they are not cheap, I'll tell you."

Something about this story was less than reassuring. I slumped down in my seat, weary. Paris and I sat in silence for the rest of the ride while Officer Cooley drove us through the woods and hummed a little tune to herself.

# Chapter Seventeen

In the warm police car, I dozed off in the two minutes it took to arrive at the guest house. I woke to Cooley opening my door. "All right," she said. "I'll be back in thirty for you."

As Paris and I entered the front room, Martha emerged from the bathroom at the top of the stairs. "Oh," she said, coming cautiously down. "No offense, but I wish you were one of the guys. This place is creepy on your own."

"Where's the cop supposedly watching the place?" I asked.

"Smoke break," Martha said, flashing the dimples. "I swore I wouldn't be bad."

"Dev will be here later," Paris offered.

"Good," Martha said. At the bottom step, she seemed to lose her sense of purpose. She stood for moment, one hand on the rail, uncertain, and then went to Paris and pulled her into her arms. "How are you doing?"

"I don't even know," Paris said. "Up is down."

"I know. Me, too. I wish—"

"I'm sorry about the thing with Sam," Paris said. "I wish I hadn't said it."

"You can tell him when you see him," Martha said. "It will all be OK. Well—not everything. But we'll find a way to salvage it. It's us."

Paris nodded, wiping away the tears from her chin. "I want things to be—I don't know. Is normal too much to ask for?"

"I want them to be better than normal," Martha said. "We have to keep in better contact, keep up better, see each other more."

Better than normal. That was going to be a tough thing to achieve. The women stood back from one another, glancing my way and now both of them seemingly uncertain what to do.

"I've got to shower," Paris said. "Before I see—anyone else. I think the water at the motel was brown. It *felt* brown."

Paris ascended the stairs and disappeared. I took a step toward my room and my own en suite shower but then stopped and looked past Martha to the kitchen floor. It seemed impossible, but I'd almost forgotten I'd have to cross a crime scene to get to my things. The kitchen had been roped off on one side where the stain of blood and wine still lay. A white sheet carpeted the allowable path around the kitchen island and out the back door. For a long moment, I couldn't move.

"They took the screwdriver, at least," Martha said. "I mean. They also took—they took his . . . he . . . him."

Her face crumpled. The tears started quietly. She turned from me, looking for escape, and then bent double, emitting a strange keen. She straightened enough to move, stumbling along the sheeted path through the kitchen. Just as she reached the door of my suite, she collapsed on the floor, ruined and howling with abandon. I hurried to her side, but she slapped me away. I pulled her to her feet anyway and kicked open the door to my room.

With real reluctance, I guided her to the bed. I had wanted the comfort of those sheets and that puffy comforter, of this quiet oasis, all to myself. She turned her back to me and wailed into the pillows.

"Would you like some water?" I said.

No response came but more crying, but the question seemed to bring her back from the brink. I sat on the edge of the bed and waited it out. Around the room, I noticed little things out of place. My suitcase, tossed. My flashlight, left behind in the ambulance, had been returned to a table near the door.

After a few minutes, the choking sobs turned to sniffles and then quiet. Martha pulled her face out of the pillow. A curl of her hair was matted against her cheek.

"Why are you being so nice to me?" she said. "I've been nothing but terrible to you since I got here."

"I was once the recipient of a lot of kindness," I said. Many people had sat at the edge of my bed in the days and weeks after Bix's death. Not all of them. Some had strangely evaporated, not knowing what to say, I suppose. Not showing up for the funeral, not making a call. But many had hung in there with me. Through the first few months, anyway. Call it karma. Call it paying back into the great wheel. I could offer a small piece of comfort. "And you haven't been terrible. You just wanted to be with your friends and here I was, in the way."

I truly didn't think she had been horrible to me. It was Hillary she and Paris had excluded. Hillary, who should have been made to feel welcome. But that was a different issue.

"I was talking to Paris about how you all became friends," I said.

Her look drifted into middle distance. "Did she tell you the short story or the long one?" She swiped the hair back from her face. "College. That's the short version. We started hanging out, pairing up into couples the way you do at that point in your life." The faltering smile she managed had a bit of a wink in it. Sam must have come by his crush on Martha the hard way, through youthful dorm-room exploration. I had seen the way he looked at her. Sharing a room here at the guest house had to be hard on the guy. "The long version— well, it's weird, but I don't remember how we ended up the five of us. It's just always been that way."

"Six before your friend died."

Martha looked caught out. "Paris told you about her?"

"Malloy did first, a bit. He didn't tell me much, actually. Paris said you were remembering her as part of your weekend."

"Tash. Natasha, but everyone called her— She was great," Martha said, her lips starting to tremble. Her bright red lipstick had smeared in all the crying. She looked as though she'd been slapped. "She was depressed, I guess, and you wouldn't have known she was struggling. She was my roommate and we had such a good time. We didn't talk about things like— real things, you know? You don't talk about it when you're young. Or not so young, either," she said. "I don't think we have figured out yet how to be without her."

I thought about what Malloy had said. *Some of us are not finished mourning.*

"She was Malloy's girlfriend."

Martha looked up, surprised. "They weren't at the time,"

she said. "It was . . . fluid. Although, yeah, they were together for a while, and then he and Paris—"

"Paris was after Tash?"

"Yeah, but I guess I thought Malloy and Tash might . . . I mean, never in a million years did I think—" She stopped.

"That Dev and Paris would last?"

She rolled her lips inward to show me she wasn't talking, the dimples popping into view.

"So then, five of you, together again," I said. Five was an awkward number. Who was the fifth, the odd man out?

"Four, now." She took a shuddering breath. "We were just casual friends at first—and then when Tash died . . . We pulled together, you know? I can only hope we pull together this time." Tears welled up in her eyes again. She wiped them away. "No more of that. Malloy would not have wanted us crying. He would have said it was wasted time—but you know, sometimes it's OK to get it out. Don't you think?"

Even though she had already lost Tash—a close friend by her own reckoning—she didn't seem to know yet that grief was a bottomless well. No amount of getting it out ever depleted the supply. Only with time could you get any relief—and then of course the sadness could come rushing back anyway. What caught you was the element of surprise, when a lone sock found behind the dryer reminded you of everything you had ever lost. The end of the box of cereal he had opened but never finished. A magazine he'd subscribed to, finally running out.

"Sure," I said, just to finish the conversation. I had to take a deep breath to shove that lone sock from my mind. "You said your friend was depressed. You believe she did it on purpose?"

"I don't want to talk about it," she said. "It was—it was a bad time."

"But you came here in part to talk about her?"

"With people who were there," she snapped. "The people who went through it."

"I get that," I said.

We sat in silence for a while.

"I'm sorry," she said. "It's another bad time right now, obviously. I feel guilty about what happened to Tash. I should have been there with her, and I wasn't."

"You can't blame yourself for that."

"Not just myself," she said. "But I left her alone. She needed me, and I didn't know."

You could know and still not save anyone.

"Can I ask you a question?" she said.

Ah, here it was. My fear of the dark had come all the way through the original group. Only Hillary, the outsider, was left to discover my secret.

"Why did your husband want to spend your anniversary here?" she said. "I mean, it's nice and everything, but . . . there must be a thousand places like this between here and Chicago."

I was so surprised the question of my phobia hadn't materialized that for a moment I didn't answer. And then I realized I couldn't. I didn't know. "Honestly? He never told me. He made the reservation as a surprise and then—it was a surprise, for sure. After he died, I found a note about the reservation in his papers."

She stared at me expectantly. "That's it? He never told you? He wasn't a stargazer? He didn't want a telescope for his birthday or something?"

"He had taken up an interest, but not in a serious way." In the last few months of his life, he'd grown a little more pensive. He still rushed around, still got distracted by any problem anyone brought him, but he also spent more time at work—or "at work," I now knew—and, when he was at home, more time on the back porch, looking up at the sky. In Chicago, though, you'd be lucky to see a single star, and if you researched it, that one bright spot was more likely a planet. Planets were the brightest objects, the only celestial bodies bright enough to fight through the city's light pollution. That must have been where the idea had come from to visit the park. He was missing out. He hated to miss out. "I guess he thought it was something we could enjoy together." He would have liked hanging with these people, a handful of years younger than he was, drinking their wine. He would have stayed up all night with them.

"If you don't mind me asking . . . you said he died in a car accident. Was it storming or something?"

She hadn't wanted to talk about her friend, but apparently my life was available to be picked clean. But—sometimes a story wanted to be told. "The roads were clear," I said. "He was late coming home, and there was a lot of talk on the news about an accident closing down the highway—"

"Oh, no," she said.

"—and then it was his accident, his death closing down the highway, closing down half the city."

"Do they know what caused it? The accident?"

"A drunk driver," I said, shutting out the details. "Four people. And Bix."

Martha raised her hand to her mouth, an O of horror. "I'm so sorry. How did you hear it was him?"

"They came to the door. The police." And when they had asked me a few questions and left one of the officers with me, a nice woman with a ponytail under her blue cap, I went around the house, room by room, and turned on every light in the place, the only thing I could think to do, the only thing that had ever worked for the bad nights, the worst nights. *Ma'am? Ma'am?* the officer had called after me, her voice rising into nervousness. *Ma'am? Can I call someone to come over for you?*

They had not taken me to the hospital. It was understood, then, that hope had passed. I could not cry. I could not think. I stalked from room to room, lighting the way, with the officer following.

"You're here for your anniversary," Martha said. "Today? Tomorrow?"

"Tuesday," I said. "It would have been ten years. Ten great, terrible, wonderful, messed-up years."

Martha was giving me a strange look, so I tried again. "You think it's going to be a romantic story because we were married and marriage is the goal girls are sold along with our Barbie dolls," I said. "But marriage isn't endless romance. It's not like we crossed the wedding-day finish line and everything since has been him carrying me across the threshold and laying me down on a bed of rose petals."

I didn't want to go into the cheating thing again. Hillary knew, so eventually the rest of them would, surely. I couldn't imagine a secret lasting among these people.

"Wait," Martha said. "Were you happy?"

"I loved him." I had just noticed the blanket over the window had been pulled down. The police, having a look around. Outside the sun was still high, the rays of light and the ripples of a breeze across the water turning the surface to diamonds. "I was devastated when he died," I said. And then devastated again, of course. The woman at the funeral. Some of the devastation was private, but much of it turned out to be public. So many people must have known before, and after the accident, everyone did. If Paris wanted to see what a fool looked like, here she was.

"Of course," Martha said. "A few days ago, I wouldn't have been able to imagine that kind of loss. But now . . . I should have been nicer to Hillary. What a position to be put in. I mean, if we don't think she killed Malloy, that is. God. 'If she killed Malloy' is a thing that I just said. I can't believe this. Do you think she did it?"

I thought it was less likely she did than any other single person in the house, but I didn't want to say so. I was sitting alone in a room, comforting a suspect. But then maybe that's what Martha thought of me.

"I'm embarrassed by how we treated her before—*before*," Martha said. "I'm actually a functioning adult, you know. I just haven't been showing it here this weekend."

"You're a lawyer. That sounds pretty adult to me."

"Just a clerk at the moment. I handle a lot of paperwork. Divorces and wills and powers of attorney. All the sexy stuff. But if you say you're a lawyer and then wave your hands around while your friend is being railroaded into a confession in a small-town jail, at least you can advise him to shut the hell up and stick around to make sure he does."

"He's staying in town as long as he can," I said, watching for disappointment. But Sam's crush seemed to be one-sided this many years later.

"He's probably embarrassed, too, about the watch," Martha said. "He just wanted something to have of Malloy's . . ." She looked uncomfortable to suggest it. She would have to work on her courtroom skills. "I don't know," she said finally. "Up is down, for sure."

If only this place weren't a crime scene. I could have taken a nap. "Can I ask you a question?" I said. "Did you happen to see anyone using my phone?"

"You still have your phone?"

"No, I mean the other night," I said.

"I didn't see anyone using a phone that I could tell was yours," she said, with a weird look, but then this was a strange line of questioning. Or maybe this was a lawyer's way of evading a question.

"Just trying to figure something out," I said. "Do you know who came up with the idea for this trip?"

"Well, Dev made the reservations," she said. "Malloy—"

Somewhere in the house, a door opened. The front door, screen door first, slowly, then the storm door. Each opened and closed gently. Someone was making an effort to be quiet. We looked at one another. Martha nodded and rolled off the bed. She noticed the flashlight on the nearby table and picked it up. I stood by, too close to the open door for my liking, while Martha slipped behind it. We listened as small noises of movement made their way across the front room, toward the kitchen. Footsteps paused there and then continued. Martha raised the flashlight over her head.

The door between the kitchen and the back hall was standing open. A dark figure stood there, like one of those silhouette cut-outs in the park, backlit. My breath caught and then

Dev stepped into my room. Martha's arm started its trajectory. "No!" I yelled and reached out to halt her progress. The flashlight hit me on the knuckles, hard.

"Oh, no, are you OK?" Martha reached for my hand, but I was cradling it to me, waiting out the rush of pain. I sucked at my teeth, trying not to say terrible things aloud, though twisted and hissing noises escaped instead.

"What just happened?" Dev said. He made no movement to assist. Some doctor.

"Eden took the brunt of a flashlight in your place, you maniac," Martha said. "Why are you skulking around?"

"Didn't realize walking around in broad daylight was skulking."

"These days? Through a crime scene? Yeah, that becomes skulking pretty fast."

"Or maybe your racism is showing? Fear of the brown man."

"Come on," she said, tearing up again. "Malloy's blood is out there on the floor. I just—"

He held out his arm, and she rushed at him, crying. He patted her back and made a few comforting noises.

I should have been amazed at how easily these friends could forgive each other anything. One of them was a killer. But it all reminded me of our friends, Bix's and mine, and how quickly they wanted to get to the part of grief where they could remember him fondly and chuckle over his foibles. To tell the stories.

My hand wouldn't close, and the area around the knuckles was puffing up. "Something might be broken," I said.

"Is Paris around?" Dev said.

"She's in the shower," Martha said.

"I could use an ice pack," I said.

"She's *showering*, in a *crime* scene?"

Dev released Martha, turned, and marched out of the room. Martha watched after him, but when he didn't stop in the kitchen for ice, she trailed out into the hall and called after him. "I didn't think of it that way. What's going on?"

"I'm packing," he said.

Martha disappeared through the doorway. "Hey," I said. "A little help here?" I followed her through the kitchen and to the foot of the staircase.

"What's the hurry?" Martha said to Dev's retreating back.

"I'm not spending another minute here," he said. "Not as long as she's here." He was up the stairs and past the closed bathroom door. Martha stood on the landing, left behind.

"Who? Hey," she called and then started after him. "Don't go. If you leave, that strands three women here, alone."

I hadn't thought of that. I had only been thinking about the accusation of sleepwalking, the texts on a phone that Dev might have put there. I couldn't decide—did I feel safer with Dev in the house, or knowing he was leaving? Martha took to the stairs after him. I hesitated and then followed, up the stairs, past the door with the shower running behind it, and down the hall to the bedrooms, which I had never seen.

Dev entered the first room on the left and closed the door. Martha pressed herself up against it. Something about the shape of her body against the door embarrassed me. I glanced toward the bathroom door.

"Dev? You won't stay here another minute if who is here? Do you mean Paris?" Martha said into the door. "Or do you mean Eden?"

When she noticed me there, she opened the door, stepped inside, and closed it firmly behind her.

I was left outside, wondering. What had just happened?

# Chapter Eighteen

My mouth was open. Me? Dev wouldn't stay in the house because I was here? It was a form of mental whiplash, comforting Martha only to have her feed me back out as fresh bait.

Enough. I had only a few more hours of daylight in this town, and I would spend them barricaded behind one door or another. It didn't matter which one. And if someone got locked out of a motel room and found my door, it was staying shut—*locked*. I didn't give a damn who came knocking. They were all trouble.

Cooley would be picking us up soon enough. My hand throbbed. I would need that time to pack, one-handed.

As I started to turn for the stairs, I noticed the yellow scene tape across the door at the far end of the hall. And then the open, not taped door next to it. I went to this door and peered in. Most of the room was tidy, except for the bed. Someone had kicked the covers out at the foot of the bed on one side, while the other side stayed tucked and neat. A wineglass with a sizable serving left in its bowl sat on the dresser, a few bits of jewelry resting against its foot. Rim, bowl, stem, foot—I'd heard Sam filling in the vocabulary the night they were pouring Malloy's last drink. Wineglass vocabulary, as if anyone cared but Sam. And Sam did seem to care so much.

A powder blue overnight bag peeked out from underneath the bed.

Through the wall, I heard Martha's flirty laugh. Maybe she could bring Dev around. Or if she held him there long enough, then Paris would.

If she held him there long enough, I had time to look around.

I moved as quickly as I could, rushing to the bed and pulling out the bag. Inside, a carefree packing job: panties jammed into one pocket, a cotton dress rolled up in a ball, some silly bunny slippers. Underneath, a bottle of vitamins rolled, rattling loudly. I raised my head and listened for Martha or Dev. Nothing. The bag had a side panel zipper. Inside that pouch was a manila envelope, the seal broken, and inside the envelope, a sheaf of paper in legalese. Martha didn't seem to me like the kind of girl to bring work along on her big reunion weekend, but then deadlines had a way of following you home. It hadn't been so long since I'd had a job. I zipped the bag up and shoved it back in place.

I stood and hurried to the dresser, using the hem of my T-shirt to open the top drawer quietly with my uninjured hand. Inside, men's T-shirts and boxers neatly folded. In the second drawer, some collared sports shirts, precision-folded as if for a display in a store, shorts and khakis folded as though with a ruler. The cops had been more careful with these clothes than they had with mine. The other drawers were empty. Martha hadn't bothered to store anything. Like me, she was living out of her bag. The difference was she was staying the week and I had decided not to stay at all.

Next door, something banged against the wall. I closed the drawer and raced to the door. The hallway was still empty. Martha's laugh trilled again. I listened to the musical notes of it and was suddenly overcome with the crushing loneliness of a woman who had not laughed with friends in some time. Bix had made me laugh. Despite his many faults, he was at his best in a crowd, telling a story that was only slightly exaggerated. A performance. Something he could put on, like a suit. I might be dragging from a long, bad night with him, but he would never show it. After one of the worst nights, I'd watched from the sidelines at a backyard barbecue, smarting, while he picked apart his time in Afghanistan for laughs. He lit up a room. He was flame.

At times like these I wondered how much of what he'd done I had already forgiven. Too much.

At the third door, Malloy's room, I covered my hand again and reached through the criss-crossed police tape.

We had promised not to mess about in the room, but what harm could it do to take a peek? They'd already worked over the room for fingerprints and that kind of thing, right? Martha could work out the legalities of it. I ducked under the tape, contorting into smallness that, once inside the room, I felt compelled to keep. The room felt stilled, interrupted in midbreath.

I had been in a dead man's room before, of course—my own. It had been hard to return to our bed afterward, after a few nights in the guest room at my sister's, at Bix's mother's house, in our guest room. When I went back to our room alone, it was with all the resolve and accommodations I could gather. All the lights on, of course.

I paused to think of the house, the sunshine through the

blinds moving across the kitchen in an afternoon. The light switch plate I'd bought at that cute store on our honeymoon. I'd waited six years to own the home that deserved it, six years of Permanent Change of Station orders that were permanent only until the next move, six years of temp housing and dislocation allowances and all the federal acronyms that came with them, six years waiting for Bix to find the end of his Army career so I could maybe start one. That house. I'd planned to grow old in that house. I'd thought Bix and I would spend our lives together there.

Once, we'd planned to have a family. It hadn't worked out, but then our plan B was so strong—each other, forever. We'd already survived two wars together, hadn't we? We didn't need anyone else.

Or so I had thought.

Damn it, Bix. Damn it. He had ruined everything, at least twice.

I had not forgiven him that.

But if I thought about all the things I hadn't forgiven, I would be here all day. Instead, I turned to the scene at hand.

Malloy and Hillary's room was the largest of all, more spacious than even the suite. Interesting that they had arrived last and yet still commanded the largest room. What's more, Malloy hadn't even made the arrangements. Dev had, Martha said. His ownership came not from a dibs system but naturally. I couldn't imagine wielding that kind of easy power. What might he have talked these people into? Hadn't he suggested that he'd already done so? All this from admiration?

For the first time since the screaming began, a wave of real terror washed over me. I had been thinking of Malloy as maligned, as a victim of a cruel misunderstanding, something distant. Distant, even though I had touched the cooling skin of his corpse.

But I had no idea why one of these impossible friends of his had taken his life. They would have had reasons. They wouldn't be good reasons. Murder couldn't be explained away—could it? I remembered the screwdriver carefully pulled from the neck of the bottle, the wine spilled, and the glint of the tool stuck to the hilt into his throat. The blood on his fingertips—he must have tried to pry the screwdriver from his own neck. A whisper, a moan. The smear on the wall from his hands as he slid to the floor. Gently, though, or I would have heard the crash, surely. I shivered.

To the culprit, the reason for Malloy's death would make sense. It would have seemed . . . deserved.

The room was awash in sunshine from a series of windows along the two outside walls. When I checked, Malloy's things were stacked all together in the bottom drawer of the dresser, leaving the others for Hillary. In one of hers, I found the slinky new sleepwear tucked into a corner. Everything was a little loose from having been searched.

I don't know what I'd been expecting to find. The police had already combed over my belongings, theirs.

Movement caught my eye, and I looked up to find a patch of light dancing on the wall. I went to the window and stood in the path of the light, which turned out to be a reflection of sunlight off the shimmering lake. I stood there, the glare in my eyes, wishing things had gone differently and I could walk the beach. I hadn't dipped a toe in the water or taken a single photo—

*Click.*

An actual click.

I pressed my face to the window to search for the source of the noise below. I could see almost straight down to the back door, but not quite. Nothing. Traveling the length of the room, I searched each window, but the lawn was empty, the shore desolate.

Down the shoreline on the public beach, a lone woman, thick in a bright blue jacket, walked with her head canted toward the water. Something in the way she had tilted her chin toward the waves made me wonder what she was mourning. It was a shame to spend misery upon such a gorgeous landscape—we had that in common. She reminded me of someone, maybe only myself. I left her to the beach and kept moving along the windows, past the corner of the room to the last of them, where I could see all our parked cars awaiting their drivers. One of the sheriff's cars was also down below, with an officer's uniform leaning in at the window. When the guy shifted, Officer Cooley was behind the wheel. She wore sunglasses but by the set of her mouth, I could still tell she was pissed. Dev. She must have dropped off Dev to get his things, and was waiting for some of us to come out for a ride back to town. One car, six people to shift. I hadn't packed a thing.

The noise, though—what was that? I went back along the windows but couldn't find anything out of place—and then I saw him. Sam emerged from the back of the house, laden with something heavy. He disappeared from my view for a moment, keeping close to the back of the house and out of eyeshot from where Cooley was parked. Where Cooley and the supposed guard of the crime scene were complaining about us.

When at last Sam reappeared, he was hauling the carrier bags of wine away from the house, two in each hand.

Is this what he considered packing?

He checked over his shoulder, then headed toward the lake at a shallow angle to the shore. At the water's edge, he veered south, away from the beach and toward the headland, that curling peninsula namesake of the park.

What was the plan here? That stretch of land thinned to a point that ended in Lake Michigan tides.

I crossed the room, climbed quickly back out of the tape, and pulled the door closed. Fingerprints. I used the edge of my shirt to wipe the door handle and, satisfied, turned around, straight into Paris.

"Were you inside Malloy's room?" she asked.

She wore a thick pink scalloped towel tucked around her, her slim brown shoulders still wet. Her braids were pulled back into a spiky twist at the top of her head, the dark crown of an angered queen.

She'd seen me leave the room, so I saw no point in answering. I tried walking around her toward the stairs, but she blocked me out, a feint to one side and then the other until she had backed me up to the railing that overlooked the living room. I felt the dig of the wood into my hip as Paris forced me into the bannister, her face close to mine.

"What were you doing in there?"

"Nothing," I said. "Just having a look around. I have to—"

"What? Are you Nancy Fucking Drew now?"

I hadn't thought of it that way. In my head, I'd only been Nosey Fucking Parker.

"Are you involved in all this?" she demanded, her eyes terrible. "Did you kill him?"

The railing groaned with my weight. I pushed away from it and slipped past her. "No, I just—"

The door behind Paris opened. She turned and found Dev standing there, looking between us.

"You're here," Paris said, her voice gone soft and grateful. Her face relaxed into sweetness.

Martha's curly head peeked out from behind Dev's shoulder. Paris stiffened. "What's going on? Why is *she* in our room?" she said. The distance in her voice from speaking to Dev to scolding Martha was a vast, cold wasteland she'd crossed in a split second.

I left them to it, taking the stairs two at a time and reaching the front door just as Cooley opened it from the other side.

"Now what?" she said.

"Old friends working out some differences," I said. "I have to—"

"Is anyone else dead?"

"Not that I know of, but I—I haven't looked in the suite yet."

The joke fell flat, deservedly. Cooley leveled me with a heavy gaze. "You haven't packed? What have you been up to? Cheese and crackers, hurry up. I have a job, you know—"

"Get *out*!"

We both looked up. Paris, still in her towel, her eyes wide with rage. Dev stood between them, his jaw set. Martha's neck was pink and blotchy but her chin was thrust out, daring.

"—you're a vulture! Every man—"

"—you never—"

Their words tumbled over one another in chaos, the two women flinging insults and their hands at each other across Dev.

"Hey," Cooley barked. "Did you take a *shower*—"

"You just can't be satisfied with anyone but the ones who don't belong to you!" Paris screeched. "If you couldn't have Malloy, then it had to be Dev."

"Tell me where you're better," Martha said. "You treated Dev the same way. He'd still belong to you if you actually wanted him!"

Dev held the women apart with the span of his arms, stoic.

"He still— You don't know anything about our relationship," Paris said. "Stop pretending that you know *anything* about relationships at all."

"I know plenty," Martha said with a wink in her voice.

"Sleeping with other women's men doesn't count," Paris scolded. "Of course, if one of them knocks you up, then I guess that's a *kind* of future."

Martha glanced at Dev. "What are you talking about?" she said, but her confidence was gone.

"You haven't had more than a sip of wine since we got here," Paris said. "The guys might not notice, but, sweetheart, I'm not dumb."

"You are," Martha said. The taunting voice was back. "It's all happening under your nose, but you're too distracted by that second-mortgage diamond ring to notice."

Dev's eyes blinked to life and found mine. "Let's get packed," he said. "Let's go."

"Nice try," Paris said. "Not that you would understand what a mortgage is, either. You never owned a thing in your life except that three-buck dye job."

"Come on, now," Cooley tried.

Martha crossed her arms over her heaving chest. "Pare

baby, if it's pawned beyond your ability to ever pay for it, you don't own it, it owns you. That's a mortgage, and you're in it up to your padded bra."

"Don't worry about us," Paris said, flipping her head. The beads in her braids, still twisted at the top of her head, flicked against one another. "We're fine."

"Fine until the estate recalls that loan Dev took," Martha said.

No one moved. Estate. All eyes turned to Dev.

"What is she blathering about?" Paris said.

"The loan he got from Malloy," Martha said. "To keep you in the lifestyle you demanded, I'd guess. To buy your status-symbol diamond. Your engagement ring was paid for by Malloy. Just like you always wanted. Well, maybe not *exactly* like you wanted."

Paris stared at Dev, who watched the floor.

"It's in his will," Martha said breezily. "The loan's not forgiven just because he died. His heirs will want that diamond and anything else you bought with his money. And since he's dead, I wouldn't be surprised if it was all due immediately."

I remembered the paperwork in the pocket of Martha's overnight bag. Legalese, pages and pages of it. Martha handled divorces, she'd said, and wills. Martha, running after Sam claiming to be his lawyer. I looked between them. Was she Malloy's attorney, too? What was a twentysomething man in the fit of health doing with a will? Even Bix, years older than these people and a big believer in both military action and life insurance, had died without one. And Malloy hadn't just died, despite Martha's tone. He was murdered, and now money, secret money that would not be forgiven, was in play. Motive. I shot a glance at Cooley, who stood looking up at the trio above with her mouth hanging open.

"How could you take money from him to—to buy my ring?" Paris said. She held her left hand out as though to admire the sparkler there, but then couldn't seem to look at it. Her hand fell. "Of all the things—"

"Well, we didn't have the money," Dev said. His voice seemed strangely hoarse from being silent so long. "Not while I was in med school and residency. And you had to have the best."

"We could have made do another way," Paris said. "Pulled money from some other fund—"

"You don't get it," Dev said. "There is no other fund."

"'Made do' was never your thing," Martha offered. "Except in boyfriends—"

"Shut up," Paris screamed. To Dev, she said more calmly, "But what about—"

"It's spent," he said. "All of it. The second it's earned, it's gone, on some scheme of yours or some ridiculous thing—it's spent."

"The wedding fund, then," she said.

He met her eyes at last. "Who do you think started one of those? My parents? *Yours* haven't," he said. "What's the point? You were never going to marry me. At least with the ring . . . at least with the ring on your finger we could pretend for a little while longer."

The group stood in the stunned silence for a moment.

And then Dev turned his head and spoke into his shoulder, "Which heirs?"

"What?" Martha said. The smug look dropped from her face.

"You said Malloy's heirs would want the loan back," he said evenly. The triangle closed off, and only Dev and Martha existed. Paris crossed her arms and shot Martha daggers over Dev's shoulder. "Which heirs do you mean?" he said.

"What does it matter? Get down here," Cooley said. She checked the door behind us, muttering. "I can't believe anyone thought it was a good idea to take a shower in a crime scene."

"Well," Martha said. "I didn't draft the will—"

"But you seem to know all about it," Dev said.

"My colleague said . . . OK, I may have seen a draft," she said. "Malloy asked me for referrals and my colleague—"

"Stop saying *colleague*," Paris said.

"Which heirs, Martha?" Dev said.

"Well, he named a few beneficiaries," Martha said. I had never seen her so cowed, her vibrant, colorful personality dimmed to a reedy, pleading voice. "His parents, of course—"

"Is one of the beneficiaries unnamed at the moment?" Dev said. "Unborn?"

Martha's color had begun to rise. She lifted her chin again, the playful dimples turned defiant. The rest of the house had gone still. "Yes."

"Hillary?" Paris said. "Did he put her into his will? He's too trusting."

"Shut up, Paris," Dev said. To Martha, he said, "How far along?"

"Three months," Martha said.

"His? You're sure?" Dev said.

The steady look between Dev and Martha made me uncomfortable. How much did it matter to Dev that Martha's heir was also Malloy's? How long ago had Martha's grand tour stopped in Dev's city?

Just as I had the thought, Paris must have had it, too. She launched herself across Dev at Martha, a wild thing. Dev flinched as Paris's ring dragged across his cheek but dodged in to keep the two women apart. He pressed Paris against the railing and blocked Martha with his back.

"Jesus Christ, can you stop?" Cooley yelled, only barely loud enough to be heard over the shouting. I glanced away from the ruckus above—the blasphemy came as an actual surprise—and in the moment she looked back at me, defensive, daring me to say a word, we both missed the end game at the railing. A loud cracking noise pierced the melee. We both looked up in time to see the railing break away from the wall and Paris pressed into the void. She fell, arms reaching for Dev, for Martha, for anyone, and then crashed to the floor below, the shape of her body on the floor awkward and tragic.

Dev bellowed and raced down the stairs to her while Martha stood above, her face a mask of shock. She stood precariously close to the hanging railing her friend had just fallen through, reaching idly with a hand for the bannister, just out of her grasp.

"She's fainting," I said, and ran up the stairs. When I reached her, she fell back against me. I dragged her safely away from the edge, where she buckled to the floor on her knees and fell sideways in a heap. I sat with her and let her grasping hands clutch at mine. "Is she—? Is she?"

"I don't know," I said. The words caught in my throat.

All I could see was the shape of Paris's body in the pink towel passing from above me to below. Downstairs, Cooley radioed for help. Dev shouted Paris's name. I listened for a noise underneath this: crying, moaning, anything. There was nothing.

"Is she?"

"I don't know."

Martha turned her head, lovely red curls falling across her face, and passed out.

## Chapter Nineteen

I first met Bix in an emergency room.

He had fallen off a roof. Rescuing a kitten, I liked to say when I told the story later. And that wasn't far from the truth. On leave, he'd been helping an elderly woman fix a piece of flashing around the chimney on her roof to stop a leak. He didn't know the woman. He'd only just met her, at the hardware store. She hadn't promised anything in exchange. Her roof was dilapidated and shouldn't have had anyone climbing around on it, especially an amateur. When a loose shingle tore off under Bix's foot, he slid down the entire length of the roof and off into the void. Two stories. He was lucky he hadn't fallen on his head, or at a bad angle that cracked his neck or spine. That's how he spun in, telling me the tale in the waiting room, as he waited to be seen by a doctor. Casual, grinning over the episode as though it had happened in a movie he'd seen. This was flirtation.

I was there in the emergency room with my sister and her kids. My older niece, a toddler at the time, had a fever that wouldn't come down. Things that had seemed easy now seemed dangerous. I sat with the baby sleeping in my arms in the corner of a busy waiting room, and only because Bix was the kind of man who needed to meet everyone, hear everyone's story, did I get the chance to tell him mine.

"Yours?" he had asked, nodding to Blythe's newborn body formed against me. She was small and hot. I was sweating from the extra body heat but in love with holding her, in love with the idea that I might have my own someday. Michele had been called back through triage with Emmeline, wan and pink-skinned.

He was settling into the chair across from me with one arm held awkwardly against his chest, wincing a bit. "What happened to you?" I said.

"Just another attempt at superheroism, foiled. Is she OK?" He had dark hair and bright eyes. A blue-eyed devil.

"Her big sister has a high fever." And then against my better judgment, I asked about the arm and the heroic story. I had a thing about men with dark hair and bright eyes, with broken wings. By the time Michele came out and said Emmeline would be fine, I had stars in my head and his number in my phone. If he was going to supply a lifetime's worth of heroics, I wanted to watch.

That roof story didn't seem like a heroic story to me anymore. The shine had worn off that old yarn, but also those like it that I heard later. Like the time he'd been arrested for trespassing and breaking-and-entering, fingerprinted, and shut into a cell in downstate Illinois before anyone could find out the truth, which was that he'd been helping someone he'd just met pick up a few things from the place he was moving from. Except that it wasn't the guy's stuff. Or his house. Bix had a million stories like that. After I'd heard enough of them, I couldn't see the point. It was recklessness, derring-do. All I was left with was worry, at which point I was pushed into the role of caregiver, of mother. Of killjoy. Of a person I had never intended to be.

Until he took one last chance, and I was left with the role of widow and the remnants of a story, but not a full one. The pieces left behind didn't make sense. Our life together hadn't made sense.

When Michele and I had finally taken the girls home to their beds early that morning after the dangerous fever, we drove the empty streets in shock that the world still existed as it had just hours before. The air was crisp and reviving but I kept the window rolled up to keep it from hitting the dozing girls in their car seats. Michele had gray rings under her eyes from the weekend's missing hours of sleep. Five years older than I was, she had always gone through so many passages before me, but I had been beginning to worry I wouldn't follow her on this one. Marriage, kids. It wasn't for everyone, was it? I thought of the man grinning over his broken arm the entire drive back to Michele's tidy little house, carefully keeping the number and my phone safe in the front pocket of my jeans.

"There's a slim line between believing in fate and letting your life be decided for you," Michele said. "He fell off a roof. Come on, Edie, be sensible."

I had not chosen sensible. I had not *chosen*. I thought I was following the magic, the strange banging together of lives in coincidence and accident. That's what love felt like in its earliest moments. Like I was being pulled along by the way things had to go. Like I had no choice in the matter and never would.

DEV WENT WITH Paris in the ambulance and Martha insisted we follow it in Cooley's car. We had hurriedly packed our things from the guest house, Martha grabbing a change of clothes and shaving gear for Dev to tuck in with her own stuff. I could have excused myself to find another way to the motel, but then there was nothing there for me but the possibility of vermin and bad TV and running into Hillary. I went along to the hospital in Cooley's cruiser, cradling my swollen right hand in my left and my camera bag in my lap.

"I can't believe this," Martha said, wiping at her running nose. Cooley poked a tissue through the mesh of the divider between us, and I pulled it through and handed it over. Martha blew her nose, then sniffed the air around us and made a face. I shook my head to keep her from commenting.

Cooley was shaken. She was muttering little oaths under her breath all the way through the park and east. She hit the siren, easily catching up with the ambulance as it rushed through town.

And then we were outside the town and—nothingness. There was nothing but water, far below. "What—"

The bridge. We were on the famous suspension bridge to the Upper Peninsula, proper tourists at last, racing along the slim precipice of the bridge with the siren screaming.

"Where are we going?" I said.

"The nearest hospital is over on the Yooper side."

I looked out at the water, my stomach doing flips. That horizon of land that had seemed not so far to me a day ago now seemed much too distant. "Where's the next nearest?"

"Not near enough."

Martha cried quietly into the door on her side of the car.

We all heard what Cooley meant. Perhaps no hospital was near enough to help Paris.

I slid down in my seat so that all I could see were the wires of the bridge rushing by, double vertical strands at regular intervals until a sudden swooping rise of wires, signaling we were nearing one of the suspension towers. One of the towers loomed into view, and then the swoop of wire led back to the ground. The wires seemed impossibly slender, the barest threads of a spider's web. If the nearest hospital was across the bridge, then I must have been driven over it already the night of Malloy's murder. Closed inside and oblivious. And again, when Cooley had picked me up and delivered me to the sheriff for questioning. Dozing, unaware. I closed my eyes. I was not afraid of heights, but then hadn't a woman just fallen through the stair railing I had been pushed against? My stomach lurched. The bridge, too fragile. The water below, too far. I was also not afraid of drowning, as a particular way of dying. I knew what I was afraid of. It should have been comforting to understand my limitations. But in the back-seat of Cooley's car, I found I was also afraid of fast-moving cars, of the narrow passage a car with a siren got from the cars pulling to the side, of the slight distance between what you expected to happen and what could happen. All I could think of was the television screen, the newscaster live on the road with the rolling lights behind her. The tangle of metal, crushed to nothingness. All the lights on in the house but knowing that darkness was coming for me.

"Don't upchuck in my car," Cooley said.

I felt Martha shift next to me.

"Not you," Cooley said. "Her."

"Slow down a little," Martha said. "Didn't her husband die in a car accident?"

"Yeah," Cooley said. "He *caused* it." But she slowed down a bit, letting the ambulance slip away, the apology coming too late. I closed my eyes.

Martha was silent for a time. "Your husband *was* the drunk driver," she said at last. "You left that part out."

"I had to," I said, taking a shuddering breath. "Bix was always the hero of his stories."

I felt her processing this new information. I'd been in this conversation a few times already. Here it came. "He killed five people."

"Four," I said, opening my eyes and looking at her. "And himself."

She didn't know what to make of me. She turned back to the window.

Cooley cleared her throat. "You'll want to get checked out at the hospital, too," she said.

My vital functions had already had a look-see at this hospital. Martha wasn't paying attention. "She means you, Mama," I said.

"I'm fine," Martha said, a hateful glance in my direction.

"You fainted," Cooley said. "Wouldn't hurt. Better safe than—"

"I know what's wrong with *me*," Martha said. "I'm not sure about anyone else, though."

We made our own way to the hospital, pulling into the emergency bay only as they were bringing Paris out from the back of the ambulance. She was gray against the white sheets and small, childlike. Dev, face bleeding from the scratch he'd taken during the scuffle, hurried after the gurney. Martha fidgeted at her secured door until Cooley got out, went around the car, and opened it, and then she was off after them. When Cooley came around to let me out, I waved her off. "Take me to the motel."

"I'm not actually a taxi driver, dangit," she said.

"You're supposed to take me to the motel," I said.

"I would dump you off there happily, but I should probably get inside and do a little bit of my real job, dontcha think, before I take Her Highness back to her castle?"

"You wouldn't call it that if you'd ever been in one of the rooms. I'll just stay here and wait."

"Get out."

I did. She glared at my suitcase until I pulled it out.

"Get the other one, too."

I reached in for Martha's soft blue bag and balanced it on my case. "What did you hope to gain by telling Martha that my husband caused the accident he died in?"

"It's the truth, isn't it?" She wouldn't look at me, though. It was not in Cooley's nature to be mean, but she was making a special effort in my case.

"It has nothing to do with me."

"Oh, really? Nothing about what he did—"

"You don't know anything about it."

She stared me down for a minute, then relented. "I guess not. Not enough to judge. I'm sorry. I'm sorry about your husband and the . . . the other people—"

"I know all about the other people."

"Yeah, I guess you would. It's a darn shame, no matter what you— I'm sorry I mentioned it."

As though this group of friends needed anything more to

talk about, but somehow I knew that my gossip would still travel among them. Martha would tell Dev, Dev would tell Paris—

The chain was broken.

No one would tell Paris. Paris might never hear it. I had forgotten for a moment that other people could suffer, that others might die.

I followed Officer Cooley through the swishing hospital doors, rolling my suitcase behind me and thinking: Did I know what was wrong with me?

# Chapter Twenty

By the time Cooley and I entered the emergency room, Paris had been whisked away with Dev pulled into a triage room to look at the gash on his face. Martha was left pleading with the staff to be allowed to follow Paris and if not Paris, then Dev. Cooley commandeered the situation and forced us to turn ourselves in, Martha, for her swoon, me for my hand.

I was given a much-belated ice pack, a sheaf of forms to fill out, and a seat in the waiting room. Martha announced her pregnancy and received a quicker response. One minute she was leaning over the desk wheedling her way into her friends' health care and the next she was dropped into a wheelchair and swept down the hall. I was left alone, at last, with my suitcase at my feet and Martha's candy-colored bag on the chair next to me.

I eyed the bag and then the other walking wounded in the area. We were all living our own private dramas. I set aside the ice pack.

Digging through Martha's bag this time, I didn't bother to be careful. With Dev's things added in, it was even more of a jumble. The vitamins rattled in their bottle. Folic acid. Should have known. And was she trying to make us believe that Malloy was the father? And what was that look between her and Dev? The envelope of legal papers was still in place. I pulled them out and riffled through them. *Patrick Malloy Halloway, sound mind and body.* Patrick? I tucked them away, not into Martha's suitcase but my own.

Which made me a thief. My hand darted for the papers again, to put them back. I didn't want to be one of them, one of the people who had used the cover of darkness to get away with wicked deeds. I wasn't that kind. Was I?

A pay phone hung down the hall. I shoved the papers back in my case and rushed for it.

When I had the earpiece in hand, all I could do was stare at the buttons. So few numbers known by heart: my own, Bix's old cell phone. No one was answering either of those. I called my sister, collect.

As I waited for the call to be accepted, I studied the other people in the waiting room. A lot of mothers with kids, a guy in work boots with a hard hat at his feet along with what seemed to be his supervisor. A handkerchief of blood here, a look of misery there. Older people, alone and in couples. Everyone, worried. It was a slender thread that held us to this earth. You couldn't help notice it at times like these, how easily you might slip between a regular moment, unthinking, into the void. How easily you might fall.

And some of us, in addition, also had to call their big sister for help. Again.

"Hello," her voice said. There was a moment of silence while Michele and the operator negotiated the release of my call, and then: "God, Edie, where have you been?"

She didn't sound worried so much as annoyed.

"Michigan," I said. "It's a longer story than you might want on reversed charges. I just wanted to let you know where I was and that I was—"

My voice strangled and stopped. I'd almost said *fine*. But I wasn't.

"What's going on? Where in Michigan? Why Michigan? Oh, no, don't tell me you went to that place—"

"Yeah," I said. "The dark sky park."

"Eden, really? Aren't you still sleeping with the lights on?"

"There's a guy here," I started. But everything I could think to say required too much back story.

"Which guy? What's going on? Are you there with someone? Are you there with a *man*?"

"*No*," I said. The idea was ridiculous. I thought for a moment about those swim trunks I'd seen first thing when I'd entered the guest house, mistaken for boxers. If only I had turned and left then. "But when I got here, there was this mix-up—"

"I can only imagine," she said. "Bix, damn it. But you didn't have to go along with it, you know."

Yes, I did, though she would never see it that way. Michele thought she and I had all sorts of things in common, but she was not widowed. She was divorced. "He planned it for us," I said. "How could I not go?"

"And he was such a good *planner*," Michele said. "We don't give him enough credit, though. He planned every step of your relationship—talked you into marriage before you knew what a mess he was, swept you off to Chicago to be near his family instead of yours. Talked you out of having kids, out of keeping that job you actually liked. He planned your life pretty well, except for the part where he fucked off and died. Oh, and the part where you never got to have a vote in anything. He didn't have to plan that."

Because I let it happen. She thought she was being supportive to recount his faults—but his faults were actually my weaknesses. Itemized. And I felt worse than before I'd called. I had let Bix talk me into the life he wanted and now I would let anyone who wanted to cut him down do it without resistance.

I tried again. "I'm at the hospital."

"*What?* What's going on? Are you hurt?"

"A little—but not as badly as a couple of people also staying in the house—"

"What do you mean? Which people? I thought—ugh, Bix, you idiot—"

"Michele," I said. "I'm scared."

I filled her in as best I could around her questions and exclamations: Malloy, Paris, the thieving, the lying, the possible cheating. It occurred to me how quickly I'd let myself be pulled into the lives of these people.

"I haven't slept in days," I said, sniffling through the last of the details. "I think I'm losing it."

"You're not losing it," she said. "Women can go a long time without sleep. Proven." Motherhood had made my sister an expert on anything she wanted to tell you about. "You're mixed up in some Agatha Christie shit, though."

"Did I ever sleepwalk? Like, when I was a kid?"

"Not that I know of," she said slowly. "Are you, now?"

"I don't know," I said, raising up my arm to find the bruise I didn't remember getting. It had softened to a dark green. "Maybe."

"So are you a . . . I mean, do they think you're a . . ." Either she couldn't think of the word or she didn't want to say it.

"Suspect," I said, more quietly.

"Oh, Eden. If you didn't kill Bix for everything *he* did, you're probably not going to kill some stranger, are you?"

"Should I get a lawyer up here?" I felt six years old, always relying on my big sister to get me out of trouble. She'd gotten me through the funeral, bodily dragging me where I needed to be, through the paperwork of Bix's death, through the weeks afterward when I couldn't quite go home. I was tired of being this woman but I couldn't stop. "What should I do?"

"Well, cooperate with the police, I mean, what else can you do? Who do you think really did it?"

I glanced around the waiting room again. "I'm not sure. Malloy is dead and now Paris is maybe, too, but that doesn't mean she didn't kill him. But that accident—I don't know what to think. Dev, Hillary, Martha, Sam—" I had simultaneously spotted Sam entering the waiting room and remembered him secreting away the bottles of wine from the house. What had that been about? How had he been left behind? "I need to go," I said.

"Who are all these *people*?" she said. "Wait, do you need me? I can figure something out, if you do. Give me a number to reach you."

"They just called my name," I lied. This was my mess to fix. "I'll call you back as soon as I can. Love to the girls."

Sam had gone to the desk to wait in the line. He stood behind a woman with a little girl who was holding her own arm in a protective embrace. For a moment, I saw Bix, grinning over his compound fracture, trying to get my number.

I shook that image away and grabbed Sam by the arm. He whirled on me.

"Oh, Eden, God," he said. "You scared me. What's going on? They wouldn't tell me anything. I saw the ambulance pull away but the cop who drove me here didn't see what happened."

His eyes darted around the room, landing briefly on the swell of my hand. Something about his anxiety seemed heightened. "If you had to guess," I said slowly. "What do you think might have happened?"

"Huh? I don't know what—what are you talking about? Was it Paris?"

For a moment I'd had the idea that Sam might know more about all this than he'd let on, that his ideas on who could have gotten hurt and who surely hadn't would help me sort this out. "Were you especially worried about Paris's safety?"

"I'm worried about all our safety," he yelled, and then pulled me away from the line and out near the pay phone while everyone in the waiting room watched. "What's going on with you?" he hissed. "Are you crazy? I'm worried about all of us, and if you aren't, you're nuts."

"Where did you take the wine?"

That stopped him. He swiped at the sweat at his brow. "What do you mean?"

"I saw you," I said. "Did you pour it out? Is it poisoned?"

"Poisoned?" He glanced out at the waiting room, where the sea of people still watched us. He grabbed my sleeve and pulled me deeper down the hall. "Did you not see the *screw-driver* in his jugular? What are you talking about? No, it's good wine, *really* good wine. I didn't—I didn't want it to be wasted, that's all."

"So you . . . did what with it?"

"I just put it somewhere to make sure it didn't disappear into 'evidence.'" He used finger air quotes. "Those bottles aren't six-buck bottles from the corner store, OK? And they're all that I have left of a promising career gone down the toilet."

"How much are they worth?"

He took a deep breath but didn't answer. He wouldn't look at me, either.

All he had left.

"Are they worth your career?" I said. "If someone back at your old job knew you had them?"

He made a noise in his throat. "That's the thing. They suspect I have them already."

"Which is why you no longer work there."

His mouth opened and closed. And then he thought of what to say. "Don't tell—" But he came up short, probably against the fact that the person he didn't want to know what he'd done was dead. "Martha," he said finally. "Don't tell Martha."

## Chapter Twenty-One

Back in the waiting room, the hospital forms lay on the chair next to me while I iced my puffy hand. If only I had reached for that swinging flashlight with my nondominant hand, I might be more interested in finding a pen.

I let my head drop. Behind closed eyelids, the chaos and brightness of the hospital's waiting room flattened to a field of dark red and photo negatives in the shape of the overhead lights. But I couldn't doze off, the way some of those around me had done. I couldn't *relax*. I had developed an eye twitch—a steady one that made the world seem like a filmstrip playing through a defective projector, time skipping a frame. Also, I couldn't be sure—but was my heartbeat also jumping, out of rhythm?

Breathe in, breathe out.

I found myself going over the things I'd learned, sorting them into little piles in my mind. Malloy's pep talk to Sam hadn't done him any good, and had maybe hurt him. *I've been known to talk people into things.* Malloy's encouragement had only created in Sam the belief that he deserved more than he was getting: more money, more prestige, more respect. More free things from the warehouse. So instead of getting that promotion he was all but destined for, Sam got fired and the wine he'd taken got spirited away to Michigan. "A consolation prize," Sam had said after begging me not to tell Martha, except I'd just heard the story, and understood that the prize was snatched before the competition had been called. The cases of wine along with the watch from Malloy's wrist—the two pieces together didn't look good, if you were searching among the group of friends for someone with a propensity for bad behavior.

"So Malloy pumped you up," I'd said to Sam. "And what you did with all that self-confidence got you into trouble."

"Yes," he said.

"So you blame Malloy for losing your job."

He had picked up a full-body spasm that didn't allow him to be still. "I never would have gone after the promotion so hard if he hadn't—"

I looked at him until he understood what he had been about to say. "Paris fell down the stairs," I said at last, handing him Martha's powder blue bag. It looked like the sort of thing a new mom would carry, actually. Congrats, it's a boy? "Dev's with her. And Martha—Martha's pregnant with Malloy's baby."

Sam blinked at me for a moment, words attempting to but not fully forming on his lips. "*Malloy's* baby?" he said finally. "She said that?"

I recalled the way Dev had pressed her the same way but before I could follow that lead, he had taken the bag from my hand and hustled away.

And I had come to rest in the waiting room, ignoring the stares.

I put my head in my hands, pressing at the side of my twitching eye. What to do? Who to trust? I had promised not to tell Martha about the wine theft. But I hadn't promised to keep anything from the sheriff. I wasn't even sure anymore what I knew, what I thought, or what was true. What mattered, what didn't.

When I opened my eyes, Warren Hoyt stood there. I couldn't be surprised. He turned up everywhere.

He smiled hesitantly, standing just off to one side as though he wasn't sure that I would remember him.

For a moment, I don't know why, I had the strangest feeling that no one could see him but me. The filmstrip, scratchy and jumping at the edge of my vision, was a horror movie. The rangy, stoic man who silently haunted my steps was invisible to all but me.

His wary look was steady, and I stared back, waiting for some word, some act, to reveal him as physical, as actual.

And then a woman with a stroller ran her infant into Hoyt's leg. He leapt out of her way with a yelp. All the heads in the room turned his way. I leaned back in my chair and pulled the paperwork off the seat next to me. He folded himself into the offered chair, pulling at the back of his neck with his hand.

"Another tough day at the guest house," he said.

For whom? I didn't agree or disagree. He nodded toward the ice pack.

"What happened to your hand?"

"Punched a Maglite in the face."

He winced and shifted in his seat. "Were you there? For the—for the . . ."

Some internal organ inside me leapt in anxiety. If I ever

slept again, I would see Paris falling in my nightmares. "Please."

"Have you heard anything?"

"No, but—" My memory showed me Paris's crumpled form again. "It doesn't seem good."

"Ah, jeez," he breathed, and I was reminded of Cooley. I missed being in her good graces. I missed her icing-coated swear words, and the soft world they let me believe in, so different from the profanity-thick world of trailing along behind an Army husband. "Ah, jeez."

I hadn't been looking closely at Hoyt before, but now I did, as though I had been invited to take his portrait. He was unshaven by a day or more, and the top button of his shirt—a faded, soft blue, instead of tidy forest ranger green—was undone. The shirt might have been a little wrinkled. Not ironed to perfection, at least. There was no polite way to ask. Was this basic human decency he was exhibiting, or did the problems at the park somehow make Hoyt's life more difficult? Public relations? Funding? Plain old marketing problems, when in one weekend, you hosted both an impromptu murder and a separate deadly accident?

*Accident.* My mind caught on the word.

Was it too strange, the timing?

I held my fingers against the twitch in my eye and tried to see the scene again. Dev, trying to keep the women apart, pressing his fiancée into the railing, and the railing—

I suddenly recalled the sound the railing had made when Paris had cornered me against it. I could have broken through. I could have been the one.

Or I could have stopped it.

I hadn't stopped it. Instead, someone else lay within this hospital fighting for her life.

I should have said something. I could have done something. I hadn't realized—but I felt keenly all the times in my life I'd had this same thought. I should have. I could have.

Would I ever be the person who could live with what she had done, hadn't done, had put up with, had acquiesced to. Would I ever fill out my own skin?

I stood up.

Warren looked up at me. "What's wrong?"

I sat back down. And then stood up again. "I have to use the ladies' room."

My eye convulsed with a renewed vigor as I hurried over stretched legs and around small children toward the restrooms. In a stall, I stood facedown over the toilet until I was sure the moment had passed. At a sink, I splashed water over my face and looked at myself in the mirror.

Could I live with myself? That was really the question I had come to the park to ask, wasn't it? I had lived with Bix. I had lived with everything he had been and done. I'd given him every chance, every free pass. Every forgiveness, until the last. But now it was me, only me. There was nowhere else to go, no one else to rely on, no one else to blame. The money he'd left me was gone. The house, my only safe place, needed to be sold. I would have to face the dark, somehow. All that was immaterial to this: Could I be the kind of person I would need to be?

A woman entered the restroom and gave me a long look on her way to a stall.

In the mirror, I was a wreck, cradling my hurt hand like a

kitten to my chest. I wetted the other hand and smoothed my hair, and then used a paper towel to wipe my cheeks. Even if it felt as though my eyelid was jumping around on my face, I could barely see it in the mirror. No one would notice. But the gray rings under my eyes, the blotchy neck. The puffy, outsized hand. Well, it was a hospital. What did they expect?

Out in the hallway, Hoyt had my empty paperwork under his arm, my camera bag strap over his shoulder, and my suitcase at his feet. He was fidgeting with a little square gadget like something they'd hand you at a restaurant that served peanuts and encouraged you to spit the shells on the floor. "I got you a . . . pager," he said, shrugging. "They said it's still going to be a while until they call you back for X-rays. Thought you might want to get some air."

Good call. We found the nearest exit and walked along a sidewalk until it petered out into one of the parking lots, my suitcase clacking over the seams in the concrete. For an area of the country that depended so much upon its scenic views, the hospital planners hadn't given much thought to making the grounds pleasant or walkable. Perhaps they'd thought no one having to spend time here would have a chance to seek enjoyment.

And yet we were never far from the lake, from the wind whipping off the water. The waves struck at a strip of sand just across the street. The temperature had dropped. Clouds overhead made the world seem small and close.

"That's the Lower Peninsula over there," Hoyt said, gesturing. "The park's on the east side, of course, not really visible from here. But that's the island right there, the source of all the fuss. There's an exceptional hotel there, the Grand Hotel. The world's largest front porch, they like to say."

I made a noncommittal noise. I had been hoping for the air, the walk, but not for the conversation. And not a *tour*.

"You'll have to come back . . . a better time, perhaps. And of course, that's Lake Huron."

I followed his gaze. "I'm afraid my Great Lakes geography isn't as sharp as I thought it was," I said. "I thought—wait . . ."

"Lake Michigan and Lake Huron are technically one lake," he said, warming to the topic. Warren Hoyt was the kind of guy who warmed to topics. He was going to make a terrific old codger someday. The world's largest front porch, indeed. "They share the same waters. The Straits of Mackinac link the two lake basins. You would have crossed over the straits on the bridge—"

I held up a hand. "Let's not talk about the bridge." Maybe the ER would drug me up enough that the ride back to the Hide-a-Way would be more forgiving. And then I pictured Paris, gray-skinned against the gurney, and that brought me up short. "I feel terrible," I said. "That railing made an awful noise when I was pushed up against it and then—"

Now it was Hoyt's turn to go pale. "Yes. I think we'll be hearing a good deal about that railing. I'm glad you didn't— what I mean to say is that I regret that anyone—"

"Put the brochure away, Warren," I said. "I'm not the lawyer and I'm not the one who got hurt. Martha's the lawyer for the group, if you want to issue any apologies."

"The guest house is solid Michigan craftsmanship," he huffed. "But the railing wasn't meant to be *wrestled* against."

A bit of a granny in a solid outdoorsman's body.

"She might be dead, Warren," I said. I had a pain in my stomach and held my sore hand there. An ulcer, just in time for the steakhouse beeper to go off. Or maybe I hadn't eaten since that morning. Had it only been that morning I'd had toast, Paris sneering at me? Paris—

It could have been me who fell, but it hadn't been. I was both horrified by what I'd seen happen and the outcome we were all waiting for and . . . elated to be alive. And, of course, guilty to be alive. If I had to be honest, this was not the first time in the last few years that I had come up against this feeling. My parents, then Bix and—the other people. I couldn't shut down the thought fast enough. And then Malloy, and now maybe Paris. People died, and here I was, still standing. I was being saved for nothing at all, as far as I could see. I could pass it off as survivor's guilt, but it was mixed with a selfishness I couldn't begin to admit to.

For a moment, I was small and wretched, like I had been standing in the viewing area in the park. The low gray sky seemed to expand out and out until I stood alone on the tilting planet, dizzy from its spin.

I reached out for something to hang on to—nothing. And then I had the sleeve of Warren's shirt in my fist.

"Are you OK?"

I turned toward the lake again and let the cold wind lash my hair into my eyes. It stung. "I'm not sure . . . I'm not . . . I can't . . . I wasn't meant for this," I said. I couldn't quite catch my breath.

"What?"

"Life. This . . . all of it. Everything. It's too hard. I think I might be broken."

"Don't say that," Warren said, his voice thick. He blinked a moment. "You may not know this, but you are made of stars."

I forced myself to look at him.

Something shifted in the air around us. *Hall pass.* Isn't that what he'd said? But now I knew he hadn't meant it generally, toward the group, the day at the jail. He had singled me out. And now again—he hadn't demanded information about Paris or Dev. He hadn't come to talk the park out of liability with Martha. He wasn't giving Sam the ten-cent gesturing tour.

Warren Hoyt was *into* me. Oh, jeez indeed.

Now I knew where we were, how things stood. I found that my mouth was open and closed it. I loosened my grip on his sleeve and let my hand fall. "I'm sorry, I thought you said—"

"Stardust, to be more accurate, which doesn't sound as . . . well, *romantic* might not be the right word for the moment." Warren Hoyt, red around the collar. He cleared his throat. "But it's more accurate, you see. The planets, the sun, the many suns around which innumerable planets spin, and us, we are all made from the same star stuff. There are two trillion galaxies in the observable universe—observable with telescopes, obviously, not the naked eye—" He struggled over the word *naked*.

"—and countless universes beyond that we may never know. But this third rock from this sun just happens to be the perfect spot, warm and well-lit, and with potable water rushing up on the shore here." The brochure seemed to run out. When he started again, he sounded less like someone leading a tour group. "And we really have made a quaint little pantry of the place, building up cozy places to rest for the night and keep away from the bears and wolves and things. Before everything else we've done and built, we were little specks of the same stuff that lights up the night sky.

If only people would step away from all the shiny technology. The phones, the tablets. The beeping mechanisms of daily life that seek to make life so connected yet make them so . . . empty." He held up the ER beeper with a faint air of disgust.

I had been trying to say that I didn't deserve any of it. And now I wanted it all. The beeping mechanism of my daily life had been turned into the sheriff for evidence—I wanted that back, for sure. But more than that. Now I wanted to be star stuff. I wanted to be made of stars. I felt as though I had stepped through a door, only to find that I couldn't walk back through. I was Alice, having sampled the cake. I was bigger.

"What?" I said, all other words fled from my brain. Warren Hoyt? Buttoned-up Sir Warden Warren? I finally realized what Warren's job was. Not a peace officer, not even an officer of the natural law like the conservation officer mentioned by Cooley. Not a ranger and not a functionary, the likes of Erica Ruth. He was a storyteller. A poet. They'd put a poet on the grounds, to make sure that everyone's sights were raised to the heavens.

"How did you learn about all this?" I said, not sure yet what all this might entail. The universe had a lot of pieces. How much of it can one person understand? How big was this tour? We'd already covered infinity, after all.

"School, a bit. Reading, mostly." He shrugged.

I liked him, I realized. I didn't know why, exactly. He was a goody-goody, wasn't he? Not my type. But then I had decided to stay as far away from my *type* as I could from now on. If I could see them coming.

It had been a while since I had met someone new that I liked, that I could imagine talking with, willingly sharing a beer with. Willingly spending time with, and on. Anyone, at all, that I could be bothered with. Dev, maybe, but that was something less noble. He had held my secret in his hands, and he had saved me once. He displayed moments of kindness but I didn't trust those, not anymore, not since the sleepwalking thing. Sam? No, someday I would forget Sam's name. Hillary, too, was a figure of something less than acquaintance. She was only waiting for me to ruin her.

What about the others? Dev clung to Paris, and Paris— well, in the absence of the one she would have chosen, Paris had allied herself with Martha. Sort of. She had no plans to put Martha in that wedding that might never happen. And then Martha, who wouldn't give Sam the time of day but was pregnant—with Malloy's baby? The pairings should have been tidy. Two by two by two. Except without Hillary, who had they really been? Who was the fifth man? Who was the one who'd been left out? Not Malloy. Not ever Malloy.

"If you're interested, I could suggest a book or two," Warren said.

*Click.* I came back from where I'd gone to find Warren smiling at me in a way that made me nervous. "A book?"

"Basic astronomy. I could suggest a few titles," he said. "Of course for most people, it's enough to visit the stars once in their lifetime, and you've done that."

"It might not be enough," I said, turning toward the lake again. I couldn't look at that soft blue shirt, almost rumpled, creased where I had grasped at the sleeve. I didn't want to be a person who grasped at others anymore.

The square of technology in Hoyt's hand buzzed and flashed violently. "Well," he said, with a sigh I thought I understood now. I was embarrassed and didn't know what to say. The poor guy, to try and enter this thin atmosphere. I said nothing. I didn't let him off the hook.

"Well," he said finally, "let's go get you fixed up."

## Chapter Twenty-Two

O ut," Cooley said as she pulled up outside the Hide-a-
Way Motel. She hadn't even entered the parking lot,
but had drawn up to the corner and pulled to the
side of the street, motor running.

Sam and I waited. For all her dramatics, Cooley would
have to come let us out.

Back at the hospital, when the pager had gone off, I'd finally gotten a scan of my knuckles. I returned to the waiting
room with a splinted but unbroken hand to find Warren Hoyt
still waiting for me, offering me a ride. I'd chosen instead to
wait for word about Paris and catch a ride back later. It was
still only midafternoon. I'd stay all night in the bright lights
of the ER waiting room, if necessary. Somehow, checking in
on Paris seemed the right thing to do, and I was in no hurry
to see the inside of a Hide-a-Way room. It was also far less
awkward than the drive into town with what Warren Hoyt
wanted the chance to say to me.

And so I waited with Sam, or near Sam, or in the same
room as Sam but not really with him, as other people's dramas
sorted themselves out around us. Eventually, Dev sent down

word through the chaplain. Paris was hanging on in the ICU, critical but stable for the moment. No visitors outside family allowed. The rest of us should go. The rest of us. Sam and I had looked at one another. The rest of us had dwindled considerably. "It's going to be a long night," the chaplain said. "You should go have some dinner, get some sleep."

Sure. Easy as that.

While I tried to get the info desk to call us a cab, Sam discovered Cooley parked near the ER bay, keeping an eye on us and angry about the assignment. But she agreed to cart us to the motel, one last time.

Martha was being kept overnight for observation. Now, standing in the dust of Cooley's cruiser pulling away from the curb, under the flickering neon of the Hide-a-Way, I didn't blame her for taking the opportunity to sleep in clean hospital sheets.

"I need a drink," Sam said, heading toward the bar.

"If only all that crime scene wine hadn't gone missing," I muttered. It was the longest day in known history—had I only let Sam out of my room this morning?—and it was still only just evening, the sun still far from the horizon. I decided I could use a drink, too, and dragged my suitcase after me.

Inside the bar, the same dark room. The same mild curiosity from the bar, the same churlish growl from the bartendress.

"Hillary," Sam breathed.

My eyes were slow to adjust. She sat in the back booth again, this time facing the door. She had already identified us and was scowling, proprietary, trying to make her skinny arms take up more room at the table than they needed.

"Do we sit with her or not?" Sam said.

"Oh, we're sitting with her," I said. "I have some questions."

Sam's face showed surprise. He went to the bar and asked for a wine list, then waited out the laughter and the presentation of the single wine bottle on the premises. Then he asked for a beer list. The bartender waved her slab of an arm at the two taps. "Our beer list."

"Shots," I shouted over Sam's shoulder on the way past. "Whatever we were drinking yesterday."

"None for me," Hillary said, sliding toward the edge of the booth as I approached.

"Sit," I said. I stowed my suitcase and camera bag behind the booth, then slid in next to her, forcing her in. I took a fortifying glance at the high window in the wall. No matter how dark the bar was, the window was still blue, still daylight.

"Surprised you can even come in here," Hillary said. "Dark as it is."

So there it was. The story had made its path all the way 'round the horn to Hillary, even Hillary, the outsider. I shook my head. I'd had my doubts the rumor mill would include her at all. "How'd you find out?"

"That cop," she said, her features sharper than I remembered, older. Almost haggard, but then I knew what mirrors had to say about grief. "I told him about Angel today," she said, glancing toward Sam's back.

"If you know about my darkness phobia," I said, "it shouldn't be too long before Sam knows about your kid."

"Shh," she hissed. "Or I'll talk to this entire bar about what a stand-up guy your husband was. How do you live with yourself?"

I felt the heat of shame on my neck and cheeks. It was a good question, but not for the reason she thought. "That doesn't have anything to do with me," I said.

Her cool look turned to disgust. "Your husband gets drunk and behind the wheel and kills five people—"

"Four," I said. "And himself." I couldn't explain why that mattered. It didn't.

"A guy cheated on you and then kills four people and himself—whatever the hell difference that makes—and you're here to celebrate your anniversary?" she said. "Do you know how pathetic you are?"

"Well, as you've seen," I said, "very little celebrating has been accomplished. Believe me when I say I wish I'd never decided to take this trip."

Sam arrived with the shots and plunked them down in front of us. He slid into the other side of the booth. "Man, this place reminds me of Jimmy's Woodlawn Tap, right, Hillary?"

"What?"

"Jimmy's. Where everybody drank at school. U of C." He waited for recognition that didn't come. "University of Chicago?"

"Oh, right," she said, glancing my way. "I wasn't much of a drinker." She shot back the drink in front of her, wiped her mouth. "Back then."

"Huh," Sam said, turning to me. "Catching her up on Paris?"

"What about Paris?" she said.

I waved him on. He obliged with a quick retelling of the facts so I didn't have to, skipping over the part about Martha's pregnancy. For Hillary's sake or his own, I wasn't sure. Interesting that Hillary had heard about Bix and about my being afraid of the dark—but not about Paris or this supposed heir.

"Eden?"

*Click.* When I focused, they were both staring at me. "Yeah?"

"I said," Sam said, "do you want another drink?"

I hadn't had my first, but their shots were gone. I threw mine back and slid the glass across to Sam.

When he went back to the bar, Hillary spoke up. "I'm sorry," she said, though her voice hadn't softened. She sounded frustrated, not forgiving. "About calling you names and—what your husband did, you didn't do."

There was something bitter in me that didn't want to be released entirely from blame, a hard little kernel deep down. I'd have to think about that later. I nodded that I'd heard her.

"And poor Paris," she said. "I think. You know, it's hard to know who to feel sorry for around here."

"Cheers to that," Sam said. He had brought the spirits to the table to fill our drinks. He gestured with his chin to the bar. "I just bought this entire bottle, so let's toast to whatever you got."

Hillary glanced my way. This stuff was potent. "Sure," I said, clinking my glass to Sam's. "Whatever you got."

THREE ROUNDS LATER, with Hillary's pours switched to Sam's side of the table, we started to get somewhere.

"Heartbroken," Sam muttered.

"Who?" I said.

"Everyone," he said. He gave Hillary a petulant look, in case she decided to keep too much of the mourning to herself.

"Not *every*one," I said. The liquor had calmed my eye twitch a bit, but what I knew was a subtle movement felt like a donkey kick from the inside. I remembered the tiny tic as I stood at the mirror. Hadn't I decided to be the kind of person

I wanted to be? But who was that? Maybe I could be the sort of person who got to the bottom of things. Nancy Fucking Drew. The faster we figured things out, the sooner I could go home and get to the bottom of my own problems. "Did either of you use my phone to text Malloy on the day he died?"

Hillary looked askance at me. "What? *Your* phone? But why—"

"It wasn't me," I said. "That's what I'm saying. Sam?"

"That was Paris," he said, and downed another. "I heard Dev being a dick about it to her." He pressed a nasal whine into service to act out Dev's role. "'How obvious can you be? What were you thinking?' She tried to deny it, but I guess Martha saw her, too. Your phone has a bright pink case, right?"

"When was this?"

"Well, he was grilling her about it on the way to the observation area, so she must have had it when she went into the house for the wine. Remember, Martha went to change, after she spilled?" He stared out into space for a second. "The last day."

"Where was I?"

"Leading us," he said. "And then you passed up the opening. Somewhere along there. They shut up when they saw me listening."

"Paris used *my* phone to text Malloy to meet her after Hillary was asleep?" I asked.

"*What?*" Hillary said. "That bitch!"

I waved my hand at her. Wait until she heard about Martha's news. "So who used my phone to . . . oh, that's easy. Dev," I said.

"Dev what?" Hillary said.

"Dev used my phone to call the police, and he called the park, too. He said he remembered the number, but no one remembers numbers anymore. He must have been looking through my phone. And while he was in there, he also texted a bunch of my friends and family upsetting messages that I'll probably be explaining away for the next year."

"Dev wouldn't do that," Sam said. His eyes went distant. "I don't think. Why would Dev do that?"

"Because he knew Paris had used my phone to message Malloy. And when Malloy's body was found and he knew it wasn't going to look good, he sent a bunch of other texts, trying to bury her messages in sheer volume. And in not a small way, make me look unstable—"

"Wait, the message to Malloy was from *your* phone?" Hillary said. "He never said anything about a weird invitation from an unknown number. I would think he'd have been surprised, to say the least. I mean, from a stranger?" She gazed at me for a second, then at Sam. "You *were* a stranger, right?"

She was trying to piece together the possible out of the impossible, to form sense from chaos. She'd seen Sam come out of my motel room, early morning, and now this. "Never met any of them before," I said. "And am not particularly fond of any one of them, by the way."

"Not nice," Sam said.

I hadn't given it any thought, but suddenly the answer came to me. I knew why Malloy hadn't thought the message strange. My number was unknown, but Paris had signed the message. That dumb emoji that Sheriff Barrows had been willing to allow had been a pocket-dial, the one text on my phone he'd been willing to ignore. It was no accident, that little picture. "She used a symbol so that Malloy would know it was her," I said. "A pear emoji. Pare. Paris."

"That *stupid* pear," Sam said, his syllables soft. "I've seen it. I know what you mean."

"The sheriff thought it was an apple."

"Why didn't she just use her own phone?" Hillary said. "She would have had it in her pocket or whatever, right?"

"Probably, but you said yourself that Malloy ignored calls and messages from her. Maybe she was trying to trick him into paying attention."

"Paris is such a drama queen," Sam said. "That stupid damn pear. Man, I never want to see that thing again."

It seemed a pretty rough thing to say. He might not be bothered with a text from Paris ever again. But he wasn't thinking clearly, which seemed like too good a chance to pass up.

"So whose idea was this trip, Sam?" I said. "Yours?"

"Like we ever did anything I wanted to do," Sam said.

"Except drink wine," I said.

"Except drink wine," he agreed. "Good wine, not that swill—shhh." In a lowered voice, he started again: "The swill they probably sell here. Hey! You're not drinking."

I drank my shot but didn't refill the glass or Hillary's when I refilled his. We all threw back our glasses, and I refilled his again. He was outpacing me by double, Hillary maybe by threefold. The warmth of the drink pooled around my knees. I should have been on the floor, but the alcohol only made me bold. "Was the vacation Malloy's idea?"

"Ha," he scoffed. "Malloy didn't want to hang out with us. He had her—" He hooked his thumb at Hillary. "*You*. And before that, no. Not Malloy's idea."

"He didn't want to hang with you?" This was interesting, considering he was their best—*all* their best—friend. But hadn't he said as much to me? It *wasn't even close* to his idea.

"I don't even know who made the arrangements," Hillary said. "It wasn't me or Malloy."

"Dev did," I said. "Martha said so, and at the office after we met up at the house, he realized he'd misunderstood there was a suite. Was it Dev's idea to get together, Sam?"

"Dev is the busiest of all of us," he said. "He's too busy being Mr. Important Doctor to ever do anything fun."

"What about Paris? If she wanted to see Malloy," Hillary said. "Maybe she suggested the idea and got Dev to set it up?"

The idea had merit. Dev did whatever Paris wanted, retrieved for her everything she ever desired. Even Malloy? Did it make sense that he would allow her even this, to make the arrangements for her to see the man she actually wanted to be with?

"Maybe he thought if Paris saw Malloy again," I said, "especially now when he was dating you, Hillary, that maybe she would snap out of the hold Malloy had on her."

"And get married," Hillary said.

"Finally," Sam said. He belched and reached for the bottle to peer at the label. "This stuff is *fire*. I'm pretty sure this says it was distributed from the seventh ring of hell. It is awful small print, though. So maybe I'm wrong."

## Chapter Twenty-Three

My eye twitched. I held my finger against it and judged the quality of blue at the slice of sky visible in the window of the bar. Time was falling away. "So whose ideas do you always have to follow, Sam, if you never get to suggest anything?"

He blanched. "I know what you're doing. You keep trying to trick me into saying something about my friends."

"She's just trying to get some answers," Hillary said. She looked at me. "Though I have no idea why."

"Well, I still think one of *you* is the most likely killer." Sam had to enunciate carefully around the words and then tried it again. "Likely killer."

One of the men at the bar cast an eye over us.

Hillary leaned in closer. "I loved him. I would have done anything for him."

"Anything to get him, maybe," Sam said darkly.

"What does that mean?" she said.

"I know you're a liar."

She glanced my way. I shrugged and poured him another shot. I hadn't said anything about Angel to anyone. "Tell us about it," I said. If he had managed somehow to hack into the pipeline of gossip to hear about Angel, this was good information. I had not considered Sam to be the hub of the group, but maybe he was the one they all trusted. He was cuddly-looking, innocent. Hadn't I let him into my motel room without even considering he might be the one who killed Malloy? He inspired confidence. But maybe that was how he'd walked out of his place of business with a consid-erable amount of liquid compensation.

"This bar is nothing like Jimmy's Woodlawn Tap," he said. "But you wouldn't know that because you never went to the University of Chicago, did you?"

"Just because I don't remember what a college bar looks like doesn't mean—"

"Don't bother," he said. "I sent that photo I took of you and Malloy at the water that day to my sister. Had you dead to rights"—here he made a gun with his hand and pulled the trigger—"before we even got back from the viewing spot. I *knew* you looked familiar."

Hillary's face was flat, unreadable. What had Angel said on the phone that night? That Hillary had worked *so hard* getting her GED. It hadn't occurred to me: Would a presti-gious university accept someone on those terms? A university that could probably afford to be highly selective?

"Familiar?" I said to Sam.

"Like, from-the-*news* familiar," he said.

"Let me out," she said, shoving her leg into mine.

"What did you do?"

"You go immediately to what did *I* do, just like the rest of them."

"She assaulted a University of Chicago recruiter," Sam

said. He picked up his shot glass, considered the liquid inside, and then put it down. "It was in the student paper. Big headlines on campus. I don't know how much play it got elsewhere."

"I didn't assault him," she hissed. "He's the one—"

"Trading sexual favors for an acceptance letter," Sam said. "Prostitute U—"

"That's not what happened!'

"My sister remembered you right away because she was on the newspaper staff. Boy, she went to *town* on that story. Trying to get her Pulitzer by twenty, I guess. She's at the *Trib* now." He seemed to lose track of things for a second, and then came back to the story. "I asked her to send me the article—wait, I'll see if she found it." He patted his pockets.

"They took your phone," I said impatiently.

"Oh, right."

"Let me out, I said," Hillary growled. "Or I'll tell this entire bar what your husband did—"

"My husband was a drunk driver," I announced. The two guys at the bar didn't even turn around. Only the bartender paused to look my way. "He killed himself and four other people. A family plus—" For a moment the words were difficult to get through. "He cheated on me." The bartender nodded once. It felt like a transaction. Satisfying, in a way. I had bought some freedom here, and maybe a small dram of respect, though I didn't want that. I didn't deserve that. I poured another shot and sank it.

"Shit," Sam breathed.

"And this guy," I said loudly, directing attention toward Sam, "is probably wanted for grand larceny back wherever he's from—"

"Hey!" Sam cried.

"So, you can sit your ass down and tell us what really happened," I said to Hillary.

She slid deep into the booth and stared down at the table, her hair hiding her face.

"How old were you?" I said.

"High school. A sophomore. He promised me he could get me into that school, and I believed him." She shot me a look. "That young."

"Angel's dad?"

She nodded.

"Who's Angel?" Sam said.

"And when I showed up at the school, he called the cops," Hillary said. "He made up some story about the bribes I'd been offering him. He had a few emails . . . he patched them together so they told the story he wanted to tell. They didn't investigate much. Who was I? Just some poor pregnant kid from Indiana with a diploma from the night school for poor pregnant kids."

"Did you go to college anywhere?"

She glanced between us.

"No, then," I said. "And how old are you really?"

"Only a couple years older than Malloy," she said. "I never lied about that. He knew."

"But the rest of it . . ."

She shrugged.

"So your résumé is a lie and your career is built on a faked degree."

"Faked identity," Sam said. "Hillary isn't her real name."

Hillary's gaze turned to him, hot and deadly, and then it was gone. But I'd seen the presence of resentment.

But Hillary wouldn't have killed Malloy, not when he represented the way out. A woman who loved him or even only loved what he could do for her and her kid didn't need to kill. Unless—

Faked identity? Faked, not changed.

My memory reached for those legal papers in my suitcase. What had Malloy added to that will? If he had added Hillary to it, that name change might let some unnecessary air into the legal proceedings. Was that motive? For Hillary? Or for someone else?

My eye leapt. The filmstrip skipped off the reel and then righted itself. At the table with me, a liar, a thief. And me? We had all three of us dumped our secrets out onto the table, a pile of ill-gotten gold. Nothing about this felt good. Nothing at all made any sense.

The bottle half gone, we all switched to water. The patch of blue in the wall had turned to a pale noncolor of early sunset. I'd have to leave soon. "Tell me about your friends."

Sam's eyes were slits, but not from suspicion. I imagined he was having trouble keeping me in focus. "You just want to put them in jail."

"I'm not the police," I said. "And if one of your friends killed the other, don't you want that person to go to jail?"

"Stop it," he said. The words were soft and sibilant. Hillary leaned in to hear better.

"He said, 'stop it,'" I said.

He repeated himself. "Stop using . . . logic and—what's another word?"

"*Lucidity*," Hillary said.

"*Reason*, maybe?"

"All of that," he said. "I get enough of that lawyerliness from Martha—oh, God, Martha, no." He dropped his head and pressed his fists into his eye sockets.

Hillary had too much lucidity of her own. I didn't want her sidetracked by what he would be moaning about next. "Let's save Martha for another time," I said pointedly. "*OK*, Sam?"

"She's OK, isn't she?" Hillary looked at my hand in its splint and packing. "What actually happened today? It was Paris who crashed through the bannister, right?"

"*Par*is, oh, God, no," Sam groaned, something of the livestock barn brought inside. The customers at the bar and our hostess all tended to us now.

"OK, time to go," I said.

"Wait," he said, holding out his hand to Hillary. "The bannister? You mean—the one at the top, over the living room?"

"The rail broke and she fell through it?" Hillary said, looking at me for confirmation. I watched Sam.

Sam shook his head, as though trying to clear it, blinking. "You said," he said, to me. "You said she fell down the stairs."

I had. I hadn't meant to lie. "Not exactly."

"But that can't be. No, that's not right." He put his head in his hands, then looked up, angry. "That's not possible! That means—"

He slammed his hand on the table.

"Hey, get him out of here," the bartender said from her station. "Come *on*."

Between the two of us, we got him upright and moving toward the door. His rage had given way to crying.

"You left your bottle," one of the men at the bar said.

"Keep it," I said.

"I'll keep it for you," the bartender said. "You'll be back."
I desperately hoped she was wrong.

Sam's feet dragged across the threshold out into the parking lot. The sky was bright but pink, yellow, the beginnings of a gorgeous sunset, if you liked that kind of thing.

"He's staying . . . with you?" Hillary said.

"Holy shit, no," I said. "He was only in my room because he locked himself out. I told you—they are all strangers to me. I only know them as well as I know you, which it turns out is not that well."

She gave me her profile. "I don't know any of them, either. Or—Malloy, really, if you want to know the truth. We weren't even together a year."

"Three months, you said."

"Yeah," she sighed. "Three months. You can't cut me even a little break, can you?" She struggled under Sam's arm and jostled him higher onto her shoulder. "I won't even rate in his obituary, you know? Girlfriend. What would it even say that would be the truth? His family—I haven't met them. We were so new. And yet, it wasn't new anymore. He felt like home to me. He felt just like . . . going home. I can't explain it well."

It all sounded whirlwind and romantic, not unlike my own ill-conceived marriage—and yet. I hadn't read the will from Martha's bag yet, but the presence of a will, to me, meant the presence of money. Malloy hadn't seemed like a person to flaunt his wealth, all his talk of pilgrims, his beat-up car, and the gift of an expensive watch that had no real place in his life. But the presence of money could be easily researched, collected, stored. It could be targeted.

I was too hard on people. That was the thing that Bix had always said about me, the thing that was true. He didn't just mean that I was too hard on him. No. I was impatient at cashier lines, with chitchat among waitstaff, with bankers, with Girl Scouts at the door. What he meant was that I had no charity. I had no humanity.

Maybe those were the words he used to make himself feel better, but I knew how right he was. And here under the darkening skies of this place, I had had a few chances to practice virtue. Empathy, at least. But I had failed. I was failing. If I did nothing different than I ever had, I would return home the same husk of a human he'd seen me for.

At the bottom of the stairs, Hillary and I paused to catch our breath and to allow someone coming down to get by. The woman wore a blue jacket that caught at her hips and cheap dress shoes with beads at the toes, out of place for the season and for daytime, really, anywhere. Something about those shoes and the shape of her in that jacket made me look twice, but then Hillary was pulling me toward the stairs and I had come to a decision about the person I had decided to be.

"Maybe they'll include you," I said to Hillary. "In the obituary. It doesn't hurt to ask."

## Chapter Twenty-Four

For one of my photography classes, I had brought in a photo of Bix I'd taken. He's sitting in an outdoor bar in Wrigleyville, near the baseball stadium, his hopeful striped Cubs jersey gone to black and white in the dimness of the place. He's sitting along the sidewalk, people in similar fan wear walking away over his shoulder. I can't tell from his demeanor or theirs if the team had won or lost that day.

I think they lost. They'd been losing early, and it was spitting rain. We sneaked out to the bar, to get better beer.

Quality-wise, the photo did not represent my ideal work. I spent the next twenty frames trying to capture a certain glow from the streetlight on his beer glass. The snap of Bix was just a throwaway. His face was a little blurry because he'd been turning his head away from me when the shutter closed. *Click*. But he was smiling, a laugh caught in the wild. His movement only increased the width of the grin, dragging the white of his teeth across the image, feral. There was the strength of his jaw, brightness of his eyes, mirth and joy. And then, in the sweep of his face, something hideous.

In my class, the other students tore that photo apart. That's how it went. If they loved a photo, they said a few supportive things, though no one gushed. Envy was too strong among them. The instructor took his turn next. He was a guy who had worked as a staff photographer for the *Sun-Times* for decades before they cut their entire staff, who wore a khaki vest with safari pockets that had probably once held all manner of lenses and rolls of actual film, back when film was used. His commitment to teaching was tenuous. He might spend more time on an image he found promising. But I had discerned a sort of melancholy in him, too, as though every image he thought had promise would have been better if only he'd been the one to take it. If it had been his own work, and also taken twenty years prior. Nothing of this world was good enough. He would have liked to ban digital cameras from the classroom, but the university wouldn't let him. They had dismantled all but one small darkroom for a new faculty lounge. The faculty smoked in there; you could smell it.

The teacher never said he hated a student's photograph. I simply began to understand that he hated everything until proven otherwise. But when the other students loathed a print someone had brought in, they were confident in their hatred—and loud. A pack of dogs let loose.

They had been overly polite to all the submissions prior to mine the night I showed them my photo of Bix. Penned in, until the gate opened. After a full round of torture, everyone agreed. The image of Bix had no merit, was a mistake, was not fit for human eyes. After that, we moved on.

After class, I held back so that I wouldn't have to spend any more time with them. But the teacher stayed, too. He picked the print from the display where it sat alone as the room emptied. He held the print of Bix on the palm of his hand for an extra beat before offering it to me. "Half handsome, half monster," he said, his voice almost a low hum for its monotony. "Not bad but accidental, I think. A portrait is better if it reveals character. Maybe it's like him, even so?"

Which is what I had not allowed myself to understand. Why had I brought the image in for the class's derision, when its value lay somewhere far more private than even between myself and myself? Why had it been my favorite? Maybe, I came to understand much too late, I had brought it in to test my own theory, that I was married to someone I didn't fully know. That I was married to a man with secrets. That I was married to the devil, smiling.

That image of Bix came to me unbidden as Hillary and I dragged Sam up the stairs to his room in the Hide-a-Way. I stopped short with the memory—it stung anew—and felt Sam's body weight shift in a cataclysmic way toward the void below.

Hillary and I both yanked him forward, almost sending him into the window of the room at the top of the stairs. He sagged between us as we caught our breath and regained our nerves. Below, someone getting into a car parked on the street slowed to watch what we were up to.

"He's heavier than he looks," Hillary whispered.

We pulled Sam to his feet again, exchanging a shaky glance over the top of his hanging head, and forged on.

Before we attempted the feat, Hillary had urged me to pick Sam's pockets for his room key. She wasn't stowing him in her room, and I had long cycled past the blind trust that had allowed me to shelter him in mine. His key was found easily in his pocket. Now, as I used it to open the flimsy door of his Hide-a-Way hovel, I wondered if he had always had his key. If he had only pretended to lock himself out, what did he need that night? To be near another human being after the horror of Malloy's death? Had he really found my room instead of Martha's? Or had he planned it that way?

"What?" Hillary said.

"Nothing."

Sam's room was the same as mine, in reverse. The mice, if they existed, were silent as we lay Sam on top of the covers and pulled the comforter up around him.

"Going to snoop?" Hillary said.

I'd been considering it. Wasn't sure what the right answer was here. "Do you think I should?"

"I'll watch the door."

I tried the bathroom first, but only Sam's missing toothbrush made its home there. It sat dry on the counter, unused. I caught a glance of myself in the mirror and ran my hands through my dank hair. I'd never gotten a shower today, not with all the excitement. This? This is what made Warren Hoyt blush around his buttoned-up collar? I looked like the walking dead. I ripped off the tape that kept my hand in the awkward splint and threw it into the trash.

I heard Hillary say something in the next room and went to the door. "What?"

"A car in the lot." She stood at the window, peering between folds in the curtains, shifting from one foot to the other.

Sam didn't have a suitcase in sight—probably because he'd used his packing time to secret away the wine—but his neatness at the guest house was evident here, too. A little stack of clothing sat tidy, almost prim. Carefully folded designer golf shirts, a pair of khaki shorts, a pair of boxers. A Dopp kit with tidy travel-sized bottles of this and that. In all his things I hadn't seen anything out of place, no entertainments, no hints.

Hillary fidgeted at the window. "I think it's them."

"Who?"

"Someone dropping off . . . Dev."

"Surely not."

"That's who it looks like," she hissed. "Who's left?"

Sam in the bed, Hillary at the window, Malloy in the morgue. Paris in intensive care, and Martha tucked in with a nice lumbar support pillow somewhere in the hospital's mommy ward. I counted them off. Dev. Dev was the one with mobility, but he would have to leave Paris alone. "I mean, there are other people in the world who might stay here," I said, "though I can't think of a single good reason. Do you think he'd leave her bedside?"

"If she died," Hillary said, glancing over her shoulder at me. I nodded. I was not rooting for these people, but I wasn't wishing them harm, either. "Find anything?" she said.

"No," I said. "Can you still see Dev out there?"

"Mmm, no," she said. "Maybe he went to his room? Their room."

"Didn't they have a first-floor room?" I went to Sam's bed and checked the drawers in the nightstands, but only a Gideon and a restaurant directory kept company there. A hotel-supplied plastic cup sat on the nightstand. There was a slight ring of color at the bottom. I picked it up and smelled it. Wine, of course. Then I knelt and peeked under the bed, trying not to touch my skin to the nasty carpet.

"What are you looking for?"

"Anything out of place," I said. "I guess. I don't know." I stood over Sam's passed-out form and studied him. He lay on his stomach. His cheek was smashed against a pillow, turning his face childlike, one of those Renaissance fresco cherubs. But an angelic face didn't make him innocent. That key in his pocket was something I had to consider more carefully. I hadn't given Sam the proper attention. I had given him a pass. I placed his room key next to his hand.

"Let's go," I said.

"Wait," Hillary said. "Did you learn anything?"

I gestured to her to check between the curtains again. She did and nodded. Outside on the landing, my breath clouded.

"Did you?" she said. "Learn anything?"

I had learned something but I couldn't quite put my finger on what it was. "Nothing," I said. And that was the strange thing, perhaps. Sam was too much nothing, and that was something.

## Chapter Twenty-Five

Hillary begged off and headed for her room. I waited until she was inside and the locks in her door had sounded before going to my own room.

I had left all the lights on, though the overall effect in the room was still dreariness.

First lock. Second. And then the chain.

In the bathroom mirror, I regarded her again, the haggard lady with the greasy hair who had been following me from mirror to mirror. I needed a shower in the worst way, but a good shower, with better soap than I had access to. I washed my hands and face, using two of the scratchy towels to mop up the water I'd splashed on the counter. The empty counter. My toothbrush was—

—in my *suitcase*. And my suitcase was with my camera case, still parked down in the bar behind the back booth. Damn it. I'd have to fetch it, and soon, before someone laid claim to it. Before night came on.

I hurried to the door, threw the bolts, opened the door, and—stopped. The sun was deep in the sky, the shadows filling in along the walkway and down below in the parking lot. Everything else had been coated in the glow of sunset. In my photography classes, we had called the sixty minutes after sunrise and the sixty minutes before sundown the golden hour. These were the times of day when the sun's rays were at their lowest angle. They painted the world and everything in it in a gorgeous, liquid, golden hue. Taken at this hour, every photo could be magnificent, every subject made heroic, thoughtful. The very air told the story of time, and this was the pinnacle, a moment drenched in the last rays of daylight before the earth spun us around another rotation. Light was the most reliable timekeeper, especially to a photographer. It didn't matter what time your phone said, your watch, or the clock. Light told the story. Light made the story.

I had not had a chance to think of this area of the country as beautiful since we'd been booted from the guest house, but of course it was, even here from the upper deck of the Hide-a-Way. Even from the vantage point of misery. The planet would continue to spin. Light would continue to rain down upon all that we made and were. You had to go on. The world gave you no chance to pause, to put on the brakes and say you didn't want tomorrow to happen, to say you didn't ask for it. When it came to light, it spent itself, ready or not. It poured out, spilled, wasted. The stars shined on, even if we had no chance to look up.

What would Warren Hoyt say about that?

I felt hurried down the stairs. Behind. Gasping to catch up with something I couldn't name.

Downstairs, the bar was darker than I remembered. I stood in the open door, trying to let my eyes adapt before cutting off access to the open air behind me.

"You really shouldn't leave your stuff behind like that,"

scolded the bartender's gruff voice. She came to the end of the bar where I could better see her, wiping at the counter with a gray rag. "I'm not the concierge or nothing."

"Sorry," I said. "My friend—" I stopped. "That guy needed help to his room."

"Don't wonder," she said. "You want the bottle to go with you?"

"God, no," I said. "Save it for the next time you need to peel paint."

"It worked, though, didn't it?" she said.

Had it worked? In two episodes, it had flushed out secrets, sent one of us rushing for the toilet, sent two people to bed, completely zonked—

I eyed the bottle now. How much did I need to drink to sleep the night?

"It worked," I said, and held out my hand.

My camera case slung over my shoulder, bottle tucked at my elbow, I rolled the suitcase outside and around to the stairs. The sun was falling fast now; the shadows in the stairwell were dense. It worked, didn't it? The bottle of spirits had not been corked. Why not? I downed a mouthful, waited, and then had another, then raised the suitcase to the second step before climbing up beside it. Maybe I'd be ready for sleep by the time I got to the top.

"I could help you with that," a voice said. Dev, emerging from the breezeway where the vending machines stood. He tipped back his head and dumped the crumbs of a bag of chips into his mouth, crumpled and tossed the bag toward a trash can.

"I Sherpa-ed your friend up these stairs a few minutes ago, so I guess I can handle an overnight bag," I said.

His eyes raked over the bottle. "I could help you with *that*," he said. "Is it wine?"

"No. Some kind of bottom drawer schnapps or something." He looked awful. Paris. "Is she—?" I held out the bottle.

"She's stable," he said. He approached, took the bottle, peered at the label, shrugged, and took a drink. Winced. "Barely. She's got three broken ribs, a compound fracture in her right leg, and—" His voice gave out, so he raised the bottle again. After a couple of pulls, he cleared his throat. "And maybe some trauma. To her head. Her brain. She could still—she might—" He took another drink.

"Why aren't you there?"

"Her parents are there now," he said. "I don't want to use up all their recriminations in one day, so I came to get a shower, maybe a new shirt—"

"A drink," I said, watching him tilt the bottle back again.

"A big drink," he said, wiping his mouth with the back of his hand and offering the bottle back to me. "Sorry. Here you go."

"Sam bought it," I said. "I'm sure he'd like you to have it."

"Is that who you carried upstairs? I'm starting to lose track of them," he said. "My friends." He tucked the bottle into the crook of his arm. "Martha?"

"In the hospital, still, I suppose. They're probably worried about the—"

We stood in silence, letting the word I hadn't said bounce around in silent echo. I could almost forget where I was.

"You thought the baby might be yours," I said, finally.

He made a dismissive face. "You're getting us mixed up. Martha must have had a little fling with Malloy when they were getting his will together. Just like old times, I guess."

Martha and Malloy? So far, I'd heard about Malloy and Tash, Malloy and Paris, Hillary, now Martha. His idea of *pilgrim* was different from mine. "What kind of old times are we talking about?"

"College," Dev said, waving off whatever face I was pulling. "It was a long time ago."

"It was *five years ago*," I said. "No wait. It wasn't even five. But I'm not talking about then. I'm talking about now. When you asked Martha about the heir, you were explicit that it was Malloy's," I said. "That was the thing you wanted to know. Believe me, I'm not the only one who heard it. Paris—"

"I thought maybe it was Sam's," he said evenly.

I knew what I'd seen. The answer had mattered to Dev.

I thought I knew, anyway. I tried to remember the scene, but most of it had faded against the image of Paris, arms reaching, the pink towel tucked around her unfurling, a flag of surrender. I was having trouble thinking anything through. I gazed at the bottle tucked against Dev's chest, remembered instead his shirtless descent down the stairs at the guest house that first day.

"Did you want help with the suitcase or not?" he said. "While I can still walk up and down stairs?"

I stepped back from the case and started up to my room.

The last few drinks had spread to my limbs. My fingers, trailing along the metal bannister to my room, seemed unconnected to my body. My head was awash, but that didn't stop the filmstrip from tick-ticking at the side of my vision. I could see our approach from every angle, a film shot with six cameras.

At the door, he set down the suitcase. The air around us grew heavy. "You're not coming in," I said. The key to my room felt awkward and too large in my hand and then dropped.

He leaned down and retrieved it, slowing rising until we were face-to-face, close. He inserted the key into the lock. "Are you sure?" he said.

I wasn't sure.

He pushed the door open and stretched to set the bottle and suitcase inside the bright room. I wasn't sure. A moment passed while we looked at one another and then he must have seen some agreement or decided not to wait for it. He pressed himself against me, and we were both inside, the door closed, our breath close. His unshaven chin had scratched against my cheek. I raised my hand to it. He reached for my hand and held it down against my thigh, as though to save me from something. I wasn't sure I wanted to be saved. Maybe he thought he was keeping me from visiting the moment, from thinking too much. I was remembering what he'd said about the passions of youth, of first kisses.

Using my injured hand gently, I pulled the strap for my camera bag over my head and let it swing to the floor. He took this hand, too, and pressed it to my other side. We touched only where his warm palms held my wrists to myself.

"How long has it been since you went to bed with someone?" he said, his breath hot against my temple.

"He's been dead nine months," I said.

"And before him?"

"We were married ten years—would have been."

"And no one since?"

I was teetering on the edge. Shove him away or breach the space between us? The decision should have been simple.

"You're a lights-on girl, I assume," he said.

I pulled away, slipping out from under his touch. I got the joke. He was making it easier to decide. "You can go."

"Let's drink some more," he said. "It seems like such a good idea, doesn't it? You have some glasses?"

He went to check the bathroom.

The spell was broken. "Is this how you show concern for your fiancée in the hospital, then?"

He came out, a plastic cup in each hand. "Is this how you celebrate your wedding anniversary?"

"Maybe you haven't heard," I said. "My marriage shouldn't be celebrated."

"Then we should toast its demise," Dev said. "We'll pour one out for each of our relationships." He walked to the door to retrieve the bottle. "Don't look at me like that. Even if she lives— I think she might have killed Malloy. There, I said it. How do you come back from that? You don't. Once you think the person you love—loved—might have killed someone, that's probably the end, don't you think?"

"That's funny," I said. "I got the feeling she thinks you might have done it. That you could have, anyway."

"There you go. Two toasts, or is that three now?" he said. "Are these cups clean? They were unwrapped."

"Sam opened them," I said. I found myself distracted by the shape of his shoulder under his T-shirt.

He stopped. "Sam was here?"

"He got locked out of his room last night."

"Is that a euphemism?"

I tasted the accusation, just out of reach. Was this jealousy? His fiancée prefers his best friend, but I'm the one he wants to fight Sam for? Dev reminded me of long-ago bad boyfriends, but of Bix, too, in a way. Bix as he turned out to be, so much beyond my grasp. "Just drink your booze and go. Take the cups, too. My wedding gift."

"Now, now," he said, sitting on the edge of the bed. He patted the spot next to him and then poured two inches into each cup.

I sat next to him and took the cup offered. Before I could take a sip, though, Dev had pulled at the neck of my shirt and was kissing the skin at the back of my shoulder. In my surprise, my cup sloshed and spilled. God, what an old lady I was. A young, virile man whose body I had already admired offered me a bit of escape. Did I care about Paris? If she lived or died, was it my fault? Would this change anything? I'd be gone in a day or two, surely, and they could get on with their marriage or misery, whatever came next. But—Bix. Not that I felt loyalty to him at this point—he didn't deserve it—but I was conscious of playing the hated role. The other woman. That was not who I wanted to be.

I stood up. Below me, Dev smiled at me in a way I felt all the way through. I knew that smile—the devil, smiling. But I wasn't afraid of it. As much as I wanted to taste that smile, as much as I wanted that smile to taste me, I was sure. "Good night, Dev," I said.

"Mediocre," he said. Dev shot back his drink and dropped the cup to the floor. "But it could yet be saved."

I went to the door and opened it. While I was considering Dev's advances, night had fallen. Outside, the neon sign stuttered, and the long road toward the park was empty. I stood in the doorway, frozen, until I heard something behind me and turned—

Dev knelt on the floor at the foot of the bed, clutching at his throat, gagging.

"What? What's wrong?"

His face was a terrible color, his limbs jerking and kicking at the carpet.

"Do you need water?"

My cup lay on the bed with an inch of booze left. I reached for it.

He gasped, wordless, and struck out. The cup clattered against the wall and to the floor. He reached for my arm and squeezed it until I screamed.

I grabbed for the phone and dialed for help. The extras. I would pay them no matter what they cost me. And, boy, was it going to cost me.

# Chapter Twenty-Six

So let me get this straight," Sheriff Barrows said.

The EMTs had taken Dev to the hospital, of course, but Barrows had ordered me here to the station. We'd been getting things straight for at least a couple of hours. Who had the bottle when, where? Who had access to my room? Sam, Hillary, Dev. The cleaning staff? No, this was a two-bit hovel, not the Ritz. The cleaning staff would enter the room and clean—here I heard air quotes around the word—after I left, and not a moment before.

They'd bagged up the bottle, the cups. They'd put me away in the squad car in the parking lot, someone's coat thrown over my head to keep me from beating at the black windows. Best they could do. They'd taken my camera.

Now Barrows and I sat on opposite sides of the cold slab of table at the police station, the same clock-less room.

Barrows had a stack of folders at his elbow, but he hadn't brought anything forth from them. They were for show, I was sure, in the same way the room was kept at meat-locker temperatures. I was the meat. The coat had been returned to its owner, and my T-shirt was no match against the cold. I had wrapped my arms around myself for warmth, knowing that I must look strung out and guilty. I was strung out. I was guilty, too—of certain things.

I'd have said this was the longest night of my life, but there had been so many. The last nine months flowed together like one, long dreamless night, the sky never black. Tonight, somehow, the end of it.

I folded myself in two, my pounding head resting on the table. My tongue was thick in my mouth. "Can I get an aspirin?"

"I'll get you sorted just as soon as I understand a few things," Barrows said. I hadn't seen Officer Cooley. Her absence felt strangely like a rebuke. "Like what you put in that booze—"

"Nothing," I snapped. "Ask the bartender. I was drinking it all afternoon. So were Sam and Hillary."

"They're a-OK," Barrows said. "Alive, at least, though fairly hungover, especially that guy. Sam. What about . . . how are all those young people traipsing in and out of *your* room at the motel when you're so-called strangers?"

I had no good answer for that. Because I was stupid. Because I had let my guard down, again and again. Because I was too focused on the surface of things to notice what went on beneath them. Because I was waiting for things to go how they would go. It would not be the first time that character trait had bitten me in the ass.

"An aspirin is waiting on the other side of you telling me what happened to that young man," he said. "*With* that young man. He has a pretty girlfriend, a fiancée, over in the hospital, so I *know* I must be reading too much into this."

"He carried my suitcase," I said, pressing a hand to my head.

"Sure, sure. All innocent," he said. His voice was sing-songy, as though he could get me to hum along. "Tell me you got that girl out of the way, so you could get at her boyfriend."

I looked up. "What? I had nothing to do with what happened to Paris, and if you asked any of the three other people who witnessed it, including your own officer—"

"I know you weren't in the fracas," he said. "But a little woodworking done beforehand, a little shove in the right direction . . ."

"I didn't *shove* anyone," I said. "I wasn't even on the same floor, and I don't have designs on—any of them. Any kind of designs. That's just a . . . distraction." I couldn't help thinking that Barrows keeping me cooped up in this town was half the problem. Who wouldn't go crazy, stuck as we were? "Wait—woodworking?"

"That railing didn't crack," he said, stern now instead of crooning. "Not the rail itself. It was loose at the wall, probably hanging by a thread by the time she was up against it. Of course we don't know if it worked itself loose or if someone helped it out." He pushed the stack of folders out in front of him. "The place covered in fingerprints, the timeline unknown. Anyone who's ever stayed in the guest house could have had a hand in it." He sucked his teeth. "So to speak. Our first goal is to narrow the field a bit."

"OK." I didn't know what he was getting at. It seemed like he wanted to tell me something. "How do you do that?"

"Glad you asked," he said. "We ask a few questions, of

course. Such as, Mrs. Wallace, have you ever stayed at the Straits Point Park's guest house before this week?"

"No," I said.

"You're sure?"

The tone he'd adopted made me nervous, but I was certain about this. "Absolutely sure."

"Fine. And then we collect what are called elimination fingerprints from all the witnesses—you and all the current guests, you'll remember, had your prints taken early on. Of course we can't eliminate any of you at the moment. What we can do is go through the fingerprints we've pulled from the house now on *two* occasions and find out who's been hanging around at the top of those stairs."

I had been. I'd surely grabbed at the railing as Paris shoved me against it. "I told you already," I said, sullenly. "I was at the railing earlier. I heard it groan. Paris and I *both* could have gone over."

"Lucky for you," he murmured. "*You* didn't."

"But—" I held my head in my hands. I had something gnawing at me, wanting to be remembered. And then the image developed from the mist of memory. The day I arrived, Sam had been perched high above the room on that same railing, sneakers dangling.

"Sam," I said.

"Sam's the one?" Barrows said, leaning forward. "How do you know?"

"No, I meant to say—the day we arrived, Sam was sitting on the bannister talking with Martha." My exhaustion fell away. "He wasn't just resting against it. He was sitting on it with all his weight."

"He's a pudgy guy," Barrows said, resting his hand on his own gut.

"He has to outweigh Paris by—I don't know—forty, fifty pounds. Or more. Surely if it was going to break, it would have broken on him. So that means—"

"That means it got loosened up this weekend," he said. "That narrows the field right down. One of you fiddled with that rail with an eye toward another of you leaning too hard on it."

"That's a poor plan for murder," I said. "How could you know who would be near it? Or if anyone would put any weight on it at all? That doesn't make sense."

"It's a certain amount of chance being introduced, but if you think about it, maybe there's some sense, too."

I couldn't think about it. My head hurt. My eye twitched. I didn't want to look too directly at the sheriff or, frankly, the situation. Five former classmates and a guest enter the guest house with an interloper, and one by one the friends meet with disaster? For a moment, I was back there, watching from above as though I had been standing at that faulty railing. The friends, gathered around Malloy, drawn close. Malloy, Paris, now Dev, somehow poisoned. I counted them out, picturing little red grease pencil X's over each of them. And then suddenly I saw the sense of it. It didn't matter who leaned their weight against the railing. One of them had.

"All of them?" I said. "Someone is trying to kill all of them?"

"*Some*one."

"I know what you want to believe," I said. "But I don't have any reason to do it. You're wasting your time on me and meanwhile— God, Warren was right."

Barrows's top lip curled a bit. "Right about what?"

"He said you wouldn't—"

We stared at one another. Finishing the sentence seemed like a bad idea.

"I need to— I'm so tired. I need to go."

"Go where? You got someone expecting you?"

The guest house was a crime scene. The motel room was presumably being combed over now and also off-limits. "Is there another room at the Hide-a-Way?"

"All full up. A number of surprise guests in the last twenty-four hours."

I swallowed the bile in my throat.

"Reporters. Parents of those kids. The first one's folks showed up this morning and now the parents of that girl. I suppose that fellow tonight will have parents, too." He rubbed at his chin, looking me over. "I noticed no one came rushing up to your side."

I gave him the look he deserved. "I'm a widow."

"My condolences et cetera. When was this again?"

"What?"

"When your husband died."

"Nine months ago."

He nodded, contemplating the folders in front of him. "So he's not coming to your rescue." He lowered his voice. "But I'm wondering where everybody else is. Aren't you wondering?"

I wrapped my arms around my stomach more tightly. I was shaking, though I wasn't sure why. I should have asked Michele to come up for me. She'd offered, and I'd turned her down, afraid of needing her, of always needing someone. Maybe I should have asked for a lawyer by now. I had not been smart. I had been thinking the best of people, seeing everyone in the best light, though this was a strategy that had already failed.

"Whenever someone sits in front of me and I don't hear banging on the door to let them out," Barrows continued, "I wonder who it is I'm really dealing with."

He stood up, stretched, and pushed his chair in. Taking his time. "Did you know? Even the worst of them have someone along, fighting for 'em, snapping the heads off my front-desk sergeant. Wife beaters, child rapists, murderers. Drunk drivers. They all got someone coming to tell me I'm all wrong about the accused. Who are you that you don't? *What* are you?"

I stood up. He stepped back, surprised by the sudden movement.

"Where do you think you're going?"

"Well, I thought of a bed that would be free," I said.

"Where's that?"

In bad taste, I thought of Dev's room at the Hide-a-Way. Free for the night, surely. "The jail."

He lit up. "What charges would you suggest?"

"Assaulting a police officer," I said, leaning on the chair I'd vacated. Barrows flinched. "Save me the trouble. I'm exhausted."

"Is that a threat?" Barrows tapped the gun holster at his hip with a single finger.

"It's a plea," I said. "We both know I can't leave this place tonight, now that it's dark outside. And at least if I'm in jail, and someone else gets hurt, you'll know it wasn't me. Once and for all."

Barrows shook his head. "Keeping you close by is not the worst idea I ever heard. I'll be wanting to talk to you again. And again. And again, until we get this sorted out.

At least until we know if that fella tonight makes it out of the hospital."

He picked up his file folders and went to the door.

"You never stayed on at the park before. You're sure?"

I nodded. I was sure. I thought I was sure.

He was gaslighting me now, trying to make me uncertain of my own motives and moves. They did this sort of thing, didn't they? For false confessions. I steadied myself. I hadn't done anything wrong. Strike that. I hadn't done anything against the law. "Why are you so sure I've been here before?"

"Not you," he said, opening the door and beckoning someone from the hall. "But I found a dead man in our crime scene. A *different* dead man than the one being mopped up. Your husband, of all people, crawled right out of the wood-work."

His words wouldn't turn over in my mind. My husband what?

Another officer came to the door, tall and not a hint of nonsense about him. In my shock, I had the feeling that the tall man was somehow canted toward me, looming. I backed up a step. *Perez*, his name tag said. Barrows motioned to me. Officer Perez had no reason to question the sheriff's orders. He approached and gently put one arm and then the other behind my back.

I let myself be manacled. Barrows was talking but I couldn't follow what he was saying. I interrupted him. "Wait," I said, barely able to force the words out. "My husband *what*? What?"

"He had a prior arrest—"

"That was a misunderstanding," I said. That guy had tricked Bix into helping him break and enter. He had faced no charges, in the end. Bix, damn it, and his situations. "The other guy—"

"Regardless," he said. "His prints were in the system and—"

"He's been dead for— What could he possibly—"

"Just listen for a damn minute," Barrows barked. "A latent fingerprint left by your husband—almost half his hand, that's no mistake, no possible way around it—was recovered from the scene." He waved us out of the room.

"But—"

"Until I know why, I don't mind extending a little hospitality, since you asked so nicely. We'll call it for your own safety. Suicide watch. You've just had some bad news."

Weak, I let Perez lead me away from Barrows, down a hall, down a set of concrete stairs, and into a bleak, fluorescent-lit hall lined with a handful of empty cells, two left, two right. The cell was concrete on three sides, with a heavy wire cage door. A toilet in the wall, a comfortless cot with no bedding. I framed the scene in my mind, a photo I would never take. The theme? Loss of hope. End of the road. The cell had no windows. It could have been any time of day or night. It didn't matter. It was definitely night, at last.

Somewhere nearby, there was someone talking in an even voice. A radio, maybe.

I had the oddest feeling as the officer led me into the cell and released my hands from the cuffs. I turned and watched the door slide closed with a clang. This was real. I was living this moment. What if I could go back in time and tell the three-years-ago me, the five-years-ago me, that this moment existed in our future? Standing on the cold floor of a jail cell, listening to the slammed metal door hum like a bell rung? What would that past me make of this? How had I brought us both to this place? Into this cell, this town I'd never planned to visit, this state I didn't live in—this life I had screwed up. Where was Bix? That's the question former me would resort to.

Where *was* Bix? Was it possible—? What did *latent* mean?

The officer turned to go. "Wait," I said. "Do you know how long a fingerprint can last?"

He stopped and looked me over. "Years, at least."

The flutter of hope in my chest turned tight and choking. Of course. He was dead. I knew that. I had chosen clothes for his broken body myself. "How long can they hold me without charges?"

This one he wasn't sure he wanted to answer. He hadn't pegged me for a troublemaker. "Twenty-four hours," he said, curt.

"Great," I said. My voice was tiny and childlike, bouncing against the walls. "I need at least that many hours of sleep."

## Chapter Twenty-Seven

The fluorescent light outside my cell flickered. The slab on which I had invited myself to sleep was even less comfortable than I had assumed. No prison-issued blankets or pillows had been offered. I curled up on my side and pulled my arms into the sleeves of my T-shirt. The only positive thinking I could manage was that I had the cell and the hall to myself. And it was safe. Maybe. I lay on the slab and breathed into the neck of my shirt for the warmth.

The sputter of the light, the flutter of my eyelid. It was better to close my eyes. I was wired. I would never sleep. The voice on the radio from down the hall drifted in, reached like a hand. The voice said . . . the voice said . . .

The moon? And he called it *she*.

"She's always a woman, isn't she?" the voice said. "In the myths and legends, she's a goddess, a sister, a maiden, a round-faced girl turned into the mother of our night sky. In the pocked surface of the moon, other cultures might see a rabbit or a set of giant handprints . . ."

Giant set of handprints? Horrible. I didn't like to think of it, but then I did. I thought about the moon, because the calming voice had asked. The rabbit, the lady, the face of a man laughing down on us. The same face, always. I had learned at some point that we only ever saw the bright side of the moon because—

". . . because the mass of the moon isn't evenly distributed, Earth's gravity keeps one face—the more delicate and puckered side—toward us. The highlands, the shiny peaks, which aren't mountains but the edges of overlapping crater rims, from impact with debris. Even those smooth dark areas, the 'seas' you hear so much about—they aren't formed by water. Altogether, the lunar map features twenty seas, fourteen bays, twenty lakes, and one ocean—and hardly any water to speak of."

Thirsty. I wished for a drink of water. The voice was muffled for a moment, faint. I willed it to come back, to keep talking to me. Tell me about the seas that are not seas. Tell me about the lakes that are not lakes. Tell me about the one lake created by two.

"—all made through impact. Basically, the moon gets hit with a lot of sh—stuff. It has no atmosphere, like the earth, to deflect or burn up stuff. She is up there, our moon, no protection, taking every bit of it on the chin. Thin-skinned as heck, from all the things she's already lived through. She's a pretty lady, bright, lovely, tough . . ."

Tough. It was fine to think so.

"Tougher than she thinks," the voice said. "Tougher than she feels right now. She casts a spell, though. Get out there and take a look."

Cold, dark, distant. The moon was a rabbit-faced lady. I was a rabbit-faced lady. I was a rabbit. I was small, tightened into a fist against the cold. Everything hurt.

"Why don't you sit down for a while?" a new voice said. My sister.

My back hurt. These shoes. I shifted from foot to foot. I would not lay my hand on the casket. I would not.

"Sit down," Michele said. "No one will mind. They'll understand. I can bring you a drink."

Yes, *please.*

"Not that kind of drink."

I've given it up anyway.

"For now," Michele said. "Until—oh, no. What's this about? Stay here."

People are bending down into my vision to say things, quiet things and well-meant things. I'm afraid I won't remember the kindnesses. What I'm noticing are those who are not there. The condolences not murmured or mailed. There are people who have texted me to say things that cannot be said in so few words. There are people I haven't heard a word from, who have faded into the past tense in my mind. I don't want to be the person who sorts, who keeps count. Where has that gotten me? Here.

Michele is back, and she's pulling me by the elbow. "She needs a break," she says. I think she means me. "I'm sure you can understand."

The funeral director had shown us a private family room with fussy furniture missing from someone's formal parlor but with a door that closes out the rest of the world, and a watercooler in the corner with little cone cups. Let's go, Michele says.

We stand.

But then the woman is in front of me, blocking the way. She's all I can see. The dress frumpy and too tight, the haircut ragged. Misery in a navy blue dress, shoes chosen for comfort. Crumpled tissues balled up in her hand. A thin band on her left hand cut into her finger.

"You think you're the only one who lost someone," she says.

The others. So many faces turn in our direction.

"You're not the only one," she says. "He did this. *He* did." Waving her hand toward—

Bix, stately in a suit so that I could pretend some other man, a stranger, lay in this box. The suit is a liar. They have patched as much of his body as they could find, and the suit holds it together in a man shape.

He did this. He did. It was like a dream I had had so many times. Had it really happened or did it only feel like it had happened because I dreamt it again and again, and in my waking hours, went over it and over it like a song I couldn't quite sing the words to. I can hum it.

He did this. He did.

There was one carefully placed handprint marring the shine of the casket, just where the flag draped. I reached to wipe it off.

Michele? Help me with this?

Help me?

Michele is gone. Only this woman. I will never be left alone. I will always be alone.

I woke up panting, my fingers gripping the criss-crossed wires of the cell's door. Saying something breathless to myself into the empty hall.

He did this. He did.

Sleepwalking.

I SPENT THE rest of the night curled into myself on the slab, shivering, awake. When I used to sleep well, the night seemed brief, sometimes too short. Often I had gone through the day yawning into my hand.

But now that I kept watch, the night was interminable. An hour stretched toward forever. I began to feel the turn of the earth under my feet. It took a long time to spin this ship around a full rotation. It took all night. If you were paying attention, eyes wide open, you were part of the crew on turnabout, tugging the ropes to swing the sails around, creaking timber, trying to catch any thin wind to keep moving toward the morning. It took all night.

"Eden."

Warren Hoyt stood outside the cage wire in a pool of light that made him look like an angel. Angel. Why had she named her kid that? A kid whose dad called the cops on her? I didn't believe in angels. I believed in skylights I had not noticed the night before. I stared at the pool of light at Hoyt's feet and reached toward its warmth. The filmstrip flickered desperately.

"Mike, come on. Get her out of there. Could you not spare a blanket or jacket or something?"

I had a jacket, then, someone tucking me into it and rubbing my arms. My teeth knocked together.

"Sheriff didn't say—"

"I'll tell you what to tell that shithead—"

Outside, it was another world. The sun was up, the air warm on its way to hot. It was still summer, still a grand blue sky overhead. Outside, it was day, a glorious day, cartoonish in its brightness.

"—what right he had to put you in that dungeon," Warren was mumbling as he put me in the passenger side of his Jeep. When he got behind the wheel, he looked at me for a long moment. "Eden, should I take you to the hospital? You're worrying me."

I shook my head. The hospital meant careening over that bridge. I didn't trust myself on that bridge. I didn't trust myself not to grab the steering wheel and jerk it. Left-hand turn into traffic. Right-hand turn into oblivion.

All I wanted was a minute of sleep. A second. Just one second. All I wanted was the puff of the comforter in the guest house, the sigh of the down as I submitted to it, an outline of my body, and the quilt off the window pulled over me, up to my chin. All I wanted.

"Guest house," I said. My mouth was dry.

"What? Really?"

I couldn't think of anything else to say. "Guest house."

"Not sure that's the right idea," he said, but turned the Jeep away from the sun through the windshield. West. "You've got another day in town—Barrows isn't letting anyone out of the county. Something about evidence, like he's actually trying to . . . I could take you home, though."

Home? My vision opened up to include his hopeful face.

"My home, I mean." He cleared his throat. "You can have the guest room there as long as you need, grab a shower. I'll find some clothes for you, something warmer. The nights here get really—well, you know that now. I'll put the kettle on for tea, or hot chocolate. Or are you a coffee drinker?"

"You don't live over the bridge."

"No, I'm on the troll side—the Lower Peninsula—that's what they say. My half acre butts up against the wilderness at the south edge of my park," he said. "The park, I mean. It's quiet."

"Yes."

"Yes? To . . . which parts?"

I noticed his hands on the wheel. They were good hands. I could put everything into them, just now. I didn't need to pull on the wheel. I was not the driver. I was not in command.

"All of it?"

I nodded.

"I just need to check in with Erica Ruth—is that OK? Just five minutes and then we'll go home."

We drove. Small houses, tree-lined streets, then green. Trees, fields, more trees. The sign for the park and then Warren was speaking. ". . . just a minute or two, I promise. Are you still cold? I can leave the heat on."

We had stopped. The blowers blasted, all the warm air turned toward me.

My hands were cold. I clenched my fists, open, closed, the injured one stiff and sore, warming them. I found myself looking at my own fingerprints. Was it possible? Had Bix been in the guest house? The Jeep grew warm, then hot. My vision widened to take in the empty driver's seat, the keys in the ignition.

For a moment I felt the wind on my face as I drove home, my real home, my knuckles sunburned on the steering wheel. Home. But what was home? Nothing, except my stuff might have been moved out and replaced with doll furniture, for the space. I couldn't remember the real estate agent's name. I reached for my phone to call him. Get out of the house. I will never sell the house. I need the house. I have nothing and now, not even memory, not even certainty.

No phone.

I needed the house. I needed . . . Michele.

The wind was against my face, the door open, the Jeep still running. I stumbled into the gate house, the screen door slapping behind me.

Erica Ruth turned and stared, taking in the mess of me wrapped in Warren's green uniform jacket. It hung almost to my knees. "Why are you— What happened now?"

"Could I use the phone? Long distance? I need to call my sister."

"Warren will be out in a minute."

"It won't be more than a minute," I said, crossing the room.

Erica put the phone up on the counter between us, more to shield herself, it seemed, than to offer me what I wanted.

I dialed. Michele. Pick up, pick up.

Voice mail.

I hung up and dialed again. No answer.

A third time. The dial tone purred in my ears. It wasn't like Michele not to pick up her cell phone. She was glued to it, except when the girls needed her, or when she was driving. Had something happened to one of the girls? And then I realized: something had happened to *me*. And further, she knew where I was. I'd told her when I'd called the day before from the hospital. If she wasn't picking up, she was driving. She could be on her way.

"What does your sister look like?" Erica Ruth said. "There was a woman here looking for you."

I swiped at my wet eyes with the back of my hand. "Already?" I said. Hope filled my chest. It would be OK. Someone would come rushing in to bang on the doors after all. I wiped my nose and thought it over. "I didn't call her until yesterday."

"Oh," Erica Ruth said. She chewed her lip, looked out the window. "Maybe not, then. She was asking about the Wallace reservation. I just assumed she was with you."

I didn't know how she'd arranged it so quickly but I was willing to believe. She was here already. She would whisk me away, just as she had the day of the funeral, when the woman with the navy dress—

"Are you OK?" Erica Ruth said. "Should I get Warren?"

I had seen her. The woman. The woman with the cheap haircut and the bad-fitting dress, but she hadn't been wearing the dress this time, of course. A bright blue jacket, zipped tight, even in the heat of summer. I'd seen her.

My eyes found Erica Ruth's. Impossible. But hadn't I? I could see the woman's face, clear as day. Her dumb beaded shoes, not good for walking. Those shoes, on the stairs—*passing* me on the stairs at the motel, before Dev had carried my case up for me. The blue jacket lit up in my memory, like bright bulbs on a strand of Christmas lights, back, back to the bench outside the breakfast place. Then, the same blue coat, public beach, her head tilted toward the water, as though the waves spoke to her and she was listening. I had recognized the woman's sadness that day but not the woman herself. Her. The woman from the funeral who had come to claim her share of my grief, who had turned Bix's funeral into a spectacle which had pushed even more of my friends away from me. The woman who had accosted me even in my own dreams. She. Her. Here. But—why? Why had she followed me to this place? And how?

"She was here?"

"Well, someone . . . I had to explain to her that the guest house was closed because of the— But she gave the name Wallace, so I thought—"

"She said her name was Wallace?"

Erica Ruth swallowed hard at my tone.

It made no sense. So little that had happened this week did, but this was too much. Too much a coincidence, too harsh a reality. There was the whole world, after all, an entire planet for this woman to exist upon, but she had come to the same town, the same patch of protected dark sky—

For a moment my mind went blank, black. The chattering nervous voice in my head that was my own churning wheel of thought gave out, and all was calm. The water lapped at my bare feet, and the only sound was the breeze rustling at the sea grasses behind me. Bix, holding my hand as we walked the beach to the viewing area. At night, Bix, putting his arm around my shoulders and pointing out a constellation I might have otherwise missed. Bix, pulling me to the suite behind the kitchen and dancing me toward the bed.

That's the way it should have gone. But I had not been here. "She said her name was Wallace?"

"No, she said the reservation was under that name, not that *her* name— What is it? Are you OK? I'll get Warren."

"Erica Ruth," I said. My voice was rotten, a creaking board. She stopped.

"When I checked in," I said. "You couldn't find my name in your paperwork."

She was nodding but uncomfortable.

"You found the reservation under Bix's name, or you wouldn't have given me the room. Benedict Wallace."

"I found his reservation."

"Under his name," I said.

"Yes."

The defenses had started to build internally. It was all a mistake. I hadn't seen what I'd seen. She was not here. She couldn't be. There was no reason for her to be here. So much of what I'd seen this week I'd started to doubt. Did I sleepwalk or not? Had Dev really cornered Martha about the father of her baby? Had I been here before? The filmstrip jumped and caught, my eye twitching to let it loose.

"Only?" I said.

"What do you mean?"

"Was there another name with the reservation? Besides *Benedict* Wallace?"

Erica Ruth slowly turned to the computer and tapped around on the keyboard. I couldn't tell if she was researching or stalling.

"Eden," she said. "Eden Wallace."

I took a deep breath. "OK," I said. I wiped at my eyes again, in relief. "OK." Breathe in, breathe out.

"But . . ."

"What?"

"I'm the one . . ." she said. "I typed that name. When you checked in, you gave me your name and I—I thought we'd got it wrong somehow."

I'd seen her. She was here. I couldn't breathe in or out. "Do you remember the name you had? The one that was wrong?"

Erica Ruth didn't say anything for a long time. The earth turned under us. I knew what she would say. It was the only thing that made any sense out of this long senseless weekend. We said it together. "Colleen."

My heart thundered in my chest. I didn't think I could find enough oxygen to confirm the worst, but I had to say it. "Rynski? Colleen Rynski?"

Erica Ruth frowned. "That name sounds . . ."

She dug out a clipboard from the counter and raked through the loose pages. Warren had gone to the clipboard the day Dev, Paris, and I had come to complain about the shared reservation. The clipboard was the final say? The clipboard was God.

Erica Ruth found what she'd been looking for and peered at the page. I had gone somewhere else. I had gone back to the house in Chicago, the back deck, the night sky overhead. Before I was afraid of the night, of the dark, of the future and the past, and the present, of everything. I went back to the deck, under the glow of streetlights and billboards and streetlamps at every corner and in the alley and bright neon at every store window OPEN, glow and sparkle everywhere you looked. To the deck, where Bix sat brooding, beer in hand. He'd been gone the week before, some project he had going on, some outing for work, arriving home tired and short-tempered. That night he'd gotten home late again, didn't want dinner. It was too cold for the deck, but he was out there, staring into a starless sky. *What are you doing out here?* I must have said. Something like that. And he'd said, after a little prodding, *Thinking about the ways life didn't turn out the way I meant it to.*

That had turned on the faucet of things you had to say to such sentiments. They hardly needed to be said at this point, did they? Reassurances. We both knew them.

We both needed me to say them, though, or I would have had to ask what he meant, which way had things gone wrong?

I didn't know what I was afraid of, exactly, but I knew there were words he could say that would ruin everything. And so I played along. *You're working as hard as two people*, I said, and he had laughed a little. We'd ended up in bed, like the old days, except that in the dark that night, he was different—forceful, almost brutish. In the dark, he turned into someone I didn't know. And I had wondered then, maybe for the first time: Who had he been treating like this? Whose fuck was this?

*Click*. "Eden?"

I shook the image from my mind to find Warren in the door. Erica Ruth beckoned to him and handed the clipboard over, pointing at a spot on the page she'd been reading. He stared at it for a long moment, frowning. "Who's Colleen Wallace?"

I fell to my knees.

The two of them rushed over and tried to urge me back on my feet. But my strength would not let me try. The top of me was heavy, my head, my heart. I lay forward over my knees on the dirty floor in Warren Hoyt's too-big jacket and cried into the floorboards. For a moment, I saw myself from above, and I was Hillary, wailing into the floor of the guest house. I had lost him. I had lost him all over again.

"I don't understand," Warren said.

"I thought I just had the name wrong somehow," Erica Ruth said. She meant to sound defensive but had started to cry, too. "That's what I thought."

"Well, who is it?"

I breathed into the cold floor. The silence drew out.

"His girlfriend, I think," Erica Ruth finally said quietly. "His, uh. Mistress?"

"Whose?"

"*Her* husband's."

I sat back on my heels in time to see Hoyt's expression morph into confusion. "He died, though," he said.

"After he made the reservations," Erica Ruth said. "For him and . . ." She gestured toward the clipboard.

"Oh," Warren said, prim and astonished. They both looked at me. "Not for your anniversary then."

Erica Ruth grabbed the clipboard and shoved it under his nose again. He looked where she pointed. I could see it in my mind, though I hadn't seen it written there. I had never even considered the two names used together. *Colleen Wallace.* Wallace. Not a mistake.

Erica Ruth whispered something to Warren. I heard *Rynski*.

"She was *here*?" I said.

"I don't—the morning after the—" She swallowed. Her face was blotchy red. "*Body.* I was here by myself until the sheriff came and everything was so confusing and I sent her away."

"You sent her to the Hide-a-Way," I guessed.

"It was the only place with rooms," Erica Ruth whispered. "They hadn't even sent you there yet."

"Wait," Warren said, looking at me. "Eden's husband's, uh, girlfriend showed up here? To check in?"

"No," Erica Ruth said, looking uncertainly at me. "I don't know."

I let the moment draw out, but there was no way around it. "Her mother," I said.

It made sense to me, but of course not to them.

"The accident . . ." I started over. "Bix killed four people and himself. One of them was . . ." I had trouble with the name.

I didn't like to say it. When he died, the name meant nothing to me, and now they were two syllables I'd rather never hear again. "Colleen. He killed his girlfriend in the crash. She was in his car and he was drunk, and now she's dead, too. They said on the news—they said 'his wife.' And that's how I heard. That's how I found out." And then the slut's mother had crashed his funeral and caused a scene and now she'd come all this way to hold up her hands to me and cry. *You're not the only one.* And I wasn't. Not by far. But I was the one still here, the one who could be scolded and shamed, the one shoved into the limelight. The mother wanted someone to pay, and though someone had and would, always—it was not enough. I knew how she felt. It would never be enough.

"She wanted to check in?" Warren said.

Erica Ruth nodded. "The guest house was closed because of the, *um*, but of course it was already full anyway, and that's when she started asking all these questions about the reservation. I thought she was *with* you, not— And then she asked about renting a boat, but she wanted someone to take her out, not just, you know, a rental or the ferry—I swear I didn't know what was happening because she said the name *Wallace* and she had the paperwork printed out, but we know the Rynskis. They come here all the—"

"The Rynskis?" Warren said. "The one whose daughter—" He looked at me. "Oh."

"Right," Erica Ruth said. "She started telling me things about her daughter and—"

"What did she say?" I asked.

They both turned to me.

"About Colleen. Really," I said. "I want to hear."

Warren nodded at Erica Ruth to go ahead but she didn't

want to. She put her hand to her mouth to stop the sob there. "She said her daughter had died in a car wreck, that a drunk driver caused a big accident. And she wanted to spread the"— she swallowed hard—"ashes in the lake. She said Colleen loved it here. She thought they might get—"

She wouldn't look at me.

"Engaged? Married? They might get married here someday?"

"She said their family used to come up here all the time when Colleen was a little girl. She said it would have been—it would have been—"

"Perfect," I said. "It would have been perfect, except he was already married."

# Chapter Twenty-Eight

**W**arren sighed and squirmed in the Jeep's driver's seat. We were headed back toward his house, just a few minutes, he said. If I had anywhere else to go, I would have gone there.

The sky had gone a leaden gray, with clouds hanging low. No stars tonight, which was fine by me. I wasn't going to allow any star talk. Things got confusing when he started up with that. All I wanted was the guest bed, as advertised. And maybe some of that tea when I woke up. Food. I hadn't had a meal that didn't come from a gas station in days.

Warren cleared his throat.

"What?" I said, peevish. I felt beholden to Warren and mad about that, and now he had to have a word or two, elbowing his way into my renewed grief, the stoked anger. He probably wanted to tell me how great the Rynskis were.

"People sign in under married names all the time," he said. "It doesn't mean anything."

"You're missing the part where he was bringing her here instead of me." In my mind, as Erica Ruth laid out the details, I had started to connect the dots—as simple as drawing pictures of bears and cups around clumps of his precious stars to make sense where there was none. Constellations made out of the pieces Bix had left me. Why had he planned the trip so far in advance, so against his devil-may-care attitude toward the future? Why come to the dark sky park at all, when we had never been stargazers? But most of all, why had Bix's handprint—in the system from one of his youthful dalliances with the law—been found in the guest house? Why was that woman here in town at the same time? She'd only be here if—if Colleen had been the intended guest, if this place had turned up on Colleen's calendar, if Bix's plans had been found among the ruins of Colleen's too-short life, the same way they had shown up for me among his.

It was the timing that made me understand, at last. Bix was not a natural planner. He was driven—he was Army, after all—but not pragmatic in that way, unless he was on a tear about something he wanted. Like the insurance policies he'd forced me to sell him as he tried to lure me toward a bigger career. Like the photography lessons he'd cleared my calendar for. Those hadn't been for me. They were to build a better me. I was a project at first, his one lone troop left to train, and then I was a liability. He needed to leave me, and he wanted me viable. He wanted me *standing on my own two feet*—weren't those the words he had used?

So the reservations at the guest house had nothing to do with how difficult the suite was to obtain. He was clearing his own calendar, too, giving himself a deadline, a goal. He'd given himself a ticking clock during which I could be shifted out of his life and he'd be a man free to take his girlfriend to see the stars. Not just a free man but a man with a clean conscience, a man who had prepared his wife for life without him, for when he ditched her.

His girlfriend, then, served as the center of this entire universe, the stargazer, the influence that had made Bix turn his eyes to the sky and bemoan the light pollution. From that, I could backtrack and find the moment when Colleen's star became visible upon the horizon of our marriage. They had been dating for at least a year when they died, tragic lovers. In this scenario, I was shoved into the role of anvil.

And of fool. I hadn't fully questioned his motives at all, not the reservations, not the little stack of cash he'd been hoarding. To *leave* me. Such an idiot. I had, after all, shown up to the dark sky park with stars in my eyes, hadn't I? Talking about an anniversary, stupid blushing bride. The timing had meant nothing, only that Bix was certain he wouldn't be celebrating ten years, not with the likes of me.

I'd played another role, too. One of failure. I hadn't landed on my own two feet. I hadn't launched. Instead, I'd dug in my heels. I'd refused to see because I was scared to be left alone and then—

But I didn't like to let my mind wander too far in that direction. There was a destination at the end I didn't want to reach.

"You're missing the part where I gave him credit for being thoughtful," I said. I'd wanted to give Bix credit, for paying close attention, for offering us a new beginning. It stung, the self-delusion. "You're also skimming over the part where the woman who shamed me at my husband's funeral for being cheated on is *here*, in town."

"Why do you think she's here?" Warren said.

"Well, it sounds like she summers here."

He looked away.

"The ashes," I said. "Colleen *loved* the place, didn't you hear? And I suppose her mother's been going through . . . her things the same way I've been forced to go through his. She probably found some piece of paper, just like I did."

"Why would she think the reservation would still be held? They died—months ago."

"Who was left to cancel the reservation? They were still living in secret," I said. "In secret because of *me*, the bridge troll."

I regretted the troll thing as soon as I said it. He'd fed the word to me, ha ha, people who live below the Mackinac Bridge are trolls. But it was a joke for another world, another time.

"I get to be the bad guy in their doomed romance," I tried again. "I'm the villain."

"You were just living your life," Warren said. "No one is a villain in your story."

"Bix—"

"Not even your husband."

I couldn't yet agree. I felt as though I had been apologizing and explaining away his behavior since his death, hiding the secrets he had tried to lay wide open. But now I didn't want to. I didn't want to forgive. I had no hope of forgetting.

"I used to think he was such a great person," I said. "Saving little old ladies in the grocery line who hadn't brought enough change, fastest to offer jumper cables anytime anyone had a dead battery. I've got a story about a roof he tried to fix that would tell you all you needed to know about that man." My voice strangled to a close. "That *idiot*. He was supposed to be the good one, the catch, the prince charming. And instead he turned out to be—"

The devil, smiling.

I clamped my mouth shut. I didn't want to be talking about these things at all, let alone with Warren Hoyt. Too bad, then, that my life had boiled down to Warren Hoyt being the only person listening.

I WOKE IN the dark.

I fought out from under the heavy quilt of Warren's guest bed and found the room around me bright. As bright as could be expected, anyway, given he only had an overhead dome light and a small reading light clamped to the headboard. He hadn't been expecting a connoisseur of wattage to visit.

The window had blackout curtains, though, a nice touch. Like a promise that I would sleep the night.

I sat up and pulled the covers up to my chest. The T-shirt, weathered and soft, from Warren's own supply, had bunched up around my waist, and I was naked except for that and a pair of Warren's white crew socks, which pooled around my ankles. My clothes had gone to the laundry room next door, where the gentle sounds of the washing machine had helped lull me into a deep sleep.

The washing machine had stopped. In the silence it left, I could hear a muffled voice. Warren's, on the phone in a nearby room. Something about it was familiar and comforting.

I'd had a shower and a meal before falling asleep. Non-motel soap and a full half hour of hot water, and then a bowl of bachelor's kitchen macaroni and cheese from the box, the kind with the nuclear orange cheese powder. I could have been served the sole of my own shoe and would have eaten it.

And that's how I slept, too, as though I would have dozed in any old dog's bed in the garage. A park bench. As though I could have slept anywhere, as though I had that skill.

But what Warren lacked in cooking, he made up for in creature comforts. The house, when we'd arrived, had surprised me somehow. It was homey, comfortable. Quaint. And, except for the pantry being a bit bare, the house was just that. Small, tidy, throw pillows at the arms of the couch, just so.

Married. That's what I thought as I dragged myself through the door. Hadn't he had framed photos on his desk? He's married. I'd misread the signals.

And yet no wife or girlfriend appeared as Warren boiled water for the noodles, fetched me a robe, and searched for the T-shirt and socks. No pictures of such a person adorned the shelves in the living room.

Why was I interested? I wasn't. I had taken the fluffiest towel for my shower and hidden myself away in the steam.

We had eaten the macaroni sitting at his kitchen table, me with Warren's green-and-white-striped robe tied around me and the socks sliding down my legs. Afterward I'd decided to level with him. "Look," I said. "I'm going to need to leave the lights on in the guest room while I sleep, OK? It's perfectly acceptable for you to wonder why, but I'm too tired to talk about it now."

"OK," he said. "That's fine."

"So tell anyone else who lives here not to turn those lights out, even if I'm dead to the world."

He smiled. "No one else lives here."

The pillows. Well, subscriptions to *Architectural Digest* weren't that expensive. You could learn as much from a single turn around a Crate & Barrel.

"Is that something that was bothering you?" he said.

I had not been in close quarters with a man in nine months, and now—Sam, Dev, Warren. A different kind of immersion therapy, as Dev had called it. I pictured the swimming trunks hanging wet from the newel post when I'd arrived at the guest house. A man's territory, marked. This was a man's territory, but unmarked—decorated, instead.

"Where's that guest room?" I asked.

So I'd fallen asleep almost instantly, like a child, and now lay in bed, considering. I'd been awake for most of the last—I counted them out—three days? It was Monday, unless I had slept the entire day away. Had I? What time was it? What day?

And what was Warren nattering on about? His phone conversation was almost constant, a monologue. Or maybe it was the radio? I tilted my head, listening.

". . . with everything that's gone on out here this week, I've had the chance to see our community in a way I never have before. As a place where terrible things are possible."

I rose from the bed, giving my legs a moment to regain their battle against gravity, and reached for the robe. I peeked behind the shades to find it full daylight. Still? Again?

Out in the hall, the voice was clearer. It was the radio, the same calming voice I'd been picking up all weekend. ". . . we want to think that darkness happens somewhere else."

The laundry room door was open. Another door a few steps down the hall was pulled tight. I put my ear to the door.

". . . if we don't find a way to live under this dark sky together, how do we live with ourselves in the daylight?"

I opened the door.

# Chapter Twenty-Nine

Warren ripped the headphones off his ears and reached over and hit a button on the laptop open on his desk.

"Sorry," he said. "I didn't hear you knock."

"I didn't."

He was alone. The room was windowless, dark, spare. Acoustic tiles lined the walls and ceiling. I noticed three, no, four light sources, only one of which he had bothered to turn on. My eyes went back to the laptop. "Are you talking to someone, or—"

"Ah," he said, blushing. "I do a little radio spot on the local airwaves about the park. You know, talk up our programs and that kind of thing. Talk about the stars."

I hadn't wanted to let him star-talk, but maybe that's all he had to say. "Every night?"

"Most nights," he said. "Not that I think anyone is listening. The diner down near Pellston keeps this station on pretty much all the time, but the show doesn't run until late. Not sure who's out there at that time of the night. If they're up, they probably have a better reason than looking at the stars. Or talking about looking at the stars."

"You work a lot, early and late." I stepped into the room and hit the light switch I found on the wall. A low-yield, pale yellow light came on overhead. Not enough.

He watched me ease inside, toward the next lamp. "It's a night shift kind of job, the stars."

"But you work during the day, too." I reached for the pull on a floor lamp. Also dim.

"I like to be at the park. I just—take a lot of naps. That's a three-stage bulb," Warren said as I started to walk away.

I went back and tugged twice more on the chain. Better.

"I enjoy my work," Warren said. "So maybe I take on more hours than absolutely necessary. How about you? What do you do?"

The full answer was too complicated. I had stalked the third lamp, the desk lamp that sat within reach of Warren's right hand. His hand caught my attention again, as it had earlier on the steering wheel. Tan, with twisting veins, high knuckles and fine hairs to the wrist. I stared at his hand transfixed—I had just realized that Warren Hoyt would hear what had happened—didn't happen, but looked as though had happened—with Dev. There was something terrible about the truth, but also about the truth getting out and around to—Warren Hoyt? And then Warren's hand reached for the button on the desk lamp and pushed it for me. "OK if I do it or do you need to?" he said.

He thought I was some kind of obsessive-compulsive. Fine by me. This took it out of the realm of odd and into the realm of clinical. Whatever Hoyt wanted to believe about me was fine. I was not embarrassed by my fear anymore, just tired of it. Could I lose the fear itself just as easily as I had the shame of discovery? Could I slip from it like a snake from its skin? I had to hope it was possible. But Warren Hoyt would hear the truth about my indiscretions, and all this openhearted sincerity would be wasted on me.

"I have to go."

He looked away. "Your clothes are still in the washer. To be honest I thought you'd sleep through the night after the last few days you've had. It's only been a couple of hours. I think they'll want to see you again soon. Are you sure you don't want to lie down and— What's wrong?"

A part of me had forgotten it all. Being in Warren's house was like living in a storybook from childhood. Wolves at the door, though.

"Has anyone heard about Dev?" I said. "Is he— Has anyone—"

"No word yet." His eyes dropped to where I fiddled with the long belt of the robe then to my feet, in his own socks. I was aware, suddenly, of my bare legs, of my nakedness under the robe and long T-shirt. He looked away. "I'll put your clothes in the dryer now. Did you need anything? I've got some wine open if you wanted—"

I nearly gagged.

"You're right," I said. "I should go try to sleep more. It's only . . ."

I searched the room and found the time, at last, on the watch on Warren's wrist. Afternoon, only a few hours. Monday, then. Tomorrow was the anniversary I wouldn't celebrate, the deadline I had set for myself to decide which way life went from here. Warren let me stare at his watch as long as I needed, and then stood and pushed the button on the desk lamp. I went to the door but turned back. In the reverse pattern I had turned on each lamp, he turned them off. I watched, noticing now a few things I had not taken the time to notice before about Warren Hoyt. I pulled the lapels of the bathrobe together at my neck.

"What were you saying on your broadcast?" I said.

He stood at the doorway gazing down at me. Hungrily. I had not misread any signs, not these. "About . . . how the night sky is elegant with or without our crude drawings connecting the stars. About how it goes on with or without us." He thought for a moment. "About the total accident of human existence and the eventual blaze-out of life on Earth as we know it."

He certainly knew how to talk to women.

"Nice bedtime story." I turned for the guest room before I could say anything else. I had made enough miscalculations already this week. One more was one too many.

BACK IN THE guest room, I let the robe fall to the floor and slipped back into the cool sheets. I pulled the blankets all around me, tucking them under my legs and around my arms as best I could until I was cocooned.

I was wide awake.

The trouble with subsisting on so little sleep for so long was that I had no talent for sleep when I had the chance. It was like an atrophied muscle.

I threw back the covers and studied the bruises on my hand. The swelling had gone down. I stretched my fingers, tested my grip, studied the creases that cut across the palm of my hand, supposedly unique.

Bix had been in that guest house. He had been with that woman. In this place. The guest house was theirs. I should never have heard of it. I should never have come here.

Would I ever get to leave?

Of course the prospect of going home had its drawbacks, too.

I was stuck here. Not physically, not in Michigan, in the vacation mecca of Mackinac, surrounded by fudge shops. Stuck here in limbo until Sheriff Barrows knew why Bix's hands had ever laid upon a surface inside the park, but also until I knew what the rest of my life held.

He'd better move fast. The troops were getting thin on the ground.

Malloy.

Paris.

Martha.

Dev.

I tried to set the problem in my mind like a photo. Wide lens on a scene with the shore, the house, the kayaks leaning up against the picnic table, the chairs down at the fire pit, the slim curled grin of land that protruded out into the water. And then I narrowed the focus down and down, until all that remained was the side of the house or one edge of a lone chair at the water's edge. The periphery, gone. The context, eliminated.

Sam or Hillary. Was that what we were down to? Sam, who I'd been shut in with overnight without even the slightest concern? Or Hillary, who had made herself scarce all week-end, avoiding us all? The guy who attributed the loss of his life's work to advice he got from the murdered man? Or the woman who claimed to love the dead guy but who might have lost him if he'd actually known her a little better?

Who else was left? Martha? What kind of trouble could she have caused? But she hadn't been anywhere near the bottle of booze that had caused such trouble for Dev.

I dozed off, then woke to the sound of a phone ringing, Warren's voice answering. It was time. Time to get myself put back together and go see to the end of this.

I was reaching for the door when someone knocked on the other side.

"Yes?" I said. The robe lay on the floor.

"Sheriff Barrows wants us down at the station," Warren said through the door.

"Us?"

"He sounded peeved," Warren said.

I had told Barrows that Hoyt doubted his ability to solve the murder. Did we have to come to the carpet for that? Or had something happened? My first thoughts went to Dev. Then Paris. What if something had gone wrong with Martha and the baby? God, where was Sam? Hillary? All of it came rushing back.

I didn't want to go. I'd relaxed since being at Warren's house. I felt safe and—protected? Cared for.

I was afraid of that, too. No. I was afraid of that more than anything. It was definitely time to go.

# Chapter Thirty

The lobby of the police station was empty. Warren and I were passed through to the back and escorted into one of the cold interrogation rooms, together.

Warren's knee bounced under the table as we waited. I caught his eye, and he stopped, glancing down at the logo on the warm fleece he'd lent me. *Straits Point International Dark Sky Park*, it read in white stitching. My jeans were still damp at the seams.

The door opened. Barrows strode in and motioned for Warren. "Just the man I'm looking for," he said. He pointed to me. "You stay here. I have plenty to talk to you about, too."

Warren went with Barrows, throwing a last encouraging smile at me over his shoulder before the door closed behind them. I had been fine with sitting still until the sheriff had taken Warren away, but now I felt caged. I stood and paced around the table once, went to the door and listened at it, took another turn around the table. I had a bad feeling and couldn't figure out where it was coming from, other than not knowing what was happening. What had happened already.

So many lives hung in the balance. They were not lives I had cared about or even known about four days ago, but now we were strung up together. Bound, in the way of hostages.

The door opened. I hurried to sit down.

Officer Cooley entered and sat at the corner of the table closest to the door. She opened her notebook and lay a pen across the empty page, crossed her arms, and finally looked at me.

"Haven't seen you in a while," I said.

"Yeah, I was off duty when you sent the last one to the ER," she said.

"I had no part in— Is he—"

"He's alive. His girlfriend is not fine, but she's probably going to make it." She shot me a look. "And in case you've lost count, that first guy is still dead."

"So what was it? What happened to Dev?"

"Let's wait 'til Sheriff gets here," she said. "He's the one who gets to ask the questions."

"I don't care who asks the questions," I said. "I just want answers to some of them."

She picked up her pen and leaned over her notebook. I peeked, caught a glimpse of a little dog sketched in the corner of the page. Cooley could be a hard case. Would not say a foul word to save her life and then when she got near me, something barbed and cruel inside her came out. Something about her reminded me of my sister. My big sister who loved me, cared for me, took care of me—and yet charged me dearly for every favor in what she might say about me and my life choices. It had always been this way. Five years older, she treated me like the kid she was sitting whose parents were late to come back. "What's your deal, Cooley?"

She looked up, surprised. "Maybe I don't like people coming into my town and messing it up."

I thought maybe she didn't like people coming into her town and reminding her that her town wasn't the only place in the world. She didn't like the park much, either. In the same way, the depth of the universe must remind her of a shallow life.

"Your town, frankly, can go to hell." Nice enough place, but I guess the world's largest front porch didn't have a seat for me.

The door opened again. Barrows made himself comfortable at what I had come to think of as his usual spot. Cooley flipped the page on her notebook and sat back. "OK," Barrows said. "Your friend Hoyt shouldn't have sprung you like he did this morning. I could have him arrested for aiding and abetting, if I had half a mind to—"

"But I wasn't under—"

"*But* I don't, and now you stink a lot less than you did when I put you in there, so that's all right. Now. Let's get back to where we were yesterday. In fact, let's start at the beginning."

We started at the beginning. The time I arrived at the guest house, in which order I met the others, what I'd heard and learned about each of them as the afternoon passed and I had decided to stay on. Each step drew us closer to the natural end of the story. I began to live in dread of it.

"And you were there to celebrate an anniversary?" Barrows said.

"Celebrate," I said. "No. That was never the right word. It's really not right now that I know how his handprint got left here."

"Hoyt filled us in," he said. "He was here with another woman?"

"This trip—it was for her," I said. Cooley had stopped note taking and gazed upon me with what could only be pity. I glared back until she started writing again. "I came here to . . . I'm not sure. *Honor*—such an Army word. Recognize the little bit of who my husband had been in life, and move on, if I could. But it turns out I was wrong to hold on to even that tiny shred of him. I never should have come here, and he never meant me to."

"And you had no prior relationship with any of those people? Think hard," he said. "Not through work, church, met on vacation or—"

"I don't know them," I said. "Well, I didn't. I feel like I know them now."

"Well enough to have the will of one of them in your suitcase?"

They'd searched my room again? Because of Dev? I'd forgotten about the will. I didn't know what to say, what to admit to. The truth seemed, at last, like the best bet. "I stole it."

He nodded. "And why was that?"

"I thought," I said. "I don't know—I thought there might be something in there that would help me figure out what was going on."

He let my words drift in the air for a moment. "And why would you need to figure out what's going on? Bit of a busy-body, aren't you? A voyeur, maybe?" Barrows said. "I heard you were a *photographer*."

Barely true at this point, and he'd said the word distaste-fully, as though he'd mixed up photographers with bank robbers. Or pornographers. "I'll allow that I own a camera,"

I said. I had, anyway, but maybe it was going to be lost to finger-quotes *evidence*, as Sam had worried about his bottles of wine.

"We took a look at that camera, as a matter of fact. But there are no photos on it," he said. "Strange, wouldn't you say? Where are the photos?"

I looked between them, waiting for a question I could understand.

"The memory card was professional-grade wiped," Cooley said. "The tech guy took a look."

"Oh, no," I said. "No, that was a brand-new memory card in the camera. It's never been used."

"You bought it for the trip but haven't used it?" Barrows said. "People come up here with cameras, they usually don't hold themselves back."

I had been trying to tell the truth here. He was begging me to lie. "It's not *brand* new. Look, the truth is I don't take photos anymore," I said. "I see them everywhere I look, but I can't—I haven't, at least."

"Haven't what?"

"Pulled the trigger," I said. "Not since Bix died."

"Interesting choice of words," Barrows said. "What did you take photos of before you stopped?"

"Anything," I said. A smear of paint on a wall that shouldn't have been there. A shadow falling sharp across a lonely street. A face lit up by a neon sign in the ramen shop window. Chicago provided the canvas. I was drawn to a shiny surface or a rain puddle reflecting a street scene, to scratches and dents and other textures of life. "Whatever caught my eye. Whatever I wanted to pay attention to." The image of Bix's stretched smile came to me. Whatever I wanted to understand.

Someone knocked on the door. Barrows winked at me and stood up. He disappeared through the door and closed it behind him.

After a bit of silence, Cooley spoke up. "So you . . . stayed in the jail last night? Rather than go outside in the dark? Looks like you got a cozy place to stay tonight. Whose sweatshirt are you wearing there?"

"You panty-thieves stole all my clothes," I said. "Warren just—"

"War-*ren*," she sang, schoolyard-style.

"—let me sleep in his guest room for a few hours. He's being nice. So little of that going around," I said pointedly.

"That's not him being nice. That's just him being a hero."

I sat back. I didn't want a hero. I'd already outlived one, just barely. "I don't need anyone to save me."

"Warren Hoyt's known for plucking drowning things out of the lake," she said. "You're just one more."

Was I drowning? "Officer Cooley, I think you've mistaken me for some kind of damsel in distress." I glanced toward the door, willing it to open and for things to get moving again. Shadows shifted in the strip of light under the door. "What drowning things has he saved?"

"I was thinking of you more as . . . a sack of kittens nobody wants, but prove me wrong and I'll apologize."

"*What* drowning things?" I said.

"Oh, he rescues people all the time. Mostly drunk b-holes trying to impress their friends on the lake. He's in the papers practically every summer," she said, "getting a plaque from somebody."

She couldn't even say *butt*. Yet she had said cutting things to me, harsh things. True things.

In my visits to the park's info station, Warren's office there, and now his home, I hadn't seen any plaques. But then maybe I hadn't found the right room. God, what if they were on his bedroom walls?

"Is that why you don't like him?" I said. "He gets too many gold stars, instead of you? He outshines the brightest Emmet County tin star?"

"I didn't say I didn't like him," she said, looking horrified. "Nothing wrong with saving people, even if they are b—"

"B-holes, yes, so then why the attitude?"

Cooley flicked at the corners of the pages in her notebook with her pen. "It's nothing to do with him. Or you, even."

"What then?"

"They told me today, official. They won't get me another pup to train. No room in the budget."

"Oh," I said. "I'm sorry. Are they going to make you ride with another officer, then? The human kind?"

"No, that's all fine. But— I mean, I don't want anyone in the car with me if it's not a dog."

"But surely a person is better company—well, no. I guess not some people."

"Dogs are great company," she said. Her eyes lit bright with enthusiasm as she started to expound—we were suddenly friends again—and then the door opened.

Barrows pointed another officer into the room. He carried a laptop in and set it up with the screen facing me.

"What's this?" I sat up. The image on the screen was black-and-white, a video, stilled. I recognized the hallway downstairs, the cells lined up two and two, and my own sleeping form curled up on the slab.

"When you're ready," Barrows said. The officer, young,

buzz-cut blonde—this one's name tag said Jahlmersson—hit a key on the keyboard. The tech guy, I presumed.

The image didn't move, but then I did. The me captured inside the cell did. A foot twitched, then kicked, my folded arms squeezed more tightly around my chest.

I looked up at Barrows. He nodded me back to the video.

And then the video-me sat up. The footage had a tint of green in the highlight areas, and so my face appeared pale, sick. The details were lost in the grainy footage. All I could tell was that I was moving, first seated and jumpy, then on my feet and erratic, walking in one direction until I encountered a wall and then another direction. The video had no sound, but I could see my feet shuffling, see my lips moving.

In the interrogation room, watching the footage surrounded by Cooley, Barrows, this Jahlmersson kid, I was cold, despite Warren's fleece. I did not like myself in pictures, had avoided video of myself as best as I could all my life. I stayed behind the camera for a reason. Watching the green-faced girl on the video sent me somewhere else for a moment, but I brought myself back—*click*—in time to watch her do what I knew she would do. She went to the door and twined her fingers through the wire hashes of the cell and spoke—

*He did this. He did.*

But of course the video mouth moved without a soundtrack. I looked like a fish out of water, mouth gasping. She stood at the cell door for a long time, and then stopped, looked about her, returned quickly to the slab, and curled herself upon it.

"That's enough," Barrows said.

Cooley's pen, which she had been holding between her teeth, fell to the table. Jahlmersson hit the space bar on the keyboard to pause the video, picked up his laptop, and headed for the door. Barrows marched around the table until he was directly on the other side of it from me, then leaned on his hands. A slick of sweat had collected on his upper lip.

"Now," he said. "What was that?"

"A bad dream," I said.

"A bad weekend," he said. "I'm no expert, but that looked like sleepwalking to me. Let's start again. At the beginning."

# Chapter Thirty-One

We started back at the beginning, again, the sheriff and I—back to the moment when I had entered the guest house and stood looking at the pool of water dripping from the pair of swim trunks hanging from the newel post at the bottom of the stairs. Back to the moment before Dev sauntered regally down to meet me. My breath caught, thinking of myself, there at the bottom of the stairs receiving a visit from royalty. I hadn't known. I'd thought I'd already gone through the worst of it. I had been apologizing and cringing for all that time, wishing away the one terrible thing Bix had done that had wiped out all the other good he'd put out into the world. Fine, one of the few terrible things. But the other things had only been done to me, and I had forgiven him. Expediently, as with an eviction, which is what it was.

The sheriff and I went over the story and over it again, but I had stopped being able to tell new information. I couldn't tell the story the way Sheriff Barrows wanted to hear it: in full, linearly, competently, using the words he expected, that he needed, to hear. When I stumbled over something or got something out of order, he made me start over at the swim trunks, Dev on the stairs. I couldn't. I couldn't do it anymore.

"Could I have a drink of water?"

"Let's just get through this one time," he said.

"Come on, Jeff," Cooley said.

He frowned at her. "Fine. Go get her some water."

"Let's all take a break," Cooley said. "Maybe if she had a break, used the bathroom, got some water, maybe got some *sleep*, we could do better tomorrow?"

We'd been at it for a few hours now. She shouldn't promise anyone that I would come back better rested. It was a dead end, that promise.

A few minutes later, I emerged from the ladies' room to find Cooley guarding the door, a bottle of water in her hand. She watched me gulp down half of it. "Better?"

"Thanks," I said. "For that. I don't know if I can tell it any better, though. It's weird how fast stuff leaks out of your memory."

"You're doing OK. Seen worse, for sure. Like—well, I shouldn't name names."

"Hillary? I bet Hillary is the worst."

She smiled. "She's pretty bad. I don't think she was paying attention to anything other than her good-looking boyfriend." She looked at me shrewdly. "But you were paying attention—pretty well, actually, even if you weren't taking the pictures you wanted to take."

I drank down the rest of the water and then turned to the water fountain to refill it. "You can see how well it's working out for me."

"What if you told it using pictures? Like, instead of words?"

"I told you. I didn't take any—"

"No, I mean you'd have to use words, of course, but if you told us what you remembered through . . . I don't know what I mean. It's dumb. Come on and I'll drop you off at the motel."

"The motel?" I looked down the hall toward the lobby door.

"We sent him home," she said. "Your room at the motel is available again. Your stuff is there. Your clothes. On the way out, we'll grab your camera. And your phone."

"My phone? And my keys? When can I—"

"Don't get ahead of yourself," she said. "Soon. Come on."

We turned toward the lobby just as the door to one of the other interrogation rooms opened and an officer emerged. Behind him, inexplicably, Dev in rumpled clothes.

"Oh, my God," I said. Finally, finally, some good news. "Are you OK?"

Dev's black eyes brushed over me and away. He walked past without acknowledgment. The officer gave an apologetic shrug and followed him to the security door and through it.

"What was that?" I hadn't anticipated a warm welcome or anything, but—what had I expected?

"I guess his, uh, feelings have changed."

I shot her a look. "No *feelings* came into it. It's fine," I said. "Was he—poisoned or what? I suppose he thinks I did it and so therefore I did everything else, too? What was in that bottle?"

"Nothing's back from the lab. Something nasty in that cup, though."

"Nastier than the liquor we were drinking? I told—wait. Just the one cup?"

"Probably both, right? He might have saved your life by drinking first."

"Who would—" But I had been trying to tell that story for a day now. Sam had been in my room. Hillary had been in my room. But I couldn't take it past that. I couldn't begin to accuse Sam of tainting the plastic cups in my motel room while he brushed his teeth, having stayed a gentlemanly distance from me while I slept. I couldn't imagine a valid reason why Hillary had come all this way with Malloy only to kill him. She wanted a proposal, not a funeral. Neither of them had been at the railing when Paris crashed to the floor below.

None of the scenarios made any sense.

"Come on," Cooley said. "He's probably gone by now."

Like he was some boyfriend I was feuding with.

Outside, my phone in hand, I waited by the back door of Cooley's cruiser to be let in.

"You can sit up front," she said.

It was a measure of trust I hadn't expected. I bowed my head to hide the tremble at my lip. A tiny bit of friendship, after all this, was the feather drifting down on the scales that tilted everything toward a breakdown. "Thank you," I said, my voice thick. I cleared my throat. "So, what kind of dog makes a good police partner?"

IT WAS ALMOST 8:00 p.m. by the time Cooley dropped me off at the motel office, where the man behind the desk hesitated to give me a new key. He finally handed it over, warning again of the extras. I had not eaten since Warren's macaroni and cheese but didn't have the energy even to face the clerk at the gas station. With the two bucks I found in my pocket, I went through the breezeway behind the stairs to the vending machine and leaned on the glass, sorting my options into food groups. Fruit group: candy-coated apple pie, fruit chews, cherry cough drops. Chocolate group: with or without nuts, without or without caramel. Dairy: Milk Duds. The potato chips constituted the first vegetable to cross my path in many a day.

In the end, I selected the cheese crackers to make up for the ones I'd brought with me from Chicago, the ones the others had swiped. I had just enough cash for a bottle of juice from the drink machine. Something with electrolytes, whatever that got me.

I turned to go up to my room. It was the golden hour again, the orange rays of sunlight shooting across the wall of the breezeway like a stab. It was beautiful. Beauty, right here at the Hide-a-Way.

I was staring at it when I realized someone stood at the base of the staircase out front, watching me.

The woman from Bix's funeral. Colleen's mother.

I wished for darkness. If only night would fall, *click*, in an instant, I'd be hidden here among the shadows.

She had seen me. It was too late to rely on the collapse of the solar system.

She wore flat-footed sandals and white capris, her tender, pale legs thick and exposed. Her bad hair was damp at the temples, curling and dark. At first I thought she would continue up the stairs and leave things as they were. Why break things that were already irreversibly broken? And then—

"You know who I am, right?"

I nodded.

"And why I'm here?" she said. Her tone was tart.

I looked down at my dusty shoes and nodded again. I felt like a child being scolded.

"Look at me," she said.

I did.

"That's all I wanted," she said. "Back at the funeral. I just wanted someone to see me. I just wanted to say her name again."

I understood that.

"It's just—it hurts so bad," she said.

"I wish it didn't," I said.

Her head bowed. I felt myself holding my breath. I let it out.

"I wish that for you, too," she said to her sandals. "I wish I weren't so—angry? I suppose that's all it is. Angry that she went around with a married man, angry that he was *married*. That's fair. Angry that he bothered her, that he paid her any attention at all. I'm so *mad* . . . that he was so *charming*. I warned her about him, did you know? I always watch out for charming people."

"Charm is the worst."

She smiled, but her cheeks trembled. "I'm sorry I came to his funeral. I wish I could undo that. It was disrespectful to do what I did."

All she had wanted was for her pain to be acknowledged, but what did I want? I wanted for my pain to be diminished. I simply hadn't come across the remedy yet that might work. I couldn't go around what had happened. Couldn't leap over it or tunnel under it. The only thing to do was go through it.

"I've been wondering," she said. "I don't know who to ask."

We both waited until she decided it was me.

"Did he—was he—I don't know how to say it, and not break your heart," she said.

I had to go through it. Was there any reason to take anyone else along with me?

"He was drunk." I reconsidered. "He had a drinking problem. And PTSD, from the front line."

She nodded. She wanted to believe that I had come to the end of the truth.

"I wish I'd made him get help," I said. I could do this. Please. Let me get through this. "He loved her," I blurted. "I mean, I don't know, exactly. He never told *me*. But I think he must have. I think he would have made a life with her. With Colleen."

She took a deep breath and let it out. She stood a little straighter. "You made her sound like a real person just then," she said. "It's been a while."

We stood in place for another moment, but there was nothing left to say. The golden hour ticked down. I felt the shadows grow long around me. At last, she turned and heaved herself up the stairs, one at a time, trudging, weary.

I waited there by the vending machines, long past the sound of her feet shuffling overhead, of her door opening and closing. Long past, until I was sure of my own legs, and could follow and get out of the dark that was coming.

## Chapter Thirty-Two

Edie, oh, my God," Michele's voice said when she picked up on the first ring. "Where the *hell* have you been? Emmeline, I *know* you didn't just pinch your sister. I expect you to act like a grown-up, or I won't ever treat you— Blythe, *stop* pestering your sister or so help me . . ."

Some part of me was disappointed that I had reached Michele at home, having a normal day. Even though I'd discouraged her, I'd been so certain she would come for me. Come for me and bang on the doors, the way Sheriff Barrows had said even murderers' families did. Another part of me was relieved. She hadn't bothered. I wouldn't have to make up for this. I wouldn't have another rescue on the scorecards.

"Sorry about that," she said. "They are testing my patience in a big way this week."

Something about using up all the stockpiled school supplies while it was still summer. I listened for a while, trying to stay in the moment. I was calling from my motel room with my cell phone charging in the socket behind the nightstand. I had just enough battery for the screen to light up and about a half a bar of service. What did people use up here? Tin cans and string? My vending machine dinner awaited me and I had spent the weekend as a murder suspect, so I didn't have much patience for stories that focused on the misuse of glue sticks.

"I think they're letting me go home tomorrow," I said, interrupting her.

"So they figured out you didn't kill that guy?"

"Not sure. I think it's more likely they haven't figured out how to prove I did. I mean, I didn't—you know that. Which is why they can't prove it." I sighed and rubbed at the headache forming behind my eyes. "You know what I mean. They don't have anyone in custody for that and then—"

I'd told her about Paris falling when I'd called from the hospital, but it seemed suddenly ridiculous to add Dev's neardeath to the list. And how would I explain that I was the prime suspect for the act, since it had happened in my motel room?

"How's that woman?" she said. "The one who fell down the stairs?"

"Not great, I think. They suspect someone fixed the railing to crack, though. It wasn't an accident."

"Shut up—are you serious? Why are you still there?"

"I was needed for hours of interrogation, Michele, what do you think? Hours. Multiple days. If I could leave, I would."

"Oh, yeah? Right now you would?"

I glanced toward the windows. It would be dark behind them soon. "Thanks for reminding me of my shortcomings. You've always been so helpful that way."

"You know I love you, even with all your crazy. If you could get over that particular phobia, I would love you more."

"Why?"

"So you could babysit . . ." she said coyly.

"Really. You have a hot date or something?"

"Maybe," she said.

"You do?" I said. "Who?"

"Just someone. I met him through my friend Belinda at work, you know Belinda . . ."

Michele always assumed I knew everyone she knew. I had never heard of Belinda, or of my sister having any interest in dating again, not since she'd split with her husband right after Blythe was born. More than ten years. A long time to be alone. A long time to be stuck. I could easily see the years stack up for me.

Instead of telling Michele about seeing the woman from the funeral, about Bix's intentions, his plan and how much it had backfired, but on me, I found myself wanting to tell her about Warren. I couldn't admit to the temptation Dev had presented, but I also hesitated to speak Warren's name. It was nothing. It was all nothing. I'd be home by this time tomorrow, and I'd get back to the business of being a widow. Hillary would have to do something similar. Dev would have to figure out his new life, with or without Paris. Sam would have to find a job. Me, too. I would have to sell the house, and then stretch whatever I made in the sale to last as long as possible. Life would have to go on. Oh, and Martha. Martha would have to get back to lawyering or whatever, and maybe raise a dead man's child, too.

"Sorry, what?" I said.

"I said I gotta run, OK? They're killing each other—I mean. I need to go break up a battle. Got to go."

"OK, I'll call you when—"

She hung up. I put the phone on the nightstand to charge

and reached for my bag of cheese crackers. Hillary, Dev, Paris, Sam, Martha—there was something there in the way I had been thinking of them that made me feel uneasy, nervous. What was it?

I took a cracker out of the bag and popped it into my mouth. In my head, I saw Hillary nibbling at the same kind of snack, like a rodent. And then shoving a handful into her mouth to keep from answering some question from Sam. He would have been on to her cover story by then, or at least suspicious.

They'd eaten the entire box of crackers that day. They hadn't come prepared at all, had they? Except to drink and maybe paddle out onto the water, the exact kind of people Warren must have to pull out of the lake on occasion. No food, no initiative to go get any. No one in charge. No one with any plan.

I'd forgotten how young they seemed that day. Ducklings, hoping someone would lead them somewhere.

Huh. I held a cracker up to the light. It worked just like Cooley suggested. If I could call up an image from my memory, a photo I hadn't taken, the image gave me access to some of the finer details I couldn't call up under the glare of Barrows's questions.

Is that what she'd meant? But—what? I was supposed to tell the story of the weekend's events through images? Would that work? I felt a little insulted, as though someone had slid a picture menu across the table at me and asked me to point to what I wanted. But I had to admit that it might work. I sat back and pulled out my camera, and pointed it at the foot of the bed, where I'd sat with Dev, so recently, so long ago. *Click*.

# Chapter Thirty-Three

After a few hours, I took a break and had a shower. When I got out, I turned on the radio on the alarm clock and scrolled around until I heard Warren's voice. Space again, this time a new planet.

"The biggest sky news we're likely to get in our lifetimes—those of us that just missed the moon landing—is the announcement of Planet Nine. Sounds like a sci-fi movie title, doesn't it? Well, get to writing that story now, because it shouldn't be too much longer before we track down Planet Nine—within our own solar system. How do I know Planet Nine is out there? Well, scientists can tell something's out there past Pluto—now demoted to a dwarf planet, by the way—way past Pluto, actually, nearly 45 billion miles next door, something big is pulling on the gravity of other planetary bodies. They've got the world's strongest, most precise telescope trained on a sliver of the night sky right now, but even with all the technology and all the top minds we have on the problem, we don't yet know where it is."

I had not had a chance to listen to Warren doing his thing, knowing it was him. I opened my suitcase to find it in disarray. Ransacked. The clothes there seemed like remnants from another life, dinosaurs unearthed. My pajamas, long-lost treasures. I changed into them, noting that the copy of Malloy's will I'd swiped from Martha had been confiscated. Martha's *colleagues*—I hated that word, too, and hadn't blamed Paris one bit for telling Martha to use another one—would have to be consulted. But would Barrows think of it? Not my problem anymore. It had never been my problem. As long as they were handing over my car keys soon, I could cut out the curiosity. Malloy's killer could go unpunished. It was no matter to me.

I folded a few things and put them away into the suitcase. Tomorrow was the day.

"What does it matter, if we find Planet Nine or not?" Warren was saying. "Why do we do all these explorations, anyway? Why can't we just be happy with the paint spatter of the Milky Way, as it appears Wednesday, weather permitting, at the reopening of our own Straits Point International Dark Sky Park? I'm not going to lie, folks. When I hear about some of the deep space explorations we are doing, with unmanned craft, with that little dune buggy we wrecked on Mars, with the Hubble telescope, which brings us back photos of things we can't comprehend, I feel . . . I mean, have you seen a photo of a nebula? The Eagle Nebula has these vertical pillars of dust that make it look like a castle made of clouds. But what it is? A cradle. Honest. A cradle for newly formed stars, seven thousand light-years away. We don't fully understand the things that our explorations tell us. Even with all the science there is, we are still feeling our way through the universe, inching our way forward like, like . . . like someone in the dark."

I shivered and sat on the edge of the bed, remembering the way I felt in the viewing area, small and alone. I had the rest of my life to feel that way. I didn't need Warren telling me. My hand reached for the dial.

"It's a scary thing, our world," he said, his voice quieter. I stopped and listened. "And beyond it, a limitless, uncomprehending, unknowable—forever. And that's scary, too. The more you understand how vast it all is, how small we all are—but I don't get on the radio to give you fuel for your insomnia. I guess I happen to think that it's just fine to stand out at the park and look up at the sky without aid of a telescope, to enjoy the view, not even bother with the names of things, the shapes of the constellations—who cares? Those are just stories someone told once. What's real is that people just like you and me have been looking up into the sky for as long as humans have walked this rock. All that matters is that we are here. But it's only a minute or two. It's a blink of the eye."

His voice was less comforting, more direct. Direct, as though he spoke to me. I could picture him at his desk, frowning a little into the laptop, headphones in place. It all meant so much to him. It all scared me so much.

"Planet Nine is out there," he said, almost a sigh. "All the math tells us something big is out there. Something big, if we only keep watching. Who would look away, when the capacity for—I don't think I have the right word for the *magnitude*. When something comes along that could change life as you've understood it, why would anyone deny that gravitational pull?"

I held my breath.

"You have your reasons, I suppose," Warren said, and then signed off.

THE IMAGES CAME to me in no particular order. When I remembered something, I jotted it down. The notations would mean nothing to anyone but me, but after I was finished and sat back, I felt as though I had captured the chaos of everything that had happened and pinned it to a board, shapes built from nothing by connecting a few dots.

Tomorrow, I could lay it out in front of Barrows, and he could do whatever it was he would do with it while I collected my keys and headed home.

Wide awake and preoccupied with my assignment, I didn't notice the night fall. In the small hours of morning, I might have even gotten a few hours of sleep if I'd thought to try. But I had remembered Photoship and reached to unplug my phone. Paris and the others had said they kept in touch there, hadn't they? I'd not had a phone and reception in the same place all weekend to check it out. I pulled up the app and waded in.

How to find any of the friends there, though? I hadn't learned any of their last names. But wait—I did know the full name of one of them, thanks to his will. Patrick Malloy Halloway.

I shouldn't have worried. He had found a way to go by Malloy, simply Malloy, which made him quite easy to find. I paged through his photos, the phone's glow on my face. People laughing, someone's cute dog, someone's red-faced baby growing into a pigtailed little girl in saggy diapers, marathoners lined up with their numbers pinned to their chests,

Malloy in the middle. In every image, Malloy in the middle. The last few weeks, he had uploaded an astounding number of photos of himself, with Hillary.

Through those photos, I found Hillary's profile, too. Her images, it seemed to me, had been carefully curated to avoid including Angel and work. Nothing much was left to document other than the last three months of happiness. Malloy and Hillary over a checked table cloth, Malloy and Hillary in hiking gear on a trail. Malloy and Hillary, a photo he'd taken himself, his arm stretched out to hold the camera high. They'd taken a lot of their photos that way, always just the two of them. Where had Angel been, all this time? She was part of the story, too, even if no one except Barrows and me knew about her.

Sam's collection of images was tidy and spare. Wine labels, a few corks with the name of the winery printed on them, a couple of nice landscapes. Vineyards. And then a few photos of Sam with other people. Work friends? There was something staid and reserved to Sam in these pictures; he seemed like a different person altogether.

At this, I remembered the blankness of his rooms at the guest house and motel, his neat wardrobe, no reading material, no amusements. You knew a person through the way they spent their time, but I had no hold on Sam. Just as the sheriff wondered about me, because no one rushed forward to my defense, I wondered about Sam. Who was he?

Paris's Photoship profile was jammed with photos she had taken and uploaded, saved, shared, or had had taken of her, shared by other people. She was a star in every image, a beacon, central to every group—

A head injury. A lot depended on her waking up soon,

whole. How much would she be dimmed? The photos I thumbed through showed what a terrible loss it would be.

After a little trouble tracking down Martha's profile through her friends, I finally discovered her under the name "Marty." Sure, OK. A nickname on a public site kept her law colleagues, and her clients, out of her private life. Plus, Malloy had called her that, bringing out the dimples. The photos she shared were mostly other people's, reshared: flowers from a garden, a misspelled roadside sign, a decadent dessert.

Very few photos of Martha had been connected to her profile. There were a couple of old photos, one of Martha with another girl's arm thrown around her shoulders. The setting was a dorm room, maybe, the walls covered in posters. I paged through her photos until I found one of the whole group hanging around a picnic table, throwing peace signs and flipping off the photographer. The background was an anonymous patch of green. Paris's hair was out of its braids and big, dramatic; Malloy's sideburns were too long. Sam wore a regrettable argyle sweater vest. Dev, sporting a short beard that didn't suit him, was half in profile, eyes on Paris. She really was beautiful. They all were, chewing the scenery with their beauty, with youth. Martha sat at the end of the bench, dimples in place, happily surrounded.

Who was behind the camera? But I knew that, too. Tash.

My phone was quickly losing charge again, so I plugged it in and lay on the bed with it, my hand over the edge so the cord could reach the wall.

For a moment I wavered. It would be so easy to click over to the much-visited memorial websites and check in with a few comment sections I had been trying to wean myself from.

No. Not time to wallow.

Tash. I scrolled back to the image of Martha and the other girl. What was there to learn about the woman who had brought all these people together? Barrows knew about Angel; he had probably dealt the presence of Angel into this poker game. But did he know about Tash? Malloy had never gotten the chance to tell me—how had he phrased it?—*the sordid details*. What was there to tell about Tash?

Natasha, Michigan State University, about five years ago? Was it enough for a trail?

It was. I was not surprised to see that she had died not approximately five years ago, but precisely five years ago. They were here for an anniversary, too, just as Paris claimed. Just not a happy one.

I read, not minding the dark and then not noticing the orange fingers of sunrise that reached through a breach in the curtain. I read until they came for me one more time.

## Chapter Thirty-Four

The knock on the door was quiet but insistent. And early. I peeked out the curtain. A neat man in Sheriff's Department browns stood out on the walkway of the motel. When I opened the door, he said, looking over my shoulder, "I'm to take you in for more questions. You and—" He consulted a piece of paper in his palm. "I think this says Holly?"

"Hillary," I said, yawning and pointing to the room two doors down. My eyes were bleary. I'd fallen asleep at some point after dawn, the phone falling from my hand and unplugging itself. It hadn't fully charged, but the clock worked. The man at my door looked familiar. After a few blinks, I placed the formal demeanor and his inability to look me in the eye. This was Officer Perez, the one who'd shut me up in the jail. "What's happening? Why so early?"

"Don't know. Sheriff said to come fetch you. And to be quiet about it."

He went to knock on Hillary's door. The door between opened and Martha stuck her head out. "What's happening?"

Had she been there the whole time? Minus a night in the hospital? "Not sure," I said. "We have to go to the police station again."

"I'll get dressed."

"They didn't ask for—" But her door closed. Who was I to say they didn't need her, anyway? I should have insisted on a lawyer a long time ago.

"Bring your bags," Perez said to me while he waited for Hillary's door to crack open. She appeared with bleary, puffy eyes. "You, too, ma'am," he said. "You're both checking out now."

Hillary peered around the doorjamb to see who had been included in the invitation and then disappeared again. I retreated, too, quickly throwing things at my half-jumbled suitcase. Pajamas, wet toothbrush in, jeans and T-shirt out. At the last minute, I pulled out the fleece Warren had lent me, for the cold station. Cautiously optimistic it was the last time I would need it. I was going home.

Perez and Martha chatted pleasantly by his car as I dragged my suitcase down the stairs, clacking with every step. Hillary was just behind, dragging her case at her heels and blinking into the severe slant of the early sun. Perez hurried up the stairs and took our cases from us, lifting them and walking carefully. How quiet? Avoiding-the-reporters quiet?

"What about the others?" Martha said.

"Who are we missing?" Hillary said. "Paris is in the hospital, Malloy—" She recovered herself. "Dev is—Eden, how *is* Dev?"

Perez rolled our cases to our feet and scratched at his chin. "At least one of them's at the station already."

Ominous. Martha and I met eyes. He could only mean Sam or Dev. Martha hopped into the front seat, leaving Hillary and me to shove our cases into the backseat between us, a barrier that we treated as impermeable all the way to the station.

Inside, the lobby was full of people I didn't know. After a few seconds, they sorted themselves. Paris's parents, maybe a sister. Everyone jangled and paced, except a white-haired couple sitting quietly. Dev rushed at us, brushing past me to accost Martha. "Tell him not to do it," he said.

"What's going on?" Martha said. The quiet couple had caught her eye. Malloy's parents, had to be. Something was indeed going on. Hillary dropped her suitcase and hurried to them. I didn't get the chance to see the introduction. Dev moved in the way, pressing for Martha's attention.

"He's—" He looked at me and turned Martha away.

"Mrs. Wallace," Cooley said, leaning through the security door to the back. "You're up."

Martha marched up behind me. "No, not you," Cooley said. "He's turned down counsel. *Especially* yours. His words."

Dev pulled Martha back into a huddle, everyone too busy talking to bother with me being taken out of the room. "What's going on?" I whispered to Cooley.

"Can't say, but who's missing?"

I counted them out. Sam. "Where is he?"

She popped me into an interrogation room and closed the door. "He came to confess. Sheriff's getting the story now."

"He—confessed?" Sam? The day before I would have said he was a top prospect for the guilty party, but now the idea struck me as hollow. But that was just Sam: he was un-knowable, blank. The only thing I knew about him was that he dealt in wine, but he'd been stripped of that. Without that, what was he? A killer? "He's confessing to Malloy's murder?"

Cooley huffed impatiently. "What else would he—never mind. He said he had things he wanted to say. So Sheriff's in there with him now."

"I don't believe it."

"Why? Because he doesn't look so tough? Don't be fooled. Maybe he filed away a lot of resentment and snapped—"

"He snapped," I said. "From what?"

"Hey, I don't know," she said. "Seeing his old-time friends again and everybody else has a job and a pretty girlfriend or a future, at least. Instead of getting to listen in, I'm arguing with you. So let's just do this real quick and the sheriff said I can take you over to pick up your car."

"Just like that."

Her face twisted into disbelief. "You've been demoted from suspect to witness. Be happy about that. You've seen the jail, remember? Come on, sit. Start at the beginning and tell me what you think would be helpful to this case. You may be called up for the trial, you know. So on the day you arrived . . ."

I started to sort through the images. Wet swimming trunks on the newel post. A handsome couple, fighting as I arrived. Sam riding the stair rail.

I went through the day, snapping and sharing the photos that existed only in my head. An Adirondack chair with the slim peninsula in the background. Wine splashed out of a glass. Paris, her chin out, defending her bridesmaids' yellow dresses. Malloy's wry smile at his phone, when he must have received a text from Paris from my number. Later, Dev's expression of disgust when he saw my phone case, presumably because he recognized it from Paris's efforts with Malloy. The clearing, with the others paired off.

I skipped over the feeling I'd had there, of raw and hopeless panic, alone, small, against an endless universe. Grief as heavy as the world. Maybe I understood why Sam had done it, after all, if he had ever felt that vast emptiness from within. Was that it? It all came down to loneliness, of the loss of hope?

During certain crucial moments, no images were available in the memory bank other than the shadows cast on the wall of my room by the artificial light of the lamps. The noises in the kitchen, then the hall, the door slam.

"Were there no fingerprints on the back door?" I said. "From the person running out that night—there would be fingerprints, wouldn't there?"

"The door was clean. Wiped."

"When?" There'd been no time—but these were people who had stayed in the house waiting for the police, people who protected one another. Dev. Dev had been through the back door, with my phone to call the police. And then he'd led me through, covered in the blanket from my bed—hadn't he lifted the edge of the cover at one point? My "train," he'd called it, as I emerged into the night for the first time in nine months. But why? Because he had touched the door, too? Someone was buying up an insurance policy, there. I backed up the story and included the detail of the tug on the blanket. Who was he saving? He didn't think Sam should confess, so who did he want to take the blame? Did he know that Sam hadn't done it, because *he* had? Then why not let Sam take the blame?

"And then what?" Cooley said.

And so on: the smeared kitchen wall, Malloy with the

screwdriver in his neck, the wine bottle overturned, the corkscrew lying in a pool of red.

"Blood?" Cooley asked.

"Cabernet."

I'd gotten one thing right. A friend had done it. The closeness
of the attack, the screwdriver pulled out of the cork to begin
with. Two friends having a drink, gone wrong. The screwdriver,
easy to hand. For a moment, the image wavered. A screwdriver?
Why not the corkscrew, so close by and certainly sharper?

Back to the still life photos of my memory: Hillary kneeling
on the floor. Martha in Sam's swirling robe to cover the blood
on her nightgown, the bottoms of her feet dusty, attending to
Sam after his swoon. The beautiful face of Paris, snot dripping
from the tiny gold hoop in her nostril as she cried.

This image was interrupted by one far later in the week. I
saw Paris in the parking lot of the motel, mourning the loss of
the life she'd had planned, not just Malloy but also Dev, her
friends. One of them had done it. Did it matter which one?
Just as the fixing of the railing had assumed that someone
would lean against it and fall—one of them, but it hadn't
mattered which. Had it?

I squeezed my eyes shut and concentrated on the kitchen,
leaning over Malloy's body to check for a pulse. The softness
of his skin at his temples. The blush of red wine stained to
his lips.

"And Ridiculous Red," Cooley said.

"What?"

"He had a little lipstick there, along with the wine stains,"
she said. "Ridiculous Red. Hillary had a tube in her cosmetics
bag."

I was there, crouched over the poor man's body with my

hand reaching for his neck, letting this new information fold into my own photo, details developing out of the mist like a Polaroid. "You're sure?"

"That's what it was called. They always have names, I guess," she said. "Everyone said they'd been kissing all day."

The images petered out after Malloy's pulse could not be found. "I guess that's it, as far as the crime scene goes," I said.

Cooley, who had been making a few notations in her pad, looked up. "Why were you so surprised about Sam coming to turn himself in?"

I shook my head. "I spent a lot of time with him this weekend. It's—weird, I guess. The whole time, he was the one."

Now the image that came to me was not one of Sam sitting uncomfortably on the chair in my motel room so that I would have the bed to myself, but of his face, cracked with grief, when I told him I'd seen him carry off the wine, when he'd confessed to stealing it from his old employer. That admission I'd believed. *Don't tell Martha.* A man that broken up over the admission of theft had murdered someone? Had tinkered with railings and poisoned hotel room cups? Sam's face, when he heard that Paris had broken through the rail he'd been riding sidesaddle.

"What did he do to the stairway railing, supposedly?"

"Uh, loosened it from the wall, I think, right?"

"Yeah, but how? With what?"

"A screwdriver, I guess," she said, and then turned wide eyes to me. "Yikes."

"Not the same screwdriver, surely," I said.

"It could be—if the railing was done first," she said. "Which I guess it must have been? Probably? You guys found the screwdriver in the cabinets looking for a wine opener, right?"

That didn't sound right. I stalked a feeling of unease back to its source. "It was from one of their cars," I said. And then I remembered: Sam's rosy neck when Martha admonished him to keep his thoughts off her trunk. "It was from Martha's car, but she and Sam drove over together. Maybe he brought it in to open the wine. He was very into getting the wine open. They all were." Until the murder, and then Sam had wanted the wine spirited away, safe. The good stuff needed to be preserved. Presumably somewhere he could snatch it back, the second he and Martha were released to go. Which might not ever happen, now.

Why would he have saved the wine, if he'd planned to turn himself in? Or, what had changed since he'd hidden the wine away that made him decide to confess?

Or—was it bad wine? "Did he say where he hid the wine?"

"Who? What are you talking about?"

The photo untaken: Sam carting away the carry-all bags of wine left behind while Cooley herself waited on the other side of the house for him and Dev. To the woods? He hadn't had much time.

"No fooling," Cooley said, taking more notes as I drew the picture for her. "I wonder . . ."

"What was Dev poisoned with?"

"The labs still aren't final," she said, "but they couldn't find anything lethal. He's fine now, seems like."

"I don't understand. You started to say—"

"This is all back before we had the confession. Now we just need the labs to know what the one guy—"

"Sam."

"—poisoned the other guy—"

"Dev."

"—with. You're off the hook."

"But—" There was something to my sleepwalking. I had been sleepwalking through the last two days, surely, not to understand fully what had been attempted. I held my head just so, letting it catch up with me.

The poison, however it got to him, was not meant for Dev. Dev had no business in that room. The poison, whatever it was, could have only been meant for me. So the whole time I had allowed Sam to sleep in my room, to use my toothpaste, he'd been looking for an opportunity to put something in place that would harm me?

That scheme, however, had had randomness introduced to it from the outside—from the spur of the moment decision to let Dev into my room. If the game was to kill any one of the friends at all, Dev's attack was an outlier. It didn't belong.

"Is Sam admitting he killed Malloy, and set the trap for Paris, and poisoned a bottle he'd been drinking from? He did all of it?"

"Am I sitting in on that conversation? No, because once again, I'm the freaking chauffeur."

Cooley closed down the interview with a snap of her notes and led me out to the hallway and then to the front desk to sign for my keys. The others had gone from the lobby—but where? Now that Sam was behind those doors and would soon be behind bars, the rest of us might scatter. Paris, laid up. Malloy to the cold ground. Sam, to jail. The rest of them, wrested apart. Me? This was where I came in. Alone.

# Chapter Thirty-Five

Driving away from the station and Mackinaw City toward the park, I had the worst feeling. I was leaving something behind that would never be recovered.

Cooley flicked on the radio. I braced myself for Warren's voice, but she found a song she liked and started humming along.

I went through the checklist. My suitcase was in Cooley's trunk. My purse sat in my lap, my phone and car keys inside. My camera bag, at my feet. I had unburdened myself of all I knew back in the interrogation room.

The feeling was akin to slipping out of town in the dark of night, though it was broad daylight. I would pick up my car from the guest house's property, maybe take one parting glance at the lake, and bid it farewell until we saw each other again on the other side in Chicago.

I might have to make a hotel stop somewhere along the way home to wait out the night, but damned if I was going to stay in this town a minute more than I had already. The scenic, friendly town that had attracted so many, including the likes of a murderer.

I patted the fleece sweatshirt in my lap. If I passed the gate house to the park and saw that Warren's Jeep was not in residence, I'd stop by and leave it with Erica Ruth. If the Jeep was there—

I hadn't decided.

I had a plan for the fleece, that's all. This was not creeping off, on the lam. I had not gotten away with a thing, and neither had Sam.

But someone had.

The revelation came unbidden. I felt it in my bones. Could no one else see it?

As we turned onto the road that led to the park's entrance, something shiny in the woods caught my eye. The pinpoint of light was a flare of sunlight on the hood of a car left off the road, parked precariously angled into a drainage ditch, a couple of kayaks strapped to the top. Was that—? My curiosity was squashed as we turned into the park entrance and drove up to the gate house. No Jeep. Erica Ruth's beater was missing, too. A *Closed* sign hung on the door. The park was a ghost town, a green sawhorse barricade across both entrance and exit.

"Dangit." Cooley unbuckled her seat belt, got out and pivoted the barricade out of our path, got back in and drove us through. Then she parked again, got out, and moved the barrier back into place. She climbed back into the car and put it into gear, letting something in the dash ding at her for not fixing her seat belt. She heaved a sigh, ignored it.

The whole time I was stewing in my seat, gnawing at my thumbnail.

I had decided I didn't care if Malloy's murderer went unpunished, so why did I care if the wrong person took the blame?

I didn't. Did I? I should be gleeful to be my own person again, relieved to be on the road. But the doubts had a taste, a back-of-the-throat taste of bile and burn. Sam was a liar, a thief many times over—

But none of it was murder. Sam's punishment would not fit his crimes and someone would get away.

Someone would get away with murder.

"Cooley, someone—"

"Do you think—" Cooley started, pulling at her seat belt to stop the bing-bing of the alarm.

We were both distracted by the other, Cooley even more so by the seat belt, and then out of the corner of my eye I saw that silhouette of a figure at the side of the road, but then it wasn't a silhouette at all but a real, moving person. Real and darting into the path of our car. My hand shot out and yanked the steering wheel. Right-hand turn into oblivion. The road curved left, but we weren't on it. I'd turned the wheel too harshly, and yet not hard enough. We smacked something, the heft of it hard against the window on my side, both of us screaming but neither of us able to stop the car, as it careened off the road into the grass and hurtled down an incline and toward the trees at full speed.

It was all so quick. When the tree rose up into our path and stopped us, Cooley jerked out of her seat and toward the dash, cut to silence. The echoes of my screams rang in my ears until there was only the sound of ragged breath. Mine. No, Cooley's. She lay against me, across the center panel and heavy. We breathed. We waited.

Someone would come.

Something in the undercarriage of the car ticked to silence.

Someone would find us.

And yet.

The green barricades across the road. Do Not Enter.

Where was Warren today? Where was the young woman . . . I couldn't remember her name for a second. Erica. Ruth. Where had she gone?

No car at the entrance. No entrance. No people.

But there had been a person.

On the road.

I opened my eyes. Had the sun moved?

I'd heard something. Someone was speaking.

I opened my eyes again. Trees. Sunlight. When had I closed them? I opened them again. A cloud had passed overhead, and I was cold.

Someone would find us.

No, they wouldn't. The barriers would stop them.

Someone, speaking. I raised my head. The voice seemed far and also close by. The radio? Was it Warren?

The police radio.

"Cooley," I said. "The radio."

I reached for a pain in my neck. The taut strap of my seat belt cut into my skin there. I plucked at it.

Seat belt. She hadn't been wearing her— "Cooley," I said. "Cooley, wake up."

She was heavy against me, thrown from her seat. I reached under her and unsnapped the buckle on my seat belt. Once it retracted, I pushed Cooley up, scooted out of her way, and gently lay her back in the seat. Blood. She had blood trickling dark along her hairline.

"Cooley," I said, only reassured by the sound of her breathing. But it was hoarse and reedy, struggling. I looked at the dashboard of the car for the radio. I had never used anything like it. I smashed a few buttons. "Hello? There's been an accident," I called into the handheld piece, pushing this button, then that one. It might have made sense to someone not stunned, not exhausted. "Hello?"

Nothing happened. I dropped the radio and tried instead the door behind me. The car was canted at an angle so that the door swung out heavily. I fell out backward into pine needles and dirt upturned by our tires.

I stood and leaned on the door until the world stopped spinning. Below me, Cooley wheezed. The windshield showed a web of broken glass. It bowed out, struck from the inside. Her head, oh, God. "Cooley, hang on, OK," I said. I grabbed Warren's fleece from the floor and tucked it around her. "I'll go get help."

I had my phone out of my pocket, climbing out of the woods for the road when I remembered the sound against the car, the weight of someone or something against my window.

"Oh, no." I clawed up the incline onto the road to find the hunched form of a man, sitting on his heels, his head of dark hair lowered. "Oh, God, are you—"

It was Dev.

"Dev," I said. "Oh no, oh no. Are you hurt?"

He grimaced, trying to stand. A red plastic gas canister lay at his feet. I rushed to him and helped him up. "What are you doing here? Should you be lying down? We *hit* you, right? The car—but what, what in the world, why are you here?"

One of the silhouettes hailed from the side of the road. If Dev hadn't been running out from behind one of those cutouts, maybe Cooley would have seen him.

If she'd been wearing her seat belt, maybe—

I looked at my phone. No service, of course. The trees? Because we stood up at the top of the world, at the land's end?

"Try yours," I said to Dev.

Dev, dazed, patted at his pockets and drew out a phone, the screen shattered. He tried to revive it, but the screen remained black and useless.

The gate house. But it was far, and closed, and my phone didn't work there, anyway. A text might work. Could you text 911? Who could I text? The only number I had in my phone, thanks to Paris, was a dead man's. I tried it. Maybe it would go off in the evidence locker, who knows? Send help dark sky, it read. Park. Officer hurt.

The little timeclock symbol churned and churned. Sending. Sending.

Not *sending*.

The beach. Hadn't someone—Cooley, oh no, Cooley—someone had said the reception was better on the beach, away from the trees. We were closer to the guest house than we were to the road, anyway. Maybe one of the officers was still guarding the crime scene.

"OK, stay here and I'll run for help."

"No," he said, holding himself on his left side. He reminded me of Bix, grinning over a broken arm, but not because of similarity—in contrast. Dev's haunted eyes searched from side to side, then shifted down the incline to where Cooley's cruiser was hidden among the trees. He had a lightning-strike streak of blood across his face. "Please don't leave me alone."

He sounded scared. I was scared, too. Cooley. Cooley needed help, fast, and Dev, too. And maybe me. My head swam, the edges of my peripheral vision shimmering with the promise of a blackout.

But Cooley, first. We had to get help. I blinked through the swoon.

"Can you walk?" I said.

He reached for the gas canister and gasped, quickly pulling his hand back and tucking it against himself and the pain.

"Just leave it. We can get it later."

He shook his head, his eyes dragging across me to the tree line again.

OK, I said, and led him, haltingly, down the road toward the guest house and the shore.

# Chapter Thirty-Six

Dev panted, shuffling and shifting the gas canister to his other hand.

"Let me carry it," I said.

He shook his head, shifted it back.

"Why did you run into the road like that?"

"Was . . . in a . . . hurry."

Broken ribs, probably. He couldn't talk and walk well at the same time, so I let it go. We needed whatever speed I could urge into him. Cooley. Cooleycooleycooley and her dumb dog-smelling car, when she should have been wearing a God-danged seat belt. A *damn* seat belt. I could say it, even if she couldn't.

"I saw your car out off the road. You ran out of gas?" I said. "Never mind. Save your breath."

We shuffled a few feet. "Were you going to the hospital? Is Paris OK? Just nod or whatever."

He frowned in my general direction but didn't answer. His feet seemed to require his complete attention.

"I haven't had a chance to say," I started, trying to find an angle into the night in the motel. "The other night—"

"Stop," he gasped. "Please."

Which part of the night didn't he want to talk about? How I had turned down his substantial charms? How I had supposedly poisoned a bottle from which I'd been drinking, too?

"I didn't do anything."

"We all did . . ." He took a shallow breath and tried again. "Our part."

This seemed like an apology to me for a moment, and then a confession. And then an accusation. "I had no role in this."

He frowned again, over my shoulder. "You do . . ." he breathed. "Whether . . . you like it . . ."

The end of the saying floated in the air.

"Or not," I said, since this was how I felt. I had no part and wanted none.

Again he pointed a furrowed brow at something over my shoulder. I glanced back to see what had caught his attention and saw a sparkle through the trees. The lake. "We're getting close," I said. "Come on, hurry."

We hurried as best as Dev could while I pulled him onward with my mind. Cooley. His wheeze provided a soundtrack to our slow pace. It was asthmatic, almost as though he was allergic to the—

"Oh, my God," I said, stopping. "You weren't poisoned. You drank from a cup Sam used for wine. Red wine."

He didn't say anything but hitched the gas canister up a bit.

"Why didn't you just tell them? They're trying to figure out how one person killed Malloy, fixed the staircase to give way, and poisoned you—and that's not even how it went."

I wish I'd heard what Sam had confessed to. How many crimes had he claimed, and how many were still unaccounted for?

"You were just being a dick, not telling them about the allergy," I said. "You wanted them to think I'd poisoned you because it took the focus off all your friends."

Dev shuffled ahead of me toward the guest house with a focus I wouldn't have given him credit for. I followed.

When the sharp angles of the house came into view, I could have wept. I pulled out my phone and tried for reception. No. It had to be the beach. We had to get out of these trees and find some open space.

My car sat alone in front of the guest house. No police presence, then. I checked the sky. Time ticked on. Five hours home, at least, and if the sun set by 10:00 p.m., I had to leave by . . .

The urgency to leave scratched at me from the inside. But Cooley lay like a sack in her own cruiser. Nothing was yet settled. I brushed Dev off and ran for the corner of the house, around the picnic table, and rushed for the shore.

Nothing. My phone had never heard of reception.

"What? Come on." I hurried out to the water, shoes in the surf, but still no bars appeared. I walked south along the curve of the water to that skinny peninsula that struck out into the lake. It was the furthest from the trees I could hope to get, this pirate's ship plank, and if this didn't work, what next? I glanced down the beach—no one. Only Dev lurching around the edge of the house. The kayaks were gone.

He was trying to yell something at me, but couldn't get his breath.

"What?"

"How do I . . . get in?" he called.

"Why do you need in the house?"

He said something I couldn't hear.

"What?" I said.

"We . . . forgot some things."

"They can get you into the house later," I said. "We need to worry about Cooley." I turned my attention back to the phone. Nothing. What to do? There was no landline inside, no other houses or buildings on the park land. I turned my phone off so I could turn it on again, a fresh start the last option.

As the screen went black, I turned back to the house, where Dev still fussed at the back door.

"Sam took the wine out, if that's what you're looking for," I called. "I don't know where he put it."

He waved me off. Stubborn. He sat the gas canister down heavily, the gas, a dark line inside the canister, sloshing. He hobbled around the side of the house, using the picnic table as a crutch as he turned the corner, out of sight.

The kayaks were gone.

I watched the logo of my phone company appear on the screen, thinking.

The kayaks. They'd come in on Malloy and Hillary's car but now were strapped to Dev's car back on the road where he'd stalled out. What did it matter?

It mattered to me, for some reason. It was a little bug in the nape of my neck, inside my throat, deep in my ears, an itch I couldn't reach or quell.

Dev came back around the house, shaded his eyes, and peered up at the second-story window that looked out upon the lake. Malloy and Hillary's room, from where I'd watched Sam stashing his pirate booty away.

The kayaks were gone. What was it about that fact that bothered me?

Dev was stripping the place for parts while his friends lay in the morgue and jail, his fiancée in the intensive care unit. But that was uncharitable. Seen from another angle, he was collecting the pieces they'd left behind. He was rounding up the loose threads. He was moving his group of friends out of the building where one of them had been killed, another hurt seriously. He consolidated their belongings as well as their need to return to this place. I didn't blame him for wanting to get out of here, once and for all.

A wind rose and fluttered my hair across my eyes. I peeled the strands back. In the shadow of the house, Dev approached the back door, fretted at the handle one last time and then at its hinges, his back hiding his work. His foot nudged the gas canister, the high dark line of liquid shifting as the gas slopped inside.

The kayaks were strapped to his car. He'd already been here, scavenging. And then had left and come back. He had carried the canister to this spot, but—

The gas container was heavy. It was full.

I heard a sound and realized it was from my own mouth. The start of a question, a clarification that had no words, no form.

Dev glanced back at me. In his hands, a screwdriver.

I darted toward the shore to get off the point's dead end but stumbled on a rock, twisted an ankle, and fell knees first into a patch of gravel. When I stood, I was skinned and bloody, my jeans ripped at the knees, and Dev was hurrying to meet me.

"What did you say?" he snapped.

"Nothing. I—" The tool in his hand caught a glint of sunlight. The photo I would not take: Dev, shoulders wide, the screwdriver dangling from his hand, a jagged arc of dried blood streaked across his cheek. He saw me looking at the screwdriver.

"It's not the same one," he said.

"It wouldn't have to be."

He snorted. "If this is the worst thing you have to survive, you'll be fine. This part doesn't concern you." He looked at me strangely as he caught his breath. "But you're wrong if you think you had no part at all. None of this would have happened if you hadn't been here."

"I had nothing to do with this."

"Try again," he spat, walking toward me. I backed up, stumbling on the turned ankle. "But I don't give a shit about what happened to Malloy. Couldn't have happened to a nicer guy. I should thank you."

He had cut off access to the mainland and was backing me up almost to the tip of the headland. Straits Point, the very end of the world, where my phone might work again. On the strength of the reboot it had finally finished, it came alive in my hand, buzzing with messages and alerts I'd missed in the last few days. My attention jumped to it. Dev reached out, grabbed the phone, and threw it to the ground, where it hit a stone and shattered into three pieces: back, battery, cracked screen.

I screeched.

He looked surprised, even apologetic, at the destruction. "It's your fault—you and your phobia coming to this place, of all places."

"How is this on me? Maybe it's my dead husband's fault, since—"

"Everything has been so far," Dev said. "Why stop blaming him for it all now?"

That got me boiling, screwdriver or no screwdriver. "You don't know anything about him," I said. "And don't pretend that you care that he ever existed, or you wouldn't have tried so hard to get in my bed." But I didn't want to talk about that night in my motel room. The whole thing had nothing to do with Dev. Even when he was looking at me with that devil's grin, it had never been about him. Especially then. But Dev was right. I had put so much at Bix's feet. The sleep-deprived part of me wondered if I had willfully misunderstood the reservation I'd found among Bix's papers, just to avoid knowing what I now couldn't deny.

"I feel sorry for the guy," Dev said. "No wonder he went out on you."

Were we going to start keeping track of who went out on whom? "You're just being cruel because you can be. No one's here to make you your better self, the way you're always after Paris to be a certain way."

"Leave her out of this," he growled.

"Then you leave Bix out of it."

"You're the one who brought him up," he said. "Again and again. Let the guy be dead already. I assume that's who you meant that night."

"What are you talking about?"

"'He did this. He did this,'" he mimicked. "You were there. You really don't remember?"

*He did this.* Colleen's mother had shrieked something like it at Bix's funeral, and I had come away with it, like a song I couldn't get out of my head. He did this. "He did?"

"He did," Dev said. He stepped forward, a beseeching look on his face. I took a step backward and felt the earth give way to sand. He came at me again, but I couldn't decide if he meant me harm or only wanted to get things clear. "Malloy did. Didn't think the accusation would come from you, but he did. He broke her—over Paris!—and then she shoved her mouth full of pills. In secret, alone, with a belly full of wine. She never had a chance and she didn't give us one. We just wanted to help."

His voice choked off.

*We all did our part.* "How did you help?"

His eyes jumped all around me. "They were just to help her get through finals, she said. Just this one time, so she could study for exams."

"You got them for her. You were . . . pre-med? You had pills?"

"I knew someone—but then I don't know what happened—Sam found her body and—" He put the heel of his hand to his eye, as though in pain. "We were all complicit. All of us. But he did it. He did."

"Tash." Malloy broke her heart. Paris was the reason. Dev got the pills. Sam found the body. A belly full of wine? Maybe I understood which death Sam had confessed for, though even Dev didn't seem to know. And Martha. Where was Martha in all this? She was like a child they protected.

"Everyone thinks he's so perfect, but he killed her, just as if he'd fed her the pills himself."

If I was following along, Dev was skipping over the part where he himself had fed Tash the pills. "I was saying that," I said. "I was sleepwalking and saying that."

"So I took you to your room and shut the door, but then

what you'd said—it broke everything wide open." He took a step, reaching for me. I teetered backward, into the shallows. The water didn't stop him. He splashed in after me, his eyes pleading for something I wasn't sure I had. "It was everything we all believed. Everything we knew. We went to bed, but then I got up because Paris—I knew she was meeting him! I saw those messages she sent on your phone. Am I an idiot? I made her go back to bed, but I don't know . . . That screwdriver sat in that bottle like a gun on the counter."

There'd been several guns on that counter—the screwdriver, the bottle opener, which was far sharper. Hadn't Martha pulled an actual knife out of the drawer at one point? Everything he was saying pinged around in my head. "Over Paris," I said. "Malloy threw over Tash for Paris. Then how . . . how did you—"

"Well, it didn't take, did it? He threw her over, too, almost immediately. Because he was—he was what he was. And then she chose me because I was going to be a doctor, but I only decided to become a doctor so she would choose me, so who won that battle? He did. He gets to do whatever he wanted—nothing, usually—and she still loved him best, anyway."

"Paris?"

His eyes were wild. I had seen that shine before. A bad night. We would have had all the lights on. "All of them," he spat. "Everyone. Do you know how hard I worked? In school and to fit in and to be—correct? Not too foreign, not too Asian, not too anything. The American dream my parents wanted—it all rested on me, but everything came so easily to him, while he never deserved it. Never tried at anything. Never worked a day. He's a millionaire, did you know?"

"Is he?" So that's why a twenty-seven-year-old pilgrim on

the earth felt compelled to have a will. The pilgrim had sig-
nificant assets. "Born to it?"

"The Halloway's Heavenly dairy empire's prince," Dev
said. Halloway's Heavenly? I remembered Paris's hot eyes on
the pint of ice cream in my hand at the gas station. Now the
feverish eyes belonged to Dev. "An ice cream king in the making," Dev said. "Can you stand it? Milk-fed, from the ground
up. A damn silver ice cream spoon hanging from his smug
mouth, while he ruined everything around us like it didn't
matter. He was never sorry. He never felt a day of guilt in his
life, while we—we all—"

"Is that why? Why you killed him?"

He went slack, blinking at me. "I didn't kill him."

We both looked down at the screwdriver in his hand. We
stood up to our knees in the gentle water. He threw it away.
The splash several feet away should have made me feel safer.

"I didn't," he insisted.

"What's the gas for?"

He faltered, gaping up at the house. "This place," he said.
"This place took them from me." The place was also covered
in evidence, none of which he could live with. Who would get
out alive?

"But what about—" Malloy was dead, but Dev had said it
didn't matter, not to him. Sam had confessed to at least some
of the group's crimes. He would go to prison and so he was
lost, too. I was afraid to say Paris's name. Dev watched my
lips for it.

"Martha," I blurted. "Martha needs you."

"Martha doesn't need anyone," he scoffed. "Not Tash, not
Malloy. Not . . . Paris. Oh, God, Paris. What good is it being
a *physician*, when—" He shut his eyes and let his head sink

back on his shoulders. I started to wade away, but he opened his eyes and caught me by the arm. "And Martha certainly doesn't need me. She got what she wanted—"

"You'll go to prison, Dev," I said. My thoughts grasped, grasped. "Think of the baby, then."

"The baby," he mused, his grip on me going loose. "That baby is the new prince of Halloway's Heavenly. He'll never want for a thing."

"A father," I said.

He laughed. "He will, that. He'll have to be tough like me, then, instead of soft and creamy. Won't that be something, if he turns out like me?" There was something final in that. Whatever the child turned out to be, Dev didn't think he would see it. The smile left on his lips was the devil's own.

I shot out of his grip toward the house, dragging through the calf-deep water, but Dev was faster. He grabbed me by the hair and pulled me back. I fell, went under, came up choking and clawing.

"Why are you—" I swiped at his face, at the open wound, and tore out of his hold. I ran, but didn't get far.

Before I knew what was happening, I was stumbling, flailing, falling, my knee cracking against something hard under the water. I splashed forward, screaming. On hands and knees, I blinked at the rush of dark flooding the water below me. Blood? Under the water, my fingers brushed up against something unexpected. I grabbed at it.

The arc of the bottle of wine rising out of the lake was slow, solid. Full. Full like the gas canister. Loaded like a gun.

The bottle cracked against Dev's head and smashed, cabernet dark. He fell backward into the water, splashing out of sight. I crawled over another bottle, another, my hands clawing and clawed at by the bottle my knee had smashed. I scrambled to find a foothold in the sand toward the shore.

Crouching in ankle-deep waves, I hesitated, stood, and turned back.

He was not coming after me. He had not surfaced. I held the shattered neck of the wine bottle until my hand shook and the glass slipped from my fingers.

I started for the house, then redirected for my phone, in pieces on the peninsula. Then turned back and rushed into the waves, stepping on and over bottles and broken glass, raking at the water to get to him, the man I killed.

He floated, eyes closed, head bleeding. I pulled him toward the shore, then onto the beach as far out of the water as I could. Was CPR just the chest compressions now or just the breaths? I couldn't remember. I did both. I was breathing for him, watching his chest rise and fall, when I heard the wail of sirens under my own cries. I did this. I did.

## Chapter Thirty-Seven

At the hospital, they sewed up a gash on my knee and tweezed pieces of glass out of both hands while Sheriff Barrows and Officer Perez pelted me with questions. The resident working on me listened with wide eyes. After my hands were cleaned and bandaged into two useless mitts, I dragged myself to the waiting room. No one waited for me.

In the corner of the lobby, a few reporters gathered. One of the sheriff's men kept them at bay.

I wore sodden clothes, ripped, bloody, and wine stained. My shoes squelched as I walked. I didn't mind. I had not had time to mind.

Cooley was safe. We had arrived by ambulance, beckoned by my ham-fisted attempts on the police radio. During the ride, I'd forgotten all about high bridges or dark skies. I worried about Cooley, about Dev, about what I had been a party to. About who I had become.

The pay phone beckoned from across the room. I should call Michele. Shouldn't I? But what would I say? What would I say, ever, about what I had done?

I found myself wondering where Warren was, how it was possible that Warren Hoyt was not here. Losing Warren's goodwill meant that I must have used up all the goodwill in the world.

I had nowhere to go. I slinked deeper into the hospital, dodging into the gift shop. The magazine rack was filled with smiling faces, scandals, women in aprons holding crockery out to the reader. There was still a world out there that cared for such things. I pondered gifts: flowers? A card? What did you get for the fiancée of the man you had killed?

Finally, I decided on an item and paid for it.

"We've sold the entire stock today," the cashier said. "I had 'em for months and then, boom. Weird, isn't it?"

I could not follow what she meant, and then my purchase didn't quite fit in my purse. In the elevator ride up, a kid stared at it, then me. His mother noticed the stains of my shirt and pulled him close.

On the fourth floor, I got out. The hospital was small, the room easy to find. No one shooed me away. I sat down in the chair at her bedside.

Paris was a lovely disaster, tucked in among white sheets. Her color was better, but her lips had chapped. She wouldn't have liked that. Her eyelids fluttered. I let my purse and camera, returned to me from Cooley's car, slide to my feet. What would I say if she woke up? Not the truth. The truth was too much.

Footsteps at the hallway. Martha rushed into the doorway, stopping short when she saw me.

"What are you doing here?"

"Paying some respects," I said.

"They're only necessary thanks to you," she hissed. Her

eyes were puffy, her red lipstick smeared at the corners of her mouth. "Are you satisfied now?" She walked to the other side of the bed and patted Paris's hand. Paris's head was turned in my direction. She flinched at the touch.

"I didn't mean to—" I gestured to Paris, shaking my head in what I hoped was a scolding manner. "I didn't mean to."

"That's a sloppy job, then," Martha said. "Because you did." She pulled a chair to the bed and sat down. We regarded one another over the body of her friend. "Looks like we were right about you in the first place," she said. "What's it like to kill a man?"

A muscle near Paris's mouth twitched.

"She might be able to hear us," I said, finally explicit. "You may want to—"

"I hope she can," Martha said. "She'll find out soon enough."

"But maybe," I said calmly, as though speaking to a toddler, "maybe it's not the first thing she needs to be aware of. If she's your friend, why not protect her a bit?" Don't tell Martha, indeed.

Martha turned her profile to me.

"Talk to me about Tash," I said.

Martha freckles disappeared in the heat suddenly in her cheeks. "Why should I?"

"Dev said something about—"

"Stop saying their names!" Martha cried. "After what you did!" Paris grimaced.

"OK, you tell it, then," I said, lowering my voice in the hopes of lowering hers. "What happened? D— *He* said you were all complicit in—*her* death, and that Ma— OK, I need to use some of their names or I can't make sentences."

"Tash overdosed on some pills she got hold of," Martha said. Her eyes welled. "She was pulling all-nighters to study. She was competitive. She wanted to be the top of our class, and Dev was right there with her, sailing through his pre-med classes."

"You two were roommates," I said to nudge her along.

"She was a riot," she said. "She brought us all together. She was our center."

I must have pulled a dubious face, because she knew exactly where I was caught up. "Malloy, right? You thought Malloy was, and I don't blame you." She smiled toward the window for a moment. "No, in the beginning it was Tash. We were roommates, and she was dating Malloy, who lived in the same building as Dev and Sam and Paris. Tash was the string that pulled us tight. And then when she died . . . it wasn't the same."

For the first time, I fully understood that I had encountered these people at the end of their story, not at the beginning. Their youth threw me off track. But they had all lived a full life, ups and downs, before colliding with my story, which was also, I suppose, nearing an end. Not *the* end, only *an* end. I had miles to go. But that must have been what Malloy thought. Dev.

"Well, that's college," I said. "Afterward, everyone goes their own way."

"Shouldn't you be going yours?" Martha said.

"What?" I looked at the clock. "Plenty of daylight left," I said, though of course I would have to stay another day.

Martha smoothed one of Paris's braids off her forehead. Paris frowned, but again only I could see it. The poor woman wanted to be left alone. "What are you talking about?" Martha said. "What about daylight?"

"You *know*," I said. "You're well within your rights to make fun of me."

She looked at me blankly.

For a moment I didn't understand the disconnect. And then I did. She didn't know. Out of all the chatter flying around about my neurosis, none of it had reached Martha. Don't tell Martha. "Nothing," I said, watching Martha straighten Paris's covers. Nesting already, and using her friend's comatose and probably aching body as a dress-up doll. "Never mind." I stood and pushed my chair back quietly and grabbed my things. "No offense, but she doesn't seem happy with your fussing over her," I said. "You might leave her alone."

"I will never leave her alone. I'm all she's got—have you thought of that?"

"No, I didn't mean—*alone*. Of course you should be with her. I just mean she's a little restless when you—you know what? Never mind. Do what you want."

I walked to the door. Martha crooned over Paris, pulling the covers up around the woman's chin. "There," Martha said. "She's gone now. You wouldn't believe how much we've had to put up with since you fell."

At the door, I turned in time to see Paris's features contort. Her eyes rolled, opening, closing. She reminded me of a fish pulled from the lake, gasping for water.

"Paris?" I said. "Can you hear us?"

Martha raced around the bed, pushing me aside. "Pare? Hon?" she said, her voice shaking. "Can you hear me? Are you in there?" Martha looked up, her expression one of full panic. "Get the nurse."

At the nurse's station, I reported Paris's status. The nurse at the desk took the news laconically and shuffled off to see if there was anything to it. Martha calling Paris's name reverberated through the halls. For a moment I stood there, torn between witnessing a miracle and remaining outside what would happen. I had, as Martha suggested, done enough. From where I stood, miracles were hard to come by.

# Chapter Thirty-Eight

At the end of the hall, Barrows and Perez were leaving another room. I waited until they were down the hall and then approached the room and slipped inside.

"Dang," Cooley whispered when she saw the shape I was in. She didn't look much better. Her head was bandaged, but a dark bruise peeked out from under the wraps. A bag of clear liquid dripped into a tube stuck in her arm. Her voice was hoarse, weak. "And here I was thinking I'd win the beauty pageant. Didn't even make it to the swimsuit round."

I dropped the stuffed dog I'd picked up at the gift shop onto her bed. "Arf," I said and turned to take a chair. On a ledge in front of the window, several more of the same stuffed toy dog formed a conga line. "Oh, now I get why they had a run on these things."

"The guys at the station," she said, looking pleased.

"How are you feeling?" I said, sitting.

"You ever see a documentary where a baby is born and it's all covered in goo and yelling and seems like maybe it's a little chucked off to be alive? That's how I feel." She smiled. "Except where I'm happy to be alive. It just hurts to be, is all. Thanks for calling for help."

"I'm not convinced that was me."

"Some of the buttons you pushed on my radio were the right ones. You just need take your fingers *off* the button sometimes, so people can talk back to you," she said. "So what part of that"—with gestures to my bandaged hands, the blood and wine on my shirt—"is our accident and what part is bar brawl?"

I catalogued the injuries. "Interesting that you call it a bar brawl—"

"They told me about your wine bottle, slugger," she said, her eyes falling closed for a second. "Also you smell like the floor of the Hide-a-Way bar past three in the morning."

"Sorry."

"No apologies necessary." She opened her eyes and seemed a little stronger. Mad. "He was going to burn down the house! What kind of—" The boundaries of her vocabulary failed her. "Why would he do that?"

"I'm not sure," I said. "To destroy evidence, maybe? To burn the house from the face of the earth, I think."

"He tried to hurt you?"

"It seemed like he might." I raised my hands to my face but stopped at the sight of the mitten bandages. "I don't know. There were moments when I thought he would kill me, but then there were others . . ."

"What?"

"There were other moments when it seemed as though he couldn't possibly have hurt anyone, that he just wanted me to—catch up. Like he wanted something from me, but never got around to asking for it. Or maybe he was asking the whole time and I didn't understand."

She scooted upright a bit, sucking her breath in pain. "Always wear your seat belts, kids. What could he have wanted from you?"

"Not sure." I stared at the stuffed dog's stupid face. Its tongue hung out in a pink felt half-moon. "Paris is waking up. Anytime now."

"She's got a lot to take in when she does," Cooley said, another twinge of discomfort crossing her face, either at her injuries or the topic or both. "Look, from what I hear, you didn't have much choice. And then you tried to save him. That's his blood on you, isn't it? From dragging him out of the lake? From giving him CPR?"

"He said he didn't kill Malloy," I said. "But I killed him. I *killed* him." I was a good guy. I had always meant to be, anyway.

"We hit him with a car, Eden. I'm not sure your wine bottle did all the damage. Anyway, you wouldn't have hurt anyone if you didn't have to," Cooley continued more gently. "I don't know you that well, but it seems to me you wouldn't." She walked the toy dog across her bedsheets a few paces. "Would you?"

"The screwdriver—I thought—"

"But he threw it away, right? That's what the sheriff said. Perez recovered it in the shallows there."

"He threw it away."

"But you couldn't be sure. Why set the house on fire? To destroy evidence—but against which of them? Himself. That's what the sheriff thinks."

And probably why I was wandering around unescorted.

I hadn't killed Dev; I had killed the killer. I was impatient. "I'm sorry that I don't care about that house. I'm sure the taxpayers of the state of Michigan care. I'm sure Warren cares—"

"War-*ren*," Cooley sang, then got serious. "OK, I'm sorry. You don't think he deserved to die, and he didn't. Even if he meant to set the place ablaze, even if he killed his friend. Even if he meant to kill you?"

"What does Sam have to say about all these crimes he confessed to? Are they his or are they Dev's?"

Cooley plucked at the blanket over her knees. "Well, I'm not sure I can divulge police business—"

"Cooley, come on."

"I can say he confessed to drinking red wine from a cup in your room, but that's no crime." She sniffed. "Made for a hard night for that other guy and his allergies, and he should've just *said* so."

"I barely remember the wine," I said. "Sam drank it all." He'd finished the cup he'd poured for me that morning as I slept. *Hair of the dog.* Maybe Sam hadn't gotten fired for the theft of wine by the bottle. Maybe he'd been sacked for all the wine he'd stolen, sip by sip. He hadn't rescued the wine from evidence because of its street value, my guess. It mattered more than money to Sam to know where his next drink would come from.

"He also suggested that he might have broken the railing Paris went through," Cooley said. "He remembers sitting on it that first day."

"But no one *broke* it," I said. "It was fixed, wasn't it?"

"He didn't seem to know that," Cooley said.

We looked at each other. A man who confessed to crimes

he hadn't committed only injected further chaos into the situation, but for what purpose? What was the point? Who did it protect?

And then I saw it.

Himself.

The empty jail was a safer place than the motel. Malloy. Paris. Dev. A murderer was loose, and Sam had decided not to take any more chances. He knew *he* wasn't the killer, so he knew he wasn't safe.

"He didn't confess to Malloy's murder at all, did he?" I said. "He confessed to causing accidents just to take himself out of the game. But not to the murder. Though I bet Barrows is giving Sam the time to think about other crimes he might have committed. Did he happen to fess up to anything . . . older? Like, five years older?"

Her eyes widened. "How did you—" She sat up straighter in the bed. "I mean. I can't say."

Tash's belly full of wine. That and the pills from Dev, but neither had known about the other. Neither had been willing to admit their participation.

*We all did our part.*

Malloy broke things off with Tash for Paris. Paris felt guilty.

Dev got Tash the pills she asked for. Dev felt guilty.

Sam plied Tash with wine. Sam felt guilty.

Martha? Martha had left Tash alone. Martha felt guilty.

Except if they'd only conferred, they might have been able to sleep at night. "He won't go to prison for that, surely."

"Not for that," she said. "He's being held as a person of interest, but then you—well, *Dev* seems like a better suspect, but he's—"

I looked down at my shirt, pink with wine. There was a

smear of dark red-brown across my stomach. Dev's blood. "So that's the going theory? That Dev killed Malloy? I'm not convinced."

"You didn't really have a thing for that kid, did you? Thought you'd be tired of guys with a body count by now."

I wouldn't look at her.

"Come on, that's a joke. Just not a funny one, I guess."

I shook my head. I couldn't talk.

"Why are you crying? I'm sorry. I won't make any more jokes, honest."

I couldn't talk. I concentrated on the light coming through the slats of the blinds. "Bix," I whispered.

"Your husband," she said, nodding at me to pick up the thread of the story. "Look at the doggie and tell me. Tell the doggie. Your husband was in a car accident with his—*friend* and they both died, along with a couple more people . . . jump in when we get to the sore spot."

"A family," I choked.

"I heard that," she said and now she looked at the dog instead of me. "A kid."

The photos in the paper afterward haunted me. I visited the online comment sections of the local newspapers and community pages, just to read the names they called Bix. I wasn't trying to get it all out, as Martha had suggested. It was not a purging. I stuffed it back in, force-feeding myself the punishment, the entire dose for both of us. "He was four years old."

Cooley didn't have to say a word.

"And—" I gulped.

"And?" she said.

I felt hollow. No, worse than that. I was turned inside out so that I wore my shame on the outside, black heart and all.

"Bix was at fault," I managed.

"He was drunk," she said, gently. "I read the medical reports, Eden. He was bombed. He drove down the wrong side of the divided *highway*. I mean, how out of it do you have to—"

"He did it," I said. "On purpose."

Cooley's mouth fell, and then she turned her attention back to the toy dog, pulling at its pink tongue.

"He did it," I said. "He did."

"How do you know?"

How did I know? I had only ever been the person tuned to his station for his mood, his rage. My bones still hummed his desperation. He had built me from his misery. No version of myself would have ever been the right one. The irony was while he tried to piece me together, he was the broken one. No amount of trying to put Bix together would have ever done the trick. It had just taken me a long time to understand that, much too long to save them all. In this, I was no hero. But neither was he.

I would never know if he remembered, years ago, the car that had roared past us in the night, the one he'd spotted first and then saved us from. I remembered. *He's going to kill someone*, I'd said, even though the road was empty, the hour late.

*If he was going to kill someone*, Bix had replied. I had never heard the rest. But I knew what he'd said, now.

If he was going to kill someone, he would have turned off the lights.

Like Bix did, when the time came. If it didn't matter who was killed, and you just wanted to make sure someone went with you, you turned off the headlights and you drove. You closed your eyes, maybe. You put things in the hands of luck and you drove until something stopped you.

"He didn't want to live anymore," I said. Cooley leaned forward to hear the words through my sobs. "He didn't want to live."

"He was military?" she said. "Did he see combat? PTSD?"

I closed my eyes.

"Did you? See combat?"

My eyes flew open. "He didn't mean to," I said, thinking of the barbecue we'd gone to the day after the worst night. Bix holding court, me in long sleeves to hide the bruises. "It was just once. Twice. He didn't know what was happening, he was so out of his mind on the bad nights—"

"Was he in treatment or anything?"

I shook my head.

"He needed to be. You both did. Did you ask him to go to therapy?"

Here was the tricky part. I had never insisted. "He got better," I said. "Just one day, I realized that things had been quiet, calm. No more bad dreams. No more screaming in the night. The neighbors stopped calling the cops. He got better."

Cooley stroked the toy dog's ear and gazed toward the window. "Just one day? Like that?"

"We moved from base to base and I thought, maybe once we settled down, saw his family more often." I went along with it all. Any plan that might work, I went along. And then the house, the dream house, the stability. Surely it would work. "I thought if he could stay in one place for a *minute*—"

"But then he met the other woman?" she said. "Or, you mean he got better because of—"

"Colleen." I wasn't even afraid of the name anymore. It was just a name, not an incantation. She would not appear before me if I said it aloud. She would not appear, ever.

I couldn't even hate her anymore. She had paid for her decision, hadn't she? She had paid the bill, all right. His, hers, mine. "He was better. I didn't know it was because he was somewhere else, taking it out on her."

Or maybe I hadn't wanted to know. My specialty was surfaces, the slant of light on the outside of the thing instead of what went on underneath. I had not been paying the proper attention because it was easier not to notice.

"You *know* he did it on purpose?" she said.

I nodded.

"But you didn't tell anyone? Because of insurance or what?"

I had needed the insurance, it was true. But I'd kept it to myself because I didn't want to face the full truth. I didn't want to put it in words. Even now, to Cooley, I didn't want to say it.

He had loved Colleen enough to take her with him.

When the time came, when he really meant forever, he chose Colleen. He chose Colleen and . . . not me. He had *killed her*, and still I wondered. Why not me, Bix?

He had led a thousand troops into war, trained them and led them and sometimes cradled them as they died, but when the time came, he left one behind.

"Never mind," Cooley said. "Does anyone else know he did it on purpose?"

I swallowed the lump in my throat. "No."

"Who would it help if you told the whole story?"

"I'm not sure."

"Who would it hurt?"

I pictured Colleen's mother, wrapped up in her blue coat, cold to the bone despite the heat. She had wanted the truth but needed the lie.

"Would it hurt more than it helped?" Cooley said. "To tell the whole truth?"

The whole truth made me a horrible person. I knew that much.

"It's OK to stay uncertain about it," she said. "You weren't there. You don't know."

"What about . . . justice?"

"Did you want me to side with justice? I can do it." She gestured toward a cabinet near the door. "Grab my shiny badge from the closet."

"I just thought—"

"Whose justice? Will you feel better?"

I didn't answer. I would never feel better.

"He was drunk. He drank a lot?"

"Yes."

"He was a sick man, your husband," she said.

The lights on all through the house, and Bix raving. A bad night. The worst night. Bugs just under his skin, crawling. Lashing out. I was the enemy. And then crying when he realized, crying and wanting to go home, and yet there we were, in the only home he'd had since he was a kid. He didn't mean home. He meant—before. Before all the things that changed him. But his was another youth lost and unavailable. His mother hadn't realized. He hadn't wanted her to know. Bix was her war hero, her cherished son and clean soul, unassailable. She would have been no help. I was no help, and I didn't ask for any. When Michele made jokes about how I went along with it all, never made a peep, never stood up for myself—I could barely take the insult. She had no idea what I'd gone along with.

Only Colleen had helped, but then she had only helped me.

"Sick," I said, but I didn't mean Bix. "It's just that it's—"

"What?"

"Lonely. To be the only person who knows."

"I guess it would be," she said. "But now you're not."

## Chapter Thirty-Nine

Cooley lay back in her bed, blinking. Exhausted. I felt the same but hadn't managed to snag a hospital bed for the night. I had no place to go. No room at the Hide-a-Way, and the guest house was still closed. For a moment I was sorry I hadn't gone back to Warren's house. I could have messed up that neat arrangement of throw pillows. I spent a few minutes imagining how, but then forced my mind back to the events of the week. Even the jail would be occupied, at least one cell.

"Why don't you get some sleep, Cooley?"

"I'm all right," she said, but by the time she had said it, her eyes were closed. I stood up, fetched the dog from her bed, and went to the ledge to place the toy among its peers.

All six of the dogs faced out, the pink felt tongues razzing me. I started to turn for the door, but went back, reaching for my camera and then stopping. Six dogs. Six of them.

One, Malloy. I plucked it off the shelf.

Another one, Hillary. She had everything to gain and everything to lose, but I couldn't assign her Malloy's death. I didn't believe in it. I tucked the two dogs under my arm and faced the last of them. Four.

Sam, who had chosen police custody rather than face what was happening. Who did he protect by confessing to things he couldn't have done? Himself? Or someone else? Dev, who had decided to burn the whole world down, to destroy or protect, no one alive knew which. Paris, I counted out. Martha. None of these people were whole. I couldn't separate them out.

I put the dogs back, lining them up prettily so that Cooley could enjoy their smug little faces when she woke up. All six of them.

Six.

But it wasn't six, anymore.

One, Tash. I moved one of the dogs off the ledge. Five.

Paris, who stole the boyfriend, and could not move beyond him, though he was long lost to her and wouldn't take her calls.

Dev, who supplied the pills, but had locked himself into a future of doling out pills, a future he wouldn't have chosen if he had known how to defy momentum, how to get the girl any other way.

Sam, who brought the wine, who always brought the wine. Who had developed a life around wine and then smashed it to pieces.

Martha, who left Tash alone. Martha, who could not stand to be alone.

The last dog on the ledge was Malloy.

What had Malloy said about the friends coming together for the week? *Some of us have not had our fill of mourn-*

*ing.* But Malloy had. He had called himself cruel, an asshole. And then a pilgrim, but for what? To work through a few things—but not him. Not Malloy. The work belonged to others who couldn't move on from the role they each played in Tash's death. But Malloy was fine. Malloy would always land on his feet. But the rest of them hadn't.

They didn't love him.

They didn't love him at all. They hated him.

It all made sense to me now. How they couldn't be together comfortably. How they had followed, me, the stranger, around while they figured out how to be in the same room. They feared him, maybe. They wanted something from him he couldn't give. They wanted him to be someone he wasn't. But he was not the center. There was no center, not without Tash. He was only comfortable, while the rest of them suffered. He was merely charming. The problem with charm was that it masked a multitude of sins. Charm was the worst.

I wandered, dazed, into the hallway. Time did not exist inside the hospital. There was no time to get to Chicago. There was no time even to embark. I had lost my suitcase; it would be somewhere among the flotsam of the accident. My shattered phone had been pieced back together but would not quite come back to life. Its power cord, anyway, was in the suitcase. Untethered, I wandered the halls until I found an elevator and took it down to the lobby.

There, the windows were dark. I hurried away from them, my ears buzzing with anxiety, and found an interior waiting area with thickly cushioned chairs. I sat, waiting, but for what I could not say. I was not comfortable.

I got back up and followed the signs for the cafeteria. But the cafeteria was glass, the night sky pressing inward. I backed out of the room and took a hard chair at a table that someone had dragged into the hall. The last occupant had left behind an array of sweetener packets. I chose one and fidgeted, letting the contents run like sand in an hourglass from one end of the paper sachet to the other. I had never felt so closed in, so trapped. I gathered the sugar packets to me. Six of them. I laid them out like a hand of solitaire, lining up the edges just so. This one, Malloy. This one, Dev. Paris and so on.

"Eden?" Warren Hoyt stood above me, his hands in his pockets. For a moment, he didn't seem real. He didn't seem possible. I reached out for the soft blue cuff of his shirt and then faltered. He glanced at the arrangement of sugar packets. "Looks like you're . . . what are you doing? Are you OK?"

It was the worst thing to be alone. To know how small and cast off you were from any shore. Just a tiny island.

"Who bought you the throw pillows?" I said. "Who's in the pictures in the frames on your desk?"

He knelt in front of me. His worried eyes darted over my face then down at my wrapped hands. "What happened?"

"If it was just you, that's one thing," I said. "But if someone else got the pillows for you—"

"Nieces and nephews. In the frames. Me on a hiking trip with some friends." He reached for one of the gauzy mitts and held it gently. "There's no one else," he said. "I just have impeccable taste. In throw pillows and—and in everything."

"You could do better."

"I don't think so," he said. "I wouldn't want to."

"I'm afraid of the dark," I said.

"I heard that."

I was caught off guard for a moment. I blinked into his earnest face. He'd heard about it? Had he also heard about

Dev or would I have to explain? "I'm the villain," I said. "You don't know what I've done."

"Maybe not. Rumor tends to run around me, like water around a rock."

I stared at him.

"You know how water runs around—look, it was dumb. My jokes are dumb most of the time, which is why I try not to make any."

"No, it's not that," I said impatiently. "But if rumor runs around you, how did you know about my fear of the dark?"

"Well, you made it fairly clear at my house that you wanted the light left on," he said. "But I had already heard about it before then. I don't know—Barrows or one of his people, I guess. No, I remember now. Erica Ruth—"

"Erica *Ruth* heard about it? While she was stuck out in the gate house of a closed park, she heard about it?"

"Don't feel awkward. Fear of the dark is not as unusual as you might think. Last year we had a . . ."

He nattered on while I tracked the news of my affliction from me to Dev to Sam to Barrows to Cooley to Paris. Somewhere along the line, the tale had splintered off on a course of its own, from Barrows to Hillary, from Erica Ruth to Warren.

And yet, Martha hadn't heard. How? Because they all protected her like a child? Don't tell Martha.

Martha, who had been brought to the group by Tash. Without Tash, though, there was no gravity keeping them tied to one another. They were an expanding universe, pulling away from one another. Martha who talked of *colleagues* instead of friends. The only one of them, I realized, who had not denied planning the reunion.

"What is it? Eden, are you OK?"

I visualized the kitchen of the guest house. After hours, late and dark, a drink between friends. Paris wanted to talk to Malloy, alone. But Martha had followed Paris into the house. Dev had called Paris out for using my phone to text Malloy, but it was *Martha* who caught her. Dev prevented Paris from sneaking to the kitchen, but no one kept Martha from going.

One friend is supposed to arrive but then another does.

Malloy pulls the screwdriver out of the wine bottle, pops out the cork with the opener. Now both opener and screwdriver lay at hand. Perhaps Martha is taking the opportunity of Malloy all to herself to flirt. Show the dimples, see if she's still got what it takes to turn his head. She wears a ridiculous red lipstick, too—actually wears it, doesn't just carry it around in her makeup bag, hoping it will look better on her next time she tries. She had already talked them all into coming to the lake. She might talk him into anything.

Or maybe she gets down to business. She's carrying his kid from their hookup a few months before. Except Malloy is a man with a new lease on life, a fresh and unmarred love affair, a new commitment to the family business, which will make him a richer man than he already is. He sits at the head of the table at a feast of life and opportunity. Maybe when he says "pilgrim" he does not think of humility. Maybe he thinks of empire, of conquering. He is, by his own words, cruel. He will not mourn. He will not be sorry for past sins. He will not be who Martha wants him to be. He never was.

Things go badly. There's a screwdriver right there. It goes into his neck—not because it is the only tool or maybe even the closest tool or the most deadly lying there on the counter. The screwdriver is from Martha's car. It is hers. It is familiar.

Malloy reaches for it, his fingertips bloody, and perhaps Martha helps ease him quietly to the floor. Eases him to the floor, an arc of blood smeared on the wall, before panicking. Does she think to wipe the handle of the screwdriver? She does.

She rushes through the back door, letting it slam against the wall, and away from the house. And then back around to the front and inside, because where else can she go?

She runs through the front door. And starts screaming.

*Click.* When I snapped out of it, Warren was leaning over me, concerned. "Eden?"

"She would have been the first one there," I said. "She threw herself on top of his body to cover for the blood she would still have on her. And I can't prove any of it."

"Any of what? What are you talking about?"

"Martha," I said. "Martha killed Malloy."

"How do you know?"

How did I know? Because the worst thing in the world was to be alone. Martha and I had both felt the open maw of solitude coming for us. We reacted to it differently. When real connection was lost, I had chosen isolation, to avoid attaching myself, to avoid making a nuisance of myself, to avoid having to admit what prowled after me in the shadows. Martha had chosen to surround herself, to make her tour, as she had called it. And what a tour it had been, with each of the men worried to hear who the father would turn out to be. You almost had to admire how she had forced them all here. She was not yet done mourning, but it wasn't Tash she mourned. It was how the people they'd been came together over Tash's death. As time went on, they'd splintered and grown apart and then—

What had changed? The pregnancy. And Malloy's will? Something the *colleagues* had drawn up that Martha wasn't supposed to see? In any case, the center wasn't holding. They were spinning away into their own lives, and Martha . . . Martha hadn't planned for solitude.

How did I know? Because it made awful sense to me. I had stood in that open field made for stargazing in the bright light of day and felt the vastness of the universe swell out around me. Underneath my skin and hers, we might be the same sleepless, helpless howl of a girl, alone in the field, alone in the world. But that's not how I recognized her.

It was Bix she reminded me of. Empty in the eyes, wearing a daytime mask of dimples and coyness, laughs. Devil may care. But where he was a hero, emptying himself out in a flood of activity that kept everyone away from his tender scars, Martha offered her body, her services as bridesmaid, the tools from the trunk of her car. Anything to be useful. Anything to be needed, to be anything necessary on this earth to anyone. It didn't matter which one of them.

Although—

I thought it might have. Martha stabbing Malloy was an act of the moment, reaching for the nearest most familiar tool. But the familiar tool was already in the house before it had been used to try to open a bottle of wine. It had already been used to tweak the bannister, just in case anyone sat on it. Just in case anyone sat on it *again*.

"Sam," I said. "She meant to kill Sam." Not Malloy—that was frustration or rage, a hot moment and then regret. And then Paris—that was a mistake, a miscalculation.

It was Sam she meant to deal out of the group. The accident she had orchestrated with the stair railing would force the rest of them together, thick as thieves. The circle closed, again.

Sam was the expendable one. And he knew it.

He hadn't, though, not until he heard what had actually happened to Paris, when he'd understood more than the rest of us. *That's not possible. That means—* And then he'd turned himself in to the police early the next morning for any crime he could think of. Not because he thought someone else might get hurt, but because he thought *he* might. He probably hadn't even heard about Dev's "poisoning" by the time he went to confess.

He had loved her, but he wasn't good enough. No one person was. Martha wanted them all.

And if she couldn't have them all, as many as she could get. Sam would have been collateral damage.

Martha, rushing to Malloy's body, blood soaking into her dark nightgown to hide any spatter that might have occurred during the murder.

Martha, tending to Sam after he swooned at the sight of Malloy, the soles of her feet dirty from her run from the back of the house to the beach to wash her bloody hands, and then around to the front of the house.

Martha, not protected but overlooked.

Martha, saying she would never leave—

"Paris," I said. I stood up.

"What is it?"

I wasn't sure. Maybe nothing. Paris, twitching at Martha's touch. Probably nothing. But *nothing* hadn't been the case all weekend.

"Paris. I left her alone—"

I rushed away from him and down the hall. The elevator

would take too long. I spotted the fire exit stairs and ran up, quick on the first few stories and wheezing by the last. Warren fell behind. When I slammed through the door and out onto the floor of the critical unit, I was alone. The ward had gone dim, the nurses station temporarily abandoned.

I approached Paris's room cautiously. It was darker than I liked, lit only by a small lamp behind the bed, lighting a small circle on the dark shade pulled down on the window. I fought the itch of my skin and stood in the doorway.

Paris lay as I had left her. Her chest rose and fell evenly.

I let out the breath I had been holding and walked in. At her bedside, I glanced nervously behind me, but no one was there. All that talk about never leaving Paris alone, but Martha had, and for that I was grateful. And maybe she would continue to leave her alone. If she'd only wanted Sam, maybe she was done hurting people. But things had gone wrong, and no one knew her state of mind. Now that Malloy was gone, Dev, Sam hiding from her. Paris was all that remained, which seemed to me a bad place to be. Who could withstand the intensity of Martha's love, alone?

Below me, Paris's breath was soft and untroubled, her head turned toward me.

"I won't let her hurt you," I whispered.

Her eyes opened.

"Paris?"

She blinked, finding focus and then me. "Dev?" she asked, licking at her dry lips.

Another widow welcomed to the sisterhood. I had done this to her. I didn't know what to say. She had loved him best, after all.

"I'm sorry." I looked away from the deep confusion in her

eyes and found instead the dark square of the window. For a moment, I was not sure what I was seeing.

I had thought the shade had been pulled down, but instead it was rigged up, yanked open all the way to the ceiling. It was not an opaque covering I was looking at but the dark hole of the night sky. Paris's window faced the lake, so the sky above went on forever, all dark.

The most beautiful thing. I was alone with the sky.

Below me, Paris whispered, "Dev?"

In the window's reflection, I could see my own shape, lit by the weak light at Paris's bedside. But then behind my own form stood a black silhouette, like those that darted into the park road. Only this one moved. Behind me, the door gently closed, *click*.

"Martha," Paris said.

The movement in the reflection stopped. I blinked down at Paris. She wasn't talking to Martha, but me.

"*Martha,*" she said, a crease forming between her eyes.

It was not a warning. It was an accusation. Someday soon she would say my name the same way.

Whatever she had learned or remembered, it was enough to force urgency into her faint voice, enough to force me to react.

I dodged as the dark figure in the window leapt forward, throwing myself at the nurse's call button at the side of Paris's bed. I bounced away just as Martha landed on the bed, the old silver knife from the guest house kitchen in her hand stabbing down and into the mattress. Paris made a terrible sound, not quite as human as a scream.

I darted for the door while Martha pulled the knife out of the bed. I was almost there—one of my gauzed mitts managed to graze the handle—but then Martha grabbed a fistful of my hair and I fell to the ground.

The knife came down. I rolled out of reach.

The strike to the floor jarred the blade loose from Martha's hands. It clattered away.

"Stop it!" Paris screeched. "Help!"

I jumped to my feet, yelling, and leapt as Martha clawed for me, landing again at the door. Through the glass, I spotted Warren and a security guard rushing toward us. I put one mitt up to the glass and reached for the handle with the other.

Something punched me in the back, hard.

The wind had been knocked out of me.

My breath. I couldn't catch it.

The padded mitten at the door handle pawed, pawed, faltered.

Somewhere far away, Paris made another gut-wrenching noise. But that was miles away and years.

I couldn't think why any of it mattered.

I was up at the railing over the room. The guest house. No, a different room, white, and if I reached down I could move the people around like dolls. Martha, and Paris, fallen out of the bed. Me, sprawled with the tarnished silver blade in my back. I was a troop at war, down there, belly-crawling toward the door.

A tug at my back: Martha pulling the knife.

The door opened. A security guard entered, stomping and kicking Martha's hands away from me, and behind him, Perez and Barrows, guns drawn.

The room had gone dark, dark, and far away. A slice of narrow room, folded into an accordion and closed, closing. And quiet.

The knife fell soundlessly to the floor, red. Martha scrambled backward, her red lips stretched in rage. She would have her reasons. They would have everything and nothing to do with me. I was forgetting who she was, even as she swept a curl out of her eyes and left a smear of my blood across her cheek.

Far, far. Warren, too. And then he was close, pressing his face to the floor. His mouth opened and closed but I heard no sound. Warren, out of my reach. He was—

*Click.*

*Click*, damn it.

It was dark. That's what it was. I wasn't afraid. But I didn't want to be in the dark just now.

I slammed back into awareness. Around me, all the sound in the world, keening and wailing and yelling. None of it was mine. All the pain and hurt. Mine.

"Eden," Warren said. His cheek pushed to the floor. Blood, there. "Stay with us."

"War-ren," I said with effort. Like Cooley's song. Someone, ouch, pressed at my back. Two giant handprints on the moon.

"Yes, yes, anything," he said. "Stay with me."

"You need . . ."

There were many people now, new sounds and shouts and a blanket from Paris's bed pulled down and wrapped around me. Warren lay on the cold floor. He had such a nice face. Such a nice, worried face.

"A nickname," I wheezed.

"You can give me one," he said, wiping at my cheek. Blood. He looked scared. I didn't like to think of Warren as scared, as anything other than the guy on the wall. Buttoned-up, in control of the chaos. Naming the stars as though he owned every one. "You think of one," he said. "You think of a nickname for me."

"Where do you . . . keep them?" My voice sounded cold, chattering.

"What? Where do I keep what?"

Hadn't I said? "The plaques," I said. "For saving everyone."

"Stay with me," he said. "Stay with me, and I'll show you."

"I want to see," I said.

"The plaques," he said.

"And," I said.

"Yes?"

"The stars," I said. "Show me the stars."

His tucked his head into his chest, not really a nod here on the floor, my blood on his face, and then he was back.

"You got it. They're yours."

# *Now*

Cooley's puppy has knocked over my tripod twice. His name is Bronco, which was cute when she first got him, at seven pounds. Now he's almost a year old, and indeed truck-like. Fast as lightning as she tries to get him to obey her commands. He's too hyped up by the activity in the viewing area tonight. He wants to sniff around my equipment. He wants to greet each of the amateur photographers as they show up. He's a fantastic greeter of people who show up. He dodges between their legs and shoves his head into their camera bags. I am expecting twenty photography students to join me tonight, though of course I never mind a drop-in.

"Are you going to cover how to shoot star trails?" one of the early birds wants to know. He's wearing one of those khaki vests with the loops for film, just like my teacher used to. The vest means business.

Star trails. I am. We're going to shoot long exposures and find the threshold between when the stars photograph as prim little pricks of light and when the exposure catches them stretching and twirling around Earth's axis. It can be a matter of a second, the passage of time made visible.

Yes, we'll be shooting the whole range. Satisfied, the guy lurches away.

One of the other early attendees is a young woman with smooth dark skin and black braids tied in a ponytail. When she turns her head, I'm sure it's Paris. I look for the nose ring, for a moment of recognition, for a flare of hatred.

The last time I saw Paris was when we crossed paths during the legal proceedings. I watched her giving testimony from a closed-circuit TV down the hall by special permission. Under the circumstances, my presence in the same room wasn't welcome.

Listening to her, I'd learned a few things. She had used my phone to text Malloy to meet her because she wanted to talk to him about Dev. She suspected he'd been unfaithful. Something wasn't right. And then Martha, after compelling them all to the guest house to honor—Martha's word—Tash's death, had played with that concern at the bannister that day. Hints and dimples, always, but they were all Paris needed to understand that Martha would have taken anything from her, if she could. "Some people are like that," she said nervously. Her braids were out and her natural hair glorious, a dark crown. You couldn't look away from her.

I go back to my setup. I use a fisheye lens, a full-frame camera. These are all things I had to learn, like how to sleep again, like how to let the sun set, all the way through the golden hour and beyond, into night. I had to learn to be still, to breathe. It takes a long exposure to film anything but the brightest objects in the night sky. A long exposure takes patience, hands off, and trust.

I keep looking up at the woman, though, to make sure it's not Paris.

It's been a year since the anniversary trip. That's what I still called it, shorthand for everything that happened and the outcome.

After a few legal delaying tactics, Martha is in Ypsilanti, at the women's facility there. I think she must not get too many visitors. So many of her friends are unavailable. Malloy, Dev—I still hate to think of Dev, though it turned out Cooley was right. The car striking him caused internal injuries that caught up with him there at the shore. But of course I did that, too. He would have been half mad and half gone by the time I swung a bottle at his head, and some might say he'd been half mad to buy the gas. I understood what he'd meant to do, though it was hard to explain to people who hadn't gone through what we had. With Malloy dead and Paris down and probably gone, he didn't care who did it. He wanted to burn the world down and see what was left standing.

Sam's still in the wine business, but not visiting anytime soon. He's in the west somewhere, working off a bit of debt to his former employer, but they hired him back, with caveats, I've heard. I'm not sure how he can stay sober and still sell wine, but then maybe he can't think of anything else to do. Maybe he can't think of anyone else to be.

Hillary works at Halloway's Heavenly for Malloy's parents. They don't much care about her past or any degree and where she got it. They found her name in their son's will. Her name, the real one along with the new one, and Angel's, too, written into Malloy's will and notarized by one of Martha's colleagues. None of us knew how Malloy found out about Angel, or why he built them into his will so quickly. Love? Someone more cynical than I have turned out to be would have to make that call.

What there had been no provision for in the will: further heirs. It would have taken a court case and a lot of money Martha had not yet earned to wrench a slice out of Malloy's estate. But no one thought it had been about money for her, and news of the baby has been quiet. Maybe Terry and Clare had taken the child in or found a good home for him, if he was indeed the prince of the dairy.

In a way I didn't want to know what happened to the kid. It's better not to know.

I mean, I'd like to know. There's just no one left to ask.

Malloy's kid? Or Dev's, or Sam's?—oh, yes, Sam's. I had revisited the open wound of Sam's face as he pined for her, the hopeful knock on my motel door when he meant to strike for hers, the lost key in his pocket. But why had he stayed? Maybe he'd really thought he'd lost the key. Or maybe since he hadn't found Martha, any other human would do.

Was it even true, the baby? But as long as Martha carried the child of one of them—didn't matter which one—as long as that part of the story was true, the friendship had a future. Without it, what was it all for? It was too much loss. You couldn't look directly at it.

I don't know where Paris went, after. Which is why I see her everywhere. I want her to show up one day, leading a small child by the hand, a child with Martha's dimples and Dev's black eyes. I don't see how it can be possible, but it's the story I tell myself.

The timer on this camera body is tricky. I fuss with it, absorbed, until a shadow falls over my hands. I squint up at Warren. I hadn't thought of a nickname. Sometimes I call him Hoyt, like we are teammates. I like him the way he is. I don't want him repackaged or changed. When I first came back to Michigan after selling the house, I didn't move in right away. I lived in a rental cottage north of the area, on the Upper Peninsula, a place out of season and cold. A blue cottage that faced down the lake, overgrown, a mosquito's daydream had it been summer. I spent a few months watching storms come in and waiting for the power to go out.

Not that I hadn't visited. Not that I hadn't found ways to mess up those throw pillows on his couch. Not that I hadn't slept in his bed.

Except I had my own bad nights, now, waking from dreams in which Bix's old truck careens away from headlights off the dark road somewhere near Chicago and lands, inexplicably, in the dark waters of the Straits of Mackinac. It sinks, sinks and I sit up, choking and gasping, scaring us both. He always stays up with me, trying to make it right.

It will not be right. Not the past, anyway. I won't force things into shapes that fit a story I'd rather have lived. When I think of Bix, he's there, in the past. I try not to hold a grudge. He taught me to stand on my own two feet. Just not the way he meant.

I live with Warren now. I have seen where he keeps the plaques. One of them props up a corner of the unbalanced washing machine.

Michele thinks I'm crazy. Or maybe she's just mad that I didn't let her shape the next stage of my life the way I let Bix command the first part. I miss her, and when I call, I don't have any favors to ask, except to put the girls on for a minute.

So I live in a tourist destination now, and I'm happy. Cooley brings the dog over to the house to knock things off the coffee table. I work at an insurance agency in town, just office work, and teach these sessions for the park. A regular life, lived in one spot. Loving and being loved, who knew? It was the equivalent of having the lights turned on, all the time.

Warren's looking out toward the water at some kids, ever watchful. It's getting dark. People do things in the dark they would never dare otherwise, but there were people like him, too, those who will practice kindness, even in darkness.

When the kids come away from the water, Warren turns his attention to the clearing. He puts his warm hand on my back, near where the knife went in. Corona Australis, he calls the spot in my back where the skin was pieced back together into a fisherman's hook, a raised golf club of a scar. Which is, I guess, the shape of that constellation. I'm still learning them. He makes them up, sometimes, when he walks into a room I'm in, reading. "Lady with a book," he might say, and I know he sees the shape of me in stars. "Man with spatula," I might say, to get him to make me eggs for breakfast.

On either side of the thin white line of the long scar on my back are small white dots left behind by the stitches. The skin is puckered there, so calling it the southern crown is another kindness. By naming the scar, he has tidied the pain, the loss of blood, the nicked lung, the near death into myth and legend.

My hands, though. He traces and re-traces the scar tissue in the palms of my hands from Sam's bottles, looking for constellations. He has no end of heroic stories for what he finds there. He tells a story of a woman who was once afraid to go out at night, and it does feel as though he's making it all up. Who would leave the lights on so long, blotting out the world around her?

The class is filing into the clearing, getting set up while

there is still light. In a minute, we'll get started with introductions. Maybe they'll be friends, or maybe some of them
already are. Then we'll start taking a look at the horizon,
where the sun is finally setting. First star, a cheer goes up.
This is a good group. It's going to be an OK night. They'll
have a good time, getting a chance to see each other in the
glorious light of the golden hour. Shutters will start to click
because everyone is so pretty in that glow. So pretty.

We'll move quickly from there. There's not much time.
They'll have just one chance to see each other in the best
light, and then we'll turn toward the stars.


The End

# Acknowledgments

This book would not be what it became without my editor, Emily Krump. Thank you. Thank you to the entire HarperCollins William Morrow team, especially Liate Stehlik, Jennifer Hart, Michelle Podberezniak, Amelia Wood, Julia Elliott, and Serena Wang.

Thank you, as always, to Sharon Bowers.

Thank you to Margaux Weisman for green-lighting this project on the basis of three words—"dark sky park."

Thank you to Julie Schoerke, Marissa DeCuir, Angelle Barbazon, Sydney Mathieu, and Ellen Whitfield from JKS Communications for all their assistance.

My deep appreciation goes to early readers Yvonne Strumecki and Kim Rader.

Thank you to the Headlands International Dark Sky Park in Mackinaw City, Michigan, for providing the model for my fictional park. I had to borrow the silhouettes, but I took great pains to leave your wonderful new observatory. Go visit a dark sky place near you by searching http://www.darksky .org/idsp/finder/. Thank you to YouTuber Marianne Else for her video tour of the Headlands, which was very useful in the early days of researching this novel. Thank you to Devi Bhaduri for her insomnia expertise (and *yikes*). Thank you to Michael Rader, Sherry Novinger Harris, Susan Courtright, Walter Gragg, Julie Nilson Chyna, Jamie Howard, and Mariah Watson for their military and married-to-the-military expertise. Errors made within the story are definitely mine. Thanks also to Robin Agnew, the Mackinac Island Library, and the Grand Hotel.

I would like to acknowledge the writers of Mystery Writers of America Midwest Chapter for all they've done for me and continue to do for other up-and-coming mystery writers. Thanks also to Sisters in Crime and International Thriller Writers. I couldn't begin to name all the generous authors who have helped me along my career, but I do want to thank Sara Paretsky, William Kent Krueger, Lou Berney (not fair!), Larry D. Sweazy, Terence Faherty, Susanna Calkins, Leslie Budewitz, Caroline Todd, and Ann Cleeves for their enthusiasm and support.

Thank you, again and always, librarians and booksellers.

Thank you to Erica Ruth Neubauer, Martha Cooley (and sister Bridget Cooley), and Dab Holt for naming characters for charitable causes.

Of course I have to thank my family and friends for putting up with me during the rough patches of writing, revising, and promoting. The biggest dollop of gratitude is always reserved for my patient and supportive husband, Greg. Pretty sure he's the reason I write so many happy endings.

## About the author

## About the book

## Read on...

Insights,
Interviews
& More...

# Written in the Stars: Meet Lori Rader-Day

LORI RADER-DAY is the Mary Higgins Clark and Anthony Award–winning author of *Under a Dark Sky, The Day I Died, Little Pretty Things,* and *The Black Hour.* She lives in Chicago, where it is very hard to see the stars. Her life has intersected with the stars a few times, though. Just for fun, here's Lori's life, written in the stars.

### I once lived in a dark sky community, unofficially.

From the age of twelve, I lived in a house in the middle of nowhere, Indiana, where our nearest neighbors were a quarter of a mile away. We had no continuous outside lights at our house, so the countryside at night got as dark as dark gets. To see the stars, all I had to do was go outside. Once I picked up a few constellations I could identify, I could actually see them without going outside. I could see them from my bed. Now that I can barely see a single star in the sky from my backyard in Chicago, I miss having easy access to the night sky.

### I was (briefly) a shooting star.

At my junior high school, eighth graders took a multi-week science class unit on the constellations, which culminated in a famously difficult test. We were given a single piece of paper with nothing but dots—and we had to connect the dots to make the constellations, naming as many as we could. When the teacher revealed the highest scores in reverse order, the last score revealed was . . . mine! I was a pretty good student, but this might have been the first time I was the "best" at anything, especially, let's face it, at science.

### I have a relative (kinda) in the space game.

I am tangentially related through my grandmother's family to astronaut Jerry Ross, who participated in seven Space Shuttle missions and is tied with Franklin Chang-Diaz for the record for most spaceflights. In 2017, Jerry and I met up when we were both authors at a book fair in Indiana. His book about his flights is called *Spacewalker*.

### I am not the star of our household.

I spotted our dog as a five-pound puppy on a rescue website: a black German Shepherd mix who looked just like a little black bear. Before we had even applied to adopt her, I knew her name: Ursa Minor (named for the constellation, translated to "Little Bear"). She is now ten years old—and looks even more like a bear.

### I am a space movie nerd.

I am a sucker for a space-related movie, stemming from a teenage obsession, perhaps, with *Space Camp*. *Space Camp* the movie, not the actual camp. *Space Camp* starred Tate Donovan before he was on *Friends* and *Scandal*. Caveat: If you can't suspend your disbelief, don't try watching *Space Camp* now. It's too late for you. My sister Jill and I call this phenomenon—when you can't revisit ▶

**Written in the Stars: Meet Lori Rader-Day**
*(continued)*

old favorite shows because your tastes have, ahem, matured—"Dukes of Hazzard." As in, "Jill, don't pause on that channel. That movie is so Dukes of Hazzard." (I think you can guess why we chose this particular reference. I loved the Duke boys at age eight, but it's best not to revisit them.) Other favorite space movies: *Apollo 13*, *Arrival*, *Contact*, *Wall-E*, *Galaxy Quest*, and *Hidden Figures*.

**I love a good space story.**

One of my all-time favorite books is *The Right Stuff*, by Tom Wolfe, about the original crew of Mercury 7 astronauts as well as the jet pilots who refused to tow NASA's line, and therefore were passed up as astronauts. I read this book for my master's in journalism, when I thought I might want to write the type of long-form nonfiction known as literary journalism or creative nonfiction. I never attempted it outside of classwork, but thank goodness writers like Wolfe, Erik Larson, Melissa Fay Greene, and Susan Orlean are on the job. ⌒

# Musical Playlist for *Under a Dark Sky*

I always make a playlist for my books, but not as a marketing tool. I actually do write to music. Many writers say they can't listen to songs with lyrics while they write because the words are distracting, but I find that music, even with lyrics, helps me focus and get work done. Songs have to do some work for me to be on the list; just liking a song isn't enough. Here are the songs that helped me write *Under a Dark Sky*:

### "TWILIGHT" BY SHAWN COLVIN

"Twilight is the loneliest time of day," Shawn Colvin sings. In *Under a Dark Sky*, Eden is a photographer, trained to watch the light upon surfaces and subjects. Since her husband died, she has folded the activity of her life into the daylight hours, and she's always aware of what time it is and how far off the dark is. It's a countdown to twilight, though most hours are just as lonely to her.

### "TOMPKINS SQUARE PARK" BY MUMFORD & SONS

"I only ever told you one lie/When it could have been a thousand/It might as well have been a thousand." A lot of liars populate *Under a Dark Sky*, but Eden has been prepared for them by her husband's betrayal. ▶

**Musical Playlist for** *Under a Dark Sky*
*(continued)*

### "YOUR EX-LOVER IS DEAD" BY STARS

Not a spoiler, but he is. "Live through this/And you won't look back."

### "YOU'RE MISSING" BY BRUCE SPRINGSTEEN

I saw Springsteen play this on *Saturday Night Live* and was devastated. It's from his 9/11 album, *The Rising*, so it's a devastating song among many devastating songs. The lyrics go: "Coffee cup's on the counter, jacket's on the chair/Papers on the doorstep, but you're not there." This song reminded me while I drafted *Under a Dark Sky* that Eden's life as a widow was still new and surprising to her. This song is what heartbreak sounds like.

### "CIRCADIAN RHYTHM (LAST DANCE)" BY SILVERSUN PICKUPS

Each playlist has one or two songs that turn out to be thematically or musically—or both—important to the book I'm drafting. When I find that song, I put it on repeat and listen to it over and over as I write. It might technically be considered hypnosis, I don't know. For *Under a Dark Sky*, this was the song, along with "The Yawning Grave" by Lord Huron (see page 8). I don't want to know how many times I listened to these two songs writing *Under a Dark Sky*. I wouldn't tell you if I knew. You might worry for me.

### "SLEEPING LESSONS" BY THE SHINS

This is just a good song with a fortuitous title for a book about a character with insomnia.

### "24 FRAMES" BY JASON ISBELL

I'm a big fan of Jason Isbell. Twenty-four frames per second is supposedly the rate of a film reel, but maybe we can say that Eden's photography gets a callout here.

### "SCREEN" BY BRAD

"Well you'll never know just how dark this screen could be." I have been listening to this song since 1993. I don't know where it fits into the story, but it does.

### "THE NIGHT WE MET" BY LORD HURON

This is simply a beautiful song. The chorus reminds me of Eden's predicament when the book starts, and how shattering it is not to have Bix in her life, despite his flaws. "I had all and then most of you/Some and now none of you/Take me back to the night we met." And of course I had to show how Eden and Bix met.

### "TO BE YOUR HONEY" BY GEMMA HAYES

This song was used in a commercial that a friend shared on Facebook, and while the commercial was lovely, what I needed immediately was to hear this song in full. I offered a bounty on social media for the person who could track down the title and artist, and was soon shipping a signed book to the winner and enjoying an addition to my playlist. The hushed voice of this song helped me write the scene at the motel between Eden and Dev. The lyrics: "I'm not scared of the dark/But I'm terrified of those who don't see it." ▶

**Musical Playlist for *Under a Dark Sky***
*(continued)*

### "AFRAID" BY THE NEIGHBORHOOD

[NSFW] This song has a creepy vibe that helps with darker scenes. I wonder what I would write if I listened to Broadway tunes.

### "PLANETS" BY JOSEPH

Nothing wrong with a little planetary inspiration when you're writing about the stars.

### "REFLECTING LIGHT" BY SAM PHILLIPS

Every playlist has to have a waltz. That's not a rule; it just happens. This song is a bright spot in this list. This is the song used in *Gilmore Girls* when Lorelei and Luke first dance. I knew you'd want to know that.

### "THE YAWNING GRAVE" BY LORD HURON

If you haven't noticed, I really like Lord Huron. This is the other song that helped shape the book from the very beginning. I have listened to this song more than any one person should listen to any piece of music, possibly more than the band itself. "Darkness brings evil things oh, the reckoning begins," go the lyrics, but it's really for me about the dark tone of the song. Have you ever heard of people talking about synesthesia, in which they taste or hear colors? I get as close to understanding that as I'm able when I say that this song sounds like the book I wanted to write. ("The Yawning Grave" is the second waltz on this list. Apparently I like waltzes.) ༄

# Q&A with
# Lori Rader-Day

**Q: How did you decide to write about a dark sky park?**

**A:** I had never heard of the term "dark sky park" until I saw a notice somewhere about a new one being designated. I was immediately intrigued, since location—especially a location in the Midwest, which I'm partial to—is such an important factor in crime fiction. There's so much story potential in a setting that is created to be dark. I did a little online research about dark sky designations and learned about light pollution from the International Dark-Sky Association's website, www .darksky.org. I also searched online to see if anyone had written a murder mystery set at a dark sky park. At the time I started writing it at least, no one had. When I saw that you could stay at a guest house in one of the parks, the story started coming together.

**Q: What kind of research did you do for this book?**

**A:** For the year I worked on *Under a Dark Sky*'s first draft, I didn't have time to visit the park I had chosen as the model for the fictional Straits Point International Dark Sky Park. That park, Headlands International Dark Sky Park, is situated way up at the tip of the Lower Peninsula of Michigan. The long drive and then the winter kept me from visiting. Instead, I relied on Google Maps, YouTube videos created by the park and visitors, and ▶

night-sky research materials like *National Geographic Guide to the Night Sky: A Stargazer's Companion.* Over the summer of 2017, I was invited to speak at the Mackinac Island Public Library about my third novel, *The Day I Died*, and I jumped at the opportunity to finally make the trip. I was able to add a few last-minute details to the book because of that visit. Unfortunately, the night my husband and I visited the Headlands Park in person, it was a little cloudy. All the more reason to visit again!

### Q: *Why did you write about a widow?*

**A:** One of the things I try to do as a writer is write about things that challenge me because I don't want to write the same book twice. I don't tend to design characters and their flaws before I start writing. All I knew about Eden when I started writing was that she was a young widow, because that gave me a chance to talk about something I feared, and that she was afraid of the dark. I made that decision for Eden not knowing exactly how it fit into the larger story because of a fascinating essay I read once by Gene Weingarten, "None of the Above," collected in *The Fiddler in the Subway*, about an American who did not vote. Casually, Weingarten reveals deep in the essay that the man who has never voted, among his many characteristics, is afraid of the dark. To me, that said more than pages of exposition could about that person. Of course in nonfiction, Weingarten could simply drop that fact. In fiction, I had to investigate it.

**Q: Why do you write about social issues like post-traumatic stress disorder in your work?**

**A:** Crime novels are the social novels of our time—as Dickensian as you can get in 100,000 words. However, I would never advise someone to write a novel based on an "issue." That smacks of manifesto, and that's not what I like to read. Most people in the mystery section of a bookstore would agree. But when I started writing my first book, *The Black Hour*, an issue cropped up. And then when I wrote my second, *Little Pretty Things*, another issue showed up. What happens, I think, is that when I spend as much time with a novel as I have to in order to finish it, I start to bring things I care about to the page. As I write and perhaps especially as I revise, these things I care about that helped me make my word count start to coalesce into what an English lit course might call a theme. The trick is to make sure the themes never take over fully. As a reader and a writer, I want the story and the characters to do the work.

**Q: You write about characters other than the traditional cops, lawyers or private investigators we find in so many other mystery/thriller novels. Why is that?**

**A:** Can I be honest? I'm not a cop or a lawyer. There are already some great books in which these characters get a chance to solve crimes. How can I compete with that? The research I would have to do! I'm not the kind of person who reads instruction manuals. I'd rather ▶

get started writing and then find out where I need research to get me through, what kind of expert I need to be.

But even more honestly, this is the kind of book I like to read. I do like a Tana French police procedural; I love Charles Todd's Inspector Rutledge series. But what I love most is a mystery led by a person with a regular job, a regular life. To me, it's more interesting imagining what a crime will do to a tranquil, mundane life than to try and imagine a crime that will shake a career cop. All this to say that one of these days, I'd love to write a PI novel or a spy novel. I might try a historical at some point, too. Like I said earlier, I don't like to write the same book twice.

**Q: *Someone once described your work as "dark stories with heart." What do you think that means?***

**A:** That person got me. I think that phrase resonates with my work pretty well, because the stories are dark (this time, literally), but because the story is often told by a character who relies on humor and who travels an arc into a better understanding of themselves, the stories also bring some light. The heart comes from the characters. What I'm hoping is that readers fall in with the characters and want them to pull through toward a fulfilling ending, maybe even a happy one.

**Q: *Where do you get your ideas?***

**A:** *The Black Hour*'s premise came from working on a gossipy university campus. *Little Pretty Things* came from my wondering what I might have done for a living if I had not gone to college. *The Day I Died*'s focus around handwriting analysis came from one of my writing professor's insistence that work was an interesting writing topic. She was right. *Under a Dark Sky* came from my discovery that there were such places as dark sky parks, and from that scene in the prologue, which really happened to me, once, when I was driving with my dad. I see novel ideas like that kid from *The Sixth Sense* saw dead people. The problem is which idea has legs, which idea stands alone without me having to dedicate ten years to research? Which story is my story to tell? ❧

# Questions for Discussion

1. Eden finds solace in photography. She sees her life as if through the lens of a camera, coming in and out of focus, and in snapshots. Why do you think this helps her make sense of her world?

2. When Eden first arrives at the park, she's hoping the trip will help her reconcile with the death of her husband. How do you think her anguish affects her initial judgments of the characters she meets?

3. The residents of the guest house are burdened by the histories of their college relationships, and the kinds of people they used to be. Have you ever felt the pressure of continuing a friendship with someone you've grown apart from?

4. Eden says that the murder victim "died perfect." How does a person's death change our perspectives of their lives and legacies? Do you think recognizing a loved one's flaws makes it easier or harder to move on?

5. Throughout the story, Eden sees the group react in different ways to the loss of their companion. How does experiencing the grief of the group change Eden's understanding of her own grief for Bix? How does this change Eden?

6.  What do you think of the question Eden's sister asks her: "There's a slim line between believing in fate and letting your life be decided for you?"

7.  Before speaking to Cooley, Eden had never told anyone the full truth about what really happened the night Bix died. Do you think Eden was trying to protect Bix's reputation, or herself? How might things have been different for Eden if she'd revealed the truth earlier?

8.  We see many different versions of Bix through Eden's memories of their relationship. How does your impression of him change throughout the story? Do you feel any sympathy for him?

9.  Did the identity of the culprit surprise you? Whom did you most suspect throughout the novel, and why? Who do you think is the most at fault?

10.  Do you have any irrational fears? Do you have any suspicions about where they might stem from?  ∾

# More from Lori Rader-Day

### THE DAY I DIED

**An unforgettable tale of a mother's desperate search for a lost boy**

Anna Winger can know people better than they know themselves with only a glance—at their handwriting. Hired out by companies wanting to land trustworthy employees and by the lovelorn hoping to find happiness, Anna likes to keep the real-life mess of other people at arm's length and on paper. But when she is called to use her expertise on a note left behind at a murder scene in the small town she and her son have recently moved to, the crime gets under Anna's skin and rips open her narrow life for all to see. To save her son—and herself—once and for all, Anna will face her every fear, her every mistake, and the past she thought she'd rewritten.

"Lori Rader-Day is so ferociously talented. . . . *The Day I Died* is a terrific novel—gripping and twisty and beautifully layered. It kept me locked up and locked in from the very first word to the very last."

—Lou Berney, Edgar Award–winning author of *The Long and Faraway Gone*

**D**iscover great authors, exclusive offers, and more at hc.com.